long live
dead reckless

Safari Spell

Safari Spell

Calibre Creek Publishing
ATLANTA, GEORGIA

Calibre Creek Publishing
Atlanta, GA

Publisher's Note: This is a work of fiction. Names, characters, places, and incidents are a product of the author's imagination. Locales and public names are sometimes used for atmospheric purposes. Any resemblance to actual people, living or dead, or to businesses, companies, events, institutions, or locales is completely coincidental.

Cover design by Joe Burns

Long Live Dead Reckless/ Safari Spell. – 3rd ed.
ISBN: 9780692739310

For mom,
who taught me to laugh when I was afraid.
Now I laugh every day.

Acknowledgments.

This book only exists because many wonderful people have always been supportive of my work. Writing groups, friends, Facebook fans, and family have built an encouraging, strong community habitat for my writing to grow roots.

My husband, Brian – thank you for challenging me to try this crazy thing in the first place. Thank you for putting up with furious all-night writes, neglected dates, and lots of irrational sobbing. Not only couldn't I have done this without you, I never would have even started. Thank you for believing in me. I love you.

My Kickstarter backers – Sue Cheek, Stacey Varner, Aunt Nat, Brenda Spell, Karen Monroe, Kathy Monroe, Brett Howell, The Bartley bunch (Keith, Cindy, Rainie, CJ), Jeff Aultman, Sherry Shanklin, and Stephanie Lewis – you put your faith (and money!) in a timid first-time novelist without even knowing so much as the plot. Your generosity made this real. I've said it before, but I'll say it again: Thank you. You are my heroes.

My designer, Joe – you're pretty much the coolest artist I know, and for some reason you agreed to share your talent for this book. Thank you for being patient with my creative perfectionism and for being such a wonderful friend!

My editor, Kim – thank you for all the hard work and insight.

1

At twenty-two, I knew everything.

I knew how to pick a gravesite a dead person would die for. I knew how to dive out of a burning house and land on the cool side of the pillow. I knew how to fail an entire semester and still make Dean's List. I basically knew everything except how to avoid falling in love with the vampire who ruined my life. But in my defense, there shouldn't have even been one because vampires don't exist. At least they didn't back when I knew everything.

At twenty-three, I knew nothing.

I didn't know how to get out of my hometown of Cypress. I didn't know how to stop itching every time a cute guy realized I wasn't invisible. I didn't know how to delete mom's last voicemail from my phone. I didn't know how to keep dad out of the mental ward. Everything I didn't know made me forget there was a world outside of my own – one full of unfamiliar faces.

While my mom lay in the hospital dying, I never saw a single face – just bodies. When a hand would reach out with some soothing word attached, I took it. When a shoulder that looked strong enough for my troubles was offered, I leaned. I never questioned a kiss on the forehead back then, so I never felt the fatal one planted there. Had I looked in his eyes, I might have a different story to tell.

But I didn't, and that single moment changed the course of my life.

There's nothing special about the place I was born, but I did always think it was weird that no one moved away. Anyone who left always came back to die. Then again, some people just skipped that step entirely and disappeared instead. Usually it was an amateur diver in Radium Springs, sometimes a lone fisherman on the Flint. Always on water, never a body found.

Only in my hometown could people both vanish and never leave. Generations of families festered in their own echoes, repeating the same lives over and over again. I couldn't be one of them, that much I knew. There's nothing here for anyone with dreams, and I have days and nights full of them.

Eight months of intense South Georgia heat slow-cooks perpetual complacency in this place. It's all back roads, bars, and bad decisions, and with no fast road out of town, far too many people call it home. The truth is, some of them aren't even people. There's little to lure a stranger – especially a supernatural one. But when I was twenty-three, I met one.

I had actually known at least two others before Sage Talis walked into Goodlife Gym looking for a job, but I didn't know it then. Supernaturals fit in better than they like to admit. Anyway, it was a hot Thursday afternoon the last week of August. Around four o'clock, to be exact.

It was the kind of day where the sun radiated down in actual waves you could see coming off the road. It felt like hell opened up somewhere on the edge of town to swallow up anyone who tried to leave.

When I walked into the gym lobby, my kitten heels clacked against the tile floor, causing the normal ruckus. A few heads turned my way, but they recognized me and went back to work. I first noticed him standing at the front desk counter. His back was to me, his head down, his left hand writing.

I stopped right there and stared. Sure it was rude, but it never occurred to me that no one else was looking at him like that. I thought we all were. A blush sizzled on my cheeks as I drew every inch of him with my gaze.

The shirt he wore hugged his gorgeous frame, teasing us all – I mean me. I knew I had to take a picture in case we never crossed paths again, so I pulled out my phone and pretended to read. It was hard to angle the camera without it being obvious what I was doing.

Actually, not hard. *Impossible.*

"Hey, Talor! If he turns around, you can get a picture of the front, too," said Kati, the front desk manager.

I scrambled to pretend I wasn't trying to take a picture of a stranger's butt and ended up with a blurry one of my feet for all my trouble. Kati chuckled as I ducked into the time-clock room to hide.

Sighing, I looked at the time. I was too early to clock in. I was constantly being reprimanded about the nickels and dimes it costs Goodlife when I clock in early.

To pass the time, I peeked out of the small window in the door to make sure he was still there. He was, and thankfully he seemed oblivious to my shenanigans. Good thing too, because I looked like a horny ghost haunting the window. Shifting on my feet, I decided to go back out and talk to Kati so I could at least get a better look at him. She wouldn't blow my cover.

Well, not a second time, anyway.

The blinds of the Assistant Director's office were open as usual, and at the desk sat a middle-aged creeper who followed me around. I hadn't walked two feet past his open doorway when he launched himself out of the chair and covered the ground between his desk and the door.

He caught himself against the doorframe while I pretended not to notice the theatrics. Focusing instead on the gorgeous stranger, I took a spot about two feet away from him and leaned against the front desk counter.

I tried not to crowd him since it would have been obvious and awkward. You know, more obvious and awkward than what I was already being. Not that it mattered. He was still filling out paperwork, ignoring my existence. His face said mid-twenties; the air about him said something else.

He came across as seasoned and poised, like a wanderer who had spent some time as a monk. He also had a wild look about him, like maybe he'd wrestled some beast to the ground just outside. The thought made my breasts swell another size.

His tousled hair made me want to run my hands through it, but I knew better. That brownish color was too close to blonde, and blondes tend to stick together like a cult. Still, I enjoyed haunting him. I mean ogling. I mean lusting. I mean looking.

A reddish five o'clock shadow edged his jaw and raced up his cheekbones, swarming around his lips. His eyes were set astride pretty much the cutest nose ever, and the most spectacular part of it all was the freckles splashed all across his skin.

There were so many freckles it was like looking at constellation camouflage, but I still saw him. Gazing at the unique dots, I imagined connecting them into shapes. The longer I looked, the more creative the shapes became.

"Sorry if I'm bothering you," I said, controlling the tone of my voice so it sounded sexier than usual.

He never looked away from the paper. At this point, I felt a little foolish. Everyone kept cutting their eyes and whispering. I was that proverbial train wreck, but I wasn't about to walk away without acknowledgement.

"I'm Talor. What's your name?"

He ignored me again. Since I wanted an excuse to lean a little closer to him anyway, I arched to see his name on the application.

"Oh, hi, Sage," I said, pursing my lips like an idiot. "You know, you don't really look like a Sage."

I didn't even know what I meant by that, but it made him put down the pen and lift his head. It felt like his eyes took forever getting to mine. Once they did, everything around us went into a haze. I couldn't tell what color I was seeing, only that the eyes were timeless, as if no sight in a world full of sights had ever escaped them.

It was something like green and gold with layers and depth – as many layers and depth as the earth itself. I think it's called hazel in sober moments. I could have sworn the irises moved in synchronized swirls like a spectacular time-lapse of the night sky, but all I knew for sure was that there was something unsettling there.

When he blinked, everything went back into focus and we were just strangers staring at one another in close proximity.

"Talor, huh? Is that with a 'y' or an 'i'?"

I felt feverish relishing in the glory that despite not being skinny or blonde, I wasn't invisible to the sexiest man I'd ever seen.

"Neither was good enough for me, actually."

"I believe that," he said, curling a corner of his lip. It was only half a smile, but it was wholly genuine.

"So...what's your last name, Sage? Just in case I want to play MASH and get spoiled on our future?"

I started to look down at the application again, but he covered it with his hand as he leaned an elbow on the counter. He didn't answer me. Or if he did, I was too focused on the hair tumbling across his forehead to notice. I cleared my throat and gave a soft laugh.

"Oh. Going to make me work for it, are you?"

"Well, you do work here, don't you?" he joked, looking away as he straightened.

I frowned before I could stop myself, but he wasn't looking anyway. It was irritating for a boy to play hard to get. Before I could come up with something clever, his focus went to something behind me. His jaw tightened, stealing away that gorgeous smile. When I turned, the Assistant Director was walking towards us.

"Well, it's nice to meet you, Sage. I hope you get the job. I know I'd like to see more of you," I said with a wink.

I know I saw the beginnings of a blush under that glorious stubble. Looking the way he did, women had to flirt with him all the time. But he didn't act like it. He was either shy or a snob, which meant he had a girlfriend (probably a skinny blonde with a thigh gap) and didn't think I was good enough for him.

I could feel my blood boiling as I considered Sage the snob with no last name. Just as I grabbed the double doors separating staff from members, I heard his voice carry from the counter.

"It's Talis. Let me know what MASH says. I don't mind spoilers. I think I know what happens anyway."

Head held high, I grinned and pranced through the doors. If he did have a girlfriend, he sure wasn't thinking about her when he was asking me how to spell my name.

2

Fate was cruel.

He ended up training with the morning crew, which was pretty much torture because I came in just as his shift ended. I used those precious crossover minutes during his first week to flirt, but he seemed even less interested in me then than when we first met.

His second week, I made the stupid decision to skip Dr. Milton's class twice so I could loiter at the front desk and attempt small talk. I made little progress getting to know Sage and Dr. Milton noticed my repetitive absences. Even the Assistant Director noticed. But Sage did not.

During his third week, another Cypress woman disappeared along the Flint. They found her bike. Didn't find her. But that was barely news anymore. The only reason anyone talked about it was because she was a long-time member of Goodlife. It felt weird trying to seduce Sage when other members stood around him crying about their missing friend, so that week was a scratch.

Even though he barely spoke, everyone seemed to like him – maybe because he barely spoke. I couldn't understand why management sentenced such a quiet treasure to close with Spencer Kaden, the resident Goodlife Gym playboy.

It was a grim fate for such a nice new guy, but it did mean that we had the same shift finally. The only thing I could come up with was that management hoped he would even out the front desk reputation. You know, with Spencer being a man-whore and all.

Then again, Spencer himself was a head-scratcher. He was a star athlete from California who somehow landed in Cypress on a swimming scholarship. He was one of those people who actually had a trust fund.

It always kind of bothered me that someone who could afford to buy a college took scholarship money meant for normal people. He didn't need a job, a scholarship, or even college for that matter. I suspected that his parents sent him away as some sort of punishment. Anyone could guess what he did.

Regardless, he was around for some reason, and his missing moral compass passed the time by smooth-talking girls into dropping panties by name introductions. Sadly, he was stupid good at that, and girls never seemed to hate him for it. I never understood why. In spite of his fatal character flaws, we were tentative friends.

That's to say he never tried to get in my pants, probably because I was teaching a karate class when he first started. He did come to mom's funeral, and we were close for a time afterwards. But recently we started doing the dance we did now, an awkward shuffle with big chips on our shoulders and lingering looks.

LONG LIVE DEAD RECKLESS

When Sage showed up, Spencer stopped being polite. He began to see me the same way he saw all women and he made no attempt to hide it. I ignored his advances, hoping they would stop as soon as they started. It was annoying, but something far more important demanded my attention: Sage.

He and I were at the point in our "relationship" that I would throw discarded pen caps at other girls who dared flirt with him. When questioned about the projectiles, I pretended some renegade kid was responsible. The girls always believed me when I pointed at ghosts. No one ever suspected I was so ridiculous. I only did that a few times, fearing it would find me out.

I can't explain those idiotic actions except to say that I wanted his attention more than I could admit – even to myself. I craved it on some level that never existed before he walked in. At first, I honestly thought I'd lost my mind. But every now and then, those sweltering eyes would wander from his solitary world and settle on me in such a way that said he wasn't just looking at me.

He was trying to *see* me.

Those moments were few, but they were all I needed to continue my quest. Since the snack area was right next to the lobby where he worked, I made regular trips there to spy on him. I spent a good twenty dollars a week on candy and drinks that I never touched. I ended up with a dragon's hoard in the nursery refrigerator. No one complained about my regular walkabouts because I had plenty of pity snacks to buy their silence.

Then one day, I got tired of just looking at him. That's when I held up a pack of Reese's to my co-worker, Larissa. I say co-worker. She's a friend. A good one. Most co-workers would get tired of the constant schoolgirl chatter about the hot new guy, but she didn't. She got a kick out of my raging hormones and his confusing disdain.

11

"So, I'm going to give you this," I said, winking long enough for it to be weird, "because I just really want something else. I'm going to the vending machines."

She was reading a book. She was always reading some book. That's what happens when you're a teacher for your day job, I suppose. She didn't look up, but she swiped the Reese's from me with precision.

"Girl, you're hopeless. Get some M & M's this time."

I scoffed.

"Oh, I'm sorry. I'll be too busy talking to Sage for that."

She looked up.

"Yeah, let me know how that goes. M & M's."

Gathering up all my nerve, I threw my shoulders back and began my journey to the front desk. It was almost closing time and all the big wigs had already gone home. I slipped through the double doors to the front lobby and tiptoed passed the vending machine area. Yeah, I was trying to sneak up on him. I have no idea why.

Sage was sitting alone at the front, his elbows resting on the counter as he read a book. My heart took an uneven turn in my chest. I grabbed at it, catching the collar of my shirt. He still hadn't seen me. I could abort. I could. I think it was M & M's, right? One foot went back, a retreat on my mind.

No. You aren't going back with candy. You're going back with something to brag about. He reads books and he's insanely hot!

I decided I was going to make pleasant conversation with him even if it landed me in the hospital. Taking a deep breath, I tried licking my lips and discovered that my mouth was so dry I literally had to pry it open with a finger. That's when it dawned on me that I had no idea what I was going to say to him or how I was going to do it without saliva.

Unfortunately, I was too close to the front desk to go unnoticed now. I turned to see Spencer and the Assistant Director in the corner, right at the door between the time clock and front desk. My heart sunk when I realized I hadn't seen them in time. On cue, everyone turned to notice me all at once.

And of course the Assistant Director had a sour frown aimed my way.

"Miss Gardin, is there a reason you're not where you're supposed to be?"

Cover blown, I just stood there like a giant fish out of water. Oh no. I had to answer him. I pulled my hand away from my mouth, but only an audible gulp came out. With a grunt, the Assistant Director pushed through the doors separating the front desk area from the lobby. Spencer reached across the counter and gripped it tight so he could lean over it and into my personal space. He smelled like the salty ocean air, which was something I had never noticed before.

"Hey baby, don't let him scare you."

He slid back behind the counter so fast I thought I imagined it all. A moment later, the Assistant Director was standing over me. I couldn't make myself move. Fish face, tree branch arms, nothing. To me, he was a T-Rex and I was going to remain still to survive. Gray eyes glared down at me, unflinching.

"Well? Do you work at the front desk or do you still work in the nursery?"

When I didn't respond, he snapped a long, bony finger towards to the hallway behind me.

"Back that way?"

I finally straightened. My tongue felt like a walrus writhing on a desert mirage.

13

"Th-ur, I'm th-orry. I was j-just..."

I trailed off. I've never been the best liar, and trying to fabricate one so quickly was not a strong suit of mine. When left with the option to come up with a believable lie or stand silent like an idiot, I always chose the latter. No exceptions. They all waited to see what I was going to say. I over enunciated my words like it would help.

"I just wanted to talk to the guys about something."

He narrowed his eyes, the age creases of his brow becoming even more noticeable.

"Work related then?"

"Um...yes."

His brow went up as he stepped to the side slowly.

"Oh. Go ahead."

When he didn't walk away, I knew I was screwed. He just pinned me with a stare, so I gave a heavy blink and shook my head.

"I mean, no? I meant no."

Sage's face softened like he wanted to smile, but he just straightened in his chair, hands closing the book in front of him. Spencer put an elbow against the wall and fluffed his hair with a sympathetic grimace and a twitch of the nose. The Assistant Director crossed his arms over his chest and cleared his throat.

"This is the fifth time I've had to tell you not to loiter at the front desk lately, Miss Gardin. Now get back where you're supposed to be or I will have a talk with your supervisor in the morning."

"Yes, sir," I mumbled, slinking off with my shoulders level to my ears. Embarrassed that it all happened in front of Sage, I felt tears starting to build and was ready to get out of there.

"And tuck your shirt in!"

I stopped. Nursery workers don't have to tuck their shirts in. My supervisor told me that when I got hired. We run after kids for money. There's no decency or order in that. Still, I wasn't going to pick this battle. After tucking in my shirt, I continued my walk of shame as Spencer cackled.

Back in the nursery, I managed to keep from crying, but I could only breathe in rapid, shallow breaths sure to render me unconscious. I paced on a thin strip of tile behind the nursery camera in the corner. I couldn't stop fuming and I didn't want my rage recorded. Larissa looked up from her book like she just came out of a daze and fanned herself.

"Girl! Whew! Where am I? Why's your shirt tucked in?"

I stopped pacing long enough to rip the shirt out of my yoga pants.

"The Assistant Director is still here. He made me look like a total idiot out there."

Her eyes went wide as she craned her neck towards the hallway and plopped her book closed in her lap.

"Oooo, I better put this down then. What happened?"

"I don't know. He was grilling me about why I wasn't back here."

She stifled a laugh. I stopped pacing to lean against the wall. My sweaty palms felt instant relief as they spread out against the cool painted brick. Larissa waved her hand in the air and lowered her voice.

"Ugh! That dirty old man shouldn't even be here, anyways. He's got a creepy crush on you."

With a grunt, she flipped open her book again. I grabbed my phone and sent a text to my best friend, Azalea Beaty.

Can I come over? Bad day. Need fun.

The reply was quick.

Yessah! I invited some people over to swim. You can borrow a suit. I'll make brownies for my bestie! XOXO

I told her I would be over after my shift. Checking the clock, I could see that meant I'd only have to survive another five minutes. I could do that. I gathered up my things and turned to Larissa, who was nibbling on her Reese's like a squirrel.

"Larissa, I need you to make sure the coast is clear before I head out there. I don't want to be at the time clock the same time as Spencer or Sage. Please?"

"So now you don't want to talk to him?"

"No, not now. I need to go lick my wounds."

"Girl, you crazy."

"God, just help me, ok? I need to go to my friend's house so I can drown in the pool."

"Say what?"

"I'm kidding."

After a long minute, Larissa nodded and marked her place in the book. Then she went around and started flipping off the lights at the other end of the room. Giving a wink, she made her way to the front along with the rest of the closing staff. I stayed behind and waited in the nursery, which was dark except for the one set of lights overhead. I could hear the clock ticking before a voice whispered into my ear.

"Hey little girl, want some candy?"

I gasped as my arm instinctively flew out, slamming my elbow against the door. Groaning, I turned to see Spencer laughing at my frenzied reaction.

"Geez, Talor. You scare easy. You ok? Lemme see."

He reached out to check my arm, but I pushed him back.

"Don't do that! God. What are you doing back here?"

He shrugged.

"I felt bad since you almost got fired coming to see me."

I touched the funny bone on my elbow and winced.

"You know I didn't come to see you. Besides, I heard you laughing at me."

He raised a brow and leaned towards me.

"Aw, that's 'cuz you're funny. I like how clueless you are. It's charming."

When I noticed Larissa waving for me to come out, I started to open the door. Spencer caught it and laid his hand over mine.

"Seriously, Talor. I like it."

His blue eyes held me hostage for a moment. I usually made it a point to never look too hard at him. It just seemed safer. But when I dared to, I could see what all the fuss was about. He embodied rare male perfection in all his features, but he was also a distinctly bad person. Plus, I now had a physical injury because of him. The tingle in my arm reminded me just how painful he could be to any unfortunate woman.

I jerked the door away from him and hurried out to where Larissa was waiting for me.

"I didn't see them. Hurry and clock out," she said.

I frowned at her.

"Wait – you didn't clock me out yet?"

"No! You said creepy creeper was here. You know I love you, but I'm not gettin' caught doin' that."

Sighing, I pushed the time clock door open to find Sage standing there with his timecard in hand. He cut his eyes towards me, making me freeze in real time.

"Oh," I muttered, wondering if not getting paid for the night's work was better than facing him again.

Unfortunately, nothing else was affected by Sage's stare. The heavy door hit me on the arm again, forcing me forward into the room. I caught myself on the counter and leaned on it, trying to ignore my second injury to the same place.

"Heyyyy, Sage. Late clocking out?"

There was pain in my voice, but I tried to cover it with a nervous chuckle. I bit down on my bottom lip as the arm throbbed. He pushed his card down in the machine and it whirled as it punched his time.

"Yeah. There was a line."

Gulping, I straightened and wrapped my arms together in front, my elbow growing red and achy. I couldn't decide if looking at him was weirder than looking at the floor, so I just watched him pluck the card out of the machine. Even his fingers had tiny freckles. It made me smile.

"Are you ok?" he asked.

My eyes went wide as I realized he just caught me smiling at his fingers like a weirdo.

"Oh, what? Yes."

He glanced down at my elbow.

"What happened to your arm?"

I held it up to see an open scrape with a bit of blood seeping to the surface. It wasn't painful now, just sensitive.

"I hit it on a door in the nursery. Spencer decided to – you know, it's really ok. I'm surprised it's even bleeding," I replied, frowning at the scrape.

18

He looked away and cleared his throat. Finally finding an empty slot, he shoved it down with the kind of aggression usually reserved for people who owe you money. Only he could make punching a time card look sexy.

He grabbed another card and held it up. This time it was mine. I nodded. I thought he was going to hand it to me, but he pushed it down into the machine. I guess Sage wasn't scared of the Assistant Director.

"Is everything always so hard for you?" he asked.

"Hard?"

His lip curled.

"You know, going through doors? Coming up front to say hi?"

He was flirting *now*? Attempting an emotional regroup, I stuck my hand in my hair and tried flipping it. Unfortunately, I was sweating like I'd run a marathon. As a result, hair caught in my fingers and spun a web.

Panicking because he was looking at me and there was no hiding my struggle, my hand flopped around like a rabid raccoon to free itself. I think I even made the same noise. Pulling hard, it came loose with a carcass of hairs strangled between my fingers.

Out of the corner of my eye, I could see something like tumbleweed resting just below my chin. My tangled hair rebelled in a giant jumbled mess between my neck and the shirt collar. Focusing back on him, I just gave a sheepish smile and died inside.

In that moment, I knew I had two choices: either quit my job or own the shame on my shoulder. I opted to pretend he was blind to all of my faults, and he played along like a perfect gentleman.

To my surprise, instead of his usual indifference, he had this humorous look on his face. I struggled to think of a clever retort like when we first met. Nothing came. It was hard to focus on words when I just wanted to touch that face full of stubble. I was jealous of facial hair for the first time in my life. I wanted to be that attached to his skin.

"I like the hair on your face. Thanks."

Silence. *Wait...what did I just say?*

He gave an epic side eye while slipping my card back in its holder. Without a word, he turned and took the first aid kit off the wall.

Right then, Larissa flung the door open.

"Watch out. Here comes –"

She took one look at us, blinked, and let the door close in front of her. Sage and I shared an awkward look and then he took out a Band-Aid and some alcohol wipes from the kit. Offering them to me, his hand brushed mine in the exchange. It was only a second in time, but the sensation of his skin against mine was warm and soothing.

Nothing ached anymore except my heart. I dared think he might kiss me out of nowhere, but he lowered his eyes and withdrew his hand, sliding it slowly across the counter in retreat.

When the door swung open this time, it was Spencer.

"What the hell, man?" he complained, throwing his back against the door so it stayed open. "I'm ready to get out of here. I've got a party to get to. I'm thirsty."

Spencer chomped his teeth like he was biting into something and gave a sly smile. Sage narrowed his eyes at him, but it made Spencer chuckle as if they were sharing an inside joke that was only funny to him. I turned so I could see them both.

"Alcohol makes you more dehydrated, Spencer."

He gave a lazy blink and leaned forward, chucking me under the chin like I was a little kid.

"Aw, Talor. You're so cute. Talis knows what I mean."

20

I frowned. Of course he would try to make Sage look like the drunk. Sage didn't take the bait. He closed the first-aid kit and put it back on the wall. Trying to help, Larissa pushed Spencer off the door despite his protests. Sage caught it and held it open for me to go through.

"Don't feel so bad about the doors, Talor. Guys should be holding them for you."

Feeling a blush rise, I stopped a moment and looked at him, but his expression was blank. Larissa drew her lips into her mouth and quickly hooked my arm in hers, peddling us off towards the parking lot. Over my shoulder, I watched Sage linger a moment before disappearing to help Spencer switch off lights.

Once we got outside, Larissa released my arm and squealed.

"Girl!"

"What?"

"That was serious."

Shaking my head, I made my way to my car as she chased me. I tried to stick the key in the door, but I kept missing because my hand was shaking. Sage had touched that hand.

"Talor, did you –"

"You mind telling me why you waved me out when nobody had left yet? Thanks for nothing."

"But they weren't up there," she argued.

"That's because Spencer was busy harassing me in the nursery. Dear lord. I told Sage I liked the hair on his face and then I said thanks! I mean, what the heck was that?"

The corners of her mouth dropped in thought.

"Ok...you do like his stubble. You talk about it a lot."

"Not to mention my crazy hair! Look!"

21

I clawed at the tumbleweed under my chin. The tangled mess behaved, but I lost a few more dozen hairs in the process. Larissa watched me fight the beast, pushing her lips together until they formed a straight line.

"Uh, I don't think he cares. I think he might like you. Did you hear what he said about holding doors?"

I launched my purse in the car and drowned my face in my hands with a sigh.

"He thinks I'm incapable of opening my own doors, Larissa."

"No, he didn't mean it like that. He was being sweet. He was saying –"

I dropped my hands to my sides.

"Hey, you don't think Sage is a big partier or anything like that, do you?"

"You talking about the thirsty thing?" she asked, turning her mouth sideways.

"Yeah, that was weird, right?"

She looked like she was searching for the words in the sky.

"Girl, you know Spencer always be talkin' about booty. I don't think Sage's like that, but you never know. Boys their age be crazy. They into everything."

I shook my head quickly and held up my hands between us like a fence keeping the comments from sticking in my head.

"Booty? Ugh. Ok, well anyway...I've gotta go. I'll see you tomorrow."

On the way to Azalea's, I rested my hand on the first aid stuff that was sitting in the passenger seat. Sage had given it to me, sure, but it was his job...kind of. Larissa was wrong. Sage didn't like me. He was just concerned for a coworker. Thoughtful. Polite. Cute. I brought my hand back to the steering wheel and stroked where his freckled fingers had touched my skin. It still felt gentle. Wonderful. Warm.

I was excited to tell Azalea all about what happened until I pulled in her driveway. There were a handful of strange cars parked there and only one I recognized.

It was expensive, sporty, and had a California license plate.

3

I could just leave. Text Azalea and say I was too tired.

I could avoid this. But instead, I watched the red line on the dash land on PARK...and I let go. Once I turned the key, the engine went quiet. I don't know why I decided to stay. Maybe because I felt I had more right to be there than he did. I held tight to the steering wheel and considered my options.

For a guy with only one motivation in life, Spencer was complicated. He pursued me more in the weeks since Sage showed up than he had in the entire year that I knew him before. Larissa explained the dramatic shift in behavior as old-fashioned alpha male competition.

I told her to stop applying Animal Planet to real life, but somewhere deep down I knew there was some truth in it. I couldn't come to terms with Spencer at Azalea's house. I couldn't imagine how they even knew each other. At least I knew she would be on my side. Plus, she wasn't helpless with men like me. She could tame them. That solitary fact brought a flicker of hope that he would fall in love with her and leave me alone for good.

Muffled voices broke my concentration. Laughter and splashing was coming from the pool area on the side of the mansion. Oh no. I forgot about the whole swimming thing. I wasn't going to get half-naked in front of Spencer. I peeled apart the Band-Aid and put it on the scrape. My elbow didn't hurt, but it was still a little bloody.

Once I made sure the bandage was on tight, I forced myself out of the car and faced Beaty Mansion. God, it was beautiful. It was one of the few standing original buildings from the Civil War. It sat on at least twenty acres of pecan groves and open fields and it had actual servants. There was a homey charm to it despite its size, at least to me.

The front lawn was dark except for a few gas lanterns that led the way to the double balcony wraparound porch harboring two shadows near the door. Walking up, the toe of my shoe caught an uneven stone sticking out of the walkway, and my keys flew out and made a loud clattering sound on the cobblestone. The shadows went still as I bent to scoop my keys. Azalea's brother Jesse stepped out of the shadows shirtless and with crooked glasses.

"Oh heyyyy," I said, giving a slow parade wave.

"Everybody's around back. You remember Kyoko?"

Kyoko, a pretty girl with short black hair and freckles, mumbled something to him before leaning her head out where I could see her.

"Hey Talor," she called nervously.

From her awkward position and slumped shoulders, I could tell she was also topless. I pressed my lips together and nodded.

"Yep. I'll go around then."

I hurried off. The tiki torches helped ward away late summer mosquitos and the string lights cast a gentle glow over the water. At first glance, I counted six people, but there had to be a dozen. Some pervert sixth sense must have gone off because Spencer noticed me right away. His grin was visible from space.

"Everyone, shut up and say hi to Talor," Azalea yelled, throwing a beach ball at the back of some poor guy's head.

A million sets of eyes found me. I recognized some of them from the plays at Cypress College. I hugged myself around the waist, pretending my body was some broken thing I had to hold that tight to keep in one piece. I smiled at no one in particular.

"Hello...strangers...ok, well, I'll just be inside, Azalea."

Azalea pouted, putting her arm around me.

"No, you have to swim. We're closing it up in a few weeks."

"I can't. I hurt my arm. I don't want to get blood in the water. Especially with a certain shark here."

Azalea furrowed her brow.

"Huh?"

"Nothing."

Everyone had already gone back to whatever they were doing. That is, everyone except for Spencer, who was strolling over with wet hair plastered across his forehead. Azalea clapped her hands and directed to him.

"Oooo, yay! Talor, this is –"

"Oh, I know," I interrupted.

Spencer playfully shook water from his hair before leaning his head towards my arm.

"You want me to kiss that and make it all better?"

His voice sounded different. Deeper, more like testosterone than usual.

"No, thanks," I said flatly.

Azalea stared hard at him as she cupped a hand over her mouth towards me.

"I don't know. Might actually work. I mean, look at him."

I jerked her hand away from her mouth and strangled her wrist.

"Azalea. Why is he here?"

Clenching her teeth, she fought a smile.

"This is the Spencer you hate? Really?"

We both looked at him. His hands were low on his hips, framing the body he cultivated with non-stop exercise and professional grade skirt chasing. There were muscles on him that I swear don't exist on other men.

Water raced down the crevasses between the streamlined muscles that stretched along his body and dove beneath the top of his low-hung shorts. I only assumed they kept going. I made myself look up to his eyes. It was the lesser of two evils, really.

"You talk about me, Talor?" he asked, a wicked grin twisting on his lips.

"I say bad things about you."

"You know you like saying my name."

Azalea's eyes went wide and her chin rumpled. Before I could dropkick him into the pool, Azalea intervened.

"Um, Talor, I need to talk to you, like, right now."

She took my elbow and carted me off into the glass sunroom where a cooler of beer sat along with two blenders full of margarita. There were all different types of brownies scattered on the table, and a girl standing alone beside it.

She paid no attention to us. She was looking at her phone. Azalea introduced her as Valerie anyway. She had thick-brimmed glasses, a wide

28

mouth, and dark hair tied up in a tight, thin ponytail. She looked like a standing railroad spike.

"Nice to meet you, Valerie," I said, forcing a smile.

She looked up but didn't respond. It was like she didn't know what language we were speaking in. Forcing a smile, Azalea took a blender by the handle.

"Valerie is a stage hand for most of the plays."

I nodded, pretending it was the best thing I'd ever heard. Valerie wasn't even paying attention to me. She was already on her phone, doing whatever was more important than being polite and social. Without saying a word, she walked past us back outside. Azalea poured herself a margarita.

"So, yeah, she's kind of weird now. But anyway, back to interesting stuff. Seriously, that's the guy you've been complaining about? I actually question whether or not he's human. Those eyes – whew. So blue! And he is all up on you, girlfriend."

"Oh my God, he's 'all up' on every girl. You have no idea how trashy he is."

"I could imagine...well, he looked bored until you got here."

"He's Rose's boyfriend."

She held up a hand.

"Whoa. What? Rose the Presbyterian?"

I cocked a brow at her.

"What? She's pretty."

With a bewildered stare, she offered me the margarita. Recoiling immediately, she rolled her eyes and grabbed my forearm.

"Sorry, I forgot you're a better Christian than me."

"Azalea, I don't think –"

"So, which swimsuit do you want to wear?" she interrupted, peering towards the pool area after Spencer. I guess she was over it that fast.

"How do you even know him?"

"Huh? Who?"

"The ego with a shaved chest."

She popped a brownie in her mouth and made a funny face at me. She couldn't look ugly if she tried. Snorting, she took my hand and started leading me back to her room.

"Jesse's friend. I just met him. I really want you guys to hook up. Hey, I'm thinking of having a mystery dinner party for Halloween this year. What do you think?"

I stopped.

"I wouldn't have come tonight if I knew he would be here."

She spun around and planted a fist on her hipbone.

"Well, ok, miss bossy. Sorry. Now come on."

She dragged me the rest of the way to her closet where she plucked a colorful two-piece off the rack.

"Here. This one always looks good on you."

I took it with a sigh. It was purple and pink with light blue. It made me look like cotton candy all swirled together. I'd worn the swimsuit several times before, but I was never self-conscious in it. It was the only one Azalea had that I could wear, actually. I was curvier than her, and this bikini was cut larger. Holding it now, my stomach turned hollow.

Azalea took another sip of her margarita and thoughtfully twisted her glass in her hand.

"You should mess with him. Flirt like crazy. He'll want you more but still get nowhere. Talk about frustration. Ta-da – you win."

"You don't know this guy. Flirting is a very bad idea."

30

"Flirting is fun. Trust me. Do that and then ask him to break up with his girlfriend. He won't do it. A guy like that knows he can always get some girl who doesn't care that he has a girlfriend. It's a control thing. Think about it."

Azalea didn't wait for me to respond. She closed the door on her way out and I was left alone with the cotton candy bikini. Once it was on, I studied myself in the mirror. Being blessed in the chest and butt was sometimes a curse.

Basically, when shopping. Nothing ever fit off the rack. But every now and then, curves were way better than a single digit size could ever be. The more I straightened the bikini to the comfortable position, the more I started to think Azalea was right. My body was a weapon.

Here I was, wrapped up in a pretty little cotton candy package to tease. He wasn't used to me turning the tables, so it might just work. Besides, there was no way he was really interested in me – he just wanted to win the alpha male competition. I would call his bluff and he would ease off. Spencer was constantly bothering me. It was time to bother him right back.

When I got out to the pool area, everyone was either swimming, dancing, or standing around cackling at glass shattering levels. I scanned for Spencer. When I saw him, he was across the pool talking to two other guys.

When he saw me, his eyes went over my body a few times. He was holding a drink in one hand and something else in the other. It looked like marijuana. *Ugh. Keep it classy, Spencer.*

As I walked over, he brought the joint to his lips.

"Oooo, what's that? Candy cigarette? Can I have one?" I asked.

He gave a sly smile as the other guys mumbled nervous excuses about why they had to suddenly walk away. He just took a long hit and handed it off to one of the guys.

31

He put his drink down on the nearby table and blew the smoke from the side of his mouth.

"Come to see me this time?" he asked, his tone low, oozing from his throat.

I paired my hands on my hips with my best judgmental glare.

"Hey, I've got a question if you're not too high. Don't drugs show up on drug tests? You know, like, at work?"

"Damn, girl," he said, leaning forward and using his thumb and forefinger to slide up and down the string attaching the triangle top to the knot around my neck. "Will you wear this to work for me?"

I didn't slap his hand away. That was hard.

"They actually do random drug tests, you know."

He was too busy drinking in my cleavage to care.

"I wish we worked in aquatics together. Kids would be drowning everywhere."

"That's not funny. I almost drowned when I was a kid."

He did a mock gasp as he pretended to tug on the string around my neck. Instinctively, my hand shot up to cover my chest. I fought the urge to punch him and licked my lips instead. I was going to keep my cool. I had to tease him to break him.

"So, are you getting in with me or are you just going to stand there?"

He straightened and gave a low growl of sorts as he ran a palm down the side of my torso to my hip.

"Talor, this is –"

I stepped a little closer.

"I mean, you're the only person I know here and … I just like the way you look right now."

32

With that, I spun on my heel and started down the stone steps into the shallow end. As expected, he was quick to follow. I glanced over and saw Azalea give me a goofy thumb's up. I eased myself down into the water and dunked my head back. He swam around me, his interest piqued.

"I like this new thing you're doing."

"I don't know what you mean."

"I don't even care if you're messing with my head. Just mess with the rest of me, too."

I shot him a coy smile and gathered my wet hair off my shoulders, squeezing the excess water out. He watched, fixated on everything I did like there was nothing else going on in the world. Forget the loud music and drunk yelling all around us.

"That's tempting."

Agitated, he rolled his eyes and gave a short sigh.

"You're making me a little crazy right now, you know that? I know you're into me."

He circled, inching a little closer. I wiped water off my chest and let the droplets trickle down my hand and dip back into the pool, making tiny dissipating ripples.

"I know."

He stopped circling.

"Huh?"

I twisted my legs together in the water on the ball of my foot, skating the tips of my fingers along the surface.

"Maybe I just don't know what I want yet. I think I need some help making up my mind."

I splashed him and giggled before diving under. He chased and caught me by the foot. I squealed as he spun me around and brought us up, breathless and laughing. My knees had been loosely floating against his hips, but he took hold of my thighs and pulled me closer. We bobbed against the pool wall.

There I rested my elbows on the edge.

"That's not fair," I scolded. "You're made of fins."

"I have other parts," he said, his lip curling.

He planted his hands on the concrete between my elbows on either side as the water lapped around us, still dancing the flirtatious rhythm we set off. We were silent for a moment – too close, too intimate. I had to do something or he would kiss me, so I brushed my fingers against the inner crook of his elbow and watched his skin cover in goose bumps.

"I can be what you want," he begged.

"No, you can't," I said, eyeing him through lazy lids. "You have a girlfriend. Do I look like I share?"

His gaze was steady on me as the rowdy water swayed our bodies gently against one another. I tried to pull my legs away, but Spencer caught my hips, holding me there firmly. He was not about to let anything come between us – literally.

"I won't share you, so you won't share me," he suggested, his own fingers stroking the curve in my thigh. "I swear it."

Trembling, I lowered my arms off the edge. I couldn't believe it. Spencer didn't care about anyone. He just took what he wanted and they liked it. I pushed my hands into his chest and took back my legs. We both stood up.

"But she loves you, Spencer."

He looked lost in thought a moment, like he was weighing pros and cons. I shook my head and started up the pool ladder. He pulled me down and slung me over his shoulder. Those sitting around the pool raised their beers and cheered.

34

Azalea jumped up out of the sun chair she had been lounging in.

"Turn it up! This is my song!"

The volume went up and soon the music was reverberating through the pool area. Everyone started grinding on someone else. Spencer held me over his shoulder like a caveman, his hand stretched out across the back of my thighs to keep me in place.

"Spencer, please," I pleaded, trying to scramble off.

With a soft shrug, he rolled my body down his chest. When I splashed back into the water, he caught me by the small of my back and began waltzing me around the shallow end singing with the song. I just let him drag me through the silky water because I didn't know what else to do.

It wasn't exactly the kind of song you waltz to, but he was spinning and dipping me at what seemed like all the right times. I was actually enjoying myself. Ninety-nine percent of the time Spencer was a pompous man-whore, but for two minutes in the pool, he was something else entirely.

When the song was over, we were standing so close that breathing fused our exposed skin. Things began to feel hazy and slow. It was kissing weather, that.

Panicking, I ripped myself away and bent one arm back to scrape hair out of my face, forcing distance between us. That's when I noticed the bandage was falling off my elbow. His head snapped to look at it, and a flash of something like desire or rage flurried in those eyes.

"I'll do it," he blurted.

"What?"

"I'll break up with her."

My breath caught in my throat. I pushed away from him, verbally incapacitated. Once out of the pool, I snatched up my towel. Looking back, I saw he was already out of the pool and something in his hand was glowing. When he brought it up to his ear, I knew it was his phone.

Azalea followed me inside.

"Hey, hey! I saw that. Awwwwwesome! I didn't know you had it in you. Wait. Where are you going?"

I ran inside and slammed the door to her room.

"That just made everything worse."

She leaned against the bedpost.

"What did he say? Oh – wait. He's going to break up with her?"

That made her start cackling, and I was so frustrated with her that I didn't even bother taking off the bikini. I just started throwing my clothes on overtop it and scowled at her.

"Seriously, he must really like you, Talor. Like, really. I think it's sweet. Kinda."

"No," I replied, tying the last shoelace extra tight. "It isn't. It's ridiculous. I'll never hear the end of it now, don't you understand?"

"Well, sorry. They usually don't do that. Don't go."

When I stood up, I felt sick.

"I can't be here. I think he just called her."

Azalea twisted herself around the bedpost and wrapped her fingers up in her wavy hair.

"Whaaat? Listen, if a guy who looks like that is willing to break up with his girlfriend – like, immediately – to get with you, then that is awesome. Believe me, there are worse things in the world than having that guy after you."

"Azalea, I know that for some reason you're really impressed here, but I need you to just be on my side with this."

"You're right. I'm sorry. He's crazy for liking you so much."

36

I stared at the wall.

"I am a terrible person who listens to terrible advice. God help me."

My tires squealed spinning out of the driveway. About a mile down the road, my phone lit up. I was scared to look at it at first. When I got a few miles further, I got brave enough to pick it up. The text was from Spencer.

It's done. Now get back here. You're mine.

4

Spencer had a swim meet the next week, so he didn't work his regular shift. That bought me some time to deal with the fallout. He did text me several times while he was gone, usually asking for a picture of me in that bikini. I always replied that he had the wrong number and the bikini in question was retired. One text he sent was almost sweet.

But I miss you.

I took a minute to text back. He was never so vulnerable. Someone must have stolen his phone or something.

Oh really? What do you miss about me?

I should've known his response would be less than chivalrous.

Those curves. Send me a picture, Cotton Candy. I'm dying over here.

Thank God that was the last one. I didn't text him back. Unfortunately, I also had a few phone calls from poor Rose, who was a sniveling mess after the idiot broke up with her. She asked me to spy on him at work to find out what skank stole him away.

He obviously didn't tell her why he broke it off or she wouldn't have been calling me at all. I felt like such a bad friend. I couldn't tell her that I was glad they broke up because I was afraid it would get back to her that I was the reason. My guilty conscience assured her that I would spy on him. It felt wrong not to grant her one request.

With the Spencer problem under control for the week, I set my focus back on Sage where I wanted it. He still never paid me much attention unless I invaded his personal space. Through snippets of haggled conversation at the time clock, I learned he was from Colorado, he drove a silver Honda Civic, and he was in some local rock band called Dead Reckless.

I thought the name of his band was weird, but I didn't ask where they came up with it. Band names never really make sense to me anyway. I did ask if they had something I could listen to, but I never heard his answer. I was too busy daydreaming about him serenading me under the blue lights of some stage.

Looking at him that day, I seriously considered quitting my job if he wasn't single. He was the one guy I would have gladly stolen from someone. It was ironic considering I had already stolen a guy from someone, and I didn't even want that one.

I was never sure when Sage would give me the time of day, but I would always be talking to Larissa about him our entire shift. She enjoyed the daily entertainment, but not everyone was so content watching my comedic love life from the sidelines. Sage's boss, Kati, grew tired of the shy silence between us. Being only a handful of years older than us, she didn't have enough age distance to keep her professional distance from romantic matters.

One afternoon she cornered me while I was waiting at the time clock.

"Talor! There you are. I've got a personal question for you."

"Oh lord."

"What do you think about Sage?"

She carefully closed the door before leaning against the counter beside me. Somehow I knew she was going to pry into my personal affairs. I felt like we time-warped into high school. Were we really having a conversation about a crush? I rolled my eyes and pretended to be too old for such a topic – even though I literally spent every shift doing exactly that a few rooms over. I tried to sound as nonchalant as possible.

"I mean, he's cute. Why?"

"Well, I was just talking to him, and he seems to like you. Y'all need to talk. You know, go on a date or something."

My face flushed as I shifted on my feet. Here was Sage's boss trying to set us up. I honestly didn't believe her. How could such an attractive guy be single?

"Me? Really?"

"Yeah, he's interested. He's just shy. I thought you felt the same way, but you guys are kind of weird around each other and I wanted to get the ball rolling. I don't want the air up here to stay this thick."

She winked and left. Before I could call after her, my phone vibrated in my purse. It was Azalea.

41

SAFARI SPELL

Don't forget about Friday night! Who are you bringing? I have an extra date if you need one, LOL! XoXo

I made my way to the nursery and crouched down in my usual hiding spot. It was perfect – just out of sight of the video monitors and far enough in a corner that I could see both entrances on either side of the large room clearly. I'd see my bosses before they'd ever catch a glimpse of me.

I sighed as my fingers hovered over my phone. Responding to Azalea required a special skill. She was unique like that. Naming her after a southern flower was only one of the ways Azalea's parents honored their deep-rooted southern heritage. The Beaty family hosted a Victorian Gala every year at their mansion thanks to Mayor Beaty's fascination with Scarlett O'Hara from Gone with the Wind.

It was a major local charity event that always took place the last week of September. Mr. Beaty was a local land developer, and Mrs. Beaty had been the mayor for the past seven years. They had a few million in the bank and a street sign with their name on it, but they were good, generous people.

The Victorian Gala was an annual chance for anyone who wasn't anyone to rub shoulders with a powerful family. For the rest of us, it was something to do in a town like Cypress. Being an avid history buff, I relished any chance to lace up a corset.

I wanted to bring Sage, but every look from him gave me a mild fever. One time he brushed against me accidentally at the vending machines and I almost fainted. No joke. I'd become *that* girl. I was also becoming more aware of the emotional wall between us. I thought we were getting more comfortable together, but he kept an upturned nose my way. I felt really good about the conversation with Kati until I remembered all that. There

42

was no way Kati knew what she was talking about. I typed and re-typed my text.

I don't know. Sage might be busy or he might not want to come.

Her response was typical Azalea – quick and sharp.

Uh, no excuses, woman. You should probably ask him. He can't read your mind! You better be there.

I shook my head and sighed as I typed my thoughts.

What if he tries to kiss me? What if I attack him? Then he would think I'm a –

A rapid tapping at the glass door interrupted my furious texting. Startled, I shot up and dropped my new phone on the ground. I was annoyed to see Spencer, but relieved it wasn't the Assistant Director, who always seemed to be peeping at me through some window or another.

When Spencer pushed through the door, my chest tightened. The last time I saw him, he was calling his girlfriend to break up. I wasn't mentally prepared to see him, so I just stared at him as he closed the distance between us.

"Texting on the job? I bet you do it in the car, too. Bad girl."

Still flustered, I wasn't quick on the uptake. I normally didn't have a problem telling Spencer off, but that was before our nearly naked bodies were rubbing in the pool.

"N-no, I'm not. I don't."

With a smooth bend, he scooped up my cell phone.

"Relax. It's our little secret, Cotton Candy."

He flipped it over and gave a raised brow when he read my unfinished message. He had invaded my privacy yet again, and I fought the urge to scream at him like a temperamental toddler.

"Don't read that. Give me my phone."

He shrugged and offered it, but when I tried to take it, he gripped it even tighter.

"Is there a picture on here for me?"

"No, Spencer. Just stop."

Somewhere in middle school, some clueless boy was trying the same trick on whatever poor girl he liked. Maybe she had less class and more fire than me. If so, he was probably laid out in a hallway holding his crotch and crying for his mother. Here in my own hell, Spencer was still holding my phone hostage because I'm too polite.

"Talor, let's do something."

"I know what you want to do," I said, glowering as I felt the burn in my face.

"Yeah, but you do, too," he smirked, glancing at the phone, "just with the wrong guy."

With a furious jerk, I pried my phone from his hand. He seemed incredibly strong, but it could have been because my hands were shaking. I tried not to look in his eyes. Many women were pulled under those tempest waves and woke up in a dirty bed somewhere as a result. Thanks to him, people already had the impression we were interested in each other. Thanks to Azalea, he had the impression I was into him.

"You're so gross," I said, turning away.

His lips were tickling my ear now.

44

"Hey, you remember when you said you were into me? Remember that?"

He was too close now, and it made the hair on the back of my neck stand up. I wheeled around and pushed an arm between us to create distance as fast as possible.

"I remember you doing drugs. Is that what you're talking about?" I replied, raising my voice and crossing my arms in front.

His hand reached out and brushed under my polo shirt at my side, his finger edging along the top of my pants against my hipbone. He didn't even try to quiet me. He was trying to do something else.

"I remember this."

My mouth dropped open. His finger felt good against my skin. Of course it did. He watched his own finger move against my skin, which prickled under his calculated touch. Frustrated, I freed myself from his roaming hand.

"You were high. I don't know what you think happened, but it didn't. I barely talked to you that night."

He was unfazed.

"Yeah, I wasn't high. I meant what I said that night, too. I'm single now, like you asked. There isn't anyone else."

"Did you know I'm talking to Sage?"

He closed his eyes and sighed, pinching the bridge of his nose.

"No, you're not. Just stop."

I held my chin up.

"Yes, I am."

He opened his eyes and looked at me as his jaw tightened.

"Talor, he doesn't like you. When are you going to stop chasing him around?"

That stung a bit. Still, I held my ground.

"I know you're used to having anyone and anything you want, but I don't have to date you, Spencer. I actually have a choice and I'm not interested. I know that's hard for you to understand."

He blinked hard and leaned his head to the side. We stared at each other for a few seconds before his brow bunched up and he gave a short, bitter laugh.

"Ok, it's hard to understand because you're lying. What is this? Don't you know you're the only reason I even work here?"

"Then you should quit."

"Go with me to the gala Friday."

I laughed harder than I expected to. I couldn't help it.

"Uh, since when were you invited? You can't buy your way into the Beaty's."

This time he laughed. He thought a girl refusing him was the funniest thing ever. He crossed his arms, mimicking me as he stepped into my space and dropped his chin.

"Your friend – Azalea – invited me personally. She wants me there. My friend – Jesse – wants me there. You're the only snob who doesn't."

My jaw dropped as I processed the fact that the trust fund jock called me a snob. I refused to believe that Azalea invited him. They had only met once and she knew how I felt about him. Even being fiends with Jesse...no, he had to buy his way in.

Just then, the nursery door slammed behind me. I spun around to see Larissa creeping in. She probably heard the whole conversation. I could tell by the fact that she was holding a book over her face as she passed by. Spencer didn't even acknowledge her.

"You'll like my car," he said, winking.

I hesitated. I shouldn't have. I held my breath, trying to think of some excuse, but I wasn't fast enough. As he slowly and deliberately pulled his shirt over his shoulders, his undershirt rode up to expose that tan, lean muscle called a body. Larissa's eyes bulged as she peeked over pages she pretended to read.

Two other female Goodlife Gym workers walked by the long glass windows separating the hallway from the nursery and giggled to each other. He jerked his undershirt back down over his chest as he savored the attention. In a relationship or single, he was still the same old Spencer. And he wanted me to be his next victim. He slowly ran his hand through his hair and threw the staff shirt over his shoulder.

"Um, why did you just take off your shirt?" I asked.

"You said you needed help making up your mind," he said, waving his hand across his body.

I paused, stifling a laugh.

"Um, no."

Out of the corner of my eye, I watched Larissa's shoulders bouncing behind the book. She was laughing hard enough for the both of us. Spencer gave a soft shrug.

"Talor, I like you. Go with me."

The clock above us ticked loudly as he waited for my answer. Just then, a parent came bursting in the room with two rowdy toddlers. I felt a heightened sense of pressure to say yes and didn't know why. The words tumbled out and I hated them as they did.

"Shhhhhhure, Spencer. As friends."

I felt sick to my stomach because I knew it couldn't be undone. I only hoped Sage didn't hear about it and think I was actually interested in Spencer. Just to make sure, I escorted Spencer out the front when he left, pretending to run up to the time clock to check my hours. When he passed in front of Sage, their eyes met in a way only men understand.

Spencer twirled his keys in his hand, winking at me.

"Looking forward to it, Cotton Candy."

I didn't like him calling me that, but arguing with him would look defensive, like I had feelings to release his way. He disappeared out the door while I bore the brunt of stares hitting me all at once. None were quite so heavy as Sage's. It was a look of everything and nothing, and my heart sunk. That hazel green splintered my confidence a thousand ways.

When he looked away, the world went back to turning. I spun on my heel as quickly as I could, burning an invisible trail of fire between the front desk and the nursery area.

Somehow, I would make Spencer pay.

5

I barely slept for two days.

When I did manage to pass out from pure exhaustion, I had nightmares of Rose stabbing hopping bunnies and wallabies in my yard and smearing liquid cotton candy all over my car. She kept yelling out some battle cry in German about the death of immortal love.

There was also a flamethrower involved. The evil instigator Spencer was there, too – clad in a leopard Speedo while he cackled and danced under a smoking umbrella. Why wallabies were roaming free in South Georgia was anyone's guess. Oddly enough, the rest of it actually made sense to me.

When I crawled into work on Thursday, I noticed the usually empty bulletin board in the timecard room had a flyer on it. It was a show for a local band. *Wait – is that Sage's band?*

Frantically, I slapped a hand against it to read the details because my eyes were moving so fast the words were jumping. Dead Reckless was playing a show at a downtown bar called Harvest Moon the next night. I started to create an excuse to go when something bright and yellow caught the corner of my eye.

It was another flyer, but this one was a reminder that all staff members had to take a mandatory CPR class to renew our certification. There were only two options – that afternoon, in exactly thirty minutes – or coming in at eight o'clock Saturday morning. I'd completely forgotten about the class. I was lucky that I came in early to work out, but I was frustrated that I would now have to spend that hour dealing with Spencer instead of running away from my problems on the outdoor track.

Sage and Larissa wouldn't be there. They were the only people I cared to see, incidentally. Sage was off and Larissa's certification from her teaching job meant she didn't have to do the class at all. I lost my loyal friend buffer for the impending Spencer confrontation.

That made me so nervous that when Spencer came in, I dashed into the women's bathroom and hid for the next twenty minutes. It wasn't my most mature idea, but I was sleep-deprived and my feet worked faster than my brain. I stole peeks out the door to see Spencer talking to some gym member with a wandering gaze looking for me. I waited until the last moment to leave my hiding spot so I wouldn't get locked out of the class.

Everyone wandered into the room, finding seats in the side-by-side chairs lining the walls. There were about a dozen people in the class – mostly fitness staff or lifeguards. I didn't really know any of them. I made sure to sit between Kati and some girl so Spencer couldn't sit beside me.

To my dismay, the girl got up to go greet her friend across the room just as Spencer walked in. I closed my eyes and turned away as a body settled beside me. I just knew it was Spencer, but it wasn't. It was Sage.

Wearing a fitted flannel shirt with rolled up sleeves, he sat back in the chair and raised my blood pressure.

"Hi," I squeaked, snapping up into good posture and hoping I looked skinny from his angle.

"Talor," he said, my name gaining a heavenly air as it rolled off his tongue.

His hair was flying out at the ends the way it does when a guy's been wearing a hat all day. I made a silent pact with my reflexes that I was going to remain calm and they were going to behave. It was the closest I'd ever been to him, and my hands were frantically searching for somewhere to hide. If they didn't get somewhere fast, they were going to reach out and touch him. I had little control over that. Spencer coolly took a seat between two cute lifeguards, who welcomed him with girlish giggles.

Kati leaned forward beside me.

"Mr. Talis," she greeted, giving him a salute, "good to see you here on your day off. You know you didn't have to come to this one. There's another one on Saturday. Did I tell you that the other day?"

Sage brushed his palms down his thighs.

"Yeah, but I was already over this way."

Ah, the old 'I was in the neighborhood' excuse. My foot bounced happily as Kati cocked a sly smile and let her jaw hang a little so we could hear her "uh-huh."

"I think there's an uneven number of people now," Spencer grumbled from his seat, stretching his legs out in front of him.

"Spencer, I didn't think you would mind the odds," Kati chuckled. "They are your favorite kind, after all."

Spencer checked out the two girls beside him and arched his lip.

"Well, you're right about that," he agreed, winking.

They pretended to be mad at him for that, but they just followed it up with childish banter so no one took them seriously. Kati slapped her hands together in the air and spread them out wide.

"See? What are you even complaining about? Come on, man."

"Nothing," he muttered, giving me the side-eye.

"Spencer's been a little moody since he broke up with his girlfriend. Don't take it personally," Kati added, looking back and forth between Sage and me.

Sage adjusted one of his sleeves.

"That sucks."

I stared down at my hands in my lap and tried not to freak out. I could feel him moving beside me since our chairs were close. We almost touched twice as his elbow bobbed near mine, straightening the folded cuff. Our eyes locked when he stretched an arm back and draped it over the top of my chair. I did my best not to blush, but I couldn't help it.

If I sat back, his arm would be around me. I rested back into the cold metal and felt his arm, which immediately made me sweat through my shirt.

"Talor, did you know about Spencer breaking up with his girlfriend?" Kati asked.

I only cut my eyes at her, not wanting to turn away from Sage. I didn't care to talk about Spencer's relationships. Especially his and Rose's, but Kati wasn't letting it go.

"Yeah, I heard."

"I just thought you'd be interested since she was your friend," Kati said, her eyes baiting me with some sort of secret.

Growing tense, I shifted uneasily in the chair. Kati had this knowing look, like maybe Spencer told her what happened. I worried what version he told her. I cleared my throat, faking a smile.

"Yes, she is my friend. Obviously, Spencer cheats a lot. She was probably tired of it."

We all looked at Spencer, who was whispering in the ear of one of the lifeguards. She flipped her hair and scrunched her shoulders to get closer to him with a giggle. Kati rolled her eyes.

"Yeah, but if she was ok with him cheating all the time before, why would they break up now? Who he cheated with probably had something to do with it, don't you think?"

I didn't respond, but the concentrated stares made me feel like I was being microwaved alive. A booming voice saved me from the awkward conversation. It was one of the EMTs – a stout man with a thick mustache and a rounded out middle.

"We'll get started if that's all right? That way we can get out of here in no time. Ok. My name's Barry and this is Mike. Has anyone here never done a CPR class before?"

The two lifeguards sitting beside Spencer held up their hands. They must have been new hires. They were young. They were embarrassed to be the only newbies, so both of them yanked their hands out of the air and stuffed them under their arms. Barry smiled.

"Don't worry, ladies. It looks like you've got plenty of old pros to help you out. Ok, first, let's go ahead and – hold on," Barry said, stopping for a moment to count heads, "get in partners. Someone might have two partners."

Spencer thrust his fist in the air. Barry pointed at him.

"I think this gentleman here has graciously taken on the task. Everyone else, please couple up."

My chest was in pandemonium trying to pretend I wasn't looking at Sage. Just when he opened his mouth, Kati's head rested on my shoulder and her fingers laced around my elbow.

"I know you're gonna hate me for this, but be my partner. I'll explain," she said in a hushed tone.

"Kati," I said, frowning.

She raised her brows and leaned around to look at Sage.

"Sorry, Sage. Girls only."

Sage gave a polite nod and partnered up with an older front desk worker sitting across the room. Sighing, I watched him get up, leaving the chair beside me lonely and cold. Barry continued giving us directions, but it was like white noise. Furious, I whipped around to Kati. While she was easygoing and close in age, I had to be respectful. She was an authority figure...of sorts.

"Explain now," I demanded.

She took me by the elbows as we both knelt to the floor. A CPR mannequin lay between us. She put a finger over her mouth to shush me.

"Wait. Do this first."

Barry showed us how to count between breaths and apply the right kind of pressure depending on the victim. Since I'd done it a few times before, I breezed through the exercise, anxious for Kati's explanation. When it was her turn to give chest compressions, she leaned far enough over the mannequin to talk to me, keeping her voice low.

"I kind of heard something about you and Spencer."

"You heard something from Spencer?"

She wrinkled her nose and bit her lower lip.

"Spencer told me why he broke up with his girlfriend. Had a little to do with you?"

I swallowed hard. Spencer had run his mouth. I shouldn't have been surprised. I never wanted that to get out – especially at work. I immediately had to know what he was telling people we did in the pool so I could do some serious damage control. I assessed the distance between him and Sage suddenly wary of them being close enough for a casual conversation about the pool party Spencer went to recently.

I shot eye daggers at him, but he was too busy groping an inexperienced lifeguard to notice.

"Wow, Kati. Well, whatever he told you isn't true."

Kati gave a soft shrug.

"Fair enough. It didn't really sound like something you'd do. He said you told him you would date him if he broke up with your friend, so he did. That part true?"

She stopped doing compressions while she waited for my answer. I changed positions on the floor and brushed the hair back that was falling in my face. The room felt stifling. Maybe it knew I was about to lie through my teeth and it was trying to crush me before I did.

"Kati, he was dating one of my best friends. Why would I do that? Come on," I said, rolling my eyes.

I tried to make the possibility of me doing what I actually did totally absurd to her. It worked. She seemed to size me up for a moment before relaxing. I pretended to care about what we were doing while she decided who to believe. She cleared her throat.

"All right. Listen, just so you know, I like you and so I'm not judging you if that did happen. I've always known that he cared about you."

I cocked a skeptical brow.

55

"Um, Spencer doesn't care about anybody. He only cares about bodies and what he can get from them."

"I'm not saying he's the most mature guy around, but...what I am saying is that he really wants to be with you and I think maybe you want that, too."

I shook my head.

"I'm sorry – wasn't it just the other day you asked what I thought about Sage?"

"Well, yeah, but that was before I knew about all this. I think you guys would be cute, but Spencer...it's actually affecting his work."

I couldn't believe Spencer's boss was rooting for him. Everyone in this place was crazy about Spencer except for me, and that was getting weird. Even in the middle of an inappropriate conversation about my love life, I still couldn't be honest. It felt like we had eavesdroppers all around us.

"I'm sorry, what? How is it affecting his work again?"

She glanced around the room.

"Preoccupied, frustrated, unfriendly."

I figured it was time to shut the conversation down. I pushed my hands back on my hips, which forced my chest out. I had to stretch my cramped back. All the kneeling and bending over was hurting my muscles.

"Well, I like Sage. Spencer just has to deal with that like a grownup," I replied, arching my neck as I rolled it back.

I caught a glimpse of Spencer's face before I closed my eyes. There was insecurity in it for probably the first time in his life. By the time I opened my eyes and returned to my CPR position, he was paying attention to his partners.

"I think you like both of them and you need someone to tell you that's ok. You're young. You're pretty. You're single. Have options. Just don't pit them against each other. I don't like getting involved in the personal lives of my workers."

I pointed back and forth between us.

"Um, yes, you do. What is this?"

"Hey now. I'm asking because I wanted to know the truth. There's too much tension at the front and I need to know what's going on."

"Maybe it's the alpha male competition. I don't know. Or karma finally caught up with Spencer."

She crinkled her nose.

"Huh? Alpha male competition?"

"Oh, never mind," I said, groaning.

She wagged a finger at me.

"Sage and Spencer are my favorites. Don't repeat that. I need this fixed. Sage is the most mature college dude I've ever met and the members just love Spencer to death. I can't lose either of them."

"It sounds like the problem is all Spencer to me, so get rid of him."

Kati turned her gaze up at the window, thinking for a minute.

"I'm going to move Sage to the morning shift."

I gave an exasperated sigh. Leaning closer, I felt like I could put a little more force behind my words without drawing too much attention.

"No, move Spencer to the morning shift! Cut his hours. We all know he doesn't need the money. Maybe you should be scolding your favorite employees about acting like adults, not blaming me for their behavior."

When Kati scowled at me, I realized that I wasn't as quiet as I thought. The two couples closest to us had heard me. Spencer and Sage both seemed to sense the commotion from where they were, so they looked over. To my relief, no one said anything.

Barry the EMT kept walking around, directing us through each exercise. Every now and then, the lifeguard twins would break the sound barrier over something Spencer said. Once we finished the next exercise, Kati leaned forward on her hand.

"Hey, I didn't mean to upset you."

"I know, but none of this is my fault."

A soft smile crept on her lips.

"Just pick one. If this gets physical and I have to fire somebody, you're gone, too. Not kidding."

The EMTs walked around and watched us all do the chest compressions next. I was going through the monotonous motions when it dawned on me that I already knew how to get even with Spencer. It was cruel, but he deserved it. I leaned forward to whisper where only Kati could hear me this time.

"Maybe you need to do a random drug test for your staff."

Her eyes went wide before narrowing into fine slits.

"What do you mean?"

I shrugged. She gave me a cold stare before glancing over at Sage and Spencer.

"Legally, I have to take what you're saying seriously. But you know if you're making this up to cause more trouble –"

"Why wouldn't you trust me?"

"Because this is serious, Talor. Did you actually see someone using drugs?"

I sat back on my heels.

"Yes."

"A certain someone?"

In that moment, I felt my blood run cold. Yes, I wanted him to lose his job and his scholarship, but I felt dirty holding the ace card to his downfall. As much as I disliked Spencer, I couldn't make myself say his name. But I didn't have to. Kati knew. Her face fell as she stared off.

"Did anyone else see it?"

"Maybe that's really his problem at work."

She smacked her hands on the ground beside her and pushed up with such force I swear she defied gravity.

"I hope you're wrong."

We caught eyes, but I didn't say anything. I just bit down on my lip, trying to act sympathetic. She paused for a moment as she passed Spencer, who paid her little attention. When she left the room, she headed right into the Assistant Director's office.

"Let's take a five minute break, everybody," Barry bellowed.

As everyone started filing out of the room to grab snacks, Spencer came over and sat on the floor across from me. He didn't say anything, making it extra awkward. I recoiled as best I could.

"God, what do you want?"

"Why didn't you send me a picture?"

"I'm not sending you a picture of me so you can –"

I gulped down the rest of the sentence. I wasn't going to say that. He smirked, finding it humorous that I couldn't suggest masturbation.

"So I can what?"

"Do...whatever you want to do with it."

"What if I send you one of me so it's fair?"

"Pass."

He chuckled and pushed the mannequin away so he could get in my personal space.

"Let's blow this off. We know all this stuff anyway. We could finish that very interesting conversation we started the other night. The one where we were pretty much naked."

Even by Spencer's standards, it was brazen. I wanted to back away, but my knees were twisted underneath me and he was leaning so close I would have to touch him.

My words went up as a shield.

"You know this is sexual harassment."

"It's what?"

"You heard me."

He dragged a hand down his face.

"Oh, right. Go ahead and pretend I'm a jerk. But don't forget that what you're doing to me is exactly what you judge me for. That makes us the same."

He eased back as Kati came through the door with a disgruntled look on her face. I was quietly thankful for the interruption. I turned my face towards the window so I didn't have to look at anyone. Spencer had me pegged. I was a tease, but I had never liked two guys at once, and I didn't like it. It felt dirty.

Kati motioned to Spencer.

"Kaden, gotta talk to you about something."

Spencer gave me a cool once over before going with her. I hadn't noticed Sage standing with Kati, too. My thoughts went to a panicky, weird place and I started to worry. *What if Sage had something to hide?* It never occurred to me. My thoughts were irrational. I knew that.

Still, as I watched them head to the Assistant Director's office together, my lungs cinched a wretched knot in my chest. Everyone else came meandering back in to finish the class, totally oblivious. The lifeguard girls searched for Spencer, but they settled sadly for each other as partners when they saw he wasn't coming back.

I could only wonder what was going on behind those tightly drawn silver blinds.

6

Sage was on the phone as I came in to work the next day. I don't even know if he saw me. I was just grateful he was still around. Spencer was nowhere to be found. At first it was exciting, but then I remembered why he wasn't there. He had the day off because it was the night of the Victorian Gala.

I didn't plan the sabotage very well. He knew I was the one who got him tested, and now I would have to deal with him at the gala. Once my shift was over, I got ready in the nursery bathroom.

While tightening a corset Scarlett O'Hara would be proud of, I discovered I was somehow missing a heel. My red satin ball gown slipped over my curves without a fuss once the corset was tight enough to kill a lesser woman. After I fastened all the buttons I could and struggled enough with the rest, I called out to Larissa for help.

"Pleeeease...I can't get the top buttons."

While I waited for her to finish whatever she was doing, I took a good look at my silhouette. It was painful, but the corset was pleasing. Why didn't women want to look this good on a daily basis? In a matter of seconds, my natural hourglass shape had gained superpowers.

I couldn't figure out why corsets ever went out of style – you know, minus the whole not being able to breathe or move thing. When Larissa still hadn't come to my rescue, I discovered I could still screech in it.

"La-RI-ssa!"

Impatient, I stepped out of the bathroom. Larissa was standing just outside with her arms crossed in front and one judgmental eyebrow set high on her forehead. She did a sassy hand wave towards my hair.

"Miss Scarlett, I don't know nothin' 'bout hookin' no buttons! Honey, what's going on with all this? Have some trouble with the curling iron?"

I looked back in the mirror. My hair was only halfway done. Lost in mourning over the extinction of daily corsets, I somehow forgot to do the rest of it. Like any true friend, Larissa took pity on me and ushered me back in the bathroom to finish my hair.

She always treated me like the younger sister she never had. I didn't mind that. She was the least judgmental of my friends and gained all my trust in only three months.

Her only fault was laughing at me all the time, even when it was only at my expense. Still, her laugh was hearty and full – the contagious kind. Being trapped in a nursery for a five-hour shift would be hell with anyone else. But working with her was a good day, and that meant every day was good. In short, it was a perfect arrangement we had – professionally and personally.

As she finished the last few corset hooks, a curious look came over her face.

"Who do you think is cuter: Spencer or Sage?"

"Sage."

She did a funny smile.

"Really? Huh. Ok. You can date both of them, you know. Besides, I've seen you flirt with him. Heat, honey. Heat."

I shook my head just in case my glare wasn't clear enough.

"What is it with everyone and that guy? Is every woman here really that susceptible to an oil-based charm?"

Larissa chuckled.

"Girl, you really don't like blondes, do you?"

"It isn't because he's blonde. He cheated on my friend Rose for a year, and he hooked up with at least two of the lifeguards this summer. They got fired and he didn't. How did you not hear about that?"

Her jaw dropped.

"Shut up! He is so bad. Did your friend find out?"

"Of course she did. Do you really think Spencer would hide the fact that he was with two girls at one time and neither one was his girlfriend? Rose stayed with him, by the way. They just broke up. I almost brought her to a hypnotist. Or a wizard."

Larissa looked oddly impressed as she sprayed hairspray on the curl that bounced out of the curling iron.

"So that's it. You don't want him to talk about what y'all do."

I fought the urge to scream. He already talked and we didn't even do anything. Larissa noticed my anger building into a rolling boil.

"Girl, if you don't get that temper under control, your curls are going to flatten from the steam comin' out the top of your head! Don't you know

I'm just messin' with you? Calm down! I'm just sayin', don't you ever wonder why Sage can't find his way back here and Spencer can? Spencer's sexy little self is here every day flirtin' with you. You should be flattered, that's all."

"I'm tired of being flattered by a frat boy. I want a mature man at this point."

She released another curl.

"A mature man? You mean a certain front desk worker who won't ask you out? The one who won't even talk to you?"

I knew she was right. Sage wasn't making any moves and Spencer was making enough for the both of them. I shrugged, tucking my chin a little as I did.

"God, I hate dating. Men are so weird."

"Oh honey, you have no idea. Count your blessings that Spencer is the worst one in your life. Serious question, though: if he treated your friend so bad, why are you going with him tonight?"

"I'm too nice. I'm terrible at saying no. I'm a bad friend. You pick."

Larissa gave a sharp exhale.

"Or you're trying to make Sage jealous. You can admit it. You know you can ask him out now? Some women's rights thing."

She was trying to be encouraging, but I was getting aggravated. I wanted to be patient and wait for Sage to make his move. Why didn't anyone understand? I was being a lady. He was being a gentleman. It was that simple. No future grandmother wants to tell her future grandchildren she wore their grandfather down.

"Larissa, not everyone moves as fast as Spencer does – and in so many different directions. Attraction takes time. Besides, I didn't know Sage was single until Tuesday when Kati told me! He acts like he's devoted heart and soul to someone else."

Larissa muttered something under her breath. Her voice kept rising and falling in intervals like she was trying to figure out a problem in her head. I finally got tired of the babbling.

"What, Larissa? What?"

"Y'all are just so funny. All you do is stare at each other when your backs are turned, but you never talk. Spencer'll get married before y'all go on a first date. All I know? You better go get your man before someone else does! I saw that cute little ballet teacher chattin' him up the other day. He looked interested."

What she was saying was true. Sage and I were doing a strange sort of mating dance and I was tired of it. For a second, I thought deep down that's why I said yes to Spencer.

"What do you want? Me to throw him in a janitor's closet for seven minutes in heaven? This isn't middle school. We're all adults here. Wait. What ballet teacher? Sage doesn't chat. Does he?"

Another girl was after him? I narrowed my eyes at nothing. Larissa rolled hers.

"Just sayin'! Like he'd complain, anyway. Don't even act like you didn't talk about seriously doing that. What was it, just last week? Or was it yesterday? You said, 'Oooo, girl, the things I'd do to Sage in a dark room –'"

Larissa was interrupted by a familiar male voice breaking in the conversation. Sage.

"Hello?"

My heart started racing. I held my breath thinking that maybe he wouldn't see me if I didn't breathe. Had he heard our whole conversation?

If so, I would have to quit. Larissa smiled as he popped his head in the bathroom.

As fate would have it, I was sitting on the toilet so Larissa could do my hair. I wasn't using it, but I didn't exactly want him to have a vision of me sitting on a toilet. Awkwardness hung thick in the air as we all exchanged weird facial expressions.

Larissa offered damage control.

"Oh, hi, Saaaaaaage. We were just talking about you!"

I began to melt in my seat when I saw that Sage was holding my missing heel in his hand. Was this real life?

"I saw this on the floor out there. I figured since you were the only one dressing up it was yours," he said.

I flashed an embarrassed smile and took the shoe from him.

"Actually, can I talk to you for a minute? Alone?" he asked, clearing his throat.

My heartbeat took a stumble.

"Sure. I think we're done here, right, Larissa?"

Larissa gave an erratic nod as she released the final curl. In a spastic fit to get out of the room as quickly as possible, she jerked the curling iron out of the wall by its cord. As it whipped out, it popped me in the eye. Larissa loosened her grip on the hot iron as she tried to catch the flying cord, but the curling iron slipped and scorched the left side of my neck.

I jumped up and let out some primal animal noise resembling a squawk. I felt the burned skin bubble and tighten, but I tried not to cry. Larissa dropped the iron on the floor.

"Uhhhhh, I'll go get some ice. Sorry!" she said, stuttering as she hurried out the door.

68

Sage took hold of my shoulder and led me from the bathroom to a rocking chair nearby. When my nose started running, I was forced to wipe it with the back of my hand since I couldn't see to grab a tissue. I was sniveling like a kid who just got bullied on the playground. Every time I tried to open my eyes, I had to shut them with twice as much force to make the rapid succession of pain subside. I bent forward and groaned.

"Are you ok?" Sage asked.

I could tell he was kneeling in front of me, so I scooted back in the seat. I didn't want snot on him.

"I'm not crying it's just...I can't see. Can you hand me a tissue please?"

It was important for him to know that I wasn't crying. I tried to look at him through my watery squint. It's terrifying to think what I actually looked like. There's nothing sexy about cliffhangers in the nose and bloodshot eyes. Sage's deep voice traveled through my ear all warm and ticklish.

He placed a box of tissues in my hand and pulled a few out, wiping my face softly. We didn't speak, but I felt myself smile as he wiped the tears.

I felt something cool against my neck. I hadn't heard Larissa come back, but I assumed she'd brought an icepack. I reached up to take the ice pack from him, but it was just his hand. Stunned, I wasn't sure whether I should jerk my hand away or not, so it lingered there. The coolness of his hand soothed the pain but set me on fire inside. I hoped he couldn't feel my skin boiling to a blush under his touch.

"Does that help?" he asked.

"Yes, thank you."

"Talor, do you mind? Your eye – can I see?"

"I don't know. I can't see. Can you?"

I heard a soft chuckle.

"Good one. May I then?"

I nodded. His hand went over my eye and started to warm against my skin. I leaned into it and the throbbing pain quickly receded. I began to feel groggy, like I'd been drugged. I was in a dreamy and relaxed state when he came into focus in front of me. His eyes didn't seem the same; they were intense and dark.

I thought it was strange, but I was quickly distracted by his sweet smile. My make-up was running down my cheeks so I knew I wasn't a pretty sight, but he didn't seem to mind. I was finally in his full attention, and we both wanted me there this time.

"How's that?"

"So good," I said, sighing softly like he was some swoony movie star.

"Here – I'll help you stand."

He took my hands in his and lifted me out of the chair. I was still a little woozy, but it was okay. We just stared at each other while he held me. After a moment, he brushed his finger across my upper cheek.

"I've been wondering about this scar. What happened?"

I couldn't see what he was referring to, but I knew what it was. It was a small strawberry-colored scar at the corner of my left eye. I became very self-conscious knowing how close he was and how hard he was studying my face. *How long had he been wondering about an imperfection on my face?*

I turned my chin down to hide it.

"Oh, that? A rooster attacked me when I was a toddler. My dad kinda kicked it across the yard. I think he killed it, actually."

He turned his head towards the door, but his eyes stayed on me.

"Yikes. Left its mark on you, didn't it?"

"Yeah, I guess so. My dad hated all chicken after that. It's all he eats now."

Sage cracked the cutest smile at me, revealing a dimple in his left cheek. Before I could swoon over it, Larissa raced back in with the ice, causing Sage to clear his throat and step back. Larissa held up the Ziploc bag of ice cubes.

"Do you – still need this?"

Sage scratched his jaw.

"Well, I think I'll go. You have somewhere to be...unfortunately."

He shot me a lingering glance as he walked out past Larissa, whose jaw was hinged open. When the door shut behind him, she dropped the ice and bolted over. She grabbed me by the shoulders and shook me.

"What did I miss? Did something just happen? I saw that look! Oooooo, that was something! Did he just kiss you? Oh my God, I can't believe I missed it!"

"No, he didn't kiss me."

Larissa furrowed her brow.

"Wait a minute! You aren't blind? Why did I go running up there to get ice? You know I don't do running."

I went and checked myself out in the bathroom mirror. It was like nothing ever happened. My eye was fine. My neck was fine. There wasn't even a scratch on me. I thought I'd imagined the whole thing, but I remembered feeling the bubbling of the burn on my neck. Odd.

I winked at Larissa.

"Thank you. You know, for burning me and trying to gouge my eye out, not for going to get the ice I didn't need."

"Oh hush! What did I tell you? He was just looking for an excuse to get his hands on you, too! Now you know he feels the same way. And you let him just walk away. I'm gonna tell you, girl – we don't get looks like that in real life. Go throw him in a closet or I will!"

As I gazed at my reflection, I looked past the runny mascara and red nose. I had a renewed sense of purpose in that moment. That look. Those hands. There were several custodial closets along the way. I felt a surge of adrenaline flood my steps as I raced out to catch him before he left.

I got to the hallway as he was making his way through the double doors. Momentum betrayed me and I failed to pull off a successful full stop in a bustle and heels. My shoulder rammed into the wall just in time for him to turn around and see it. To make matters worse, I hadn't run far, but I sounded really out of shape because of how nervous I was.

"Sage, wait!"

I hadn't really thought about what I wanted to say, just that I didn't want him to leave. I couldn't tell him that. A smile crept up on his lips as he released the door. It closed quietly. I beat my brain while we shuffled our feet.

"What did you to me about?"

"Oh, what was that?"

My whole body went cold. I was horrified. In my hurry to get out the perfect words in my head, I missed a few. I wished the curling iron had marred my face so my horrific expression would have been excusable.

There was no coming back from the missing verbs. I steadied myself against the wall, trying to pretend I wasn't nervous or breathless from running a few steps – or that I hadn't literally run into a wall trying to catch him.

"I wanted to thank you for my shoe, but I – uh – think I interrupted you. What were you saying?"

"I did want to ask you something. I was wondering if you would like –"

All of a sudden, Spencer came through the door behind him and passed him like he wasn't even there. Without a word, Sage slipped away. The magical moment was gone, and I felt cheated. I stiffened as Spencer filled my vision. Any other girl would have fainted at such a sight, but I could have knocked the fake mustache right off his smug upper lip.

For once in his life, he could have passed for a true gentleman. Head to toe, he looked like a different person. He was clean-shaven with his hair carefully brushed to the side away from his face.

He was wearing a black tailcoat and even a silk top hat. That tux was probably worth more than my car. But then again, my car wasn't worth much. His eyes snaked down my frame and came back up to rest on my chest.

"Yowsa, you look good enough to eat. Ready to go?"

Ugh.

7

I could still feel Sage's hand on my face.

There was a subtle tremor in his fingers, like they were used to the weight of the world in them. Of course, he could have just been nervous. But he was the one who'd been playing hard to get all along, not me. I was the awkward one running into walls and creeping around corners.

"Hey, let's talk about that drug test I had to take," Spencer said, interrupting my thoughts.

"What?"

He eyed me sideways as he shifted gears.

"You are being so bad lately. I'm impressed."

I watched his other hand slide along the wheel. The leather purred beneath his caress.

"So I guess you passed?"

"I don't know what to tell you, Cotton Candy. You were seeing things that night. I just hope you don't have to take a drug test."

He winked as he changed lanes, speeding around everyone on the road like they were driving pool floats.

"Spencer, are you even going the speed limit?"

"Calm down. It feels faster than it is. It's the car."

Of course I didn't believe him, so I leaned over to check the speedometer. He was definitely speeding. His hand scampered down my bare shoulders and latched around my waist.

"I can do a couple things at once."

I pulled away and leaned against the passenger door.

"Why can't you act normal? You're in costume. Play a part!"

I wanted as much distance as possible from him, but it was hard to find distance in a dress that size in a car that size. I groaned as I tried to keep my skirts down and behaved.

"This car is too small, Spencer! You knew what I was wearing tonight."

He smirked.

"Just take it off then."

"I mean, why do you even have a car like this? You're a college student."

"Uh-oh. You don't like my car?" he asked, the inflection in his voice going up with the corners of his mouth.

All of a sudden, he shifted gears and floored it, the seat beneath me kicking back like I was taking off in flight. It felt like the first big drop on a roller coaster, and my stomach got left a few miles back. I held onto the armrest like I would fly out of the car at any moment.

As we went down the winding street, the tires gripped the road so tightly that it felt like we were riding the ledge of some towering mountain. I turned my smile towards the window because I didn't want him to see it. I'd never been in a car so fast, and it was fun. He watched me in the reflection and chuckled to himself before slowing down.

"What did you see in Rose?"

He cleared his throat and leaned back in his seat.

"She's...nice."

"She held out on you. That was it, wasn't it? The challenge. You like that. You need the chase. This car proves it."

"I can't catch you though, can I? Even in this car," he mused.

"You do that, don't you? Treat everything and everyone like a new car. As soon as something new comes out, you have to have it."

He looked at me.

"You know that's not true. I've known you for over a year."

I smirked.

"So why did you start acting like this when Sage showed up? Don't want anyone else to play with your toy?"

"You're so perfect, aren't you, Talor? You barely know him and you keep holding out. We could make this work, you know? You just don't want to."

"You don't know how to be a one-girl kind of guy, and that's what I want."

"I would be with you."

I turned to face him.

"Really? Then keep your eyes on just me tonight. Prove me wrong. Maybe then I won't hate your stupid car."

His eyes sparkled with the challenge.

"You don't want me to watch the road? Ok."

I rolled my eyes. I thought he was kidding until he stared at me for a few moments too long.

"Spencer, watch the road!"

He gave a wink.

"Imagine that Sage wasn't perfect. What if he was just a deviant like me? Would this even be a competition?"

I batted my eyes and gave a strained smile.

"You can't compete with Sage, darling."

Spencer narrowed his eyes into the rearview.

"He's not good for you, Talor."

"Oh, I can't wait to hear this."

"Look, I'm serious. I've known him a while. You don't want to get mixed up with him. I mean it."

"Oh, wait. I'm sorry – are you saying I should get mixed up with you then?"

He half-smiled.

"Now you're catching on."

I tried to brush him off, but I couldn't.

"And by the way, what are you talking about 'you've known him for a while'? How? You're not even from here! Neither is he. Did you guys go to the same prep school in California or something?"

Spencer cast a knowing look my way and shrugged.

"I guess it's something like that."

"Oh my God. Ok. Yeah, that's for sure. He's not even from California, Spencer! You're such a liar."

"I'm glad you brought that up. Ask yourself where he's from. Has he even bothered to tell you?"

"He's from Colorado," I beamed. I was so glad I knew that so I could rub it in his face.

Spencer gave a short laugh.

"Is that what he told you? Creative. Ok. I could tell you some things about him, too. Things actually true and less easy to believe."

I couldn't help but chuckle. Do men actually think jealous lies about the competition works?

"Have you ever heard his band play?"

He sobered his tone. It softened as he tried to coax me into his lie. There was a hint of jealousy in there, too.

"See, that's what I mean. Stay away from them. They close places down, and I mean that literally."

"Ok, so that means they're awesome and now I have to see a show. I didn't know you were such a good wingman, Spencer."

Hands heavy on the steering wheel, he stared at the road ahead with a tense brow. His mouth was twisting as he tried to wrestle rude words into submission.

"I'm not kidding, Talor. It's – they're – he's unsafe for you, I'm serious."

I did a dramatic fake yawn.

"New subject. Your jealousy is starting to get boring now."

Giving one last concerned look, he downshifted as we turned on the long, tree-lined driveway to the Beaty mansion. There were flickering lanterns lining the drive and dozens of red taillights haunting the fading dusk.

Fireflies led the way as I rolled down the window to get some non-crazy, non-jealous air in my lungs. I listened to the gravel groan beneath the slow-rolling tires as the familiar coaxing of old world charm almost made me forget about the idiot sitting next to me.

"Ugh, how come this driveway isn't paved?" Spencer complained.

My lips straightened into a thin line as I considered just getting out of the car and walking the distance to the mansion, but he said something that kept my hand off the door handle.

"Oh hey, Talor, next time you're having one of your honest conversations, ask Sage about Adair."

I scoffed.

"Adair? Strange name. Kind of rhymes with thin air. Probably where you pulled it from."

"Ask him. I bet he won't tell you."

I pointed to the mustache.

"Sorry. I can't take you seriously. Especially looking like that."

"I'm sorry, too."

Sighing, he rested an elbow against the door as we rolled down the driveway. When we got to the mansion, he opened my door before handing the valet his keys. I couldn't get his words out of my mind. They kept looping until I was wrapped up in the mystery of a woman named Adair. He hooked my arm in his as we filed in line.

To compensate for the silence, my mind shifted to the grand garden in front of me. The Beaty Mansion was as elegant a place as ever; the crystal-laden centuries-old chandeliers scattered throughout the lawn beckoned us closer. Azalea's parents stood at the door greeting guests with Vaseline smiles.

Mr. Beaty was a good man. His humor was dry and his glasses were thick. His eyes always had playfulness in them, like they belonged to someone a third his age. Azalea was the spitting image of him, and they were alike in many other ways, too. There was little about them not to like.

LONG LIVE DEAD RECKLESS

Mayor Beaty was a quirky middle-aged woman with money to burn, and she showed no fear of the gray in her hair and the crow's nest on her brow. She was silly and genuine, and that made her the perfect hostess. She greeted us with a thick southern accent to complement her layers of lacey petticoat and eccentric make-up. It sounded like Scarlett O'Hara mixed with Eliza Doolittle. Didn't exactly hit the mark.

"I declare, Miss Gardin! We were so worried you would not find an escort for this evening. Mr. Beaty wondered what men there must be in this town that a handsome belle such as you should be without a dancing partner. What fine gentleman is this, pray tell?"

The blood drained from my face as I remembered we were supposed to play a historical role for the evening. We were meant to both dress and act the part of antebellum southerners. As if it wasn't odd enough to be a southerner without an accent, I almost couldn't remember what one sounded like.

"Why, good evening Mr. and Mrs. Beaty! Might I introduce this...fine gentleman – my dear friend, Mr. Spencer Kaden?"

I looked at Spencer, who was an entire continent away from being a southerner and ever further from a gentleman. As soon as he opened his lips, southern charm poured from them like he was born in the bygone era itself.

Mrs. Beaty fanned herself as the professional charmer took her hand and lightly kissed it. He seemed at ease with antebellum manners. Even I was lost in the moment.

"What a lovely home you have, Mrs. Beaty. Mr. Beaty, I see you are a marksman?"

He pointed to the dozens of Civil War rifles and pistols crossed on the wall above the foyer. It was a regular museum in the Beaty house. Mr. Beaty beamed.

"Indeed, Mr. Kaden. There's nothing quite like being on the hunt."

"I am inclined to agree. It gives me great pleasure."

"You must join us next week, young man. We go Thursday. How are you with horses?"

"I am quite accomplished, Mr. Beaty. I have broken a few headstrong beasts in my time, and I do enjoy a good ride."

When he winked at me, I was ready to get away from him. Mayor Beaty checked Mr. Beaty's pocket watch and gasped.

"Goodness, my dear, we must begin!"

Mr. Beaty gave a reverent nod.

"Of course. Please excuse us, Miss Gardin. Mr. Kaden. Do enjoy yourselves."

A silent butler took my shawl and Spencer's top hat. We took our place at the entrance of the great ballroom. When we were announced, couples turned and looked our way as the butler's voice echoed through the hall. Music still played by a classical band in the corner, but too many eyes were turned to us. I felt oddly out of place in my best friend's house.

Spencer noticed my nerves and offered his hand.

"Don't give yourself so much credit. They're looking at me."

For once, Spencer's smug arrogance was aimed in the right direction. I placed my hand on his and he led me into the grand ballroom. Once inside, Spencer took two champagne glasses with silver bows tied to the bottom and offered me one. I refused.

"Um, I don't drink. Don't you know that?"

He clucked his tongue.

"A silver bow means non-alcoholic. Don't you know that? I thought you ran in these high society circles."

I took the glass from him.

"No, I didn't know that. Probably because I don't have a trust fund."

He raised his glass to me with a tilt of the head.

"To possibilities, Cotton Candy."

Sighing, I took a few sips while he downed his in two swallows. There was a bubbly burn that I wasn't used to, but I drank all of it anyway. When I was done, he took it and placed it on a nearby table along with his empty one. Without a word, he whisked me onto the floor. Couples all around us were waltzing in tight circles.

I couldn't understand how he was so fast to get us into the center of the room where I couldn't get away from him easily. He had me firmly by the waist, leading me around the dance floor with my skirt in picturesque full swing. It was easy to imagine the antebellum south as I listened to the swishing of ladies' bustles and the eloquent sliding of violin strings. He really was so good at dancing.

"Remember the last time we were here?"

"Spencer, please stop talking about that," I begged, suddenly feeling hot.

"You're a horrible dancer, Miss Gardin, but somehow I still want to kiss you."

He dipped me low as the song ended, leaning in. I turned my face away just in case. He was just crazy enough to try and kiss me there. Luckily, I saw Azalea out of the corner of my eye. She was standing at the top of the grand staircase leading up to her painting room waving dramatically to me. Spencer followed my gaze, letting go of my waist.

"Can you behave yourself? Don't set anything on fire or molest anyone?" I asked, fanning myself.

"Might I do everything else, Miss Gardin?"

He kissed my hand before I ripped it away.

"You can do whatever you think will get you thrown in jail, actually."

A devilish smile spread across his face as he touched a finger to his nose and watched me slip through the meandering crowd, making my way to the staircase. Azalea grabbed my hand, leading the race up the spiral staircase to her painting loft. There was a wrought iron Juliet balcony through a set of French doors where we often sat at night and counted stars.

With only a couch, art supplies and two walls full of old books and photos, it was a small enough space to feel cozy, yet large enough for us all to move freely without doing battle for space. Gentle acoustic music played through the speakers.

There was a canvas oil painting of Azalea in one corner. It looked fresh, and I could still smell the familiar stench of paint and egos. The painting was haunting; the eyes watched me cross from the doorway to the couch. Hobbling from a sprint in heels, we both collapsed on the rug in our grand dresses.

I looked over at the painting that stared at me. Jesse was on the balcony eyeing the arriving party crowd.

"Jesse, since when do you paint haunted paintings? The eyes are following me."

Jesse ignored me as he moved across the room to the narrow, floor-length window of the grand ballroom below. He was scanning the audience. His behavior was a little odd since he was the easiest guy ever to talk to. The best part about him is that he actually used his ears to listen, instead of like most people who just used theirs for decoration.

Being artistic twins, Jesse and Azalea would paint one another whenever the mood struck. The one down side to being their friend was that I was always left sitting by the side adjusting hair and clothes for perfect translation on the easel. I had no artistic talent.

I could never work out in my mind exactly how a smart guy like Jesse could be a friend of Spencer's. They had nothing at all in common except penises. He finally glanced back our way once his gaze broke from the window.

"Hey, I thought you were bringing this guy Sage tonight? What happened?"

Before I could answer, Azalea took my face in her hands.

"She was too scared to ask."

Azalea and Jesse looked at one another. I shrugged it off.

"You guys don't know him. He's hard to talk to."

Jesse raised a brow, bringing the drink he'd been nursing up to his lips.

"Spencer said to watch out for that guy. He wouldn't tell me why."

"Jesse, I know he's your friend, but everything out of Spencer's mouth is filler."

Azalea went over to where Jesse stood and peeked downstairs at Spencer.

"Can I just say that he's not a bad back-up? He does wear a tux well. Rwworr."

I crawled over and joined them at the window. Spencer seemed at ease in the chaos. He stood alone, his back against a wall with a calm smile held fast on his lips. His attention was focused on a group of men, not a collection of young women on the other side of him. When he looked up, I dove behind a wall.

"Great. You can have him," I told Azalea, frowning.

"Oh, I brought some guy in my Physics class. He's an exchange student – Italian," Azalea cooed.

Jesse crunched on a piece of ice and cleared his throat.

"Uh, didn't you bring two guys?"

Azalea turned away and smiled at herself in the mirror with a satisfied sigh.

"I honestly don't remember. Isn't that terrible?"

Jesse and I shared a look.

"Yes," we said in unison.

Azalea covered her mouth like she was ashamed, but there was a wicked smile behind it. Jesse shrugged and downed what was left of his scotch.

"Anyway, I better go. I'm neglecting Kyoko, and with that guy down there, well, Talor, you get it."

As he started to leave, I fell forward and grabbed his ankle. It was a desperate gesture, but I was desperate.

"Jesse, you're his friend. You're my friend. Please make him go away."

"I thought you came with him?" he asked, puzzled.

"I did, but...please go do something. Friends don't let friends deal with Spencer," I cried, letting him go.

He adjusted his tux and started to leave. Azalea swung around from the mirror.

"I don't know why you're fighting this thing with him. You won him fair and square. Go and take your prize. Sage seems happy waiting in the wings."

I shook my head violently, making it clear that I didn't want any more of her bad advice.

"You know, I'm through listening to you. Spencer has been pouring it on since the pool party when I took your advice. He's trying to make Sage jealous."

Curious, Jesse stopped and leaned back into the room from the staircase. He stretched a palm towards me and wiggled his fingers.

"Wait. I'm confused. You're saying that you would rather deal with Spencer, who you don't even like, than attempt asking that other guy out? Does that make sense to women? Because to a guy, it looks like you're into Spencer."

"Please don't say that. Everyone quit making me feel like an idiot about all this. You haven't met him. He's really hard to read and God, just, freaking intimidating."

Azalea twirled her hair as she gazed into the vanity.

"Maybe he's just shy, Talor. Or, maybe you intimidate him. Happens to me all the time."

Azalea was accustomed to scores of men fawning all over her. She looked as extravagant as ever dressed in an emerald green ball gown with diamonds in her hair – probably real diamonds, actually. A cat in human form with large, opal eyes and wavy dark hair couldn't comprehend my common problems.

"Why would anyone be intimidated by me?"

She grabbed a fallen tube of mascara on the floor and started to touch up her eyelashes. It was only then that I realized the painting studio was a complete mess, but Azalea liked it that way. It "fed her muse," so she said.

"Beautiful women intimidate men. They pretend to be confident, but they're really terrified. Right, Jesse?"

Jesse, who was still leaning on the railing, reluctantly chimed in.

"Um, yeah...sure."

"Sage and I have worked together for almost two months now. Uh, when does it wear off? And another thing, Azalea! Why did you invite Spencer in the first place?" I asked, crossing my arms and tapping my foot.

Azalea was doing her lips.

"I didn't invite him. Hello? You brought him with you."

"I only brought him because he said you invited him."

Azalea laughed heartily. Jesse brushed back his hair and jerked at his jacket.

"Well, I feel a lot of male bashing coming on, so if you don't mind, I'll be downstairs where it's safer."

With that, he disappeared down the steps. Unfazed, Azalea kissed her reflection in the mirror to blot her lips. It left a fresh red stain of perfect lips among the dozens of faded ones in different shades.

Furious that Spencer forced his way into an evening with me, I gathered up my skirts and made several attempts at a sentence. I never got past the first or second syllable. Azalea rubbed lotion on her hands as I started down the spiral staircase.

"Where are you going?"

"To punch him in the face."

8

Azalea called after me, but I didn't care.

I was on a mission. For the first time, I felt like she was on his side and maybe even helped orchestrate the whole evening. I just wanted distance from them, and I couldn't get it fast enough. I pushed through the crowd, making a beeline for Spencer. He made a fool of me.

He must have felt me zeroing in because he turned and spotted me barreling his way. I thought I still had a few steps to come up with something nasty and smart, but there was too much blind fury in the way for words. I opened my mouth and nothing came out. My thoughts wouldn't connect to my lips, and he took full advantage of that.

He held me fast and close.

"Whoa, hey, calm down."

"No," I argued, trying to pry his hands off.

Shaking his head, he kept his fake accent.

"I haven't looked at another woman all evening, you know?"

"You lied to me about Azalea. Liar. Stop using that stupid accent. You sound...s-stupid," I stammered.

"God, everything about you is so sexy. Even jealousy."

"I'm not jealous. I'm pissed. You tricked me into bringing you here."

Couples rustled around us in happy little ballerina-box worlds. Spencer's hand brushed up to my cheek. He stepped close, dropping his head down and touching his nose to my forehead.

"You wanted to bring me, Cotton Candy. I just let you."

"Nope. I've had enough. Done," I cried, pushing him away.

Giving him as evil a glare as I could muster, I marched off. I didn't have to push people out of the way this time. Everyone moved before I got close, creating an easy path to the door. I decided to leave the gala on foot. It wasn't my brightest notion, but the walk would give me some time to think about what to say to Sage on our future date.

I only made it outside to the pool area when Spencer came blazing up in front of me. It wasn't well lit outside, just the glistening of lantern lights hung above in the fruit trees and candles on strategically placed stands, but he looked different. More intense. He held up his hands.

"Wait, Talor."

"You aren't even going to apologize, are you?"

"I'm sorry."

"You are?"

"Sorry it upset you. But be honest with yourself for a minute, Talor. Would you have come with me otherwise? I just wanted a chance with you. I deserve a chance, and you're so full of yourself you wouldn't give it to me any other way."

"You deserve? Wait. You did all this on purpose to screw with Sage, didn't you? That's what this is really about."

"I wanted to screw with you."

"What's wrong with you? Seriously, go away. Get yourself some help, Spencer," I cried, exasperated.

"What if I said I've never really loved anyone and I didn't know how to do it? So maybe I lied a few times. I don't know how to be in love. It's new. I know how to do a lot of things, but this? I don't have a clue. How could I do it right when I don't know what I'm doing? Please."

If it had been any guy in the world other than Spencer, I would have stopped dead in my tracks. I might have believed him. I would have jumped in his arms and forgiven him. But Spencer was good with women. If he thought a declaration of love would get him what he wanted, he dished it out like Halloween candy.

"You just want sex and you're not getting it from me."

He forcefully ripped off the fake mustache and jerked at his collar to loosen it.

"Thing is, I don't think you're really mad about me lying at all. I think what's really pissing you off is you want it to be all about Sage, but I'm in there, too."

"You really think you're God's gift, don't you?"

"Admit it and I'll leave you alone."

I didn't stop, but before I knew it, I was saying exactly what he wanted to hear.

"No. Ugh, admit what? Yes, you're a liar. Yes, I think you are one of the worst people I've ever known. And yes, I'm attracted to you, and I hate you. It makes no sense, but I admit it. That's what I think of you! Now go away!"

91

"Please wait."

I stopped trying to move past him. Something about the way he said wait. It was strange to hear that sound from his lips.

"What?"

He didn't waste another second. He forced me up against the side of the pool house, his arms forming a fortress around me.

"Enough, damn it."

When he pulled me into his lips, I thought I would fight him. I thought I would hate it, but the truth is, I was so in shock at how good a kisser he was that I just stood there and took it. I knew nothing in the world but what was going on between us.

I could tell he had lots of practice with women in dark places, and I struggled to find something to complain about – you know, except all his experience. He had mastered at least one thing in his shallow life, and I was enjoying it.

After I didn't push him away, he only paused long enough for me to gasp in a good breath. He didn't bring his lips fully away from mine, probably for fear I'd change my mind and deny them a second taste. They warmed bits of my own lips as they trembled and curved into a smile. The faint laughter from inside the mansion was the only thing reminding us we weren't alone.

He buried me in kisses, abating my hesitation. I didn't expect to be so receptive. I never wanted to like him, and I should never have let him kiss me. It's odd how I even knew that then. It felt like I didn't really know myself all of a sudden.

"I knew you wanted me," he said, his lips trading the tasks of talking and kissing.

Every time he pulled back, I grew more docile, diluted, and numb. Everything was on fire, so the itch on my wrist just blended in.

Was I getting money soon? Oh, wait...that's the palm. Ugh, whatever. Lips. Kisses.

I had never been kissed so well in my life. His massive list of conquests made so much sense. What woman could pull away from this? I was disgusted with myself, so I focused on being yet another name on his list and that did the job.

"God, I hate you," I said with a groan, pulling him closer and drinking in another kiss. What I was saying and what I was doing didn't match.

"Tell me about it," he smirked, running his hands down my hips and gripping them tight.

Tell him how I hated him? Oh, that I could do. Agitated, he pulled at my skirts, but didn't try to lift them. Just to be sure, I brought my knee up to maintain space between us.

I was glad that even in my frenzied lust, I still had a head on my shoulders. He continued showering me in a cascade of kisses, keeping me dizzy. Since I couldn't stop kissing him, I did my best to insult him between each one.

"You evil...kissing...wizard...man-whore! I want to slap your face."

That last one made him laugh. Not my intention. He slipped a hand under my knee and with a mild flick, turned it out so his hips were between my thighs. At least there were layers of ball gown between us. I was grateful for that.

"Yeah? Go ahead," he murmured.

His ability to get me in such a compromising position so quickly made me just mad enough to take him up on it. To my surprise, he let me. I hit him square across the face – hard, too. He didn't even try to stop me.

I was shaking so much from adrenaline that I couldn't believe I landed a well-placed slap. I'd never hit a man before. It was terrifying and invigorating. He just smiled as he touched his cheek.

"Hmmm ...wanna do it again?"

I shook my head. It was disturbing the way it turned him on. It was then that I became very aware that I was trapped against a wall with a guy who liked a bit of pain with his pleasure. When he tried to kiss me this time, I turned away.

He caught my chin and brought it back.

"No, no, now. Don't get all upset. We don't have to do that. Just trying to see what you're into. So far, I know you like this," he purred, sinking me again.

As he pulled back, a subtle moan escaped and betrayed me. I hoped he didn't hear it. No such luck. He nodded, taking my head between his hands and speaking in a hushed tone like some desperate prayer.

"Yeah, I know what you want and I'm gonna give it to you, but I've been thinking about this for so long, you know? He tried to steal you. But he can't have you. You're mine now."

He...who? It took me a second to realize he was talking about Sage. *Oh, Sage. I want Sage!*

I wanted him breathing penitent pleas on me – his lips, his whispers. *Stop kissing Spencer.* I wanted Sage, but I couldn't stop. Spencer's fingers softly caressed the length of my throat. His lips followed his fingers, spilling kisses down. When he came to the spot where my pulse was beating wildly, he hesitated.

"Talor, if I wanted to take you far away from here...would you go?"

I nodded, surprised at myself.

"Yes."

94

Oddly, I think I meant it. His voice was a blend of excited and mortified, like a kid riding their first real roller coaster.

"Then don't be afraid, ok?"

My eyes shut so I could sort through a sensory overload of moments I had fought so hard against having. My body was burning. I wasn't really thinking clearly myself, but I thought it was an odd thing for him to say. He took in a deep breath. I felt his tongue slide across the heartbeat in my throat and then his lips touched down, bringing something sharp against my skin with them.

It was jolting – more surprising than painful. It didn't make sense that a kiss would hurt unless...he bit me? My eyes flapped open as Spencer lurched back like I hit him. He stood there wide-eyed, looking as though he wanted to cuss me out.

"Princess?"

The next moment, he seemed sick.

His hands shot up to his head as if he was in excruciating pain and he let out a restrained growl. I started to reach for my neck to see what happened, but he brushed back the wild hair from my forehead. I saw a faint light flicker in his eyes before they went wide with fear.

"No," he wailed, his eyes filling with tears.

"Did you – bite me?"

We looked at each other like we were speaking two different languages. Suddenly, the skin on his hand crackled and split as though slashed with a fiery whip. The burn wrapped up his arm and went white hot, dropping him to his knees. He let out a sharp, guttural scream.

As he leapt up from the ground, his blonde curls twisted on their own to form what looked like actual horns. His eyes hollowed into slick, black holes as his face started to change. His teeth sharpened to points inside a face that was no longer human. His body was fast catching up.

I turned and stumbled a few steps away, but when I looked back, he was gone. All that was left was a fake mustache on the ground. My eyes scanned the edges of the forest around us, but he was nowhere. I stood there in that corner, staring into the eerie candle-lit darkness trying to figure out what just happened. I went limp against the wall wishing I smoked. As I looked across the pool, I saw a set of eyes shine from just inside the thick wooded forest beside the property. The eyes were moving closer.

I didn't dare look away.

9

I watched as a puff of smoke twisted past the eyes and towards the lonely candlelight. I wanted to run, but I froze there, my body plastered against the cold brick at my back. The reflective eyes lowered and then something small and white flew through the air, landing a few feet away. The embers burned as smoke oozed from the end.

A cigarette.

The eyes came forward into the light and revealed the Assistant Director. As he came closer, his wrinkled hands adjusted his vintage tuxedo cuffs. His voice was hoarse like he'd been yelling.

"You should go inside. There are all kinds of monsters lurking here in the dark. Don't you know any fairy tales?"

With that, he walked past me and back into the mansion. I watched him leave, thoroughly confused. Once it was quiet and I was sure I was alone, the recent memories caught up with me like an approaching train wreck in my head, screaming and crashing into each other. I bent at the waist and waited, sure I would be sick just trying to make sense of the turn of events.

Nothing came up. There was nothing in my stomach but a bundle of nerves. I'd forgotten to eat somewhere along with way. I crouched there for a few minutes anyway – at least until I was breathing normal again. Once I could think clearly, I called the only person who wouldn't ask questions – my friend, Bex. Wherever she was, it was loud.

"Oh, hold up," she yelled into the phone, and then screamed at people to shut up. It didn't work. A door slammed before her voice came back on the line. Now the noise was muffled.

"Talorrrrrrrr!"

"I need a ride. Can you come get me?"

"Where are you?"

"I'm at the gala thing."

"Say what?"

"Bex, where are you?"

"Harvest Moon."

I perked up, remembering Sage's band was playing there that night. Quickly, I made my way over to the two-acre Zen Garden on the safer side of the pool. There was more light, more people and a better cell phone signal over there. Oh, and the Zen. I needed the Zen.

Frustrated, I kicked a pebble; the garden wasn't working. I wasn't feeling peaceful. Sand squished underneath my heels as they sunk in the thick cold.

"Can you drive?" I asked, knowing the answer.

"Girl, I've had a beer. Oh! That speckled cutie of yours is here."

I stopped kicking pebbles and drawing heel circles through cold sand.

"God, Bex! Come get me."

She was a good friend, but she definitely didn't know when to stop talking.

"Yeah, I think they play next."

I clinched the phone tighter.

"Pick me up on Plantation Court – I'll be walking. I'm in a...ball gown. Can't miss me!"

She laughed in a long, drawn out way.

"Ohhhk then, crazy. I'll bring you some clothes."

"Are you kidding? I can't wear your size. Just –"

"Listen Cinderella, don't hitchhike. Your pumpkin carriage is coming!"

I gathered the layers of my dress and started walking. I passed the long row of cars lining the grand entrance and headed out onto the road. When I got far enough from the bright lights of the mansion, I realized I was on a dark road alone. As expected, I began to freak myself out. *Had I just become that stupid girl in a horror movie? Why did I leave the safety of the gala?*

I should have just gone back inside and waited for sanity to show up. Spencer was gone, but his car was still sitting in the driveway. He was probably laughing his butt off somewhere with Jesse. I started to wonder how bad a kisser I really was if he acted like it nearly killed him. Should I dare embarrass myself with Sage? And was I really a bad dancer, too? I ran my fingers along my lips as I pondered the whole thing.

I had plenty to think about on my lonely walk. It was a good thing, too, because the longer I traveled down the winding country road, the more I feared that Bex would forget to come get me or drive down the wrong street. She'd never been to Beaty Plantation before. I'd forgotten that not all my friends were friends with each other. The edges of my stilettos started to rub the sides of my feet raw, so I stopped to take them off.

As I bent down, I caught a whiff of something dead and had to cover my nose. I hoped I wouldn't trip over a dead raccoon in the middle of the road. It wasn't a good time for a twig to snap nearby. I tried to pretend it was a deer. I wasn't about to start looking around for more eye shine.

After all, it was the outskirts of the city, otherwise known as the country. There were plenty of fields and forests; protected places full of wild things because millionaires like to have miniature countries to lord over. In an effort to lighten my mood, I escaped into childlike imagination. Maybe the deer and the road kill raccoon were old friends. Maybe he was coming to pay his respects. For safety's sake, I hoped animals were that sentimental.

I knew it was something else, but I didn't look back. I couldn't muster the courage. I quickened my pace, knowing that if something strange was lurking around, it was going to have to work up a sweat to catch me. I was jogging a solid six-minute mile in my ball gown by the time Bex's headlights were on me. I could hear her ridiculous cackle and blaring beats before I got in. She didn't even try to suppress it.

"Takin' a pleasure jog in your evening gown, Miss O'Hara? Aren't you supposed to be sipping mint juleps or something?"

I slammed the car door and waved her on without answering. I was out of breath and sweating a little more than I wanted to in a silk dress and cinching corset.

As I laid my head against the window, I caught the glimpse of something in the rearview. It was standing in the middle of the road where I had just been picked up. It looked like...

"Stop!" I screeched.

She slammed on the brakes.

"Ohmahgod, what?"

As we sat idling there in the road, I turned around; I'd seen something in the rearview. It was gone now. What I saw, I didn't dare say. It wasn't real, but I was sure it was what had been following me.

I slammed down the door lock. I saw something that shouldn't be there. Something that didn't exactly exist.

"No. Just go. Go now. Go fast, please."

Shrugging, Bex hit the gas and barreled down the winding road. She gestured at a pile of clothes covering half of the back seat.

"There's some stretchy stuff in there. Oh, and you need to freshen your makeup, girlfriend."

I wiped sweat away and tried to take a body check of how I felt. I didn't feel drugged, but I had to be. What I saw wasn't real. Spencer had to have slipped something in my drink. I sifted through the mound of dirty clothes. I found one dress I could wear with my corset still on.

While it was a little tight, it emphasized all the right places. I slipped on some ankle boots and unpinned my hair. We pulled up to Harvest Moon just as I finished. Somehow, spandex could be less mentally comfortable than a corset.

When I stepped out of the car, Bex looked at me and did a lively dance step.

"Damn, kid. What did Spandex ever do to you? I don't know who's spankin' who!"

"Gee...thanks?"

Harvest Moon was packed and loud, so I waited by the car while Bex went to talk to the doorman. Wearing a tight dress around drunken men suddenly didn't seem like such a good idea. I was very self-conscious, but I didn't want the gawkers to know it. Feigning confidence, I threw my chin high in the air.

About then, everyone started filing out of the bar like kids on field trips. Some people were stumbling, obviously drunk, while others were laughing hysterically enough to need a white room. Something weird was going on inside – something that made me want to get out of there.

Bex came back pouting a minute later.

"They're closing. Somebody set off a fire alarm, so the cops are coming."

"Let's go. I need to get home. It's been a long night."

Bex squinted her eyes and twiddled her thumbs.

"Ok. Lemme say bye to some folks."

"Bex –"

"A minute," she called, waving me off.

She rounded the car to get her jacket. I buried my cold nose down in the scarf around my neck and stared at the pavement. I was glad that I hadn't asked Sage to go to the gala. He would've said no because he had a show. Just then, gray and white Saucony shoes were in front of me. Sage had a pair like that.

I snapped my head up; hoping Sage was the only guy in Cypress with those shoes. The magical moment dissipated when it turned out to be a drunken frat guy instead. He was just drunk enough to be annoying.

"Hey, what's yours name?" he slurred.

His breath was its own interesting cocktail.

"Married, thank you. Bex, look for some Tic-Tac's in there, would you?"

He turned up the beer bottle in his hand until it was empty. His eyes were bloodshot, but they looked like they were normally brown. He stumbled a little closer and almost fell against me. I moved just in time for him to fall against Bex's car. Bex stopped throwing clothes around and popped her head out of the backseat.

"Hey, get off my car!" she said, scowling.

He was oblivious.

"But do I know...you look like this girl I...I know you. It's Brandi – isn't it? That's it! It. Hey, Brandi."

I shook my head.

"Not it."

"Oh...then what's it? I'll buy you. Drink?"

He offered me his empty bottle. I knew he was basically harmless, but I had enough harassment for one night, so I started to walk away.

"Bex, can we go now?"

"Brandi?"

He reached out and tried to grab my arm, but he missed and lost his balance. He hit the ground with a thud and his glass bottle shattered, cutting his hand. Bex slammed the door shut, pointing at him. With her other hand, she waved a bouncer over.

"Greg, get this fool before I break his head over my hood."

I couldn't imagine Bex hurting a fly with her petite frame. Still, she was tough. She had a no-nonsense way about her that made men straighten up as she passed. I leaned back against a parking meter to watch. Bouncer Greg ran over and forced the bleeding stranger to his feet.

The drunk tried to apologize to Bex for not knowing her name was Brandi. Apparently a bodybuilder in his free time, Bouncer Greg grabbed the poor guy up by his collar and swung him around like a rag doll. That's when Sage came out of the side door of Harvest Moon. I glanced at Bex, who was cussing the guy out. Since she was busy, I turned to go after Sage when I came face to face with him. I didn't concern myself with figuring out how he got to me in a matter of seconds.

I wasn't sure whether I should act surprised to see him or play it cool. I didn't do either; I batted my eyelashes at him like an idiot. My default. He pulled at his hat; I think he was tipping it. I nearly did a curtsey with all that chivalry.

"Talor? I didn't know you were here."

His tone seemed surprised, but his face was a blank slate. He had to know I didn't go to bars just to hang out.

"Well, I didn't know you were playing tonight."

Never mind the huge marquee flashing DEAD RECKLESS over his left shoulder. He looked at my dress in a way that said I-want-to-stare-but-I-want-to-be-a-gentleman-too. Let's just say he seemed to like it.

"I thought you had some big...ball or something tonight?" he asked, brushing his hair out of his face.

I laughed.

"I did, but...I left. I hate I missed your show."

"Nice dress," he said, scratching a bit of his stubble and giving a crooked smile.

Before I could thank him, he reached out and took the blubbering guy up by the jacket.

"Greg, I'll take him. His girlfriend'll drive him home."

Greg shrugged and let him go. Sage helped him stumble off towards the side door. I took a chance at seeming desperate.

"Sage?"

He glanced back with a look that stopped me in my tracks. It was cold, almost angry. Sirens wailed down the road as opened the side door and pushed the guy inside ahead of him. A bouncer guarded the door as it closed behind him. I hurried after him, but the doorman held up a hand.

"We're closed."

"I was just talking to Sage. You know Sage?"

The man wouldn't budge. Bex walked up beside me and showed her hand stamp. She tried to move past him, but he blocked the entire door. He was big like that. Bex pulled out a ten and threw it in his face.

"Seriously, Dan? Have a heart – she's in love with Sage from Dead Reckless."

"We're closed."

He stared me down. He must've thought I was used to getting whatever I wanted wearing dresses like that. I didn't have the energy to tell him things didn't exactly work that way for me. No one was footing my bill because I was pretty. I was even wearing a borrowed dress. Bex had the energy to argue, but I wanted to get out of there fast. Sage wasn't interested in talking to me. Even in that dress.

I looked across the intersection to Citizen's Park, a newly renovated city project dedicated to all the missing citizens lost over the years to the river. It was a way for families to feel support for the loved ones they never got to bury. While it was once a crime-infested eyesore, police patrolled the area now. There were even a few new businesses on nearby corners.

While there was always a chance to run across a homeless beggar, the solitude and serenity of walking the river by moonlight was worth the risk. The Flint was a dirty river, muddled by the red Georgia clay and a myriad of snapping turtles and alligators, but at night it could have been the blue Nile. I needed a quiet place to think. Bex shouted obscenities at doorman Dan before following me across the street.

She carried a drink in hand as she sauntered along.

"You know my stuff's still in there? I saw him talking to you."

She nudged my shoulder. I walked straight to the swing set and plopped down. My voice sounded small.

"He just said hey."

She offered me her drink, but I ignored her.

"Thanks for coming to get me, Bex."

She sat on the swing next to me and raised the glass with a wink.

"He couldn't keep his eyes off that booty."

I gave a weak smile.

"Yeah."

She twisted her swing in a tight circle and spun out wildly. Sure, we were grownups on a playground – and she was drinking alcohol – but I needed something simple and familiar at the moment. Her laugh made me feel like a kid again. It had been a long night and I just wanted to breathe.

The men in my life were confusing and I couldn't figure out what was wrong with any of them. At that point, it seemed like everything. I closed my eyes and with each gentle swing, I felt less weighed down. Each soar through the air brought a fresh breath my way, and that felt like just enough for the moment.

10

I woke up the next morning to three voicemails from Azalea.

Questions ranged from why she couldn't find me at the gala to when Spencer was going to come get his car. Each message had a different ruling emotion. I think I liked the curious one the best. The one constant in every voicemail was that she wanted to meet me for lunch downtown after she finished volunteering.

Like most wealthy people, she spent her mornings pretending to care about others less fortunate than herself. Azalea called it the "silver spoon oath." I could never tell if she was kidding when she called it that.

She was always involved in some charity work or another, and I think she liked it – wealthy requirement or not. Her charity of choice was the Cypress Aquarium, a local aquarium of sorts just showcasing the types of creatures anyone near a creek could pluck out on any given day. She said she felt led to help the local biologists who took on the community project being that she was more knowledgeable than them anyway.

I always agreed with her, mostly because she was right. She got me painlessly through Biology the semester before. She was a genius and she loved animals – even the not-so-cuddly kind. I did feel bad about ditching the gala, especially since her parents probably spent several thousand on catering and enslaving a local concert pianist for the evening.

I got in the aquarium free with my student ID – one of the perks of being a college student longer than I was supposed to. I wore my new black boots and a flowered dress Azalea gave me from one of her magazine photo shoots. She was a good friend like that. Rich. Plus, she said it was too big for her. She met me in an over-sized polo shirt muddied with bits of grass and some type of slime – not exactly typical for her.

Still, she bore it like a champ. She hugged me with just her neck as she stuck her hands out to avoid dirtying my dress. Her dress. It was some major label; a good one, apparently, because I couldn't pronounce it.

"You're supposed to wear a belt with that. Also, turquoise. Have I taught you nothing?"

"Oh. Sorry."

"I've just got to wash my hands and change my shirt and we'll run to lunch. Do you want to try Harvest Moon? Have you ever been there?"

"I thought they closed last night."

"Yeah, restaurants do that. But they open the next day. Repeat, that kind of thing. Why did you just run off last night? Were you really that mad at Spencer? Wait, before you answer, let me do this."

With that, she hurried off with an impatient sigh. Her hands were getting to her. Turtles and alligators peered at me from behind the glass as I shuffled quietly around in the lobby listening to a looping track of birdcalls and frogs. Azalea returned in a spaghetti strap red polka-dot tank in the place of the dreary polo and fresh makeup was on her face. She waved a little piece of paper.

"I get a free appetizer volunteering here."

Being just about the only bar/restaurant in downtown Cypress with enough room for customers to actually sit, Harvest Moon was packed to the brim at lunch. People even spilled out on the streets in animated conversations while waiting for tables to open up. I tried to convince Azalea to go somewhere else, but she wouldn't budge. She wanted Harvest Moon. She had the coupon and all.

"You know they have trivia here every week? I usually go with Sara. You've met her, haven't you? You should come with us next time!"

The line barely moved. We took a single step forward. Impatient, I checked my phone.

"I don't know her."

"Sure you –"

"Azalea, I need to talk to you about something and I don't really want to be in a crowd. Can't we go eat somewhere else?"

Her eyes got big.

"Ah-ha! You finally did it. It was Spencer, wasn't it? That's why you two disappeared last night. Tell me everything!"

My heart dropped. Surely my best friend didn't believe I'd sleep with someone like Spencer. I prayed no one I knew would be standing within earshot of the conversation we were having. Azalea was a good friend, but sometimes she was insensitive. And loud.

"Are you talking about Spencer Kaden?" someone asked.

The voice was soft and unfamiliar. We turned to see a petite girl holding two menus. She was only about five foot tall with thick eye makeup, a

109

lip ring, and was not a natural redhead. She wore Toms and a black T-shirt with an illegible band name splashed across it.

In Cypress terms, she was a "scene" chick, a groupie. Not really Spencer's type, but then again, he was into any woman who would open their legs for him. Literally. Neither of us answered her.

"You're Azalea Beaty and Talor Gardin, right?" the girl asked.

I nodded. She continued.

"I guess you don't remember me. We went to school together. I'm Jill. Um, we were in the same homeroom senior year? Anyway, I know Spencer. He's a regular here."

"Oh...ok," I replied.

"So are you sleeping with him, too?" Jill asked.

I fumbled for a rational tone. Was this a normal thing now? Getting all chummy over mutual current lovers? Gross. After blinking a dozen times in a few seconds and making some weird sighing stutter, I finally found words.

"G – od, noooo! I just –work – we work – I – work with him."

Azalea had this expression like I was screaming obscenities in a church. I think she knew then that something had happened the night before. Since I stumbled through my first defense with Jill, I turned to Azalea and bellowed at her.

"God, Azalea! This is how rumors get started."

Azalea let a tiny smile escape while Jill hugged the menus to her chest.

"I just figured if he knew you, he would like you. Since you're so pretty and nice."

I didn't expect a compliment. I struggled to accept it, but I wasn't very good at that. Azalea tagged in for the save.

"Sooooo, Jill, you work here now? How's that going?" she asked, shifting her weight and holding her chin a little too high.

110

"I'm a hostess. I can seat you now if you want."

Those standing in front of us in line looked back with chilled stares. Azalea met their frowns with a smug smile. I avoided their eyes, shrinking into my shoulders as Jill led us past the complaints of those in front of us. Walking close behind her was why I noticed a bit of blood on her collar.

"Hey, Jill – your neck. Did you cut it?" I asked, pointing to where she had a Band-Aid.

It was sloppily put on, so I could make out a small puncture wound in the skin. It looked a little infected, but before I could look closer, she adjusted her thick choker over the Band-Aid, covering it for good. She gave a slight nod.

"It's just a new tattoo. Supposed to look like a vampire bite. Like it?"

I bit my tongue and forced a smile.

"It looks infected. Did it hurt?"

Her eyes rolled back in her head.

"No, man. It felt good. I only wish it had been a real bite. Eternal life and all? I'd let one bite me. You?"

I couldn't take my eyes off the tattoo. I tried to hide my grimace, but I couldn't shake it.

"Probably not, but I'm not really into tattoos or biting or...infections."

I had been so consumed by her infected neck tattoo that I didn't notice her leaning in close. When she licked my cheek, I jerked back. She lingered like she expected me to come back for more. When I just stared at her, Azalea turned up a brow.

"Seems like a good time to mention dick. As in, what we like. As in, we're straight."

The restaurant got quiet as someone stifled a honking laugh. It felt like everyone was watching and waiting on my response, so I nodded. Jill's gaze was direct and strange. It was like she was counting eyes to make I wasn't growing more or something.

"Princess, I bet. Both of you," she muttered, snarky.

A twinge of terror froze my stomach solid until ice spread across my skin. Spencer called me a princess. Azalea dangled a twenty-dollar bill in front of Jill like it was catnip.

"Well, it's been real weird, Jill. How about that table now?"

Azalea's tone was sharp, like she was out of patience. No doubt she didn't like being referred to as a princess when she had so many shining crowns from being the queen of something. Homecoming, prom, pageants – you name it, she was queen of it. Princess wasn't good enough. Looking hard at Jill, I suddenly remembered her.

She sat towards the back of the class usually. She had glasses in high school and always wore oversized black Goth pants with a chain hanging out the back pocket. She was never the one talking in a group, but her eyes were the most hungry for attention.

She had a really bubbly personality, though – always smiling. She wasn't like that now. I hoped she wouldn't spread some horrible rumor about me being part of Spencer's ever-growing harem.

Without another word, Jill took the money and led us to a table in the upstairs loft of the restaurant. The industrial building was well over a century old, and it was converted into a restaurant fifteen years before. The owner of Harvest Moon had it stripped bare years back and painted the entire inside a giant mural of stoner art.

There were large mushrooms and swirling night skies. It looked like Wonderland was trapped on the wall. As I passed confusing collages, I imagined a good Burning Man going on just out the back.

The air smelled of old, wet wood, pizza, and local beer on tap. The floors creaked as you walked along them and the fans swayed out of sync overhead. It was every bit as eerie during the day as a haunted fun house at night, but it was a popular local spot.

It was always full of eclectic people and live musicians. I usually loved being in the middle of a thriving art scene, but this one was different. The vibe was overwhelming and uncomfortable.

I felt the need to run out of there in a spastic fit, but I tried to ignore it. It made no sense. People occupied the tables around, and they seemed perfectly fine with their smiling faces and lively conversation.

What was wrong with me? No one else seemed to be feeling the fight or flight reflex, and I was on the verge of a panic attack. I chalked it up to Jill's weird juju and wild tongue. Azalea was unaffected. She slid her straw from its paper and cracked open her menu, peering at me like a sly detective over it.

"So when are you going to tell me about Spencer?"

I looked around. Strangers watched us. Their eyes darted around, trying to pretend we were invisible.

"This is going to sound really, really paranoid, but have you noticed everyone looking at us?"

She fanned herself with the menu.

"Well, we're the best looking people in here, Talor. What did you expect? For them all to pretend we're hard to look at? Even lesbians dig you. That's new."

She motioned to Jill downstairs standing at the door. Jill looked like a robot. Not moving, staring, barely breathing. There was that ice running over my skin again. I shook my head and shivered, thinking the movement would crack the sheen and free me.

"I don't think she's a lesbian. She said she was sleeping with Spencer. Don't you remember her from high school? She was crazy over every guy with a guitar!"

Azalea twisted her lips around in thought.

"Well, yeah, you're right. Maybe you're just irresistible then. Anyway, stop stalling and tell me about Spencer. I want all the juicy details. And I know there are juicy details."

I asked for this conversation, but now I dreaded it.

"Ok, so last night, when I walked outside to get some air, he followed me out and –"

"He tore off your clothes and sexed you in the pool?"

I stared at her a minute. The things my friend imagined me doing.

"No...no, listen. We argued and then he, well, we did kind of make out. Not naked. And not in the pool."

She squealed and slammed the menu down on the table, sending the extra napkins and straw carcass sailing through the air into the restaurant space below. Her eyes sparkled with curiosity. People were definitely looking at us now.

"Oh my God! Was it amazing? Speech, speech!"

I blushed as I looked up and saw the waiter standing at our table looking like he'd just walked in on his sister changing.

"I'll, uh, come back," he mumbled, clearing his throat.

"Azalea, get a hold of yourself. Geez! You can't just blurt out everything in your head."

She pouted at me over her straw.

"My, my. Aren't we touchy? I was just kidding. What happened to make you so pissy?"

I groaned and leaned forward so I could whisper.

"That's what I'm trying to tell you. I'm gonna sound crazy, but Spencer changed last night in a way that's hard to explain. He became something else, like a beast –"

Her jaw dropped.

"A beast? Oh my! Did he get all grabby and grunty and try to pull your hair out?"

"Stop. I'm serious. It's not funny. It makes me question what I was drinking last night."

She blinked hard and sat back rigidly in her chair like she was poised for a job interview with wide eyes and perfect posture.

"Oh...yeah. The governor sent my parents a century old case of Perrier-Jouet for the gala, you know?"

"What does that have to do with anything?"

"It's really old, really expensive champagne."

"Did you hear me? I'm trying to tell you what happened last night and you're talking about what people were drinking. Do you want to hear this story or not?"

Her mouth opened, but it took some time for anything to come out of it.

"It's pretty old stuff. Strong...for someone like you."

I was confused. It took a second or two before I caught what my best friend was telling me. I didn't drink. She knew that. Heck, everyone in Cypress knew that. Dad was in the loony bin because of his hallucinations while drunk. Because he burned down our house while hallucinating while drunk.

I almost died because he was drunk. He never drank a day in his life until mom got sick, but he made up for every missed drink in his life during those seven months. With a parent like that, I did not drink – not socially, not at all. That wasn't news. It was known. Her shoulder drew up defensively.

"I'm sorry. I meant to tell you, but since you basically ran out, I never got a chance."

It took a minute for me to finally get a word or two out. My teeth were grinding so hard against each other that my jaw was aching.

"So that's why I saw Spencer turn into the creature from the black lagoon. And now I'm just like my dad. Seeing things and going crazy."

"Why are you talking about a monster? How much did you drink?"

"Do you hear anything I say or are you just too busy worshipping yourself inside your own head all the time, Azalea?"

She scowled.

"What is that supposed to mean?"

I slapped my hand over my face and rubbed it.

"Spencer, like, shape-shifted into some crazy monster last night after he kissed me. Then he disappeared. It wasn't the best night, Azalea. I guess it all makes sense now. No wonder Sage didn't want to talk to me last night. Who knows what stupid crap I said to him?"

Azalea glanced back and forth while she took a long sip on her drink, which she nearly spit out.

"When did you see Sage? I'm so confused right now!"

I stood up to leave.

"You're confused? You ship a guy I hate, try to get me drunk, and insist we eat at shady bars with weird people! Who are you?"

"I'm your friend, and I'm sorry. But you aren't your father, Talor."

I grabbed my purse and shook my head at her.

"No, I'm not, and you aren't my friend, either."

Those words must have hurt, because she looked up at me with tearful eyes. I pushed my way down the stairs and just before I got to the door, a hand caught my arm. It was Jill.

"She isn't good for you. You're doing her a favor, princess."

I shot her a bewildered glare and she let go. I took the last heavy step to the door and threw my whole weight against it. It groaned as it gave way to the world outside.

Everything went white as my eyes adjusted to the bright light of mid-day, and for once, I was glad to feel the autumn southern warmth on my face. In the searing sun, my own tears began to evaporate and with them, my troubles.

11

All weekend, I had to play the bad guy in my own life. Dad called, but I ignored my phone and spent silent hours seeking the advice of wind in the wheat field instead. Even Azalea tried calling me once, but she didn't leave a message. When Jesse called Monday morning and asked me to meet him before work, I agreed, but only because he wasn't his sister.

It was obvious that Azalea was sending him as a buffer to gauge the severity of our fight. It was a juvenile move for sure, but it also reminded me that we didn't have many arguments. Our most recent was in fifth grade over the last swing on the playground, so it just proved that she was as awkward at fighting with her best friend as I was.

That was a good thing, and it gave me hope that I could forgive her. Still, after all that happened, I needed some time to think about it first. The wheat field by Bosh's house was always a hiding spot for me growing up – a shelter of sorts. It was at the end of the cul-de-sac and it backed up to several acres of forest.

Wild wheat grew so tall there that I could just lie on my back in it and hide from the world. I would imagine stories about the cloud animals passing overhead while the tips of wheat formed a moving picture frame of the sky. I could doze off for hours and feel safe there in the open arms of nature. The only alarm clock was the crickets' chirping. When it started to sound more like road construction than music to my ears, I knew it was time to go in.

I kicked off my dusty shoes and flopped down on the bed. Spreading out like a sacrificial shirt on an ironing board, I was ready to be released from the wrinkles plaguing me. The house was still. Warm. Soothing. I cut my eyes to a crumbly pair of old slip-on shoes Bosh used to wear neatly sitting beside the door.

Her small feet had worn toe imprints in the soles, so I bought her a pair of real TOMS for her birthday. She didn't understand why someone had written their name on her shoes, but she wore them every day. It was the least I could do since I didn't even pay rent. She had been out of town all weekend on a church retreat and she wouldn't be back until evening. I was alone with my crazy thoughts for a little while longer.

Looking at the ceiling, my eyes followed a slow-spinning fan blade around while I replayed the scene with Spencer over and over in my mind. I felt the well-placed kiss on my lips, plotted and perfect. His lips were so much softer than I imagined. I blushed when I realized I had imagined them.

I saw his face, the features morphing and twisting and the curls transforming. I remembered the hollow hell of his eyes, the shards of empty night. He acted like I betrayed him, but he was the one who had turned on me.

It *had* to be drugs.

That had to be the reason for the violent change in behavior. I turned every corner in my mind to find a better excuse for him. I couldn't. I felt a darkness closing in around me, so I turned my face towards the window and the light. I watched the leaves grapple with the windy gusts in the back yard. It was finally acting like autumn outside – my favorite season. But I couldn't see past his hideous face.

I came to the conclusion that I wasn't crazy and he wasn't playing some elaborate trick on me. He had simply drugged my drink. My alcoholic drink that my best friend served me. No wonder I was crazy; I had friends like them. I groaned and sat up. The grandfather clock in the kitchen clunked a solemn rhythm. It reminded me that there were still hours left in the day. Hours before it got dark. Hours before friends turn into creatures you can't explain sober or drugged.

In an effort to distract myself, I started walking around in the house. Bosh's presence was everywhere. It was comforting to be surrounded by her things. I ran my hands against the collage of artifacts from her life and the picture frames sitting on side tables. I knew the faces around me – cousins, aunts and uncles, mostly. But the half-covered black and white faces of strangers caught in time grabbed my attention and beckoned me over.

There – almost totally hidden – were newspapers stacked on top of an old photo. Figurines and books littered the corner bottom shelf. The books and papers were dusty but looked like they had been moved recently. I bent down and grasped the edge of the picture. It was then that I saw it was hanging out of a cloth burgundy album with a dragon stitched on the front.

Wiping away the dust from the crumbling cover revealed the words SHANGHAI, CHINA.

I paused.

Now, there are family photos standing guard over every corner of the house, and each holds a different chapter of Bosh's life. Well-known chapters. Ones she tells us grandkids. They're on display, and this book of photos was hidden. That was curious. It was curious because Bosh never talked about her childhood in Shanghai. Curious because no one knew why. We all just stopped asking somewhere along the way. So a hidden photo album was worth investigating, especially with no interruptions.

I rested back on my heels as I cracked open the fragile spine and peered through the pages. They were filled with fascinating photos of her family from as far back as the early 19th century. Their frozen faces were like a mysterious stranger with a steamy secret to tell. I bent forward and pulled it close, studying their faces and listening for their paper whispers. They kept their secrets.

Turning a page, I saw a piece of old stationery paper stuffed between two photos that had some strange writing on it. I pried it from between the sticky old backing. At first glance, I thought it was just poor handwriting in English. But another look told me I was wrong.

I guessed it was Russian – since that's Bosh's first language. A family photo album filled with Russian inscriptions made sense for a Russian family. Unable to shake my curiosity, I took the golden paper over to my computer and started searching the letters.

Nothing came up. Nothing. On the Internet. I thought maybe it was just because the letters needed special characters on the keyboard, and I didn't have them. I took a picture of it with my phone to show one of my professors at Cypress College. Dr. Milton might know something. He was in the military a while back.

The next picture was dated October 1886. It was a hazy shot inside a crop circle. *Wait...a crop circle?*

I brought it up to the light. I wasn't sure why I was checking it like it was a fake bill. I could see the stain of age on the edges and the uneven bubbly matte finish of the photo paper. It looked authentic, but that didn't make sense. I shook my head and put it back.

I knew where I could get some answers. Heading into Bosh's room, I went straight for the small wooden chest on her dresser. It was locked, like always. The chest was a gift from her bridesmaids on her wedding day.

Bosh once told me that each of them carved their names and wrote a memory on the inside so she would always remember whatever secrets they shared in China. If the crop circle was real, and it was the reason Bosh never talked about Shanghai, I wanted to see inside.

I picked it up and fiddled with the lock. It looked simple enough for even a novice criminal like me to pick. I considered breaking it and replacing it. Instead, I took an envelope opener into the crack and pried it open slightly.

Bending over, I put one eye against the dark open slit into Bosh's secrets, but I couldn't see anything. Unwilling to risk breaking it, I set the chest back down with a sigh. It felt like no time passed from when I put the chest down to when I awoke. I was back on the bed again staring up at the fan. I shot up to check the clock. Two hours had passed. I had less than an hour to meet Jesse and get to work.

Seeing the dirt from the field still clinging to my ankles, I jumped in the shower. Grabbing the razor, I propped my foot up on the water faucet so I could shave my leg. The monotonous motion had me lost in thought and oblivious as I tried not to nick my knee as I always do.

Then things got weird.

I noticed the shower curtain move and I felt the cold air at the same time. I checked the air vent overhead. The air conditioner wasn't on. I turned to the small window beside me. It wasn't open. I slowly raised my head and looked towards the door, which to my horror was not closed, but now open. My eyes went wide as I saw the shape of a man standing directly behind the see-through shower curtain separating us.

The beads dangling from the velvety valance on the outside of the shower curtain swayed back and forth but made no sound. I stood frozen in my bent position as if remaining still would make me invisible. It didn't. The shower curtain ripped open in front of me as if it were my last defense. My attacker was a dark shadow.

As in a ghost.

I didn't have time to scream. I instinctively lashed out at it, slapping it away. I took my razor and slashed at it several times. Even then, I felt ridiculous, but I didn't know how to fight a ghost. I knew the razor wouldn't do anything, but I had to improvise. As expected, my attacks did nothing except dissipate the shadow for a moment, but it kept gathering back together as it gave an echoing cackle.

This ghost had vocal chords, which was all the more unnerving. I finally let out something of a scream – part gasp, part whimper – before closing my eyes and cowering in the corner. I was tired of perching on a single leg like a crane and slashing at a ghost with a pink lady razor.

A flash of light burst out, warming my lids, and the ghost screeched. I cracked open an eye and saw that the overhead light had busted. The ghost was gone. I was alone. It vanished like I was imagining the whole thing.

Like I really was a crazy person. The water ran cold over me and I jumped back, leaping out of the shower and slamming the door shut, locking it. Every move was shaky and quick, like I had no control over myself.

I just wrapped myself up in the towel and let the shower continue to run. I slid down against the wall, trying to calm myself down. I didn't have my phone in the bathroom to call anyone. Thankfully, I had also undressed in there, so my clothes were sitting on the floor beside me. I scratched my forehead, only stopping once the itch subsided.

I lay down flat on the bathroom floor so I could see if the ghost was still around just outside the door. I saw nothing —no shadow feet taunting me from inches away. I decided to get dressed with my towel on just in case. I made sure balled up pieces of toilet paper blocked out the sporadic holes in the old door. A ghost could seep through cracks in the door, you know.

Every time I would put a new piece of clothing on, I would check the door to make sure that it was still locked. It could always come back. I needed to hurry. Once I was fully dressed, I turned off the shower and pre-pared to fight whatever I would face outside that door. I gathered my cour-age, but I couldn't make myself open the door for a good five minutes. I tried to remember where I put my keys and phone.

Who I would call first? My mind slowed at the thought. Wait, why would I call multiple people? Why would I call anyone? What would I tell them? Imagining the right words to describe what happened was like listen-ing for a whisper through a hurricane. *Oh, I was just taking a shower when a ghost attacked me. You know, Mondays! Sure, Talor. I know a good doc-tor you should meet.*

When I finally emerged, the constant quiet of the house wasn't soothing anymore. I wanted to get out of there. I hurried to my bedroom, locking the doors on either side. I hunched over on the bed, my hand catching my head as I closed my eyes to think. A heavy knock came on the front door.

Since we lived on a dead end street populated by baby boomers, I jumped up. None of the elderly neighbors had that kind of energy. My mind went to its craziest place, imagining all manners of people on the outside of the house lurking. Knocking, yet lurking? *Wait. Lurkers don't knock.*

I crouched down and tiptoed to the front door. I was glad no one could see me creeping across the room. Ironic that I was accusing a stranger of being a creep when I looked like the very definition moving towards the door. Thankfully, Bosh had a peephole installed. I peered through it and no one was there. I straightened up to a sigh of relief. *Wait. No. That's worse.*

No one was knocking? That wasn't alarming at all.

I was startled by the noise of a big UPS truck driving off. I peeked out the window and saw the tail end of the truck disappear down the road. When it was clear, I cracked the door. There, on the doorstep, was a plain white package. It had no addresses on it – not even mine. Why – heck, how – would a UPS truck deliver something without an address? I battled with the decision to leave it on the doorstep or bring it in. I stared it down, expecting it to move or something.

For some reason, I couldn't let it sit. It wasn't an abandoned baby, but I whisked it inside like it needed a new diaper stat. I slowly unfolded the edges. The paper was thick – like a brown bag from a grocery store. Inside was a box. It had rhinestones decorating all four corners and a small latch without a lock on the front.

I mentally prepared myself before opening it. Not that such a small box could hold a ghost, right? It was the phantom feeling of justified dread lingering inside the box that made my fingers pause before creaking the top open.

LONG LIVE DEAD RECKLESS

The truth is, I jumped before I even looked inside. My premature reaction caused me to drop the box on the floor. Once I saw what tumbled out, I laughed. Curled up at the ends, Spencer's gala mustache looked happy to see me. What else could I do but smile right back at it? Spencer found a way to make me laugh when I wanted to hide under a couch. Maybe it really was all a joke in good humor.

Leaning down to scoop up the mustache, I noticed there was something else inside the box. I turned it over to look and saw a unique key. Spencer's car key, specifically. It was wedged in the box with a folded note wrapped around it. Blood stained the paper where a cryptic sentence was written.

The car is yours, my love.

12

I stared at the package.

Who called me 'my love'? Wholly spooked, I flung the package at the couch and ran to my car. It felt as though I'd be safe if I could just get in my car. My hands were shaking as I struggled to start the car and turn the wheel.

I hoped for some solace when I got to work. Familiarity. People. I would busy myself and forget all about the gala, the car key, and the ghost. You can make yourself too busy to go crazy, right? Yes – I think.

Kati tried to talk to me as I came charging through the lobby, but I didn't even look her way. I went straight back to the nursery area. I didn't realize until later that I forgot to clock in so I worked that day for free. It was quiet in the nursery, and I was grateful for it. I needed to sit alone for a few minutes to process everything before being bombarded by a hodge-podge of screaming toddlers.

My hands had finally stopped shaking when I just happened to look over to the door where someone was standing and staring at me. I gasped, unable to breathe again. Sage gave a shy wave as I went over. Easing into the hallway, I began to feel a little safer standing next to him.

"Hey, are you ok?" he asked.

Nodding, I sighed the stress out and stuffed my hands in my pockets. They were shaking again and I didn't want him to see.

"Oh – what? No, I mean, yes. I'm fine. What's up?"

He gave me a once over.

"You're shaking. Do you need to sit down?"

I looked up and locked my elbows in an effort to still the offending arms. I opened my mouth, feeling my brow soften as I considered telling him everything. Sage seemed to actually care. Those eyes, that voice, the genuine look of concern on his face...but no. No, I couldn't tell anyone what happened. I shrugged.

"I'm just – oh god, Sage, it's been a day, you know?"

He watched me for a second. We both knew I was lying, so I couldn't look him in the eye. I stared at those gray Saucony shoes he always wore. Now they were shuffling. Running, but not running.

"Well, as long as you're ok, um," he said slowly, thumbing towards the double doors. "Kati asked me to come get you. You need to come to the front."

"What for?"

My cell phone vibrated in my pocket, startling me. I laughed it off this time, embarrassed. I grinned stupidly at Sage and he did the same. We tried to ignore the ceaseless vibrating, but it kept on. It meant someone was calling. I didn't want to offend Sage, but I thought it might be Spencer with a gotcha call, so I pulled it out. I checked it quickly, seeing Jesse's name.

"Oh man," I groaned, remembering that I was supposed to meet Jesse fifteen minutes ago. I hit ignore so it went to voicemail.

Sage politely cleared his throat. There was rare curiosity in his tone.

"Anyway, there are some cops here. They want to talk to you, I think."

I rolled my eyes and gave a short laugh. Nothing like the guy you're crushing on telling you the police are looking for you. What a freaking day.

"Are they strippers?" I asked.

Sage laughed as he opened the double doors and held one for me.

"Um, I really hope not."

I could see two cops standing there talking to Kati. One of them was familiar. He had a baby in the nursery almost every day. I only knew he was a cop because he was always wearing his uniform when he came in.

I squint to see the shiny nametag in my memory. Thomas, I think. Normally a really nice guy, he seemed much less approachable with a gun replacing the infant on his hip. I gave a nervous smile.

"Mr. Thomas?"

They both turned and the older one tipped his hat. His southern accent was thick. He was definitely a local...and not a stripper. He wasn't dressed in a uniform, either.

"Afternoon, miss. Sorry to bother you at work like this, but we've spoken to your supervisor and we'd like to ask you a few questions if that's all right?"

Wide-eyed, I looked over at the Assistant Director. As always, he stood idle and judgmental, crossing his arms. A small crowd of my coworkers had gathered to watch my undoing. Of course Sage was in there, too. He was back on the other side of the counter in his designated seat, his finger gently tapping his lower lip.

"Ok, sure," I answered.

The cops looked at each other. A few regular Goodlife members toddled awkwardly around the commotion and swiped their cards on the reader. The beep seemed to be the only sound in the lobby besides my deafening heartbeat. Officer Thomas looked around and shielded his mouth with his hand.

"Don't worry. We're only here to ask questions."

I nodded as the Assistant Director pointed to his office.

"Please use my office."

Trying to think of a way to excuse myself without looking suspicious, I pointed to the nursery area.

"Can you give me just a minute? I'm sorry. I left my purse sitting out in the nursery. You know kids these days."

Great. I'd resorted to accusing toddlers of stealing when I was about to be questioned. As bad an excuse as it was, somehow it worked. The cops politely waited while I hurried back to the nursery.

I turned off the lights when I got there. No one should see this. In my frustration, I started punching the air wildly. I looked like I was fighting someone invisible. *Oh wait...I'd already done that.*

I couldn't believe I actually did that twice in one day. Circumstances were pushing the limits of my sanity. For all I knew, Spencer was dead and I was about to be blamed for it. Once I'd worked myself into a breathless frenzy, I stiffened my arms by my side and tried to regain composure by remembering my yoga breathing.

Grabbing wildly at my purse, I heard something metal drop on the floor. In my mindless rush out of Bosh's newly haunted house, I held onto

Spencer's key and brought it with me. I stared at it lying there for a minute, not knowing if it was real. When I blinked a billion times and it didn't disappear, I bent down to pick it up.

Would be better to flush it down the toilet or risk the cops finding it in my purse? Would they search my purse? Could I drop it on the floor somewhere in the hall and pretend it was just there? I could say I took the key because he sexually assaulted me. I mean, it technically was true, but only technically.

Ok, it wasn't true at all.

I panicked. My heart shuddered against my chest as I watched the key slide into the toilet water. I felt like the guilty man in the "Tell-Tale Heart," and I was glad I was stupid enough to flush the evidence so I couldn't drag the cops back here to pull up the bloody floorboards.

I flushed it and scalded my hands in hot water before heading back out to the front. The crowd hadn't dissipated much. I was asked to sit in one of the chairs in the Assistant Director's office.

"Miss Gardin," the older cop said. "I'm Detective Case. You know Officer Thomas, I think?"

We both nodded at each other.

"She watches Jackson. Keeps him from swallowing tiny toy trucks," Officer Thomas said, smiling.

Detective Case furrowed his bushy brow.

"Miss Gardin, we're told you and Spencer Kaden were close."

He paused, ascertaining my reaction. He was looking for anything signaling my guilt. I shook my head.

"What do you mean, were?"

"You do know Spencer Kaden, don't you?" Detective Case asked.

I thumbed backwards towards the lobby.

"Yeah, we all do. The gawking masses out there included. Why are you only talking to me?"

Detective Case folded his arms.

"Witnesses say you were the last person seen with him before he disappeared on the night of September 28th. And some of the gawking masses out there say you were romantically involved."

I scowled. I know the Assistant Director told them that. Had to be him. He's the only one who saw us that night. Azalea said Spencer's car was still in their driveway, a strange package showed up on my doorstep...everything was linking together for a mounting panic attack.

"It's not true. We were – are – friends."

"His girlfriend claims he hasn't been home or answered his phone in three days."

"Oh, I know his girlfriend. She didn't mention him missing. Are you sure this isn't a prank? You know, since people go missing here all the time."

Detective Case ignored me as he peered down through his glasses at a notepad he was holding.

"Maybe you can walk us through what happened on your date? Anything you think might help us find the young man."

I looked over my shoulder out the office window to Sage. He was still standing there pretending to be working. Pretending to be on the phone. Pretending not to judge me.

"It wasn't a date. He picked me up here for the gala."

"Well, what happened after that?" Officer Thomas asked.

I swallowed so hard it felt like I had strep throat. I didn't want to tell them about the kiss. It would be in a report. I couldn't tell them about what I saw after the kiss, either. I would be thrown in the room next to my dad. I was trapped.

"Shouldn't I have a lawyer present for this?"

"You aren't under arrest," Detective Case said.

I stood up. Detective Case held up his hand.

"Miss Gardin, please. We're just trying to find this missing young man. He has a very concerned family who want to know he's all right. That's all. We need to know everything you can tell us so we can help."

"I wish I could, but I don't know any more about where he is than you do," I said, sighing.

I wanted to call them out on never finding anyone who disappeared from Cypress, but I kept my mouth shut. I knew Spencer had played some joke on me, but I didn't know why he took it this far. I was sure the woman who went missing after her bike ride weeks before had a very real, very concerned family, and it frustrated me that the police were wasting time on a case like Spencer.

Officer Thomas crooked his brow.

"Did he take you home after the gala?"

I sat back down. I didn't want to seem like I needed to escape.

"No, a friend picked me up."

"Why didn't you leave with him?"

"Because."

They waited for my answer. I tried to imagine one. But wait – that would be perjury. Lying to a cop is illegal, right? Yes. I tried not to fidget. I was going to tell the truth. Part of it, at least. The only believable part. I lowered my voice as much as I could.

"Because he kissed me and he's my friend's boyfriend."

135

They looked at each other. Detective Case scratched his head and scribbled something down on his notepad.

"I see," he mumbled.

Officer Thomas covered his mouth as he leaned closer to Detective Case. I strained to hear, but he was good at whispering. It was freakish, really. He then adjusted his uniform as he stood up from sitting on the corner of the desk. Detective Case handed me a business card.

"We don't want to take up any more of your time, Miss Gardin. Please let us know if you think of anything. Where he might be, folks he might be with, that sort of thing."

I took the card without a word. Detective Case tipped his hat as he followed after Officer Thomas. I studied the card for a moment before leaving. The Assistant Director walked out with the detectives and I was left standing with Kati, Sage, and Larissa, who had come in while I was being questioned. The rest of the crowd scurried off when I came out of the office. Larissa waited until the cops were outside before jabbing her fist deep into her hip. She still had her keys in her hand.

"Talor! You got cops coming up in here looking for you? What in the world happened?"

Kati just kept laughing.

"You just made history here, babe. I've been here seven years and no one ever had the cops come in. Tell the truth – we're your friends – did you kill Spencer?"

Sage had a strange look on his face. I stuffed the card into my pocket and grabbed the sides of my pounding head.

"Dear lord, I'm just about to lose it. You all know he did this as some sort of joke. Where is he? Is he hiding back there, Sage?"

Giving a sympathetic smile, Sage shook his head as Kati reached for the ringing phone.

"You heard the cops. You were the last person to see him. So, where'd you bury him? You can tell us."

"Oh, answer your phone, woman," I said, stomping off.

I went to the break room and sat at the corner table. It was perfect for sulking. It was usually quiet in there and it allowed me to collect my thoughts. They only thought it was funny because they didn't know what I knew. They hadn't seen the things I had. Sage came in a minute later jingling change in his hand.

It was just the two of us in there, so I was trying to think of something to say.

"This has been the weirdest day of my life."

"Looks that way."

There was silence between us as he dropped coins in the machine and pushed buttons for his selection. Whatever it was dropped to the bottom and he reached down to get it. When he straightened, he pointed to the chair across from me.

"You mind?"

I shook my head. I hoped my perspiration from interrogation wasn't visible. He sat down and started unwrapping his sandwich. I glanced at it and my stomach gave a loud grumble, much to my dismay.

"Do you want some?" he offered, holding half the sandwich towards me. I shook my head.

"Oh no, please. I'm ok. I'm just a little stressed, I think."

He gave a gentle shrug and placed it on a napkin between us.

"Well...I'll leave it here. Just in case you turn ravenous."

Ravenous? Good word. It was always nice for a hot guy to use an SAT word in conversation. I blushed despite myself. An intelligent male vocabulary would always be a pleasure point of mine. My stomach groaned again.

"You're not hungry?" I asked, placing my hand on the table near the sandwich half.

"Not really."

I leaned forward.

"If you're not hungry, why did you buy a sandwich?"

He leaned forward as he nudged the sandwich my way.

"I needed an excuse to come in here."

Smiling, I took a bite. It was turkey, lettuce, tomato and Swiss, and it tasted like heaven from a vending machine. It was depressing how excited my taste buds got over that. They burned and ached as I devoured a few bites.

Maybe I hadn't eaten all day and it was four in the afternoon, but a sandwich from the hand of Sage was food from the gods. As I chewed, Sage looked down at the crumbs gathering on the table.

"I know you've had kind of a rough day, but would you like to hang out sometime? Maybe go for something not from a vending machine?"

I wanted to savor the moment Sage finally asked me out, but I almost choked instead. All I could do was try not to cough bits of sliced turkey all over his staff shirt. Sage just asked me on a date after seeing me interviewed by police. I could feel the crumbs outlining my lips and sticking to nearly all of my teeth, but I didn't care.

I beamed a big, nasty smile anyway. I tried to play it off by licking my lips, but I wasn't great at getting out of embarrassing situations. I was doing my best to keep from sticking my finger – or my foot – in my mouth.

Saying yes before Sage changed his mind was more important than my comfort.

"Yes," I said, trying to swallow and smile and not cry.

He gave a bouncy bob of his head as he stood up.

"Ok, well, I've got to get back, but I'll see you after work. We'll talk?"

"Sounds...perfect."

He gave one last shy smile before disappearing out the door. I was too excited to eat any more and my stomach groaned in protest. I was wearing more of that sandwich than I ever got in my stomach, but I couldn't have cared less.

I finally had a date with Sage, and it only took six weeks, a police investigation, and the weirdest day of my life to get it.

13

I was so nervous about my date with Sage that I completely forgot I was angry at Azalea. I called her to ask if I could borrow clothes. I didn't remember we were fighting until she answered the phone with this awkward hello. I felt stupid, but I used it to my advantage so I could seem mature and forgiving.

"I didn't think you'd call me. I thought I'd have to go through Jesse," she said, subdued.

"Well...fighting is dumb and I'd had a rough night. I was still raw. I hadn't processed everything, but it's ok now. I'm not mad anymore. I just wanted to say that."

She was biting her lip. Or doing that smirk thing when she was pleasantly confused. I knew it even though I couldn't see it, so I waited on her to speak. Her tone was hopeful, fragile. It was rare to hear.

"Well, I'm sorry I didn't tell you about the champagne. I know it's a big deal to you and I respect that. You know I don't think you're crazy, right? Your dad isn't either. So...yeah. God, it was hard to, like, not talk to you for a few days, you know? I want to catch up. Can we hang out later? Not Harvest Moon. I promise I'll protect you from your admirers."

She gave a nervous chuckle a little at the end and I smiled.

"Actually, I kind of have a date with Sage tonight."

Just like that, old Azalea was back. She squealed into the phone and asked me a dozen questions. When I asked to borrow clothes, she said she'd be over in thirty minutes with five options. Azalea really knew how to make up. I realized then that's why she could date so many guys at once. They all forgave her because she was easy to forgive.

Against better judgment, I decided to borrow a dark green V-neck sweater, pairing it with tight jeans and fierce stiletto boots. She asked me why I continued wearing shoes that were bound to kill me one day. I told her I would never get better at something if I didn't put the time in to learn it. In this case, walking in stilettos.

As expected, Sage picked me up on time and opened all my doors. He took me to dinner first (where I did not order a turkey sandwich), and we were going to a play at Cypress Theatre afterwards. He must've known that I loved going to the plays. I always wanted to be up on stage, but I never found the courage. Instead, I lived through Azalea's theatrics – on and off the stage.

As we sat at our booth, I couldn't help but smile at him. His hair had been meticulously fixed in its wild style and his eyes had a glint in them I hadn't seen before. I think it was excitement. He shaved for our date. It was strange seeing his whole face clean-shaven. He had a strong jaw that was usually softened by a beard.

My eyes traveled down to his shirt, which fit as well as the one he was wearing the first time I saw him. He was carved from some living marble somewhere – one that was toned and freckled. I always got to work an hour early hoping to catch a glimpse of him working out in the weight room. I loved to watch his arms and chest flex when he would do pull-ups and push-ups. It seemed so effortless. I don't think he ever kept count of his reps, but I did.

"Can I ask you something?" he asked, breaking me out of my trance.

He was talking to me. Oh yeah, we were on a date thing. Time to stop fantasizing.

"What?"

He narrowed his eyes until all I could see were wet drops peering out from beneath thick lashes.

"Did you do it?"

He was flirting. I liked this side of Sage. He just kept getting cuter. I smiled and leaned forward over the table.

"What?"

"Whatever the cops are accusing you of?"

"Do I look guilty?"

He gave me a long look.

"Not of everything."

I smiled. I could get used to his smooth voice and quiet playfulness. I wanted to learn more. It was my first chance to really get to know him, and I wanted to find out everything. I reminded myself not to ask anything too weird.

"Now can I ask you a question?"

"Well, it's only fair."

"Why'd you wait until the cops showed up to ask me on a date?"

Not a great start, but it made him chuckle.

"Plausible deniability?"

I leaned my head back and laughed. How could he think I would ever say no to anything he asked? Didn't he know how sold I was on him? I tried to be nonchalant.

"Oh wow, do girls turn you down often?"

He gave a shy smile.

"I was afraid you would."

I laughed to ease the sexual tension that was billowing bigger between us, threatening to smother us if we didn't submit soon. I was smiling like an idiot at what he'd just said and I needed to change the subject fast before I admitted I was already in love with him.

"So, you're in a band, right? Do you write all your own music?"

He looked flustered, so he fiddled with the napkin on the table, folding it repeatedly.

"Yeah, we do. But I'd really rather talk about you," he replied, obviously uncomfortable.

It wasn't the worst thing a date could do – show total interest in the girl instead of talking her ears off like Spencer. *Oh, Spencer. That crazy idiot.* What had happened to him? I forced his memory into the back of my mind. I wasn't going to let him ruin my evening with Sage. I must've been silent for longer than I realized.

Sage looked concerned.

"Hey, you all right?"

"Oh, yeah, I just, um, go ahead," I said.

He was smiling with his eyes and his mouth.

"We can talk about my band if you want. I just – I'm interested in knowing more about you. More than your name and where you work and the fact that you go to Cypress, I mean."

"There's not much interesting about me, really."

"I think you're interesting," he replied, shrugging.

I looked down at my hands in my lap. Sage was a major ego boost to be around. All he did was say polite, sweet things and make a girl feel valued. I thought I would explode from all the attraction building under the warmth of authentic manners.

"You're always full of compliments, aren't you?"

"It's easy to compliment you," he answered, folding his hands on the table.

I dipped my head nervously. I kept doing that and I felt stupid, but I was caught in some reactive loop.

"Thank you, Sage," I said, blushing as I said his name. It felt so intimate all of a sudden.

"Tell me what you like to do."

Daydream about you. Talk about you. Watch you workout. Imagine what you kiss like. Wish you'd touch me. Wish I could touch you. Think about you when I touch me...I couldn't say any of my current pastimes. Still, he was waiting for my answer, so I had to come up with something.

"Um, but I'm actually very outdoorsy. I hate hot weather, though. I like poetry. I've tried to write some, but I'm not very good, so don't ask to read any."

"Ok, I'll steer clear. What else?"

"I don't like kids. Working in the nursery is great birth control, you –"

I stopped with my mouth open, realizing what I just said. I'm sure it made me very attractive to him, being so anti-kids. I couldn't think of a recovery, so I sat there staring. He blinked a few times and tried to bite the smile out of his lips. He waved me off casually.

"Hey, no judgment. I see what goes back there and I feel for you. Really. Now tell me about your family."

"I live with my grandmother right now. We call her Bosh. It's Russian for grandmother. She's Russian, in case you were wondering. You know, I just don't want kids anytime soon. I don't hate them or anything. I'm open to them in the future."

He gave an odd sort of smile as he sat back, leaving his hands resting on the table.

"Sure, I get it. So what are you studying at Cypress?"

"Oh, history and music."

"Double major, huh? Impressive. Favorite instrument?"

"I know the piano and the guitar. Oddly, the triangle."

He grinned.

"I bet you play a mean one. Do you sing?"

"I don't anymore."

"Anymore?"

I cleared my throat and looked at him. I wasn't ready to explain that I couldn't sing without thinking of mom. I couldn't tell him that she loved hearing me sing. I couldn't tell him that music was a part of my soul and that soul shattered when she died. I couldn't go there without crying, so I went somewhere else.

"So, what are you studying?" I asked.

I could tell he still wanted to know why I was a music major who didn't sing, but he took the social cue like a champ. He stretched his arms out in front of him, fiddling with the napkin.

146

"I'm not a student. I'm on campus sometimes to tutor linguistics. It's my second job."

That was intriguing. I knew he was a few years older than me, but he was basically a professor?

"That's – wow. Are you serious? So are you like a student-teacher?"

The waiter interrupted us as he brought our drinks. I had ordered a Cherry Coke and Sage ordered water. I regretted ordering a drink since he didn't. I hated feeling like the girl who gets stuff she doesn't normally because a date's paying for it. Sage didn't seem too concerned about that. He thanked the waiter as I tore the paper off my straw and plopped it in the fizzy goodness. Sage was busy emptying salt into his water.

"Is that...good?"

"This? Oh, it's just lemonade. My mom showed me how to make it once. It's always better than ordering it."

That made me feel better about ordering a Coke. I watched the unsqueezed lemon float in the water.

"Well, so far I know you're a musical linguistics tutor with strange taste buds. What are you doing in Cypress? Aren't you bored yet?"

He took a long gulp of the lemonade.

"So staying here for the rest of your life – not an option for you?"

I stared at him.

"Um, yeah, no. Once I finish next semester, I'm out."

"Going where?"

"I don't know yet. Just not here."

"Do you like to travel?"

"I've never been anywhere, but I'd love to go everywhere, so I think it's a yes?" I answered, imagining touring some ancient, romantic city on Sage's arm.

147

"That's a yes," he said, nodding.

The food came out quickly. Thankfully, dinner went smoothly and without incident. That is, I didn't do anything embarrassing like choke or smile with broccoli in my teeth. Later I was so happy that I didn't order broccoli because I smiled a lot. I couldn't stop, really.

Once we found our seats at the theatre, Sage and I sat in silence. Every few seconds, we would lock eyes and smile the same shy way only to retreat our attention into whatever seemed interesting around us.

Honestly, I was more nervous at the play than at dinner. I couldn't figure out why. I think because it would be dark. Not that Sage was handsy. Just all of my sexy daydreams about Sage were in a dimly lit place. Those daydreams happened so often I was actually afraid on some level that I'd trained my brain to attack him when the lights got low enough.

We were on the beginning of the row and the seating was tight, so when someone had to go by us to get to their seat, I had to touch him. The seats didn't fold up, so I leaned and turned my knees towards him until they were against his thigh. I was blushing like crazy every time I did that, so I was never more grateful for the low lighting.

When a large man tried to get by, Sage turned my way and put one arm over the back of my seat and the other on the armrest where his fingertips accidentally brushed against my thigh.

"Oh...sorry," he apologized.

"It's ok," I said, wishing he would do it again.

He curled his fingers up tight after that, and I wasn't going to kick my leg up to be caressed no matter how much I wanted to. Instead, after an agonizing minute, I stretched my hand from my lap and barely touched his.

He glanced down and relaxed his hand, letting the tips of our fingers curl into each other.

"It's...ok?" he asked, looking at me through the tops of his eyes.

I nodded. The way we looked at each other then, I wouldn't have known if the theater exploded around us. I wanted to stay touching all night. His body was warm and close. It felt like home. But when the lights overhead flickered to signal the curtain, the spell was broken. We took in the same breath and took our fingers back, straightening in our chairs.

Disappointed, I tried to fix the flyaways in my hair as the play began. Our hands rested painfully close on the armrests. I ached to hold his hand, or even touch him again, but neither of us made another move.

When he drove me home, I had a hard time keeping a smile off my face. He was as charming as I had imagined. I hoped he would kiss me. God, I wanted him to. He walked me to the door and we stood there like all nervous first-date couples do, trying to figure out how to end the night. He wouldn't even pretend to crowd me, so I knew no kiss was coming.

"I had such a great time tonight," I said.

He nodded. Just as I turned to walk inside, I felt him gently hook a few fingers of my hand.

"Wait."

I looked back, my heart skipping a beat. I slowly turned and leaned against the doorframe. No way was Sage going to kiss me on the first date. I had given every KISS ME NOW sign that I could, but no way would he do it. Yes, I could have kissed him, but I wanted him to have that moment. I wanted to let him be a gentleman and he wanted to let me be a lady. We fit that way.

We stood there, our entangled fingers nervously caressing like skin was a new thing. He was so close that we were both breathing the same air and feeling dizzy for it. He leaned an arm up over me on the doorframe and studied my face.

149

Oh God, he smelled so good, so male.

I wanted to stick my entire face in his armpit. Thankfully, I acted sane instead. When he'd tortured me with his pheromones long enough, he gave a little sigh.

"Well, good night," he said, pressing his lips against my knuckles.

His kiss made my knees buckle. I was glad the doorframe was holding me up. He gave a slight bow of the head and jingled his keys as he walked away. I watched him drive off until the taillights faded. When the street grew quiet and dark again, only the crickets were left in the world.

Looking up at the clear, cold sky, I thought even the stars seemed to shine a little brighter than usual.

But then again, it could've just been me.

14

All I did was think about him.

I ran into a lot of inanimate objects thinking about him. And also a lot of animate objects, actually. I'm surprised I didn't have more bruises after our first date. But I didn't actually see him again until a few days later. He hadn't called, either. I tried not to think anything of it as I walked across campus to a class I missed too many times.

Professor Milton sent an email that said I'd to be safer dead in a ditch if I missed any more of his award-winning lectures. He signed the email with no less than seven emojis to make up for such a harsh statement. He was my favorite professor.

I took him during my first semester at Cypress College, and he always seemed to like me. It was like having a really cool uncle on campus that acted more like a student than a professor. He did have a point about my absences. It was only the middle of the semester, and missing more class would delay my graduation date. Again.

As I watched a swirl of colorful leaves dance in my path, I got lost in thought. I was proud of myself for carrying on a somewhat normal life since mom died. I missed a year of school while she was sick, so it would be spring before I graduated. I only came back to school because I knew she wanted me to, but my youthful zeal was gone. I had stopped being involved in clubs on campus. I had little direction, but no one would have known by the way I pushed forward.

A familiar voice called out to me across the grassy courtyard, bringing me out of my head. I looked up to see Azalea walking towards me from a group of unfamiliar guys. Clad in a floor-length red brocade coat with a fur-trimmed neckline, she tossed her head back and gave a sly smile, nonchalantly sauntering past the big fountain across from the school library. It looked like a few of the guys from the drama department – Azalea's friends. I'd never met them, and I wasn't in the mood to, either.

"Aren't you hot?" I asked, gesturing to her coat. It was about sixty-five degrees outside.

"Always. You know this! Sit down."

Azalea pulled me down to sit beside her on the ledge of the fountain like she'd rehearsed it a million times. Her eyes sparkled as she stuck her hand in the water. She was in a good mood. Not that it was odd, but it felt like she had a lot to say and I had to go.

"Listen, I've got class. I'm already late."

She splashed me hard in the face. The water soaked the front of my cotton dress and outlined my bra.

"Azalea!" I cried, leaping up.

"What? Now you have an excuse."

152

She splashed me again, so I tried to cover my chest. My bra was out in the open now. Anyone could see it.

"What are you doing?"

"You need to have some fun. You're walking around all stiff. Is that lace? I'm so proud. I didn't know you even owned anything like that."

"Yeah, thanks for showing the entire freaking world, Azalea. I really can't miss another class, you know? I'm going to fail –"

Before I could finish protesting, she splashed me again. I told her to stop, but she just laughed, so I started walking away. She flattened her palms on the wet concrete of the ledge and turned her face towards the sky.

"It's happened, Talor. I'm in love!"

I stopped.

"In love?"

"It's why I'm so crazy today. Sorry! His name is Mannix! He's Irish! He's in the red shirt over there."

I squinted at the group of guys jabbering on the library steps. There wasn't a single guy wearing a red shirt. An accent found my ear.

"A couple of sirens splashing in the waves, aren't ya?"

I whirled around and stared into the chest of the red shirt known as Mannix. Immediately, I noticed several necklaces of varying materials. There were forms of foreign gods, things you wouldn't usually see a guy wear.

He was average looking, really, but with longer hair than most guys. It was a dark brown and messy, covered mostly on top by a slouching ski cap like a typical college musician. My gaze went up to the tattoo on his upper right arm of something like a dragon. A pierced eyebrow jutted out from behind his aviator sunglasses.

I could see myself in them, but not his eyes behind them. That bothered me. It was a cloudy day. No need for sunglasses. I couldn't tell what he was looking at, but I hoped it wasn't my lacy bra under a wet sundress. Azalea came over in a hurry, batting her eyes. She doused him with such furious kisses I had to back away to keep from getting mauled.

"Well, since you're busy," I mumbled, starting to slink off.

Azalea caught me by the hair while she was still kissing him. I yelped and pushed her hand off. She giggled.

"Wait. I want us to have lunch together!"

I forced a smile as I combed my hands through my hair, undoing the tangles she put in them with her erratic behavior. She was being aggressive and weird. I didn't care to get to known the guy making her act like that. I just wanted to get away.

"I really can't. I'm all wet and…"

As soon as Mannix's lips twisted, I wanted to retract my comment.

"Got ya fella to take care of that, darlin'? I know a guy," he murmured. Azalea laughed heartily.

"Oh, wow. What a gentleman you have here, Azalea."

She rolled her eyes and hooked my arm. Before I knew it, she had leapt into the fountain and pulled me in with her. We immersed in the water like a baptism, and Azalea wrapped her arms around me when I came up.

Her curly dark hair cascaded over my wet shoulder. She flung it back, effectively wetting several giddy bystanders. They cheered in response. Mannix reached in his pocket and brought his phone up to record us.

"How about a song, princess?"

When the crowd started growing behind Mannix, I tried to find a way to excuse myself quickly.

"I have class," I answered coolly, moving to get out.

Azalea snapped her head around.

"And I don't?"

"No, I mean class, as in college. Like campus? You know – this place we're standing in the middle of?"

Mannix shrugged, pulling out a crinkled hundred-dollar bill from his pocket. Azalea grabbed my arm and gave an excited squeal.

"A paid gig! What song, maestro?"

I shook my head.

"Azalea, the crowd is all yours."

Mannix tipped his sunglasses down slightly as he leaned forward my way. I could finally see a little of his eyes. They were a piercing kind of dark.

"Can't sing then?"

"Course I can. How do you just have that kind of money?"

"What's that phrase? YOLO?"

I frowned at him as Azalea sat in the water laughing her head off.

"Look at my shirt float. Come on, Talor! Your dress is going to look like a ghost when you lie down!"

I didn't stop glaring at him as I bent from the knees, not until I was horizontal underwater. The crowd seemed to be enjoying two women back-stroking in a fountain. When I stood up, my dress was clinging like spandex. Everyone started clapping, so Azalea took my hand and curtsied.

She sent a splash at Mannix, which he dodged.

"Satisfied now, you pervert?"

"Not yet."

He yanked her out of the water with ease and carried her off around his waist, their lips doing the only navigating as they went. Suddenly, the crowd started clamoring and scattered in a hurry. The dean was coming for us, and in a swift stride, too.

I scrambled out of the water, leaving my purse and books on the ground where I left them. I hustled from the scene of the crime to the safety of the oak tree around the front of the Art building.

Once I was safely behind the tree, I tried to remain quiet in case he had followed me around the corner. When I peeked around the tree and saw no one, I sighed.

"Talor?"

I jumped and squawked, slamming my back in the tree. It was Sage. He was trying to hide his amusement.

"Oh God, Sage! Hi. Um, this isn't what you think."

He leaned lazily to look around the tree. Cocking a brow, he took a step forward and tilted his head.

"What do I think?"

"That maybe I went swimming in the fountain because of peer pressure and ran away before the dean could expel me?"

He laughed.

"Oh, the dean, huh? Yeah, he's coming this way."

"Oh – God – save me," I mouthed, stiffening as tightly as I could against the tree. I could hear the dean approaching. I just stared at Sage, eyes pleading.

"Mr. Talis, it's good to see you," the dean said, his voice getting closer. Sage cut his eyes at me and smiled sweetly. Suddenly, he held his hand up.

"Uh, I wouldn't come any closer, sir," Sage said.

The footsteps stopped right on the other side of the tree. My heart was beating so hard I could swear the tree was shaking.

"Is – is it a snake?" the dean asked.

156

Sage shrugged.

"No, I just farted."

I slapped my hand over my mouth. *Sage did not just say that!* The dean cleared his throat and said something under his breath before retreating. I stood there against the tree, soaking wet, mouth dropped open.

We stared at each other until he winked at me, then I started laughing so hard there was no way the dean hadn't heard me. I still couldn't believe Sage said that. He pulled off his hoodie and paused to look at me before offering it. I guess I looked nervous to take it.

"I didn't really," he said, chuckling. "Sorry to be so crass. I figured it would work."

"But I don't want to ruin your jacket."

He held it higher, to my eye level.

"You couldn't ruin anything."

I took it gratefully, feeling a little exposed in my liquid dress. It was a gentlemanly gesture and an excuse to wear something that belonged to Sage. I pulled it over my head and sighed lightly as the soft fleece spread over my skin. The hoodie was warm so I blushed, lavishing the fact that it had just been on his skin.

Then Azalea and Mannix came over and ruined everything. I wanted to drag Sage away so we could stare longingly at each other in peace, but I did want Azalea to meet Sage.

After I introduced him, Azalea stroked an invisible beard.

"So this is the infamous Sage? I can't believe you're real. Mind if I pinch you?"

I slapped her hand away as she reached out towards him. She arched a brow at me. Sage adjusted his hat.

"What am I infamous for?"

I took control of the situation before Azalea could open her mouth. I ushered to Mannix.

"And this is Azalea's something...Manny? Or Manic? I'm sorry. What is it?"

Mannix stuck his chin in the air. Sage did the same.

"It's Mannix, princess."

"Her name is Talor," Sage countered.

"Anyway, Azalea is the reason I needed your hoodie, Sage. It was her idea."

Mannix rested one hand on his chest and wrapped the other arm around Azalea.

"Shame you missed it."

Sage's jaw was tight. Too tight for him to say anything, I guess.

"Mannix, see how Talor tries to make me out to be the bad one? It was fun and Talor knows it. She just doesn't want a certain person to think less of her," Azalea pouted.

Mannix kissed her on the cheek and pointed at me.

"This one has a siren inside her. At least, she wants one in her," he said, flashing a wicked grin.

Sage gripped his messenger bag tighter.

"It was nice meeting you, Azalea. I'll see you at work, Talor? I have to go."

His words were cordial, but his tone wasn't.

"I'm glad you're real and actually cute!" Azalea called after him.

When Sage was out of earshot, Azalea gave me her opinion. She watched him all the way past the fountain.

"He walks like a cowboy, doesn't he? Yeehaw! And he's *speckled* in freckles."

I smiled. I could still smell his skin on his hoodie. Naturally, I rubbed my face in it like a cat.

"I know. Can you blame me?"

Azalea tried to fluff her wet curls.

"No. You should definitely tie him up before he gets away. Need to borrow some rope?"

Mannix wrapped his arms around her from behind and leaned towards her ear.

"You know he can hear you, right?"

"You're crazy. He's way over there," Azalea argued.

Mannix ran his tongue across his teeth as he looked where Sage was just about to go into a building. I followed his gaze and noticed Sage pause before going through the doors. He didn't turn around. Mannix winked as he gave a salute. When I looked back, Sage was gone.

"You owe Talor some money," Azalea said, grabbing his chin.

"You can keep it," I answered, turning and walking away without looking back.

The money felt dirty and I never even touched it. Mannix was worth investigating a little more, and Sage seemed to know a few things I didn't. I would make it a point to talk to him about it. If nothing else, it gave me just one more reason to talk to him, and one more reason is all I ever needed.

15

Rose Warren was the first friend I made at school.

We weren't fast friends. She bullied me at first, pushing me on the playground and calling me ugly. But I wasn't innocent, either. I think I threw rocks at her. Our friendship was born the day I drew her a unicorn and she drew me a barn; I guess for it to live in. Who knows if unicorns really need barns, but the artwork ended the feud.

She spent middle and high school homeschooled, but we remained friends. A few days after the fountain incident, I went for my morning run like I did every Saturday. I had just finished when I got a call from Rose's mom. She said Rose was in the hospital because she tried to overdose the day before and had to be rushed to the ER.

Apparently, Rose had been asking for me and since the doctors were probably going to keep her for psychiatric evaluation, Mrs. Warren said I should drop by.

When I got to her hospital room, Rose was alone. Her face was towards the window with the blinds mostly drawn, but a sliver of light streamed in on her face. She was sitting up in the bed with this vacant expression. I didn't know what to expect.

I cleared my throat and knocked. It must have brought her back from wherever she was in her mind. She turned and looked at me, a flit of happiness spreading on her face.

"I was just thinking about you."

Her voice was hoarse, like she'd been screaming. I walked in holding the drawing I sketched before I came. It was a unicorn standing in a barn. It was terribly done, but I knew it would make her smile. I held it up as I approached.

"I thought you might like this for old time's sake. Sorry my art skills haven't improved since fourth grade."

She smiled. It seemed hard for her to do. I put the picture on the side table and reached out to touch her hand. It was clammy, but I held it anyway. I noticed a tray of uneaten food out of the corner of my eye. A vase of flowers and a balloon sat on the bedside table. She wasn't really looking me in the face. Her focus was on a ceiling tile. She blinked slowly.

"I'm so glad you're here. I can talk about him with you. No one else cares. I can't live without him. It feels like I'm dying inside."

I swallowed hard. I should have prepared myself for this conversation, but I wanted to get there quickly. I had to dig deep to find the confidence I was lacking.

"Well, some of us can't live without you, Rose. We need you here, ok? We want you here."

"Spencer doesn't," she answered sharply.

I squeezed her hand.

162

"So many people love you."

Her lip started to tremble.

"I don't know why he doesn't want me anymore. I don't know why. Did you find the girl that broke us up?"

I sat in the side chair beside the bed.

"Rose, what happened?"

Tears started to fall and she brought her hand up to wipe them away.

"I need him. He said he was in love with someone else, so he was setting me free."

I gulped.

"He's a jerk, Rose. I mean, when's the last time you saw him?"

Her gaze shifted to the wall.

"I don't remember."

She squinted her eyes like she was reading something small on the wall. I actually looked over. It was just a wall. Her voice was shaky, like she was afraid to remember.

"He was in some suit. I asked him why he was dressed up, but he just kept trying to kiss me. He acted like he was in pain or something. He was saying horrible things. I told him I would take him to the hospital, but he left. I haven't seen him since. I don't know what was wrong with him."

I let go of her hand and walked towards the window. I leaned against the windowsill and tried to keep my breathing natural, but the next breath kept getting caught in my throat. She just confirmed my fears.

Something really was wrong with Spencer. I didn't know how to respond. I was the cause of all the pain. I gripped my forehead, squeezing hard, knowing I would have to get through the next few minutes without losing it. I had to be a good friend since I hadn't been a good one lately.

"Why did they have to bring you here, Rose? What did you do?"

163

She didn't say anything. I looked over my shoulder and saw her looking down at her hands and crying, so I went back over and sat on the bed beside her.

"I'm sorry. You don't have to tell me if you don't want to."

She kept shaking her head, like she was getting frustrated.

"I didn't do anything. No one believes me. I didn't do anything. I just collapsed. They said I was doing drugs, but Talor, I've never done anything like that. No one believes me!"

"I believe you," I reassured her, grabbing her hand and squeezing it.

I heard a tap at the door. Mrs. Warren poked her head in. We both looked over as she brought a plate from the cafeteria. She kissed Rose on the cheek and hugged my neck.

"I'm glad to see you, Talor. Rose, honey, I brought you some of the chicken and potatoes from the cafeteria you said you liked."

"I'm not hungry," Rose yelled. "If I get skinnier, he'll come back. He'll want me again!"

She became violent then, throwing the plate across the room and screaming. Nurses came charging in to restrain her. I backed away from the fray, my hand covering my mouth. Mrs. Warren started to crumple up and cry, rushing out into the hallway. I followed, catching her in a hug. She was a petite, sweet woman, and I had never seen Rose disrespect her.

"I'm so sorry, Mrs. Warren. That's not Rose. You know that," I said, soothing her.

"I just want my baby back. Oh God! What did that monster do to my baby?"

Monster. That's not far off. I let her cry on my shoulder, so disoriented that I couldn't think of a single thing to say to comfort her. I pat her on the back as we stood there in the hall. I watched the nurses give Rose a

164

tranquilizer. It put her out in seconds. They filed out once she was sedated. When things were quiet, Mrs. Warren managed a warm smile at me through the tears.

"You're such a good person, Talor. I'm so glad Rose has a friend like you. I know your mama would be so proud of the person you are."

I gave her a final squeeze and had to let her go before the tears began to fall. I was ashamed of myself, acting like a good friend when I was the source of all the trouble. My mother wouldn't have been proud of me at all. I looked back in the hospital room.

"What drugs did she take?"

Mrs. Warren followed my gaze.

"That's the strangest part of all this, Talor. They didn't find anything in the lab tests. Nothing. But the doctors swear it was an overdose. She had all the symptoms. She says she didn't try to kill herself. Is it crazy that I believe her? I don't know what to think."

"That's not crazy to me at all, actually."

I was just standing in the middle of the Elements Coffee parking lot reliving the events of the afternoon in my head. It wasn't until a car horn honked at me that I came out of my daze and wandered aimlessly inside. It was busy. There were more people waiting on drinks and sitting at tables than I'd ever seen before.

I took a place in line and shuffled along as it moved, staring at the floor, imaging what Spencer and Rose could have been into. He was missing. She

165

was in the psych ward. The world was still turning, but it was wonky, like reality was reflecting back from a funhouse mirror. Rose had never done anything crazy before. None of it made sense. I forgot where I was again.

"Ma'am?"

The voice was a barista behind the counter. There were a few people waiting in line behind me stomping impatiently. Startled, I pulled out my wallet.

"Oh, what do you have with cinnamon in it?"

He pointed to the menu.

"We have cinnamon –"

I interrupted him.

"Never mind. Excuse me."

I didn't want anything at all. I just wanted to sit somewhere alone and cry. I felt this overwhelming sense of shame in myself. I had made out with my friend's boyfriend, caused him to break up with her, and it all landed her in the hospital. I was a bad person. Bad people don't deserve good coffee.

I moved away from the counter and bolted straight for the single stall bathroom where I washed my face. I leaned over the sink and realized I had forgotten deodorant that morning.

Using the paper towels, I gave myself a makeshift bath. I dug through my purse to see what I had in there. The only thing I could find with any scent was a trial size honeysuckle hand lotion. I cringed as I put lotion under my arms. Smelling like honeysuckles was better than the alternative. I flapped my arms up and down like a chicken trying to take off.

I gave myself a disappointed once over in the mirror before leaving. I looked as terrible as I felt. I walked to the window to watch the sunset. The autumn sky was exploding with burning oranges and velvety purples. It was soothing, so I wrapped my scarf tighter and pushed open the door. The weather had finally started to change. It was cooler now. Cold, almost. As I started past the empty iron tables outside, I heard someone rushing up behind me.

"Excuse me, ma'am!" the voice called.

I stopped and looked back. The Elements barista strolled up and held a coffee apprehensively.

"You left this at the counter."

I shook my head.

"No, I didn't get anything."

"No, a guy bought it for you. He's here all the time. Always buys the person behind him a coffee. It was you this time."

I scanned the people at the tables and on the couches inside. I didn't know anyone.

"I'm sorry. I don't – just give it to someone else."

He looked at the words written on the side of the cup.

"Are you Ta-al-lor? Cinnamon hot chocolate with whipped cream? And a cherry?"

I smiled.

"Yes, I'm Tay-lor. There's a cherry in it?"

He nodded and handed it to me before going back inside. I breathed in the creamy smell, letting the cup warm my hands. I opened the top and I stepped back onto the curb. Pulling the cherry off the top, I took a sip.

Sage walked around to stand in front of me, cute as ever. He was wearing this green beanie hat slung back on his head and those hair ends were flipping out of the sides again. Just seeing him made me smile. I held up the cherry.

"I believe this is yours, sir?"

He took the cherry and popped it in his mouth.

"So, how is it?"

"I love it. Thank you."

He nodded as he finished his own espresso shot and turned to toss the cup in the trashcan. I took the opportunity to check him out, of course. The hot chocolate settled in my stomach about the same time, making me sweat. Goodness. I was feeling better already. I had to loosen my scarf as I looked at him.

"So, espresso for you this time? Not lemonade?"

He tapped his jacket pocket. There was a tiny notebook in it.

"I'm writing songs. Never know when it might go all night."

"Wow. You must be really inspired to go all night."

I didn't mean for it to sound the way it did. He studied me for a moment and then looked away.

"I'm not – I'm not bothering you, am I? Were you supposed to meet someone?"

I wanted to laugh. Looking like this? No one would have me. I didn't say that. I was in the strangest mood. He was smiling, making me feel all confused and giddy. Hadn't I just been torturing myself for my plethora of bad decisions?

"No," I said, shaking my head as I rotated the warm cup in my hands.

"Oh, good. Then would you mind my company?"

I was not dressed for a makeshift date. My hair was dirty. I was wearing sweaty yoga pants, his hoodie, and zero makeup. Even worse, I was emotionally unstable and raw, ready to bawl at any moment. Also, I had been busted wearing his hoodie. Plus, I forgot deodorant that morning, so I couldn't offer to give it back to him in case it smelled.

I didn't remember actually brushing my teeth that morning, so I freaked out and put the cup in front of my smile. Despite all that, a cute, well put together Sage wanted to spend time with me. I decided he looked good enough for the both of us, so I would just have to deal with my embarrassing lack of hygiene. I would never pass him up – even looking, feeling, and probably smelling like garbage.

"Sure, but I don't know if there's a seat in there."

He thumbed over his shoulder.

"Actually, I know a place you'll like. Come with me?"

He led me to the end of the building and we took a left. I couldn't believe that almost hidden in plain sight was this serene garden park. It was at least three acres of garden and lawn. There was a ground fountain that spanned the entire length of the park in the middle, and there were lights on the interior sides of the walls so it was lit up at night.

At dusk, it was purely magical. Large rocks were compiled in the fountain and smooth slabs of concrete jut out on either side so people could sit beside the water. There was even a tiny garden maze. Two small Japanese maples glowed bright red like burning bushes.

Sage stepped in front of me and turned.

"There's never anyone back here. I don't think many people know about it."

"This is amazing. How'd you find it?"

"Just paying attention."

I followed him over to a part of the fountain where a willow tree dropped down. He sat down on the smooth concrete first, pulling one bent leg up on the slab and resting his back against a pillar. I sat down a few feet away, trying to think how keep my thighs from spreading out to the size of watermelons. Emotionally exhausted, I just let the chips fall. He was looking in my eyes anyway, watching me from over his knee.

"Tell me what's wrong," he urged softly, his voice soothing and sweet.

I shook my head, taking another sip of the hot chocolate.

"No, it's not a pretty enough conversation for this place. It's great. I love it. Thank you for bringing me here."

His arm draped across his knee, where his hand hung loosely.

"You seem upset. I don't mind listening if you need to talk."

I traced the plastic top of my cup. I felt myself opening up in that moment. I could never understand how or why it felt so natural to be so at ease with him.

"I just went to see one of my friends at the hospital."

"What happened?"

I felt my emotions building, so I paused until I gathered my strength back.

"She might have tried to kill herself."

His leg swayed slightly.

"Wow, that's tough. I'm so sorry."

I didn't look up. I couldn't believe I was telling him, but the words kept coming.

"It doesn't make sense. She's never done anything like that. She's not a wild person, ok? She's good. And what's worse, I feel like I didn't help at all by going. I think asked the wrong things or should have said less or something. I'm not very good with words. Maybe you've noticed."

He dropped his leg down and rested his elbows forward on his knees. He looked over his shoulder at me.

"Just being there is important. You did help, even if it doesn't feel like it."

I drank more hot chocolate while I thought about everything I couldn't tell him. Spencer. The tease. The break-up. The kiss. It all started to churn somewhere behind my eyes, collecting into tears. I would have to hold them back as long as possible. I was not going to cry in front of him. I picked at my uneven nails.

"She's not crazy. A jerk really messed her up."

He blinked and his head went full tilt.

"This isn't – the friend of yours who was dating Spencer for a while, is it? What was her name?"

"Well, yeah actually. Rose. How did you know that? Anyway, they didn't find anything in her system, but they think she tried to overdose. Everyone thinks Spencer might be involved. Like maybe he got her the drugs or something."

Sage sat up straight, looking deep in thought. His posture and expression made me paranoid for sharing that information with him.

"Sage, please don't say anything. I'm only telling you because I can't shut up and you kind of bribed me with this," I replied, tapping on the coffee cup. "And he was smoking marijuana at my friend's house a few weeks back and I just – I mean – please don't tell anyone."

"It's ok, Talor. I won't say anything," he assured me.

It was quiet. Both of us focused on the lights in the water beside us. Sage looked like he was searching for something, maybe words. I cleared my throat.

"Can I ask you something? Something a little weird?"

His gaze slowly climbed up from the water. He never gave me permission, but I went for it anyway. I sat up and flattened my palms against each other before bringing them to my lips.

"Do you remember the day you came back to the nursery and asked me if I was ok?"

He nodded, his eyebrows going up. I continued.

"Some super weird things had happened to me that day. Do you think that, ok, I know this is going to sound crazy, but do you think it's possible that Spencer is into drugs? It's just things happened that I can't exactly explain. I know it sounds crazy."

Sage's eyebrows dropped as he looked away and stood up.

"What things happened that you can't explain?" he probed, his manner introspective and wary.

I wasn't telling him that story. It had a kiss in it. Oh, and me seeing things. I stood up, too. It seemed odd not to. I chuckled and waved him off as I scooped up my things.

"Oh, nothing. I don't know what I'm talking about right now. It's been a long day. I'm gonna go. I'm talking your head off."

"But...you're going?" he asked, caught off guard.

"Yeah, I think I've taken up enough of your writing time with my crazy talk."

"Talor, is there anything I can I do? Anything at all?"

I started to move past him, but when he asked that, I stopped. It was a genuine question. He meant it. I zeroed in on his chest. It seemed very inviting. I looked up at him, my hand daring to reach out. I felt like a hug from him would make everything so much better.

Then I remembered that I was wearing lotion for deodorant. It was probably not faring well in the emotional heat under my hoodie. Ok, Sage's hoodie. His hands slid past my ribs and across my back like they knew the roadmap straight to my heart. One hand was closer to my neck than my shoulders, and it tilted my face up towards his. He looked me right in the eye.

"So beautiful, you know that? Inside and out. Just everywhere."

He guided my head into his chest and covered me in the best hug ever. His fingers stroked my hair as I closed my eyes and leaned on him, my heavy conscience feeling a little bit lighter. I couldn't believe I was in Sage's arms. He took a deep breath.

"Well, one thing's for sure, Talor."

"What's that?"

"This thing's never smelled so good," he chuckled, grabbing the shoulder of the hoodie.

I relaxed into him.

"Really?"

"Is that honeysuckle?"

He could smell the hand lotion under my arms. Maybe he thought it was lip-gloss or face lotion. It didn't seem to bother him either way. I nodded, confused and embarrassed. And happy. Oh so happy.

"Oh, yeah. It's, um yes."

He laid his head over mine. I could tell he was smiling as he spoke.

"It's a good smell. It's you."

I wanted to thank him for being the most amazing man in the world. I wanted to tell him how much he meant to me in that one moment. With a few kind, well-placed words, he turned my entire day around. I closed my eyes and savored his arms, all the while praying my happy heart wouldn't shoot out through my chest into his, killing us both in its wake.

It was a legitimate concern.

16

A week later, I received my invitation to Azalea's Halloween party. It was obvious she'd decided against a mystery dinner because she invited too many people. She didn't realize you could only have a certain number of people take part in a dinner party like that. She made it a costume party instead, including dinner.

Since our talk at Elements Coffee, I was feeling much more at ease around Sage. We still didn't have long conversations at work, but we did talk more. As a result, I was bold enough to ask him to be my date. It would technically only be our second date, but I was ready to move us into relationship territory.

The costume party was less extravagant than the gala the month before, but nothing the Beaty family ever did could be considered small scale. There were at least 100 jack-o-lanterns spread all across the lawn and along the front porch. They looked like creepy flickering faces eyeing the arriving guests.

An unseen fog machine covered a layer of the ground and shrouded guest's steps in mystery as they walked along. A menacing-looking scarecrow stood leering in the open field just to the side. I think it moved periodically, making girls jump.

A headless horseman – on actual horseback – chased people sporadically through the grounds. I was pretty sure it was Mr. Beaty from the get-go. It was something he would do. Screaming and laughing resounded through the lawn after each frenzied chase. He awarded those who survived the chase with candy from his large glowing pumpkin hanging off the saddle.

Everyone got a piece.

I stood at the gravel and watched the craziness unfold. A familiar voice startled the sleeping butterflies in my stomach, sending them fluttering without escape.

"Ariel, right? From The Little Mermaid?"

I turned to the trees on my left and saw Sage stepping out of the shadows with a grin. I beamed, spinning in my sparkly blue dress to show him.

"Yes! With the wig, I was worried people would just think I was a Texas beauty pageant queen. What gave me away?"

He pointed.

"The purple seashells, I think?"

Oh yeah. The boobs.

"Now. Let's see about you," I said, tapping my finger against my lips.

His hair was different. It was brushed across his brow and had a wave to it that normally wasn't there. Thick stubble had grown thick enough to be a beard – a real one. He was wearing a white henley with some crisscross ties dangling down his open chest.

A deep gray coat covered one arm and tied under the other shoulder. It was lined with fur on the collar and went almost to the ground. It all looked seriously vintage. A real sword hung at his side and weathered leather boots climbed up his shins. I licked my lips, unable to control the impulse.

"You're a sexy prince, right?" I asked, catching myself. "Oh, I mean, just a prince!"

His expression changed like I'd said something wrong. He shook his head urgently like he was trying to physically cast some thought out of his mind.

"Wait. The costume. Yes. Yeah, I am."

He approached apprehensively, offering a tiny bouquet of honeysuckles. I breathed them in, remembering it's what Sage said I smelled like. I hoped it was a good thing.

"You know, I'm actually impressed. Most guys just bring just me sea weed."

He bathed me in an adoring glow.

"I'm not most guys."

"No, you're not. Where did you find these in October?"

"They're still around. Just have to know where to look," he answered.

His soothing eyes settled somewhere in my soul. I was glad for the honeysuckles. I pretended to smell them again when I felt like fainting.

"Much like gentlemen," I murmured. I didn't know whether or not he heard. He didn't respond, so I assumed he didn't.

His elbow bowed out, so I slipped my hand in the crook of it and we started along our way up to the house.

"So, is that a real sword?" I asked.

He swung his coat out and tapped the sword hilt with his free hand.

"Yeah. It's actually been in my family for centuries. Kind of an heirloom, really."

"Ever use it?"

He laughed.

"Not often, no."

I laced my fingers tighter around his arm and followed him to the entrance. The Grim Reaper stood blocking the door with glowing red eyes. I stopped. Sage pulled out his sword and pointed it at the Reaper.

"Well, what else is a sword for?" he asked.

The Reaper put its hands up in surrender and moved to the side to let us pass. Once we were inside, I heard Azalea descending the stairs in a noisy, sparkly flapper girl outfit. I was afraid to look at Sage and see him ogling her like most men would. I risked it.

He was still gazing down at me, a soft smile easing my mind. Azalea spread out her arms wide and swallowed me in a big hug. When she let go, she took my arm out to the side and eyed my costume.

"Nice stems, doll," she said, joking in a typical mobster accent, moving her eyebrows up and down rapidly.

I pretended to be offended with a mock gasp and fake slap. She moved her jaw around like I'd hit her before checking out Sage.

"And for this one," she pondered, eyes going wide. "Gimme a minute here, chum."

She looked him up and down and gave me a thumb's up. He looked confused. I scowled. She shrugged and pinched her chin.

"I really expected a cowboy with that walk."

I remembered what she said that day at Cypress College when she met him for the first time. He had a cowboy swagger about him.

"But instead I see a sexy swordsman, I think?" she guessed.

"He's a prince," I corrected, my tone a little sharper than I meant it to be. I didn't like her calling him sexy, even if it was true.

"Oh. You're missing your crown if you're a prince," she said to Sage, pointing to his head.

"Not all princes wear crowns," I said.

Azalea shrugged it off and brought us into the grand dining room. It was a room so large it was almost never used. It was located at the back end of the mansion and had a stained glass ceiling. I could never figure out why a room would have a stained glass ceiling in the first place, but it added eeriness to the night since you could see the moonlight overhead and shadowy black branches from bare oaks reaching over.

There had to be hundreds of tall candles lighting the area. They made it brighter than I thought it would be in there. Four butlers dressed as statues stood in corners. Ominous music played from musicians with an oboe and violins. One servant dressed as a zombie came over to us with a tray of wine glasses holding a thick red liquid.

"Blood?"

I narrowed my eyes to look at it.

"Oh. Ew. It does look like blood. What is it really?"

"Blood," he repeated, monotone.

I shook my head.

"Ohhhk. I think I'll pass."

From the corner of my eye, I could see someone walking up as Sage visibly stiffened. It was Azalea with Mannix. Mannix was dressed as a cowboy vampire. He had longs fangs that looked real. Azalea leaned her head against his shoulder as he tipped his cowboy hat at us. I looked him up and down.

"Wait. You couldn't decide between a vampire and a cowboy? Was it really that hard?"

Azalea kissed his cheek.

"I love it! It's out of the box. Genius, right?"

Mannix hadn't said a word yet. He was just standing there with some snarky smile.

"If you were going to combine costumes, you could've been a leprechaun loser," I suggested.

Azalea frowned. Sage covered a smile with his hand. Mannix kept the same smug face.

"Well, see now, princess, those don't exist. I happen to know."

I rolled my eyes.

"Oh? By all means, let's keep it confined to reality, Mr. vampire."

Azalea took her index finger down the length of his fangs and dropped her jaw when she rubbed them.

"Seriously, that's amazing, Talor. They feel so real. Touch them."

"He'll probably bite me," I said, eyeing him.

"Go way outta that," Mannix said.

"Huh?" I asked.

"Uh, Talor –" Sage started, scratching his ear.

Unable to resist, I reached out and lightly brushed against the enamel. They felt as real as fangs on a person could feel. I brought my fingers to the sharp end.

"God, that's too sharp. Aren't you scared you'll bite your tongue?"

Mannix actually laughed. Like, a real laugh. It threw me, so I smiled. Like, a real smile. Azalea looked pleased with our interaction for once. Sage was the only one not smiling.

Mannix licked across the fangs.

"They bother you, mate?"

Sage sighed.

"Talor, would you like something to drink?"

"Thank you. Anything non-alcoholic. Azalea?"

Azalea nodded and pointed to a table across the room.

"Everything on that table is as virginal as you are," she replied, winking.

Sage started off, catching my eyes for a moment with a smile that drew my shoulders up to cover my blistering ears. I took the opportunity to glance around the room. That's when I saw a girl I recognized from the pool party. She was standing alone near the musicians, dressed as a ghost in a sheet that didn't cover her head. She was basically a marshmallow in a white poncho.

I walked over and touched her shoulder.

"Valerie, isn't it?"

She stared at me blankly.

"Yeah. Who are you?"

I walked around to her front.

"I'm Talor. We met a few months ago here at the pool party. You don't remember me?"

She looked at me like she wanted to remember, but she just couldn't. Blinking once, she pulled her phone out of her pocket and ignored me while I was still standing there.

"No."

"Oh," I said, rolling my eyes and pulling off my red wig. I'd forgotten about it. "I'm not usually wearing a gigantic red wig. Do you remember me now?"

"Can you go away? I don't know you," she snapped.

I balled up the red wig in my hand, a little surprised at the aggression. It wasn't like I'd asked her to show me her breasts. I didn't say anything back, and since she was playing a game on her phone, it didn't matter if I did. I got a few steps away from her when Sage caught up to me. He handed me a glass of clear fizzy punch. I thanked him and put my wig back on.

"Everyone, find a seat. It's time to start," Azalea called.

The crowd murmured and everyone shuffled around the table that spanned the entire length of the room. It was covered in a bright white linen cloth and real silver candelabras that dotted along every few seats.

Sage and I found chairs across from Azalea and Mannix. He pulled my chair out for me and let me sit before settling beside me. Azalea was too busy snoozing up to Mannix to notice the clockwork chivalry.

I tried not to stare at him, but I couldn't help myself. I blushed like mad when he caught me. In return, his fingers brushed loosely against his lip, going back and forth to hide the smile underneath. A woman stepped inside the room and let out such a piercing scream that I grabbed ahold of Sage's leg because it was the closest thing to me. I recoiled my hand bashfully as a zombie butler stood at the head of the table.

"The banshee has screamed. One of you will die tonight. But dinner first. It is bad manners to die on an empty stomach," he announced.

A fleet of servants filed out of the kitchen carrying trays of food, which they placed all along the length of the table. Sage and I were caught in a gaze again, our hands stretching fingers to touch.

When he finally took my hand against my thigh, I had to look away. Azalea leaned over to whisper something to Mannix and he didn't react. He just stared at us with this judgmental disgust like we were a brother and sister. It chilled me to the core.

LONG LIVE DEAD RECKLESS

I immediately released Sage's hand and sat up straight against the high backing of the chair, hoping the dinner would go fast so I could get away from Mannix. The servants laid out salads and soups for us.

I tried to pick up my fork, but I still hadn't recovered from the weird juju. The fork kept turning sideways, so I was fumbling it all over the table. I finally wrestled it into a caveman hold in my hand. I could feel people staring at me, but I didn't look up.

"Yeah, my fork is possessed, Azalea," I groaned, wheezing from stress like I was having an asthma attack.

"Maybe your date can help with that. He's a wizard with words," Mannix said, cocking a brow.

"Really?" I asked Sage.

"Give us a poem about the princess and her wicked fork," Mannix replied.

Sage shrugged and touched the fork in my hand.

"It starts at your touch, not of a rebellious nature; such a common misconception. But no; its consuming will to serve you writhes the inanimate to life. Your slightest touch tames the tenders of its restless little soul. It starts because you possess it – mind, body, whole."

Azalea and I stared at him. We barely remembered to close our mouths. Mannix gave a slow, taunting clap. I just wanted to kiss Sage right then and there. A silly little poem about a fork had me all hot and bothered. I didn't know how that was even possible.

"A poet," I told him, "that's what you are."

Mannix rested an elbow on the table and leaned forward.

"There's a lot of power in that tongue of his, isn't there, princess?"

Azalea elbowed Mannix, shushing him.

"Quit making them uncomfortable, baby."

Sage tossed the water back, drinking it like it was some hard liquor he really needed before slamming the empty glass down. It was like we were in a saloon. Maybe Azalea had a point about the cowboy thing. Mannix leaned my way.

"Talor, did I tell you my fangs retract?"

"No."

He opened his mouth and the fangs retracted back into normal teeth. Azalea gasped.

"What is it? A built-in spring or something?"

"It's magic, that's all."

"Outside now," Sage said, taking his napkin and thrusting it on the plate. He stood up and glared at Mannix, who just sat back in his chair and raised his glass.

"I doubt we duel the same way."

Sage excused himself and disappeared out the side door of the mansion towards the pecan groves in the back. I stood up and looked after him. I wasn't sure if I should follow.

"I'd leave him, princess. He's in a fragile state," Mannix warned.

"Stop calling me princess!"

"It's what you are," he replied.

"You suck, you know that?" I growled, throwing my napkin at him.

"Yes, I do," he said, catching it and bowed his head. "And God, I love it."

I had a hard time catching up to Sage. It was darker back there than it was in the front, with only jack-o-lanterns atop hay bales lighting the way. He was standing underneath a tree with one hand grasping onto a low hanging branch.

He apologized before I even got to him.

184

"I was rude in there, wasn't I?"

He stayed turned away from me, but I held up my hand anyway.

"Don't apologize. I don't like Mannix, either. He's weird and rude and a total loser. I can't figure out why Azalea even likes him. He's basically made of jerk. Not beef jerky, you know. But jerk. Like a jerk?"

"Yeah...I'm sorry if I made you uncomfortable."

"Oh, no. I just came out here to come ask where you hid his pot of gold. Has to be why he hates you. Why'd you go and do that, Sage? Steal the tiny man's treasure?"

He chuckled lightly as he shifted his weight, bringing both hands up to the branch. I saw him look at me from between his raised arm and shoulder. I wrapped my arms around myself as a brisk wind rushed past. I definitely wore the wrong costume for the weather.

"I loved your poem. Do you know any more just −" I paused, watching as he dropped his hands down from the branch and turned his head towards me, "off the top of your head?"

His mouth opened lightly as he faced me.

"You know, poetry is fragile. A gentle breeze can blow it over, really. But one perfect line of poetry can linger for centuries. Just one single breath out of the billions ever breathed. It's amazing, the power of finding the right words."

"So there's that tongue I was warned about."

His lip twitched into a smile that disappeared too quickly. He unhitched his coat from the side of his chest and shook it off the other shoulder. He brought it over and wrapped it around me. It was too big, but it was still warm from his body heat. Perfect. Another brisk breeze blew through, stirring up leaves at our feet. He brought the coat tighter around me.

"I write lyrics mostly."

"So you're a writer?"

"I'm a lot of things."

He stayed close, blocking the wind. Neither of us made a move. It was like we were consistently caught in this stupid 'almost' dance. It was driving me crazy, so it was good that he finally retreated to the tree and leaned against it. I followed, keeping a respectable distance. It isn't what I wanted to do.

"Oh, I wanted to tell you something. Do you remember my friend, Rose? The one I talked to you about that day at Elements?" I asked, rubbing my fingers on the insides of the coat sleeves.

He nodded and propped a foot back, resting his hand on the raised knee.

"I do. How is she?"

"Well, she's her old self again. I talked to her yesterday. The doctors said it was probably just a weird new street drug that someone slipped her. She's doing really well," I said, smiling.

"I'm glad she's ok. I know you were worried. I told you that you were a good friend."

"Thank you for being so nice to me that day."

I shivered, clutching the sleeves up into my palm so no wind could get through. Sage leaned his head back against the tree, but his gaze was direct.

"Hey, come here."

I looked up. He shrugged.

"The tree helps block the wind."

He didn't have to tell me twice. His hands reached out and took the outside of my covered arms, slowly rubbing up and down them to keep me warm. His brow was tense even though the rest of him seemed relaxed. There were conflicting signals all over the place, but that was Sage.

"I want to know you," I said, exhaling.

"I know," he said with a twinge of sadness in his voice.

"So let me."

He curved his warm hand against my cheek. In response, my hands attached to his chest like magnets were drawing me into his heart. We were both unyielding, both aching. There was something strange between us, and I don't think either of us knew how to push it away to get close. My nerves were tearing me at the seams as his lips separated. He bent his head slightly as though testing the waters.

When I puckered my lips, he eased back and brought my hands off his chest. He walked a few steps away before tangling his hands in his hair and shaking his head. I wanted to dissolve. Die. But not cry. No. Not that! Rather than risk crying in front of him, I tried to bolt.

He cut me off.

"Wait."

"It's ok. We can – just be – just friends if that's how you feel," I stuttered.

He took in a deep breath and one of his hands clutched his shirt close to his heart. I dared look at him from the top of my eyes, keeping my head down. There was turmoil in his face, but I couldn't understand why. He was the one who rejected me. Whatever kept him standoffish and distant, it was a prison to him as well as a fence to me.

I hurried off, his coat the only thing keeping me together underneath.

17

I ended up in a coat closet.

I'm not sure why I chose to hide there over the eight bathrooms in the mansion; maybe because the large coat closet was just inside the door, and I was too embarrassed to face anyone yet. I had to beat myself up first. I basically undid two months' worth of work in a few seconds of sheer impatient stupidity.

I clung to the empty jackets around me like security blankets. Their thickness helped muffle the hectic sounds of the outside world. People are loud by nature. I never disliked people so much as I did when I was in that coat closet. They're much more annoying when drunk and performing for their friends. Wiping my tears, I listened to the chaos. It didn't take long to hear something interesting.

Something I would regret.

"Now," said a male voice. Deep. Desperate.

"Ok," replied a female voice. Quiet. Submissive.

It sounded like Mannix, but it wasn't Azalea he was talking to. I held my breath as they walked by at different paces: hers, slow and sluggish; his, fast with purpose. The door slammed shut behind them and the party sounds took over again. I peeked out the closet.

Even though I was still reeling from what happened with Sage, I wanted to catch Mannix being a total tool so Azalea would be done with him. My first thought was to record whatever was going to happen. I felt for my phone at my hips, but there were no pockets in that dress.

I groaned. I didn't have it on me, and I couldn't waste time running to get it from my purse. My word would have to do. I tiptoed out of the closet and cracked open the side door. Before I stepped out, Sage came to mind. *Was catching Mannix cheating worth facing Sage?*

I started to close the door when a flash of something caught my eyes. It was luminous, bright, and coming from the grove. I clutched Sage's coat around me and firmly set my feet towards it. I kept scanning the area, feeling watched for some reason. But there was no one else being nosy. I was alone in that.

Crouching down, I hid among the bushes near the grove. The light was gone now, but I could hear voices. I tried peering through the bushes, but I couldn't see much – just hands and movement. I felt an insect crawl on my skin and furiously brushed it away. I held my breath, hoping I hadn't been found out, but they didn't react to my spastic fit. They hadn't heard me. I dared peek over the bush to see Sage, Mannix, and Valerie all standing together.

I wasn't close enough to make out every word they were saying, but I heard something like "you want it" and then the party noise got louder as the song changed. I could only assume Mannix was talking about Valerie.

There was a faint smile on her face as she leaned against Mannix. She was giving them her full, wide-eyed attention, and I'd never seen her give more than a second's glance at anything but a cell phone. I couldn't understand it.

Was Mannix dating her, too?

My teeth clenched tight as I squat down and moved along the ground like a crab. I scurried closer to the nearest tree so I could stand up for a better view. The sound effects machine beside me let out a loud wolf howl, causing me to squawk. I scrambled to the tree, looking around all crazy-eyed for a werewolf. When I realized I wasn't actually in danger, I turned my attention back to Sage. He was shaking his head.

He had turned away from them and was heading towards me when something Mannix said made him stop. I couldn't hear what it was. He was speaking at the right pitch of mumbling to frustrate me. I noticed then that Valerie was wearing normal clothes now, no lazy ghost costume.

Something was on her skin around her neck. It was oddly shaped. I couldn't tell if it was a choker or some chunky necklace. I thought maybe she had been wearing one underneath the ghost costume.

Mannix tossed something white and flimsy at Sage and he caught it. He carefully looked it over, gripped it tight and shook his head again. Mannix gestured for Valerie to do something, so she brushed a hand against her neck and brought it up to Sage's eye level.

Whatever was on her neck was also on her hand. Maybe mud? Paint? Fake blood? Huh. I stared hard to figure out what she was showing Sage. He took a step back and dropped the white thing on the ground. Without warning, he grabbed Valerie harshly by her hair and turned her face up towards his. It was like a dirty romance novel, the way he held her and she

191

went blissfully limp in his arms. His body language was angry, vicious and dark – not like the person he was with me at all.

He seemed to take a deep breath and plunged into her, kissing passionately. When she wrapped her arms around him, something inside me shriveled up and died. I couldn't watch any more. I closed my eyes as I dropped down in a ball at the base of the tree.

I felt the empty darkness of the night all around me, but I remained still and more importantly, I didn't cry. I just sat there with the knowledge that Spencer had told me the truth after all. Sage didn't want me.

Just then, a drunken couple stumbled loudly out of the side door. They were oblivious to everything except their own antics. I watched them fall around and cackle before hearing Mannix and Valerie rustle off from the thicket separately.

Sage was slower to leave.

I glanced back to see him standing there with his head low and shoulder blades slumping. He brought his arm up to his face and wiped across his mouth. He let his hand fall flimsily to the side and wiped it off half-heartedly on his shirttail.

Next, he pulled off his shirt and tossed it aside. He bent over and took the white thing back in his hand. It could have weighed two hundred pounds by the agonizing way he straightened. I watched his naked muscles flex and roll under the skin as he toyed with whatever was in his hand. He moved to put it on and I knew then it was a shirt. I was so lost in thought that I barely had time to get on the other side of the tree before he walked by.

I was trying to be stealthy, but my dress was not cooperating. I whipped the train of it around to my side of the tree just in time. I tensed every muscle to keep from moving. His footsteps stopped as he paused just on the other side of the tree. I held my breath as I listened to him sigh repeatedly and adjust his clothes before he continued on.

When he went through the doors of the mansion, I collapsed against the tree and gasped. Letting out a pitiful scream I couldn't contain any more, I ripped Sage's coat off and threw it on the ground. I snarled at it like it was the reason my heart was breaking.

Out of nowhere, something hit me in the head. I jolted, looking up to see Mr. Beaty riding up as the Headless Horseman on his black horse, Butch Cassidy. He leaned forward in the saddle and bellowed a hearty laugh at me.

"God bless Texas, Talor! What are you doing in the bushes, kid?"

I picked myself up, feeling foolish in general, but especially as a mermaid slinking around bushes beating up a coat. I ripped the wig off, only then noticing how heavily my hands were shaking.

"I was just getting some air. Hey, Butch Cassidy," I said, petting Butch Cassidy's velvety nose.

"Hiding from boys? Are there too many of 'em chasing you?" he asked, raising himself up in the saddle like he was looking around.

I fixated longingly towards the door Sage went in.

"None of them are chasing me."

He pulled back his black mask and winked at me.

"That makes them all idiots. What about that fella you brought to the thing last month? What was his name? We were supposed to go hunting together. What happened to him? He seemed to really like you."

I stood there holding a red wig while dressed as a mermaid talking to the headless horseman about boys. I just let that sink in before I answered.

"Yeah, that didn't really work out."

He shook his plastic sword.

193

"Huh. Ok. Plenty more fish for you, kid. You want to be the Headless Hessian for a little while? You get to chop off heads. It might make you feel better. Maybe you can chase down a fella. Butch Cassidy'll catch you one."

I smiled, shaking my head. He handed me a piece of chocolate from the pumpkin head.

"Well, go have some fun. Here's some candy to bribe some friends, you little loner."

He rode off, chasing down the drunken couple that had meandered outside and interrupted Sage's abusive make out. I opened the chocolate and mindlessly stuffed my face, the sugar high granting me a stupid kind of courage. I marched back inside to ruin my life.

When I got there, Sage was scanning the crowd. I ducked so he couldn't see me. Luckily, the sugar high didn't last long enough for a confrontation. I pushed backwards through the crowd until I made it to the wraparound porch outside.

It was much less crowded out there. I put my red wig beside me on the swing. It was chilly, but I enjoyed my solitude for a few minutes. It was nice, looking at the stars and pretending I wasn't losing my mind in the most creative way possible. I did credit myself for being inventive. Spencer's freak out and Sage's betrayal were excellent hallucinations.

By the time I was done with my 'pros and cons of losing my mind' list, I didn't know whether to let myself cry like a baby or time a scream with the sound effects blaring out of the yard speakers. A minute later, I was glad I didn't choose the screaming.

My stomach turned when I saw Sage lope out of the mansion. He hustled down the steps and into the lawn, where he was so preoccupied with running his hands through his hair and pacing that it wasn't hard to stay unnoticed.

He was deep inside his own head. I didn't want my motion to catch his attention, so I tried to still the swing by touching my foot on the porch. Unfortunately, the swing was heavy and old, so it creaked. I cursed myself as his head came up and turned.

"I was looking for you," he said.

We stared at each other.

"I can't imagine why," I said.

"I wanted to make sure you were okay."

"I'm perfect."

He looked at my bare shoulders.

"Aren't you cold out here, Talor?"

"Oh, I lost your coat. Sorry. Hope it wasn't expensive."

His hands found his pockets as he made his way towards me, hesitant. He knew I was being rude on purpose. It was unprecedented for both of us.

"Ok, listen. I wanted to apologize. I probably shouldn't have come since Mannix –"

"Probably not," I interrupted.

"But I really wanted to see you," he said.

I looked away. Why was he complimenting me? I was being rude and hurtful, but I couldn't stop. He was being too nice and I knew now that it was all a show. He was fake. No one was really that sweet and kind. I stood up from the porch swing and started towards the door.

"You see me at work. I think that's good enough," I answered coldly.

He leaned forward.

"Maybe it was, but not anymore. Not to me."

"Well, it's good enough for me."

His forehead nearly folded over itself.

"What? Why?"

I stopped.

So many nasty thoughts were clawing around in my head to get out. I had my pick of harsh things to say to him, but it was hard being mean when he was so sweet. Then Valerie flashed in my mind. He was completely different person with her. Not this apologetic guy in front of me. Then I realized that Spencer warned me about this. Sage did have me fooled.

Sage and Mannix were probably friends. Maybe they shared Valerie in some twisted threesome. That's how it looked in the grove. Maybe he wanted to see if he could get me, too. I was being played. Azalea was being played. I felt stupid, naïve.

A fire welled up in my belly as I prepared to deliver the final blow to shut him up for good. He was going down. I shot him an icy glare as I hastily descended the steps towards him in the grass.

"Spencer and I made out here. Did I tell you that? He pushed me against that wall over there. He's amazing with his tongue. Really knows what he's doing, you know? Makes me wonder what else he can do."

"You – kissed – Spencer?" he asked, soft and strained, like he didn't know what word would follow the one before.

He blinked a few times, obviously confused. His mouth was slightly open like it had been when he pretended he was going to kiss me in the grove. It pissed me off to see the dark line between those lips. It led inside him – down his throat to his heart where I wanted to be. I stopped just in front of him, ready to dig the dagger in.

"Yeah, I did, and it was amazing. You ever kiss a girl like that, Sage? Careless, furious, frenzied – violent, even? I'm glad I know at least one guy who will kiss me like that."

He turned his body to the side and cut his eyes. There was a puzzled expression on his face as he stared at nothing. A few seconds of silence passed. I waited on his response, still battle-ready. With a gentle sigh, he dropped his head. His words barely needed air, but they slapped me in the face.

"I have to say goodnight here, Talor."

With that, he raised his gaze. There was a soft sincerity in those eyes; an unflinching vulnerability that made me just freaking hate myself. He never wanted a fight. He was surrendering. I don't know what I wanted to accomplish by telling him about the kiss with Spencer. I wanted to make him jealous enough to kiss me, I guess. Competition.

Deep down, I think I wanted to hurt him in a way he wouldn't forget. He wounded my pride, rejected me. I wanted immediate vengeance for him kissing Valerie, so I went too far and it backfired. He didn't have the slightest desire to kiss me now, and that parting look said he wouldn't forget it anytime soon.

The ridiculous, jealous girl inside was shamed into submission. The sane person left behind wanted to reel in my words, but there was no getting them back. They were free now; free to swim around in our heads, hurting him and haunting me. I tried to remember horrible things about him so I could feel better. He was sadistic, two-faced, and he had played me.

I wanted to recall his faults in excruciating, vindicating detail, but I could still feel the warmth of his tender goodbye on my skin, and I could still see the longing in those sweet, caring eyes; his poetry, his warm coat, his compliments, and his humility – those were the only things I could remember. All the evils of the night couldn't contend with my pinpoint cruelty. And it was too late to apologize.

He left without looking back.

18

Days later, I was still tortured by what happened at Azalea's party. I know I had a right to feel the way I did, but I was terrified that I'd reacted too harshly. Full of regrets and thoughts, I drove to the only place I could think anymore – the graveside. Mom's grave was under the shade of a tree, next to a small holding pond where ducks would nest in the spring. I knew she'd like it there.

She always loved ducks for some reason.

She had been gone for about six months, and it felt wrong every time I visited. Like I was just going through some motion that wasn't natural to either of us. Still, I went, and I always brought a letter with me. Sometimes a poem, other times just a few lines or a memory we shared. I never brought flowers. They could be expensive and I only made minimum wage.

She would understand.

I licked the envelope and pushed the sides together. As I wiped away the debris from freshly cut grass away from her name, I rested my chin on my bent knee. I wanted to say something to her. Something loving. Something kind. Something that would give us both some peace. I mulled over the right words as if she really would hear them.

"Hi, Mom."

I paused, waiting for her to answer. There was only the wind.

"I remember the day we put you here. All I wanted was to take your place. You were needed here. I'm not. I remember wanting to skip forward a few years until it wouldn't hurt anymore. I thought that I would have three or four years to struggle through and end up ok, but...I don't know. I don't know anything. If you can see me, I hope you're proud of me. That's all. I just hope. I don't know what I'm doing half the time and I really don't even know who I am, either. I wish..."

I had to stop. Even the dead don't want to listen to sniveling. I watched an ant crawl across her name. Angry, I flicked it away. No ant would step all over my mother's good name – not today. Not any day.

I bent over, my tears like fat raindrops splashing against the stone. A heavy footstep fell kind of close so I stood up quickly and turned to face the intruder. It was an old man holding a rake. His uniform nametag said "Jet."

"Pardon me, miss?"

He looked like he himself would be in the ground any day. Being interrupted during an emotional gravesite moment seemed like a firing offense in his line of work. I forced a smile, but my tone was less than cordial.

"I'm sorry, am I in your way? Do I need to leave?"

He shook his head and hand simultaneously.

"No, please. I apologize."

I wanted to pick up the letter I had placed on mom's grave, but for some reason, I couldn't imagine not leaving her something. I cleared my throat and started the trek back to the car on the road.

"It's just −" he called.

I stopped. He looked up towards the sky and smiled. I looked up, too. There were a few gray clouds. I wasn't sure what he was looking at.

"The daughter of the king is only strongest at her weakest."

I said nothing as I walked back towards the grave. I wasn't going to leave my letter with a person like that standing around. I knelt down and pretended to clean off the gravestone so I could scoop up the letter.

Glancing around, I could see that we were alone except for a few people standing over a newly marked grave across the field.

"Yeah, I'm not a princess," I said sharply.

For a maintenance man at a cemetery, he was fairly cryptic and totally unprofessional. And he was now added to the list of weirdoes calling me a princess lately. I didn't know what they meant, but I was tired of it.

"You are the daughter of the king. What they call you is not the same thing."

"Don't you have a grave to dig? People haven't stopped dying, you know."

"The professor will point you in the right direction if you ask," he said, nodding.

"What?" I asked, a little flustered. The professor? Did he mean Professor Milton?

When I turned around, there was just a rake against the tree. There was no one anywhere. The people across the way were gone. Jet was gone. There was no way he could have gotten out of sight that quickly − especially a man that old. How could a stranger know I was planning to talk to Professor Milton about the crop circle photo? Why did he say those things?

I couldn't shake the rampage of thoughts going through my mind as I made my way to campus. I finally settled on the possibility that it was a hallucination from all the stress. My recent fight with Sage had me in a funk and I wasn't sleeping well after the ghost incident. Maybe they were to blame.

While at a traffic light, I pulled up the crop circle photo on my phone and stared at it. Looking at it again, I knew I needed answers. I turned my car towards Cypress College.

Professor Milton had this tiny Zen garden on the desk in his office. Since my first semester, he was my unofficial therapist. He was one of the few professors on campus who actually liked his students and he always had time for one of my moods.

The first time I dragged myself into his office, he pointed me to the Zen garden. It always worked. I would periodically drop by and move the little stones around the fake plants and white sand with the tiny rake because it made me feel better. I told him once that I was master and commander of a tiny garden I couldn't kill, and I liked it. That made him laugh.

I wandered down the hallway to his office, past other open offices where I avoided the prying eyes. Dr. Milton was at his desk on his computer, probably reading an online newspaper or doing some crossword. He saw me over the monitor and brightened, waving me in without a word. I plopped myself down in one of the chairs.

"Here to talk or rake?" He asked, still focused on his work on the computer.

"Both, I think."

He turned from his computer and rested his elbows on his desk. As always, he ushered to the Zen garden.

"Well, go on. You know what to do. You do know I'm not a therapist, though, right?"

I smiled at him, grabbing the miniature rake and scraping the rocks around.

"I know. You say that every time. If you were a real therapist, I wouldn't come anywhere near you. You might have me institutionalized."

He threw back his head and laughed.

"If I were a real therapist, you would be my favorite patient, but I'd never tell my other patients that. Or you, for that matter. Yikes. I'm such a terrible therapist."

"Aww, thank you," I cooed, playfully batting my eyes.

He smirked.

"So, what are we talking about today?"

I stopped raking and pulled my phone out.

"Ok. Crazy stuff. You were in the Marines, right? Like, a long time ago?"

He tapped a pen against his cheek and looked up at the ceiling thoughtfully.

"Back in the Civil War, I was in the Union Army, yes. Don't shoot, Johnny Reb!"

His good sense of humor was wasted on me for once. I looked down at the photo and wondered if I should share it. I was hesitant for some reason. It wasn't like me to be wary of Dr. Milton. Taking in a deep breath, I pushed forward through the apprehension. I placed my hand on his desk.

"Don't think I'm nuts, but a few weeks ago, I found this picture in my grandmother's old photo album. My grandfather was in the Marines and stationed in China during World War II. I just thought you might know about this since you like war and stuff."

"I like war?" he muttered, almost offended. "Nobody likes war."

I waved my hand between us wildly to slap away the misunderstanding.

"No, no – you know what I mean. You know about them. You teach them! Anyway, here."

He raised both bushy brows as he took the phone from me. Putting his glasses on, he studied the photo. He looked longer at it than I expected. I shifted in my seat a few times while I waited.

"Well, huh. This is interesting," he said, pulling off his glasses.

I sat up in my seat like I was in a doctor's office waiting the results of a test.

"I know it sounds crazy, but do you think it's real? I figured you would know."

He turned his head to the side and tapped a finger against his bottom lip.

"I'll tell you, Talor, it looks real. I'd like to see the original photo if I could. I could probably at least tell you if the photo is authentic."

"Well, I know the photo is real. It's aged and everything. I mean, what's in the picture? The crop circle?"

"I'm sure it's real, too. Not an illusion, I mean. Crop circles are always man-made. I've seen a few through the years stationed around different

204

places, but I don't think there's anything like aliens involved," he answered, handing back the phone. "If that's what you're asking."

It felt sheepish to suggest aliens to an academic I admired, so I tried to backpedal.

"Well, no, I mean –"

He propped his elbows on his desk.

"But this one – I've never seen that design before. Unique. Really large, too. I remember when making these was all the rage back before you were born. They were everywhere."

"So it wasn't like some weird phenomenon that was covered up by the government or anything? Right?"

He chuckled as he leaned back in his chair.

"You could look in the archives, but I'm not aware of anything like that in there. No historian really takes crop circles seriously," he said.

"Oh, there is one more photo, but it's a weird language, so not that you could help, but here – look," I pointed, scrolling to the writing on the photo.

When he looked at the strange writing, his whole manner changed. He was always so cheerful and friendly, but he went solemn as he pulled the phone closer and blinked hard at the screen.

"I don't know what language this is."

"Maybe Russian? It's my grandmother's first language."

He scratched his eyebrow and looked back at me.

"Could be, but you might want to ask someone over in the foreign language department. They would know more than me."

"I was told to ask the right questions."

He handed me the phone and looked me in the eye. I put it away.

"What do you mean? Who told you that?"

I shook my head and grabbed the rake again and started scraping the rocks around. I was embarrassed I even said anything weird like that. I just thought it might matter.

"Uh, no one."

He ran his hand across his cheek in thought. He was studying me through a grim look.

"Strange things to find in your grandmother's photo album. Did you ask her about it yet?"

I shrugged.

"Bosh doesn't talk about her life in China and this was a hidden photo. I don't know why she would have a picture like that anyway."

He pushed his lips together and looked towards the ceiling.

"Sorry I wasn't more help, but I'll give you extra credit if you lead a discussion in class about crop circles and aliens."

I gathered my things and stood up.

"Anyone ever tell you you're a terrible therapist?"

"Every day. Now go on and get out of here so I can pretend to work in case my department head shows up."

I headed straight for the library under a sky congested by an angry gray veil. When it broke, there was a lashing out so fierce that it battered against the windows until the building cried out in a chorus. I hunkered down in my favorite place on campus for the onslaught.

The library was soothing; old books were my favorite smell and it was always quiet there. I started by walking around the towers of books. I wasn't really sure where the crop circle conspiracy section would be, but I wasn't in a hurry. I had nowhere to be and the rain was really coming down.

LONG LIVE DEAD RECKLESS

The library was pretty dead at that time of the day, so only a handful of people were quietly studying at individual workstations and tiptoeing upstairs while flipping through books on endless shelves. I heard a faint laugh or two followed by a quick shushing from the librarian. I let my hand drag across the rows of books as I walked up and down sections aimlessly.

A rumble of thunder called me to one of the large windows lining the wall. The storm had rolled in with gusto, so I watched it send people squealing for shelter. I took a seat in a corner cubicle and pulled my legs into my chest, wrapping my cable-knit sweater jacket around.

People react to rain like we're made of fire. Maybe some are. But most of us are water, and we're even waterproof, but we act like we'll drown in a few drops. I leaned my head against the cold window, looking out across the hazy campus.

One thing caught my eye. There was a couple standing together in the rain. They weren't running. They weren't even trying to get under shelter. They were kissing like they had mere moments left to live, and with lightning flashing over their heads, they might have been right. They kissed so passionately I felt like I was peeping. But they were out in the open, so I kept watching.

"One day," I said, sighing to myself.

A minute later, I saw his reflection. Sage was in the aisle behind me looking through some books. I stiffened. If he came a few feet closer towards the window, he would see me sitting there. He hadn't noticed me through the shelving yet. I froze, not knowing what to do. I hadn't talked to him since the fight at the Halloween party.

I was angry, nervous, excited, terrified, confused, and aching all at once. He made me feel everything. I never knew that was possible before. I didn't know how to act around him now.

I mean...were we still friends?

The wind picked up and howled as it battered the rain against the window in a ceaseless tapping rhythm like it was trying to get him to look my way. I was aware of every sound around me: the whispers, stifled giggles, and chairs creaking. I was trapped, just waiting to be found out. I didn't have to wait long.

He searched book titles until he started to pluck one off the shelf. There were already a few in his hand. Intrigued, I was trying to read their titles sideways when his gaze shifted from the bookshelf. It was a sobering feeling when his eyes fell on me.

We just looked at each other a moment, neither of us speaking or moving. I blinked first. *Dang.* He really did see me. He put the book back on the shelf. Immediately, I wanted to know what it was.

"Hey," he said.

I didn't answer. I just gathered myself up and headed to the rear stairwell – the back way out of the library. I only got two steps down when he caught me by the arm.

"Please talk to me," he pleaded.

I looked at his fingers on my arm and frowned. He pulled his hand back as I faced him. I leaned on the railing beside me for support to get through the confrontation.

"I have somewhere to be," I lied.

"I'm sorry, Talor. I'm so sorry."

He sounded like he meant that. Still, I wasn't ready for everything to be ok. I was hurt. Humiliated. I held my hand up and hinged my lips into something of a smile. It was uneven and trembling, but it looked like a smile.

"No need to apologize. I told you that we could just be friends."

He slowly reached back and locked the door behind us. It was a narrow stairwell, one that didn't see much traffic. I watched him put his books down on the floor and it occurred to me that he was going to do something.

"You think that I don't like you? Is that what this is?" he asked, dropping his chin a little.

Something about his manner told me I could finally have what I wanted. I'd never been kissed in the stairwell, but I imagined it with Sage. I could have it right then if I forgot all about Valerie. For the first time, those fantasies felt cheap. I thought he was a gentleman, but he wasn't. I never thought the day would come when I didn't want him to kiss me, but it did in that drafty old stairwell. I didn't know the truth about Valerie yet.

I had dreamed about losing myself with him in every secluded place I ever passed, but when it came right down to it – it wasn't just sexual attraction anymore. My heart was in it now, and I needed answers, not fantasies. I shook my head.

"I don't know what you want."

"We want the same thing," he answered, blinking for the first time in the conversation. I guess since I was trapped, I couldn't escape so he could actually blink without fear of me running off. I retreated a step or two, but he started to follow. *Uh-oh.*

"I saw you kiss Valerie," I snapped, maintaining space.

He furrowed his brow.

"Oh."

"You know, silly me thinking you liked me when you were making out with her all of five minutes –"

I couldn't finish because my voice broke at the end. I was so mad about that. I had kept control of my emotions the whole time until then. I had to cover my mouth and close my eyes for a second to get a hold of myself. When I glanced back, he was eying me, his face softening.

"Talor, we need to talk. Meet me tonight."

"Why?" I asked, pinching between my eyes so I wouldn't cry.

"Because I want to fix this."

Fix it? Fix a hurting heart? What a male thing to say. I took a shuddering breath and looked down.

"No, you don't have to apologize. I told you, I get it. Now –"

"I don't want to apologize. You said you wanted to know me, and I want you to."

"Well, why now?"

He gripped the railing with one hand, putting his weight against it so he could lean close. He lowered his voice like someone else was listening.

"So that the next time we're in a place like this, you won't be talking about how Spencer did anything."

His gaze darted to my lips at the end, making me flush hot with the full heat of his words. He took his weight back and paused before picking up his books. So he was jealous. I started to smile, but a bang at the door startled me. It was a librarian. She peered at us through the window and pointed repeatedly at the lock. We stared at each other for a second before Sage straightened.

"Come tonight. Please?"

The librarian rapped her knuckles against the glass window again, so I scurried off in a hurry without answering. As I went out the door into the cool autumn rain, I passed the couple still kissing and found my own smile. We both knew my answer to his invitation. I didn't know why, but I would be there.

Anywhere he named.

19

Sage asked me to meet him at 3squares Diner.

I'd never been there before. I'm a Waffle House girl myself, but I had to see him after the library stairwell. Things were weird between us, and I was ready to know the truth about Sage after three months of smoke and mirrors.

I had to know about his feelings towards Valerie if nothing else. He asked me out for coffee because he knew I never turn down a late night cup in a diner. It's the closest I'll ever get to being in a '90s music video. I got there before he did. It was late and the place was so dead, I wondered if it was even actually open. There were lights on inside, and a waitress leaning against the counter reading a tabloid.

I came in, sat down, and the waitress brought a steaming cup of coffee over without asking. About five minutes later, Sage eased himself across from me in the booth with broken springs. I had tried several other booths, but they were all broken or ripped.

Seeing him again brought fresh color to my lips and I couldn't help but shape them into a smile to match his. My ignorant bliss was short-lived since I did notice something strange about him then. There were no freckles on his skin. I blinked to be sure, but no. His skin was *sans* freckles.

The plump waitress started to make her way over to us, but he waved her away quickly. She disappeared into the back and the diner became eerily silent. Our eyes met.

"I was scared you wouldn't come," he said.

After what you said earlier? How could I not? I didn't say that, but I thought it.

"You said you'd explain," I answered, shrugging.

"It's hard," he said.

"Well, it was hard for me to show up," I said shortly, coming across a little sharper than I meant.

There was no sizzling bacon, no cash register ding, and no song playing in the background. We were alone, both on the edge of our seats, sitting under a thick solemn tone. It was like he was gathering his thoughts and trying to situate them in the best order before sharing them. I poured two creamers in my coffee and stirred before he broke the uncomfortable silence.

"I know. I'm glad you're here."

I nodded graciously, trying not to torture him. He was doing a good job of that himself, wringing out his hands like they were in a gladiator match to the death. He was never this nervous, never this obvious. I started thinking wildly about what his secret could be. If Spencer was a drug lord, what was the quiet, well-mannered Sage?

212

"What I'm going to tell you, Talor...might make you laugh. It might make you think I'm crazy, but please, please don't let it scare –" he began, clearing his throat.

"Why isn't 'Have a Waffle Great Day' playing?" I rudely interrupted, not so secretly terrified of what he was going to admit.

He looked slightly confused, but quickly straightened his leg under the table and reached his hand down. He pulled a quarter from his pocket and handed it to me across the table.

"Um, this is 3squares. They probably don't have that song here."

I took the quarter anyway and I ran over to the jukebox. I slipped the quarter in and started looking through the H's. "Hard to Say I'm Sorry", "How Do I Live"...*wait!*

"Ah-ha! They do have it!" I exclaimed, maybe a little too excited.

As I came back to the booth, "Have a Waffle Great Day" started playing. I felt a little better hearing something goofy and familiar, but neither of us could escape the nerves. I wanted the truth, but only if it was convenient and tipped in my favor. If he was here to tell me Valerie was his girlfriend and they have an open relationship and he's into weird stuff, I would run out bawling and throw my coffee at him. Probably in that order, too, because I hate confrontation.

"I think this'll be easier if you ask me what you want to know," he suggested.

"I might have made a list," I replied, sitting.

"Oh. Ok. Well, go ahead then."

It suddenly occurred to me how foolish I was about to look. While I was waiting on him to show up, I jotted down a few questions – about six. The only paper I had on me was my pocket notebook one of the regular nursery kids bought me for my birthday several months back. It had fuzzy binders and a goofy phone with a face on the front.

To make things worse, I had to use my only pen – a small lipstick shaped, lipstick-sized pen – to write the list. I tried to throw it in my purse before he saw it, but my aim was off. I missed the purse opening and the pen bounced off the wall, ricocheting to the middle of the table before spinning around. He looked down at it as it came to a stop. He pointed at it and opened his mouth, but I flipped open my notebook and started talking before he could.

"Are you or Mannix dating Valerie and if so, is it a weird progressive open relationship threesome type thing? Also, are you into that?" I asked sternly. I was displaying confidence, but my arms and voice were shaking.

"No...to every part of that very personal question, actually," he said, smiling briefly. He covered his mouth and gripped his chin as he worked on trying not to laugh.

I felt myself ease up a little as I checked off the question with my finger. I didn't dare reach for the lipstick pen. He would never answer another question seriously if I wrote down his answers with that.

"What happened in the grove?" I asked, feeling the air shift as I did.

"What did you see?"

"You kissing Valerie. And changing your shirt afterwards, but mostly the kissing part."

His hand moved from his jaw to his cheekbone, stroking it deep in thought.

"Yeah, I wasn't kissing her, Talor."

"I saw you."

He narrowed his eyes.

"Wait. Were you hiding behind a tree?"

214

I swallowed hard and at first, I tried to deny it.

"What? Tree? No. Maybe. Yes. But it was dark out there, and you," I sighed, pausing to take in a deep breath. "I saw you grab her hair and – you – I know you kissed her!"

He looked across the booth at me.

"I want to kiss *you*."

Not past tense. But present tense. *I want to kiss you.* My skin flushed, so I slammed my fuzzy notebook closed and fidgeted with my hands to distract from my face.

"You obviously didn't that night."

He tilted his head a little, his expression softening.

"It wouldn't have been right."

"Because of Spencer?" I asked, not daring to look at him.

"God...him again? No, it's not about Spencer."

"Then why did you kiss her?" I demanded, feeling a little bolder.

"I didn't," he corrected, grimacing.

It seemed like he wanted to say more, but he couldn't. When he didn't say anything after a few seconds, I stuck my notebook in my purse with force.

"I don't even know why I came here. I'm just stupid about you, Sage. I should've known you'd come up with some vague excuse. I mean, what is this? What's wrong with you?"

I grabbed for my lipstick pen in the middle of the table, but Sage swiped it so fast it was alarming. He held it up in his palm. His voice gained immediacy.

"I want to tell you."

"Then tell me," I growled.

215

He adopted this pleading look then, his eyes growing a little wider as his brows eased away from them.

"Just don't be afraid of me, ok? I know you're going to be, but I don't want you to."

I took in a deep breath. Why would I be afraid? Something big was brewing between us –total honesty. Scary honesty, apparently. I looked him over again. Yeah, there were definitely no freckles.

"Where are your freaking freckles?" I asked, making a sweeping gesture at him.

He looked directly at me, trying to work out the words in his throat. There was a moment before he spoke that I thought if I blinked, I'd suddenly wake up.

"They come and go based on how much I need them."

"You're telling me that you have disappearing reappearing freckles?"

"I'm not exactly human, Talor."

"So what are you? An alien?"

He blinked.

"More like what you know as a vampire."

The jukebox played cheerfully as I stared him down. I always knew there was something strange about him; he didn't eat much, he always drank water, and he always added salt to it. But none of that meant Sage was a vampire. I started to laugh, but the serious look on his face stopped me. I winked at him.

"Oh, right! All vampires are warm to the touch, walk in daylight, and eat normal food. And they actually exist. I forgot about that."

Sage leaned forward.

"I'm different than you expect."

I just stared at him, unsure how to respond. Should I play along or leave? He relaxed back in the booth.

"Do you know what a siren is?"

"Like on a fire truck? I mean, like in Greek mythology?" I asked, correcting myself quickly.

He gave a sly smile.

"Yeah, what do you think you know about them?"

"They lived on an island, killed a bunch of people. Odysseus and a horse...I'm a bit fuzzy on that, but...they were all female and they also had wings, so," I replied, arching my neck to look at his shoulder, thinking I had stumped him. No wings. "I think you need a new origin story, champ."

"Don't believe everything you read," he said, raising a brow.

"Or everything some guy tells you to get out of explaining kissing another girl."

He looked at me like he wanted to wipe something off my face.

"Sometimes humans get things wrong about us. You know, little details and big details and believing we don't exist."

His wittiness caught me off guard. I gave an uneasy smile. I was caught somewhere between actually believing him and knowing he was in need of anti-psychotic meds. I brought the coffee to my lips and took a slow sip.

Ok, let's pretend it's for real. If he was a siren, my unprecedented, overpowering attraction to him was explained. But that wasn't enough; seeing him in a tight pair of pants would have brought me to the same conclusion.

A siren. Huh.

That would explain why he's the singer in the band. Maybe salt water curbed cravings or something. When he mentioned that he was in a rock band, I was secretly thrilled. Since we were only technically dating, I figured that's why I hadn't met his band mates yet. They were probably just like him. I guess it isn't easy introducing the girl you like to your vampire buddies. They might bite her.

"So you're half siren, half vampire? Two mythological creatures? Not a human being? You're going with it, then? You look very human to me unless there's something, um, else different? Not that I'm asking."

Mortified, I closed my eyes and hid behind the coffee cup. Was I really insinuating that he had different plumbing and actually asking about it? Smooth, Talor. I had to open my eyes because it was getting weirder not looking at him, but I didn't want to.

"I'm not half anything."

"Not even half human?"

"My mother was fully human, so everything about me, as far as physically, is normal, so yeah...to answer that question," he replied, his lips flattening against each other in embarrassment.

"Oh good," I cried, touching my hand to my heart. "I mean, good for you. That's – I'm so happy. For you, I mean."

He didn't respond, so I started stirring my coffee with my finger. I didn't realize I was doing that until Sage offered me a spoon. I took it and stirred my coffee for no reason except to give my nerves something to do.

"So I guess that means your dad was a vampire? Is a vampire, I mean. I didn't know vampires could, you know, procreate. I thought they were kinda dead. If they were real, I'm saying."

He scratched the table quietly with his fingernail.

"Vampires aren't dead, but we don't need to get into all that right now."

"Well, if you're not dead, do you age? Can you die? How old are you? Also, do you kind of turn into monsters with horns after kissing innocent people?"

218

His drew his lips into his mouth with a heavy brow.

"Like Spencer?"

I stared at him and stopped stirring my coffee. Spencer was one of them, too? He seemed so normal. Now I would have to watch Sage get whisked away to a mental hospital for delusions, just like dad. Or worse, he was doing this to make fun of me. I tried to keep myself together. I couldn't believe he was that kind of guy. He couldn't be.

"Sage, did someone tell you about my dad?"

His expression changed as he stretched his hand across the table. I pulled back, my lips quivering.

"Talor, wait. No, don't do that. Please. I don't know anything about your father, but if I said something that hurt you, I'm sorry. If I'm a little blunt, it's because I'm from a time when people knew about supernatural creatures. Now you think we only exist in the imagination, but we're real. I'm real, and I just want to help you. Not hurt you."

I didn't say anything, but I wouldn't let him touch me.

"I know you need to see them, you just don't want to ask," he said quietly.

I knit my brow, not sure what he meant. Before I had time to ask, ominous, sharp fangs extended from his gums. I thought I was imagining it, but no, there they were, the real fangs of a real vampire! His eyes dilated until there was no beautiful hazel left. They were strange and inhuman, like a wild beast was looking out at me. I remained silent and still as they retreated back into normal teeth.

My tongue had daydreamed for months about being in that mouth, but now there would be nightmares. I found myself oddly calm considering Sage was a real vampire, a creature of the night designed to seduce and kill the likes of me. It was scary. Surreal. But it meant that Sage wasn't making fun of my dad and he wasn't lying to me.

So what if he was a vampire? There were worse things in the world. I'd dated them.

"So, Mannix?" I murmured.

"Yeah. That's why I acted the way I did."

"Oh my God, I touched those things! And he's probably killed people with them," I gasped, bringing a hand to my mouth to cover the gaping hole of shock.

Things started clicking. Mannix and Sage's tense rivalry, Sage's distant personality, Mannix being a total douche bag, Azalea liking Mannix at all...*oh no! Azalea!*

"Can you hypnotize people?" I asked.

"We call it influence."

I touched my hand to my chest, afraid of the answer. But I had to ask.

"Sage, tell the truth. Have you –"

"No," he interrupted, clearly understanding where I was going with it. "You wouldn't know if I did, but I can't. I wouldn't have. My band and I, we don't do those things."

"What about Valerie?"

He scratched behind his ear, looking at me from under those cute fly-ways.

"Yeah, her. So that night...I'm not proud of that. Yes, I fed on her, but I will never do that to you. I mean it. I'm sorry you saw that. I wish you hadn't."

"I'll ever forget it. Especially now that I know all this," I murmured, dropping my eyes.

"Yeah," he said.

"Would you have killed her?" I asked, suddenly acutely aware of the cascade of secrets Sage likely carried.

"No. Like I said, the band and me, we don't do that, Talor. Not many are like us, though."

I turned a little to the side and kept my arms wrapped tightly around me. I looked away from him, not wanting to risk meeting his gaze. He just admitted they could control minds, maybe he could read them, as well. He noticed my insecurity and leaned his elbows on the table.

"Hey, I understand you're scared, I do. Don't pull away. Not now that we can really know each other. This is a major risk, but I want to be with you if you can accept me."

"Why is it such a big risk? Because you could kill me?"

"No...because of who and what I am. Please, Talor."

He offered his hand across the table. I slowly untangled myself in the booth, my fingers inching towards his. When they met, I felt the same for him that I always had. I smiled at him as his thumb stroked across my hand.

Somehow, I was relieved about everything. Strange things were happening to me. I wasn't crazy. Sage was a vampire! It felt like anything could be possible now. The night of the gala came rushing back. I saw something in the road that night when Bex picked me up.

I didn't believe my own eyes then, but I know what I saw, and I had never been so excited. My leg started bouncing underneath the table. I lurched as far across the table as I could, clutching his shirt with desperation.

"OH MY GOD, do unicorns exist?"

I was horrified that my first real question about mythological creatures had to do with a magical horse. He had the strangest look on his face – like he wanted to burst out laughing. Neither of us ever expected my reaction. Once I started, I couldn't stop the questions from tumbling out.

"Can you see in the dark? Can you read minds? Are your freckles coming back?"

"I think that's enough for one night. C'mon."

He winked as he pulled out a few dollars from his pocket and laid them on the table. When we got outside, he pulled me close until I pressed against him. It was a dank kind of late autumn cold with the rain that came through in the afternoon. I rested my chilled hands against his chest, trying to feel for a heartbeat. I didn't hide my motive well because it made him sigh.

"Talor, I have a heartbeat. Feel," he murmured, pulling open his collar and letting me rest my head against his skin. The rhythmic thump was familiar and soothing. I remembered the hug he gave me at the coffee shop. He was warm, alive, and had a heartbeat throbbing then, too. I raised my head and smiled sheepishly up at him.

"I'm sorry. It's just a lot. I don't know how I can I feel safer with you and more terrified of you at the same time."

He gave me a curious, contemplative kind of look.

"There's a word for it."

"I hate feeling this way," I said timidly, stroking a finger against his collarbone.

"I hate that I hurt you. But now that you know how I really feel, no more games. I want this. I want us, ok?"

He fiddled with my fingers against his chest and raised a brow. There was a hesitation in his movements, like he was scared I would say no.

"Ok," I said, nodding. This time I turned his hand around and kissed his knuckles.

He smiled and brought his arm tight around my waist. It did cross my mind that he could just drain me right there, knowing what little I could do to stop him. But after what he just said, I doubted I would ever be in any danger again.

As the streetlight flickered above us, he looked at me in a way that I knew he wanted to kiss me. My heart was racing so fast I thought it would burst there on the spot and save him the trouble of killing me.

He leaned down. Instead of going for the lips, he turned his face into my cheek. The stubble brushed against me as it crossed my mind that he could be going for my neck. The second between fearing what he would do and knowing what he would do was eternal. His lips stopped as they grazed my ear.

"I missed the rain, didn't I?" he asked, his voice smooth and steady.

He was talking about what I said that afternoon in the library. About kissing in the rain. *Oh wow.*

"You heard that?" I asked, blushing madly.

He eased back.

"Yeah, well, my hearing's pretty good, but my timing's not. I'll be watching the sky, though."

He pointed at the sky and held out his hand to feel for raindrops. When he felt nothing, he pouted. I smiled. Could he get any cuter?

"Well, anyway, we have a show tomorrow night at The Journey. If you come, you can hear me sing and, I'll introduce you to everyone," he said, shrugging.

I agreed, but as I drove away with the 3squares Diner sign fading in the rear view, I couldn't help but wonder if this siren would lead me to my own death.

223

20

When I drove up to The Journey the next night, my stomach was threatening revolution with every churn. I'd never heard a live band before, and a vampire one at that. I pretty much spent all night trying to figure out if I really believed him. I hadn't decided yet.

I stepped out of the car wearing my tightest jeans, my kitten heel boots, and a violet-colored low-cut sweater. I almost ditched my boots considering our history together, but they did wonders for my butt. It was worth the risk. I just hoped no one but Sage would take much of an interest in me.

As I locked eyes with a group of young guys loitering around outside the venue, I suddenly wish I had worn sweat pants and a hoodie. To avoid going by them, I stopped and looked around for Azalea. I invited her to the show for safety reasons. I didn't tell her why I wanted company and thankfully, she didn't ask. I saw her waving me over near her car, so I pushed through the massive crowd gathering around the entrance.

"There you are! I've been looking everywhere for you," she said, wrapping her arms around my neck and giving me a good squeeze. "Sage is going to fall off the stage when he sees you in those jeans! So, where is he? Is he supposed to get us in?"

I shook my head and got on my tiptoes.

"He just told me to call when I got here, but I don't know how he would hear his phone with this noise!"

I couldn't believe so many people were there to see them. The noise from inside the building was reverberating under us, but we finally made it to the entrance. The doorman was large and imposing; he had earrings everywhere on his face except his ears.

"Hi! I'm Talor. Sage from Dead Reckless invited us," I said, smiling up at him.

The man studied me as if he was going to be given a test on my every feature. I was a little intimidated, but I stood up as tall as my heels would let me without tittering over. He looked on the clipboard in his hand. He pulled a strange-looking ink stamp from under the table and marked my hand. He ushered to Azalea.

"Is she with you?"

I nodded, so he stamped her hand, too – but hers was different from mine. Mine was so iridescent it looked like I didn't have anything there. But the letters "LLDR" began to glow faintly after a few minutes. Everyone else that walked by had "PAID" in typical blue block letters. *Weird.*

I wondered how many people got the shiny stamp. I figured maybe Sage said to give me a different stamp for backstage access. The doorman ushered for us to move along.

"They're about to go on. Hurry. Stand on the far left side of the stage," he said.

226

As soon as we got inside, the lights on the stage went low. I hurried over where the doorman told us to go. We made it just in time. The restless crowd was anxious, the air thick with anticipation. And then it was total darkness. No lights, no music, nothing. A few people from the crowd yelled excitedly out of sync. I held my breath, suddenly aware of how vulnerable we were. No one else knew what I knew.

Suddenly, the stage lit up with a hundred dazzling lights, and there was Dead Reckless. Sage was center stage. The four of them stood still and poised, sharp eyes swimming over a sea of young faces. There were smirks and nods, as dozens of arms rose up in the crowd and screams chased the tails of each other. Smoke oozed from mist machines on the front of the stage.

Sage shot a quick glance over my way before turning towards the crowd and belting out an electrifying yell into the microphone as the drum beat began and the music swelled. How could he know where I was in a crowd that size? Then again, he was different. Or so he said.

The bassist was a character, moving and jumping around on stage effortlessly. Every now and then, the guitarist would lean back-to-back with him as they played. Whenever they could, they went to the front of the stage and reached out for the fingertips of the crowd. The drummer moved like the fluid motion of a centipede on the run, his arms sweeping across cymbals and drums with incredible ease.

Azalea tossed a crooked brow over at me, bewildered. I think I had the same expression. This was no small town garage band. They were clearly seasoned professionals. Sage moved around very little, but his presence was commanding. His voice caressed the ears like the hushing hum of a lullaby. It didn't match the type of music they were playing.

I looked around, wondering how people would react to the strange mixture, but everyone seemed to love it. The crowd went absolutely wild. It was like everyone in the audience except for us was under some sort of trance. People were trampling each other trying to get close to the stage where the band was. They pushed forward and cried out, their hands arching almost out of socket to get to Sage. He never came close enough to the front so they could touch him.

The notes would come from the bottom of his lungs and he would kick across the mic stand, his tongue extending as he held a penetrating and powerful note. Then he would stomp down on the amp nearest to him and ripples would vibrate off like waves reaching for shore. Sage was otherworldly on stage. It was a jolting, alarming sort of feeling being hit by those sounds.

It's why people were swaying so much. I could see it, but I don't think everyone else could. I knew in that moment that I'd heard the most unique sound on earth. It was right then that I believed him. Like, truly, wholeheartedly, actually believed him. I could see what he was doing. I could see the power he had, and I knew I'd heard a real siren.

I had no doubt that I had never – and would never – hear anything like it again in my life, or in this world. My breath broke from my lips as I looked around, knowing full well that I was the only one who had heard it. It was a tearful realization that no one could witness what I was witnessing, and suddenly, in a room full of bodies, I felt as lonely as the edges of the universe.

When a mosh pit started, several big, burly men pushed the crowd back so the stage wouldn't break. At the end of the set, the band had to hurry off stage as the crowd tried to chase them. Everyone acted like they were the most famous band alive and I had never even heard of them. I watched in awe from our safe spot on the edge away from everyone throwing punches to be the first to follow the band.

"Oh my God, wow, that was amazing!" Azalea said breathlessly. "He has such stage presence! I thought he was shy. Isn't he shy?"

"Uh, he is shy. His voice was really surprising," I blinked hard. "It was...soothing."

"What are you talking about? He was screaming the whole time."

I was confused. She looked at me crazy, like we had listened to two different bands. I had heard a soulful singer and she heard a screamo rocker. She looked like she was about to say something when a tall, lanky guy came over. He had strange hair, like he only had enough money for half a haircut. I tried not to stare. That took a little effort. He looked me up and down.

"You're Talor," he said, waving me over. "Sage said to bring you back."

Just as I opened my mouth, I saw Sage over his shoulder. I smiled and he smiled back. We had a moment that was just ours. He moved towards me, but stopped after a few steps, staying hidden behind a mountain of Dead Reckless merchandise near the wall.

"Oh, there's Sage right there," Azalea cried, pointing.

The lanky guy bobbed his head and stepped aside. I gave Sage an awkward hug. I wasn't sure why I didn't hug him like normal. My emotions were full of static about then. I hugged him with my butt sticking so far out I was almost bending over. Azalea giggled.

"Um, have you guys never hugged before? What was that?" she asked. "Awkward!"

Sage and I cut our eyes away. He exhaled sharply.

"Those stage lights are hot. I don't blame her for not wanting to drown in my sweat."

"Trust me, she really wants to," Azalea muttered. I jerked my head around to glare at her.

"I'm glad you came tonight," Sage shrugged, wiping his forehead off with his arm. "What did you think?"

"Oh my God, amazing," Azalea cried. "They were about to tear apart the stage!"

"Yeah, they about did," he laughed. "The stage was shaking."

There was a moment of silence where no one really knew what to say.

"Well, I know I enjoyed it," Azalea replied, glancing casually at the door. "I probably need to head out."

"I'll walk her out," I told him, following her. When we got outside, Azalea turned to me, grabbing me by the shoulders.

"Ok, there's something going on. All you talk about is how you want to make out with him! Now you're hugging him like he's a leper? You're keeping something from me. What is it?"

How do best friends always know when you're holding back a secret? I tried to bide my time by pointing out some rowdy cat-fighting groupies near her car. It didn't work. She pressed me.

"Spill."

"What? We're just at that awkward stage," I answered, huffing.

I tried to reassure her, but I know she could hear the hesitation in my voice. I couldn't tell her yet; it was all still too new to me. She pursed her lips, which I've learned means she doesn't want to stop from saying whatever is building up steam behind them. She swallowed hard.

"Ok. Well, whatever it is, I'm going to figure it out," she said, turning on her heel. I watched her leave, wishing I could tell her the truth. Just not yet. My thoughts were interrupted by footsteps closing in. I caught the glimpse of a shadow behind me, so I jumped and let out a squawk. It was Sage.

"Sorry! I was trying to walk slowly so I didn't interrupt," he apologized, jamming his hands down in the pockets of his dark-wash jeans.

He'd changed shirts. This one was tight, white, and clean, and it might've liked him more than I did. I forgave him immediately. I didn't really have a choice, him looking like that.

"Um, you were incredible in there," I said, looking down at my hand.

"Thank you. I hope it wasn't too loud."

"So how many girls get the sparkly stamp? I've never had one do that before. It's fancy."

Sage took his hands out of his pockets and stepped closer. I looked away as he took my hand and pulled back the sleeve. He just stared at the letters like they were some hidden treasure. After a few seconds, he still hadn't said anything.

"What does L.L.D.R. stand for?" I asked, turning my head sideways to look at it.

He looked hard at it for a full minute. Finally, his brow unclenched.

"If I had to guess...I'd say, long...live...Dead Reckless."

"Oh...ok. That's neat. Well, long live Dead Reckless," I replied, balling my hand into a 'rock on' gesture.

He bit his bottom lip and looked me square in the eye. It was the same look he gave me by the time clock that time. Something was wrong and I couldn't figure out what. I already knew he was a vampire. What else was going on here?

"I didn't tell her anything," I assured him, darting my eyes towards where Azalea had drove off.

"Oh, yeah, no, I know. So...did you like the set?"

"Honestly, your voice didn't fit the music, like, at all. Is it weird if I say it was beautiful? You're so talented."

His eyes softened and he took in a deep breath. He seemed so far away. Finally, he pat my hand sweetly and shifted his weight back. With a smile, he laced his fingers with mine and leaning away, gave a playful tug.

"Come on. Ready to meet everyone?"

I had so many more questions for him before meeting his band, but between that smile, those dimples, and that tight shirt, I just followed. I knew then that I would follow him anywhere – even straight into the lion's den.

21

Following Sage through the dark hall backstage, my heart was racing just trying to keep up with the questions in my mind. *What kind of mind control did they have? Why was I not affected by the music like everyone else?*

My thoughts kept returning to the holographic stamp on my wrist. It was weird, and it made Sage act weird. I couldn't dwell on it long because we soon came to a spray-painted black door that separated us from the band. Even in the black lights, I could see all kinds of bumper stickers littering it; some were less than PG.

The door separated my old life from this exciting new one, and while I didn't know whether the band mates were as safe and likeable as Sage, I wasn't going to let fear keep me from finding out. Oddly enough, Sage could sense my faltering faith. He paused, squeezed my hand, and turned the knob. The door opened and soon the sounds that were muffled behind it surrounded me at full volume. I stood in the open doorway slightly behind Sage.

"Hey, this is Talor," Sage said, stepping to the side so they could see me.

I felt naked without him sheltering me from their gazes. They had been horsing around back there, laughing and talking, but they went quiet as they saw me. Somewhere, a cricket chirped loudly as we all had our first good look at one another.

All but one had dark hair. They looked like typical band guys: slender, torn jeans, flannel shirts, tattoos. They shared no similarities except height and intimidation factor. I put on my bravest face.

"Hi," I said, my voice seeming small and mousy.

The lead guitarist came over first. He had shoulder-length black hair tamed back with a bandana. His eyes were so dark it was hard to make out the pupil. They seemed dilated until he blinked. Then they were green. He had a kindness about him that seemed like a constant smile under his olive skin. That smile was also hidden somewhere in his face, as if at any moment it would come out. He stopped a polite distance from me and stuck out his hand.

"Talor, I'm Tomahawk. Don't worry. We won't bite," he stopped, and then slapped his hand against his forehead. "Oh wait."

I forced a smile. A bad joke on my account? Now I was indebted to shake his hand. His fingernails were tough and long – like fake nails you'd see in a costume shop at Halloween.

They were painted black, too, so it was hard not to stare. I was honestly jealous he could get such strong, long nails like that and keep them. I would have asked his secret if I didn't already know it. Even after the warm welcome, I didn't want to know how a vampire could get a nickname like Tomahawk.

"Do you go by Tom...ahawk?"

He shrugged.

"You can call me Tom."

He waved the rest of the guys over since I wouldn't move from the spot I deemed safe. Sage rested his hand softly on my lower back and urged me forward, providing enough comfort for me to take a step inside the door so he could close it. A new guy was in front of me when I looked up. He was regarding me with much more energy than Tom.

"Hello there, little lady," he replied, touching his forehead like it was a cowboy hat.

"Oh yeah, meet Mika," Sage said. "The one kind of all in your face right now."

Mika was the least imposing stature of them all, and his eyes were wider than everyone else's. Judging by the two or three shades of lipstick smeared on his neck and cheek, he must've spent centuries perfecting the charming playboy persona. He had been mauled by a harem of groupies before they made it backstage. Looking at him, I could see how they could be drawn to his warm smile and wavy hair.

He reached over the table beside me and grabbed a Monster energy drink from the cooler. It was odd that there were drinks on ice and a platter of snacks on the table when I was the only one in the room who ate. I started wondering where the warm blood was kept, and then I remembered that venues wouldn't actually know a vampire band was playing. They also wouldn't believe vampires existed.

"Do you want a Monster? Other than Sage, I mean," Mika asked, raising a brow as he held up the drink to me.

His misplaced enthusiasm and great sense of humor were oddly comforting. I nodded and he dropped it into my hand. I wasn't thirsty, but taking a drink called Monster from a chipper vampire with a joke attached was a bucket list imperative. It would be one of my greatest regrets at the end of my life if I passed that up.

Mika moved back and settled on the arm of a couch. There was only one band mate left to meet, and he wasn't nearly as forthcoming as the others. Sage pointed to the drummer, who seemed to have only one piercing eye – a bright blue. The assumable other eye was covered by long bangs.

"You should've talked to us first," the drummer said, extending a hand towards Mika, who gave him a cigarette.

I actually felt the harsh glare from him, noting how impressive it was to feel so threatened by only one eye. Sage was unaffected.

"We did talk. Talor, that's Ash."

Ash made it easy to believe everything Sage said in the diner. He looked less like a human and more like a creature in a man-suit. He had the icy energy of a dancing cobra. He seemed to toe the human line only as long as it suited him, but it was never known when he would strike.

He seemed like he'd be cool to the touch, and I had no interest in shaking his hand. Luckily, he shared the feeling. He slackened his frame against the wall, flicking the end of the unlit cigarette with his finger like it was a bug. It immediately burned bright as he drew a long breath on it, the frail ashes falling fast to the ground. I watched in awe, only tearing my gaze away once he looked up.

"Anyway, hey," he muttered, crossing an arm over his chest.

I said the same, still a little insecure to look at him for long. Having done their polite duty to Sage, they all relaxed about the room in various places; Mika perched on the arm of the couch playing on his phone, Tom lazily stretched across another one, and Ash kept to the far wall, still giving Sage a warning glare that would have run me out of the room.

Sage brought me further inside so we could sit down on a large loveseat. Mika pushed another cigarette between his lips and offered me one. I shook my head.

"Don't smoke, huh?" he asked, humored.

"No, it's kind of bad for you. You know, it kills you and all," I replied, feeling weird having to explain not being a smoker. I noticed they all smoked at some point and I hoped Sage didn't. I couldn't imagine Sage being a smoker, but I never imagined him being a vampire, either.

"Oh yeah. That mortal thing," Mika said, chuckling.

I hoped he wouldn't light it up after I said that. I hated the smell of cigarette smoke. It was a major pet peeve. He pulled it from his lips and slipped it behind his ear, smiling at me. I smiled back.

"So what does she know?" Ash asked from the other side of the room, drawing us into conversation. Everyone got quiet as they focused on Sage. I looked at him, too, not sure how I was supposed to know or not know. He made a motion for me to go ahead and speak, so I cleared my throat.

"Just that you actually exist."

Silence.

"How do you feel about fallen angels, Talor?" Tom asked.

I placed my hands on my thighs and sat forward.

"Um, I don't know. I've never met any."

"Are you sure?" Ash asked, moving from the wall towards us.

"Well, I think I'd notice wings," I said, unsure why it was a touchy subject.

Mika stuck his tongue in his cheek.

"Wings? Really?"

"Anyway, if you haven't seen one, that's good. We can blend in, but they really can't," Tom said.

I began to wonder about anytime I had actually been in a crowd and if there had been an angel in it. What would an angel look like? I shook my head; perplexed. I hadn't seen one. I didn't know why they were asking me about angels when we were talking about vampires.

"What do fallen angels have to do with any of this?" I asked, half serious, half joking.

"Only everything," Ash grumbled.

"As in?"

Mika did a little dance step and waved his arms around while he hushed everyone else like he was an outfield baseball player trying to catch a fly ball.

"I got it, I got it! First, here's how it works, little lady. You ready? One of us gets hungry, finds a person who looks a bit tasty, seals them with what's called a cicatrix – got it? It's like dopamine, oxytocin, all those feel goods rolled together every time you think about us. Following?"

"Um, ok, emotional steroids...yes?"

"So, our signature's on you. Then we feed off each other. You get some, we get some. I do mean that literally, too."

"Ugh, stop," I groaned.

Mika slapped a hand to his chest and gasped. It made me laugh. Sage threw a stray energy bar that had been lying on the couch at him. Mika caught it and cheered for himself before finally sitting down again. After a playful punch or two in the arm from Tom, Sage looked at me.

"Anyway, Talor, there's a side effect to the cicatrix. We were never meant to mingle blood, so our blood diseases yours...right down to the soul. There aren't any symptoms until a human is abandoned. The disease isn't physical, but that's how it manifests. Addiction, Alzheimer's, mental illness, cancer –"

"Wait, wait...cancer?"

"Yeah."

I stared at him as I started to piece together a dirty secret in my mind. Someone had been messing with my parents, and I wanted to know who the bastard was. I made a mental note to hold onto that thought and ask Sage when we were alone.

"So you heal that?"

"Yes."

How many people died of diseases that weren't actually physical? Was he saying humans were meant to live forever and vampires were only allowed in the world because they make us mortal? *Why would a good God do that?*

I felt for the cross around my neck, wondering if the God I'd known all my life was any good at all. It felt like my brain was expanding at a rapid rate, and the only thing that slowed it was the face of my dad. When he popped in my mind, Rose followed, and then – finally – mom. I took in a deep breath, my lips trembling as I spoke.

"God won't even heal cancer."

"Well, He can, and I –"

"Where were you six months ago?"

I tried not to sound angry. Sage hadn't known me when mom died. But he could have saved her. It was only months ago. Only *months*... Our eyes locked, unmoving, unbroken. He reached a hand out to cup the side of my face.

"I'm so sorry. I would have saved your mom if I had been here," he said, tears forming in his own eyes.

I could only nod in return, battling my own tears back. We were suspended in that moment. It was sad, but it was nice to feel understood. Tom cleared his throat politely.

"The point is, if we don't go around doing what we do, the Grigori gain power. All the shootings, bombings, and general chaos you see in the news? That's what happens when the balance is off. What Sage does – what we amplify – breaks that stronghold, so they hunt sirens."

"Grigori...where have I heard that word before?" I murmured, wiping my eyes.

I tapped my finger against my teeth while I thought. It suddenly came to me from a religious studies class lecture I heard once. I stretched an arm against Sage and gulped, nearly choking as I tried to get the question out.

"Oh – my – God! Are you – no! You can't be! Are you those angels – the ones that caused the flood? Is that why you asked about fallen angels?"

Ash, Tom and Mika all looked at Sage. They each gave their permission in some gesture. Sage held my hand for the next part. I guess he wanted to make sure I felt safe with the information I was about to get.

"Those are our fathers," he replied.

"Your fathers? So you are –"

"Nephilim," we said together.

I stared at the floor. It was incredible to imagine sitting in the presence of creatures I'd only ever read about in a book – a book whose authenticity most scholars question. I didn't remember everything about the story, but I knew the Nephilim were violent creatures that nearly wiped out mankind.

They were much worse than the fallen angels that fathered them, and I was sitting in a room with four of them. My anxiety must have shown because Sage made it a point to stroke my hand as if I were some pet he was putting to sleep on a vet table.

"Hey, we aren't like the ones you read about," he said sweetly, ushering for Tom to grab a bottled water.

Tom opened it for me and I took it without looking, gulping. For some reason, a fallen angel cursed into a vampire wasn't nearly as hard to grasp as sexualized zombies slinking around in shadows seducing and biting people when they're hungry. When I finally found my voice, I think I sounded calmer than anybody expected.

"But you look so normal."

He raised a brow.

"Ok. We can stay in this form if we want because our mothers were human. And because our fathers are what they are...well, I think the easiest way to explain it is that a human like you can't manifest your soul in the flesh, but we can."

"Why? How?"

"Our blood."

I let that simmer a good minute.

"So, hold on – are you saying you're like some sort of spirit animal?" I asked, trying not to smile as I said it.

That seemed to hit the funny bone on Tom and Mika, who had to bury their faces in the crooks of their elbows while their shoulders jumped. Even Sage smiled a bit. I wasn't offended. It was kind of funny imagining them all running around as super-powered house pets.

"Um, kind of? Maybe not in the sense that you think, but yeah, something like it. Whatever creature we are, it's the closest thing in nature to our truest self."

"Well, what are you? What does it look like when you become it?" I asked, looking around to each of them.

"We're all different. We'll show you ours if you show us yours," Mika said with a wink.

I blushed.

"I'm pretty sure I can't do anything you can do."

"We don't evo around cities. And it's too risky with all the Henches running around in a place this saturated," Sage said.

Mika sighed and dropped his shoulders dramatically. I exhaled, releasing the tension from expecting a bunch of mythological beasts to start raging through the room.

"Henches? Evo? Huh?"

Ash spoke up.

"Henches are the bad guys. That's all you need to know."

"Ok then."

Sage nodded.

"Yeah. Anyway, is it making sense?"

It all rolled around in my mind, the pieces of the puzzle starting to fit. Vampires aren't dead, they're just fallen angels. That's why Sage isn't cold to the touch. Supernatural creatures were created from angels mixing with mortals. It all actually made sense. I seriously thought to ask about the unicorns again.

Instead, I sat up straight in the loveseat, showing I was both willing and able to follow him down the crazy rabbit hole of supernatural family trees. But the unicorn question needed to be answered at some point. I kept trying to think of a roundabout to ask. I looked at each of them, scratching my head. It was the first moment since Sage had shown me his fangs that I really thought I was the butt of some elaborate joke.

I rolled my eyes.

"I don't know. If vampires are going around biting people, how does no one ever catch it on camera? You're talking about at least hundreds – if not thousands here, right? How do you avoid being caught?"

Sage sighed like he'd been expecting me to question the authenticity of a clinically insane fantasy. His eyes held their fervor, and the steadiness of them sent all my self-assured confidence to the floor with a thud.

"Remember what I told you about influence?"

"Yeah, but I thought you said you don't do that. Can't was your exact word."

"He doesn't," Ash replied.

"Does that mean you do?"

"In case you were wondering," Mika piped up, still steadily typing away on his phone, "no, we don't feed on anyone without permission. We're old-fashioned like that, little lady."

"Well, since you...do you...go to blood banks, that kind of thing?"

Just then, the same guy who came out front to get me after the show came in the back door. He jammed his fists down into his pockets and fell back against the wall. He giggled oddly, as if he was laughing at a joke only he heard. He brought a cigarette to his lips and took a long drag on it. On his neck, there were bites marks. Fresh.

Ash's lip curled as he cut his eyes at me.

"Yeah, that kind of thing."

I swallowed hard and choked on the cold, hard truth. I knew I was standing in the middle of something bigger than a crush. Supernatural creatures did exist and thank God – there were a few actually on our side. Still, the shifting eyes of the others told me there was much more to Dead Reckless than playing shows to heal humans of supernatural marks.

243

I gave a false smile in spite of myself. I wanted to seem calm and seamless to the fantastic creatures around me. I must've looked faint, because
Sage touched his hand to my forehead. It was warm. That helped.

"Not going to pass out on me, are you?"

"No, no. But I'm just confused. If it's so dangerous to heal people of
these cat – what did you call them?"

"A cicatrix," Sage answered.

"Yes, that. If the Grigori are hunting you because you're doing that,
then why do it?"

Tom sat down on the armrest across from me.

"Do you need a reason to do the right thing when you know it's the
right thing?"

"No," I replied.

"It's the same with us. We broke from our fathers because they believe
mankind is food. They call us the Dissent or Prodigals. There isn't always a
siren in the world to rally behind, but the Dissent has always existed. We
get stronger and have real, well, for lack of a better word, influence when
there's a siren.

The Loyalists – we call them Henches – kill men senselessly and brutal-
ly. We don't kill anyone. We only feed from the willing and we never seal
them. But that's not the only reason we do this. Our mothers were human,
just like you."

We shared a smile.

"What he really means is that we also need humans to survive. The fact
is you're the only thing on our menu. We still bite the neck that feeds us,
we just don't rip it open," Ash added.

I didn't want to be a little kid who just learned that Santa Claus was a
vampire rock band named Dead Reckless and instead of delivering gifts,

saved humans from zombie-status by supernatural hybrids. These were – at best – flawed heroes from what I could tell. Tom fiddled with the couch cloth for a moment.

"Talor, you need to understand that Sage is...honestly, he's irreplaceable. He's the only siren. As in the only one in the world right now, understand?"

I always knew he was one of a kind, but putting it that way, I felt myself shrinking rapidly. His singing was the secret weapon against the forces of darkness? No wonder he could be so picky with women.

"Ok?" I said, not really understanding why Tom was pleading with me like I was holding a gun to Sage's head.

Ash paced with his spinning drumstick.

"Moving on. Do you know what happens if the siren's song is heard by a mortal?"

"Don't," Sage snapped.

"It's just a question," he replied.

I nodded, remembering what happened in mythology when sailors somehow escaped the song of the sirens. The truth hit me so hard I gripped the top of the loveseat for support. Sage would die? I heard his beautiful voice during the show, but it wasn't my choice.

All this time, I was afraid of him leading me to my death...had I killed him instead? I couldn't reconcile such a thought. My lip started to tremble. I wheeled around to Ash's pointed drumstick my way. He tried to catch my eye, but I wouldn't look directly at him.

"What did our music sound like to you?"

I gulped. I could lie, sure, but this was a room full of vampires. They could hear my heartbeat and sense my nerves. It wouldn't be a great idea. I looked at Sage.

Tom attempted to grab Ash's shoulder.

"Hey, we have to trust Sage on this."

Ash jerked away from him. His words cracked like a whip against my ear. They even made me flinch.

"Henches have been infesting this area. There's a royal seal somewhere. Where's the stamp from the door?"

Sage shook his head and stood up from the couch, pulling me with him.

"She doesn't have to prove anything. That isn't why she's here."

"Why is she here?"

"Let's go, Talor."

Sage stared them all down before moving to the door. All at once, Ash snarled and tossed his drumsticks aside. It happened so fast it's amazing I could see it. Ash's skin became a scaly blue as a trail of smoke snaked out of his lips. His face began to change shape and fangs extended, his fingers evolving into menacing claws as he grew larger.

I clutched my mother's necklace on my throat, and when one of the claws came at me, I shut my eyes; certain when I opened them I would be with her again.

22

I felt the intense heat of fire before the room went silent around me. I curled up on the ground, my eyes squeezed as tight as they would go.

"Take my hand," Sage urged.

When I opened my eyes, the stamp was vibrant under my skin. The light from my wrist was strange and bright and purposeful. It extended about two feet all around me almost like I was in a bubble.

Everyone kept their distance from me except for Sage. He reached through the light and it suddenly dissipated. My ears were still ringing with confusion and distorted voices when he stood me up.

Ash was hunched over a few feet away, his palms stabilizing against his knees. He was muttering, groaning, trembling. The noises he was making were ungodly, and my ears finally gave a pop, bringing me back into the room. Right about then, he pushed himself up and arched his back until it cracked. There was a faint smell of fire and the sound of sizzling.

The roadie laughed hysterically in the corner of the room until he fell on the floor. He was the source of the fire smell. He was on fire, but he oddly knew to stop, drop, and roll.

Dazed, I swiped at my purse on the floor, ignoring its scattered contents littering the path between the door and me. There was a tampon in there. Ok, enough! Sage gathered his fingers around my chin and turned my face side to side.

"You ok?"

I nodded.

"She's a princess," Mika murmured.

Ash's eyes and fangs bulged as he aggressively extended a pointed finger at Sage. The veins in his neck were so large and swollen it looked like slender fingers were wrapped under the skin and choking him from the inside.

"Are you going to tell us now that you didn't know? You? Would you do your own brothers like that?"

"Dios mio," Tom groaned, nervously latching his hands together behind his head and pacing.

Mika couldn't stop staring. He was looking at me like I was going to pull his heart out and eat it.

"Did Spencer know?" he asked.

Spencer? How did they know Spencer? I gripped tight to Sage, feeling the billowing suspicion. I didn't want them to know what happened the night of the gala. But I knew then that something bad happened to Spencer.

Aside from Tom's pacing, no one else was moving. Well, aside from the scorched roadie rocking himself back and forth on the floor. The shifting eyes all landed on my wrist.

"How long have you had that?" Ash asked, boring a hole through my soul.

"Since the door?"

"Not the stamp, genius. The seal."

"Just sing again," I said, turning to Sage.

"Even a siren can't save you, princess," Ash said.

I stared past him, eyes wide, fingers digging deep into Sage's skin. Sage, who still hadn't said or done anything. I did the only thing a panicking person could do: I looked down at the visible LLDR and tried to rub it off. It was beneath the skin like a tattoo now. *So...not coming off.* It began to glow so bright everyone in the room could see it.

"No! Tell her not to do that. Don't call him," Ash cried, pointing at me.

Sage caught my hand, stopping my frantic attempt. I blinked up at him.

"Why can't you take this one off? Isn't that what you do? You and only you?"

Sage bunched his brow together, trying to work out what to say. I could tell he wanted to make me feel better, but there was nothing good to say. Ash tried to cover his face with his hand, but it was shaking.

"After everything we've been through, *bràthair*. When did you know?"

"That doesn't matter, Ash."

"It damn well does. You owe us that. Did you know before we came here?"

"No."

Mika and Tom sighed in unison. Ash just stared.

"So many Henches around makes sense now. I thought it was just us," Tom said.

"We need to haul ass," Ash said, his brow releasing. "But it might already be too late."

My thoughts felt scrambled as every eye in the room fixated on my wrist like it was on fire, so I hid it behind my back.

"I want to go, Sage."

Ash clapped at me sarcastically. Venomous words coiled in his throat, and he loosed them on me with one painful, well-placed strike.

"Yes, you go. Leave now that you've ruined his life."

"She hasn't ruined my life," Sage warned.

I took in a deep breath to defend myself, but I couldn't figure out what to say. I had no idea how I got a Grigori's seal. I had never been careless with men.

I just glared at Ash, frustrated that the first time I met the people central to Sage's life, it all went horribly wrong. I couldn't say anything, despite the screaming in my head wishing to be cleared of any suspicion in Sage's eyes. The truth was, I didn't have any answers.

"Soon your husband will come for −"

"Husband? I'm not married. What are you talking about?"

"And if you go with him, you'll kill the only siren left in the world."

"I just want to go home," I cried, letting Sage protectively take me into his arms.

"What name is it?" Ash growled, his beady eyes glaring down.

I felt Sage tense beside me. I wondered how long he would allow Ash's tirade. Why wasn't he getting me out of there? I didn't dare try to leave without him. I thrust my shaking wrist towards him.

"It's j-just letters," I stammered.

"You do know. That is, unless you can't count how many names have been between your legs."

"Apologize," Sage said, stepping forward.

Ash lowered his eyes, still indignant.

"You're too important for this. What we're doing is bigger than just you and her–"

"I know who I am and what I do. I don't need you to remind me. I need you to apologize. That's what I need and right now."

Sage's tone was icy, but his words burned. He was pulling rank. Ash's arms were stiff at his side, his fists all balled up. His shoulders slumped forward like a little kid forced to return a stolen piece of candy. His jaw was tight and grinding, and he didn't look at me when he said it.

"Sorry."

I reached forward and timidly took Sage's hand, pulling on it until he eased back. Ash moved his head erratically and retreated, turning his back to us. Tom sighed.

"The fact remains. It's on her. So, what do we do?"

"Do you remember anything?" Mika asked me, his fingers tapping like a pianist against his lower lip.

"Too important for all this," Ash mumbled.

I ignored Ash and shook my head, weary of the heightened stress.

"I wish I did. I don't want this. I don't," I answered, dropping my head onto Sage's chest.

Ash looked hard at me one more time over his shoulder before he walked off, flipping over the couch with the flick of a few fingers.

Tom and Mika reluctantly followed him outside – presumably to calm him down before he went full evo in the parking lot. There was muffled talking and thumping music from people outside our four walls, but it was quiet between us. Ash left such heaviness in the air that we were both trying to carry the weight of it.

"Well, that's – you know, I never should have come," I whimpered, flinging the door open and dashing out.

251

I got just outside it before Sage caught me. It was dimly lit, but I could see the reflection of the overhead lights in his eyes. It was like coming across an animal in the woods with a flashlight. I didn't have time or the energy to freak out anymore than I already was, so I stood still, terrified that he actually believed Ash. I held up my wrist.

"You knew."

Without a word, he tenderly brought my hand up to the light. I watched his eyes start to change as a dark truth was revealed. I didn't know what was wrong, but he seemed overwhelmed. His next words were chilling.

"I would have saved you, too."

My heart dropped. Was he saying I was going to die? I wondered how sick I was already. How much blood did it take? I was too far-gone for even a siren to heal, and healing is apparently all a siren does. Words stumbled through my lips before I could trip them.

"Why can't you?"

Sage brushed back the hair from my face. Sliding his hand behind my ear, he cradled my head. I could tell his age now; no normal man could have perfected such a dashing move in only a couple of decades.

"I'll find a way," he whispered, nodding.

I nodded with him even though I had a feeling that I was doomed. It was his eyes that said it. They were swarming with pain. I knew he was holding onto something terrible. He leaned his forehead against mine. His words were a shivering quiet, as if we were standing in a tomb.

"The seal on you. The name...it's my father, Rami."

23

"My father's eyes are gray now. They used to be brown," I said, handing Sage a photo.

I wanted him to see what my dad was supposed to look like. Sage needed to know a different man raised me than the one he was about to meet. I stared down at my boots and pretended to fiddle with the buckle on the side while he looked at the photograph.

It took every ounce of my courage to call Sage after meeting the band backstage two days before. After everything that happened, I considered just quitting work and school and finally running away. It wasn't a new thought, but it had a new motive.

The only thing that stopped me was the hope that I could make things right before being taken away by someone called Rami. Rah-me. The more I looked at the eerie stamp, the more I actually saw the name. It was backwards, but the letters were there and they got darker everyday.

Soon people would think I'd gotten a tattoo. That wasn't the worst part, really – explaining what it really was, well, that thought made me sick to my stomach. So I decided I had to use my time wisely. Maybe Sage couldn't save mom and maybe he couldn't save me, but he could save someone, and that was my dad. All I had to do was ask.

Sage said nothing as he studied the photo, his eyes scanning over the smiling face of the wonderful man in it. I cut my eyes to look, wishing the father in the photo would be returned to me as soon as Sage did whatever he could do. Even now, those eyes still look at me with the same level of love and tenderness I grew up knowing.

I had a better idea of what happened to him, but that didn't make losing him at the same time as I lost mom any easier. Maybe I was technically an adult, but I still needed my parents, and I had a chance to get one of them back.

"Talor?"

Sage was holding the picture for me to take. I took it from him and stared at it until my eyes blurred. Clearing my throat, I stood quickly and forced it back in my pocket so hard it crinkled. As I straightened the wrinkles on my shirt from sitting, Sage rose slowly beside me. I looked up at him like an innocent child.

"Are you sure it's safe to do this?"

"Yeah, but I need to say something first," he replied.

I shuffled uneasily. I was hoping we could talk about the argument with Ash and the whole 'my dad wants to marry you' thing, like, never, but I wasn't going to deny him an apology if he was going to tack it with a self-less deed. His eyes shifted to watch a man meandering alone on the lawn. Once the mumbling man moved past us, Sage focused back on me.

"I should never have allowed Ash to say those things to you," he replied, stopping for a moment to check my reaction.

I nodded, remembering the jab about my legs spreading and it being my fault if the whole world died and all. It made me blush even then, so I glanced away, scratching my head.

"No one's ever said anything like that to me before," I admitted, my nose scrunching up.

"That's because no one ever should."

I rubbed my hands together to warm them. Sage was good at apologizing. It was weird because he was so perfect. How could he ever have done enough of anything wrong to master that skill?

"You don't think that I – what I mean is – that I have done that with anyone," I sputtered, not sure what I was saying. I think I was trying to tell him I was a virgin, but I had no idea why it was important to say that right then. I grimaced. Couldn't rewind the words now.

"I know," he answered thoughtfully.

I almost asked how he knew, but I figured it would lead to a conversation I wouldn't survive. I turned towards the entrance.

"Well, ok. So, I know this is a weird way to do it, but I'm excited that you get to meet my dad."

I shrugged. He took in a deep breath.

"Remember your friend Rose?"

I nodded, a furrow building in my brow. I was worried he was going to tell me there was some side effect that I wouldn't like. Instead, he looked insecure and shy all of a sudden. It was hard not to smile at him.

"Did you ever wonder why I didn't come here and help your dad when you first told me about him?" he asked, his head lowered.

"I actually just figured there was so much going on, you just...but maybe a little."

He shook his head and stepped closer as a chilly breeze blew around us.

"It's because I wanted you to introduce me. That kind of thing – it matters, you know?"

I could see him swallow; it was like he was afraid I wasn't going to like his answer. And some girls might not have. They would have been angry that their father was sitting in a loony bin while the guy they liked could have healed him in a snap and made everything all right. They might have been furious that the boy was being old-fashioned about something like that, but I wasn't. It just cemented Sage's character to the core in my mind.

He was honorable, respectful, and above all, selfless. With mom gone, I only had one parent left. I wanted my dad to meet the man I had fallen hopelessly for – even if was afraid to admit that to myself. I didn't realize it then, but that's the first time Sage was really saying that he was in love with me. A vexed expression flashed over his face then, and I realized I hadn't responded yet.

I quickly sunk into his chest as my tears spilled onto his shirt.

"I feel really stupid crying right now. I'm just so grateful," I said through sniffles.

"Crying is courageous," he said, stroking my hair.

I lifted my eyes. I felt like I should be embarrassed, but I really wasn't. Sage was gracious, and he never looked at me the way anyone else did. If he thought I was just a silly girl with fickle emotions, it never showed. Even at the Halloween party, he didn't judge me. It was peaceful being around someone like that.

"How's that?" I asked, wiping my eyes.

"Crying is that hardness melting inside you. Every time you cry, you're gaining strength and rapidly, too – so cry often, and cry hard. It keeps your soul polished like the diamond it is. Trust me on that, ok?"

I nodded, less convinced than I wanted to be. Sage knew what words to say mostly, but that didn't always mean I believed them. He took my hand and together we walked into the doors that held my father hostage. A kind older woman with wrinkle-guarded foggy blues sat at the desk. She eyed us as we moved; her interest piqued. She gazed at Sage and smiled through dentures.

"Hello there," she greeted, her voice as fragile as the translucent skin barely clothing her bones.

I smiled, but I don't think she even looked at me.

"We're here to see my dad," I said loudly, trying to gather her eyes away from Sage. He didn't seem bothered by her stare.

"You brought your boyfriend?" she asked, finally addressing me.

I blushed, releasing his hand. Sage gave a pout and took my fingers back.

"Do we need to sign in somewhere?" I asked, trying to move the conversation.

I glanced around the counter in front of me and saw a clipboard with a solid black pen attached by chain. It reminded me of being a kid in the doctor's office and always batting at the cord while mom signed me in. When she would sign our last name, the chain would always retreat like a metal snake off the clipboard and I loved hearing the grating sound of the free-fall.

"Here, honey."

It was said in a way I knew meant she was repeating herself. I'd gotten lost in thought again. I gave an apologetic smile and filled out the paper.

She asked for our IDs, and after she looked us over, she scanned two visitor badges and handed them to us.

Seeing the red flash across the barcode made me tense up. I stole a glance down at my wrist to see the faded LLDR. It had become disguised in the veins along my skin, with nearly no visible way to distinguish what it once was. I sighed and looked at Sage, who had just attached his visitor badge to his shirt.

"They just came back from lunch, so he will probably be in the common area with the others. They like to talk and play cards sometimes, but Mr. Gardin...hmm. I'd check his room first," the receptionist suggested, dipping her chin to study me. "But you probably already knew that, didn't you, honey?"

I nodded. As Sage turned towards the door, the old woman touched my hand and winked.

"Your dad will like him."

She patted my hand and hurried off – or, as fast as someone her age could hurry – and for the first time in that place, a real smile found my lips. I knew what was coming, and for once, it was something good.

Dad was sitting in the same place I left him. He was on the edge of the old pleather chair, the rips on the edges showing the wear of hands moving and gripping those places the most. Dad was still, his gaze fixated on the window ahead. He was at the end of a corridor, so it was quiet near his room. The door was open, like most are for safety.

My stomach knotted up at the sight of him. I could only see the true sorrow, the true pain in unguarded moments like these, when he didn't expect me or see me yet. For some reason – maybe something to do with being a parent, I didn't know – he put on a good show for me every time I visited.

It was always like he was better, or at least not any worse than the day he was brought in. I think he wanted me to believe we would be a family again. I ignored the times I caught him crying at the window like it was his only friend. I guess I was playing a role for him, too.

He was bathed and freshly dressed, but it was still hard to see the aging around his eyes and mouth. Those eyes were so full of fun and love just a year or two before. That mouth told me wonderful things that every daughter needed to hear from her father. But they weren't the same. They were weathered with despair and depression, beaten with the knowledge that nothing would ever be the same again even if he could be.

There was no hurry in his mind to heal for the outside world. It was empty without mom in it. I think being strong for me was too heavy a load for him to bear, but I was ok with that. I told him as much once, but the way he looked at me, I could tell he only saw a little girl with missing teeth proudly showing him some horrible art project. Even if he heard what I said, he didn't believe the words. A baby had said them. *His* baby.

They could change his clothes, but they couldn't change his sickness. Only Sage could do that. And Sage was here. Sage's thumb rubbed against mine, pulling me out of the sullen moment. His warmth filled me with peace. I smiled at dad even though he couldn't see me yet. Redemption had arrived, and I brought it through the door.

"Dad?"

He shuffled and wiped his eyes quickly, probably hoping I hadn't noticed his attempt to rid his tears before I got close enough to see them. He coughed and stood, whirling around with a grin. He stopped when he saw Sage.

"Peanut – oh...who's this?"

I looked between them and stepped forward, letting go of Sage's hand.

"This is Sage. He's my friend from work. I hope it's ok that I brought him?"

Dad nodded vigorously and gave a quick smile at Sage. He straightened his collar and brushed off his jeans as he strode across the room in two steps.

"Yes, wonderful. Please come in, son," Dad replied, pumping Sage's hand like they'd just agreed on some major merger.

Sage gave a sweet smile.

"Thank you. It's an honor to meet you, sir."

After I hugged him, we all settled into the chairs around the room. Dad tried to keep the same bright-eyed, friendly manner, but I could tell he was exhausted. He probably didn't sleep the night before, but he wouldn't tell me that.

"Sage, was it? You a musician? You look like one," Dad said.

"Yes, Mr. Gardin."

Dad slapped his knee.

"I knew it. My little peanut is a musician, too. It makes sense that she'd be interested in someone like you. She's very talented. Have you ever heard her play the piano? Or sing? Such a beautiful voice. Just like her mother does – I mean, did," Dad said, suddenly stopping.

His eyes caught mine and we stared at one another. Every time either of us mentioned mom, we were brought back to the same moment in time –

the funeral. It was there that we caught eyes for the first time in days. It was a fleeting look, but we cycled back through it a billion times over since that day.

It was a somber, soulless look – one that acknowledged the void we would suffer the rest for our lives. The one that said she was really never coming back. It was a place of no tears. We could only feel the agony of loss, and we shared it because it was the only way we could keep from feeling totally, utterly, completely alone in the world. Dad broke away first, looking down at the ground. I was equally shattered, unable to speak.

Sage had come for my father, but he decided to save us both then.

"No, sir, I haven't had the pleasure, but I couldn't imagine a single thing about Talor not being beautiful."

Dad sniffed as he brought his attention back up, his gaze softening. There were still fresh tears glistening in the gray, but they started to clear the longer he looked at Sage.

"You're exactly right, son. A blind man could see that about my peanut."

"You're exactly right. A blind man could see that about my peanut."

My cheeks burning, I fiddled with the frayed edges of my own chair.

"So, Dad, how have you been?"

He sat back in his seat.

"I've been good. Good. I think my time here's just about done. Dr. Andrews said this week that he was going to submit a letter about my condition to the court. With medication – which I don't need, but I do take," he said, raising his voice as sat up and leaned to one side of his chair, looking into the hall, "I'm well able to go home."

Home. Oh, you mean my childhood home? The one you burned down with me inside it, Dad? I tensed at the unwelcome angry thoughts rising up in me, trying to remind myself that it wasn't his fault. But still I frowned as Dad sunk back into the chair. Letting out a silent breath, I righted my emotions before he looked back at me, but I know Sage caught my quiet anger.

Dad smiled and shrugged, his knee jumping along with the twitch in his hand. I watched it do that, knowing he was unaware of it. He couldn't focus on more than one thing, and he was trying to control his facial expressions the most.

"That's great," I said.

"So you won't have to come back to this crap hole again, honey," he said, winking at me.

"Oh, well –"

"As long as I don't see anything else. Or hear the voices, or...anything like that. I know I'm getting better. I know I am. I want to so much. I want to. And the things I was seeing, those things are starting to go away. There were things in that house, I'm telling you, but I'm not seeing anything anymore. I've been sober for nearly a year now, Talor. Did you tell him that?"

Sage sat forward in his chair and brought his hands into a steeple against his chin. It looked like he was getting ready, and so I leaned forward on the armrest and raised my voice a bit so dad would listen instead of ramble.

"I'm glad, Dad. Listen, the real reason I came here today is because I know that you're not crazy. I've always believed it, but Sage can prove it. And even better – he can make it all stop."

Dad ignored me and focused on Sage.

"You seem like a good boy, you know that? You don't let anyone make fun of her because of me. You take up for her. I know her little friend Azalea is good to her, but I want her to be with a man who can defend her good name."

"No one makes fun of me, Dad," I interjected, almost embarrassed that he suggested that to Sage.

Though technically, I suggested the same thing to Sage that night in the diner. Dad kept going, like he had to get all the thoughts out. Like they were a breath being held in too long. Like he needed to take a deep breath and all those thoughts were in the way.

"I only tried to burn the one I could see, son. I know there were three other demons in that house, but I could only see the one. It was just a shadow, but I saw it. It kept laughing at me. I really thought if I burned that corner of the house –"

"Dad, please stop. Listen to me," I interrupted.

"There wasn't a body after the flames had been put out. There wasn't. I even showed them where to look, but the body was gone. That isn't right, son. Someone moved it, I said. I grabbed the guy's collar. Maybe I shouldn't have done that, but –"

Sage looked at me, and I could only meet him with tearful eyes. Dad kept babbling, his eyes focusing on some non-distinct part of the floor. Sage nodded to me and slowly stood up. The chair began to slide away from him and the door closed. I could only watch the scene unfold with wonder. Sage's skin began to glow with a soft silver hue as he knelt before dad.

There were voices down the hall coming to the commotion of dad going into a fit. Dad's voice fluctuated from hysterical to polite and back again. The paint on the wall began to vibrate with such fervor that the world became as loud as sound could get right before the eardrums burst. I felt something cool like blood ooze from my ears as the ringing took hold of the room. Sage watched dad as though nothing was happening.

I think he was listening to the whole story. I think he wanted to know it all before healing him. When dad's lips stopped moving and he finally looked up, Sage reached out and touched his lips. A flash of light passed from Sage into dad, and a miracle unfolded before my eyes.

The babbling, a thing without a face or identity apart from its host, materialized in the air and melted as it tried to transfer to Sage. The warm light glowing as a circle between them acted as a machine drawing impurities from the soul and flushing them with Sage's immense power. It was like watching a star burn up close, glorious and terrifying.

Once the disease my father had suffered was gone, Sage's skin hummed back into the gentle familiarity of freckles. The room slowly took on its volume again. The voices remained down the hall. The door was open. Sage rested back in his chair with the collar of his shirt soaked in sweat. His eyes were shut, his lips parted slightly. I felt my ears for blood, but nothing was there. I went over to him and touched his shoulder.

He reached up and touched my chin, giving this weary smile. I was almost afraid to look at dad and see if it had really worked. A part of me still didn't believe in miracles and magic, even though I knew the supernatural was real in the world. But I had accepted that dad would be a paranoid schizophrenic for the rest of our lives, and I had to talk myself into looking at him now.

When I did, I saw my real dad, not the silhouette soul he'd become. The weathered look had evaporated from his face. The fear, the pain, and the distrust – they were all gone. There was a real smile on his lips. The same lips we shared.

The smile reached all the way up to his eyes. The same eyes we shared. There was true hope, true joy, true happiness – all of which in that moment

– we shared because we weren't alone anymore. And there was a flicker of light in that void.

Something good.

24

Bex called me Sunday afternoon to see if I wanted to go to Citizen's Park. It was a cold day, but as luck would have it, I had recently bought a new sweater I wanted to wear. I agreed to meet her after six. My phone had been pretty quiet all weekend, but my thoughts were quite the opposite. I hadn't heard from Sage after he healed dad.

While I was happy that dad was ok, part of me started to worry that Sage thought I was only taking advantage of him. I developed a bad habit of checking my phone religiously while I waited him out.

To make matters worse, I felt like I had a fever all night, but I didn't feel sick. It was probably the insanity of obsessing over a relationship I'd never have taking hold of me. Then there was the whole open "investigation" on me since Spencer was still missing. Bosh didn't know anything about his disappearance, the police investigation, or Spencer's car keys left on our doorstep. I had kept her safely out of the gathering storm.

But there was still the matter of Rami. Thinking about him made me brush a finger against my wrist. I noticed it looked like it'd started getting infected the way a real tattoo does – with a slight redness highlighting the letters. Remembering not to touch it, I jerked my fingers back and used them to wrap a scarf around my neck.

Before I left, I made extra sure Bosh didn't get close enough to feel my skin. Even without actually having a fever, she would object to me doing anything outside in winter.

She glanced up from her newspaper with sharp brown eyes.

"Button up your jacket, honey."

"Ok, Bosh."

I did the button quickly. It seemed enough to bolt out the door unopposed. As the day dipped below the tree line, I relived the healing at the clinic. I remembered the painful wincing of Sage's face as the entities absorbed inside him and dissipated.

He hadn't done that on stage when he healed hundreds that time at The Journey. I didn't know why it looked more difficult to heal just one person at a time. It didn't make sense, but then again, nothing about it did.

There were a ton of cars parked up and down the street when I walked up. I could hear a crowd, but it just sounded like white noise. There were bright lights set up like those at an outdoor concert. A few sugared-up kids pushed past me as they chased each other towards a long, loud line. It wasn't until I got closer that I saw what the line was waiting for. Bex wrapped a bear hug around me from behind.

"Free ice-skating! Whaaat? The only problem is the line, and the people in general. But come on, we saved you a spot."

She took my arm and started leading me through the crowd.

"Since when does Cypress have an outdoor ice-skating rink?" I yelled, trying to compete with the clamoring voices. I felt silly yelling, but it was the only way to be heard.

"I don't know, but I knew you'd love this! Everyone's here," she said with a wink.

"Wait – what do you mean everyone?" I screeched, my jaw and stomach tightening in anticipation.

With that, she pushed me ahead to the front of the line where Azalea, Jesse, Larissa, Kyoko, and Sage were standing. They had their skates in hand. Sage was smiling sweetly and holding a pair for me.

"They should be the right size," he said, shyly offering them.

To keep from melting, I looked to Azalea and Larissa, who had the goofiest looks I'd ever seen as they hugged me.

"Surprised?" Azalea asked, letting a devious smile slide across her perfectly lined lips.

"The hat is so cute," Larissa cried, grabbing it and pushing it around on my head.

"Ugh, no," I sighed, knowing my hair looked wild once again. Sage bit his lip and released it quickly.

"Happy Birthday, Talor," Jesse and Kyoko said in unison.

"But it's not –"

Azalea slapped a hand across my mouth and pulled me close.

"Shhh, don't finish that sentence, trust me."

"Oh."

"Now be polite and thank everyone."

"I definitely didn't expect this," I said, nodding and giving a thumb's up.

So they were throwing me a fake birthday party so I could hang out with Sage. I wouldn't ruin it. Satisfied, they gave each other high fives. Once we were able to find a free bench beside the line, we all got to work putting on our skates. Sage sat across from me. I wished I'd worn more make-up. And not taken that late nap. I was still groggy.

"I missed you at work," I said.

"Larissa mentioned that."

I kept my head down.

"Oh she did?"

I watched him do a double knot on his laces.

"I missed you, too," he said.

My mouth dropped open as I finished my laces. I knew he was smiling at me, but I didn't dare look. I glanced back at Azalea, who was busy bossing Jesse and Kyoko around as they got out on the ice. When I finally found the courage to look him in the eyes, I felt better. He was good at that.

"You have good friends, you know?" he asked, chuckling as he stood and pulled me to my wobbly feet.

I looked around. Jesse was holding the side for dear life as Kyoko pulled at him. Bex was scoping out the single guys skating. Azalea and Larissa were still giving each other high fives for some reason. They were really proud of themselves. And they'd done this all for me. I smiled and felt it all over my body. Good friends.

"Yeah, I know."

Sage went out first, steadying me as I followed.

"I'm not amazing at this," I warned.

Everyone in the group was pretending to have lots to talk about as we passed. I know they were just watching us. Sage held both my hands and skated backwards, careful to avoid other people on the ice. I wasn't bad, but he was better than I was.

Once we'd gone a turn around, he bent his elbows and pulled me closer, lacing his fingers into mine. His hands were strong and slender, and they wielded mine with some primal masculinity that made me want to curl myself up into a ball small enough to fit inside them. He grinned when I squeaked every time we hit a slippery grove in the ice. I really wondered how we would skate on melted ice from the looks we were giving each other.

"You're not mad at us for inviting him, are you? No? Ok, don't mind us. I'm getting pictures of his butt for you," Azalea yelled.

Embarrassed, Sage and I both laughed and leaned into each other so we could stop ourselves against the wall. He rested an elbow on it, holding me at the side and blinking rapidly. Confused, he arched back so he could check out his own butt.

"You want pictures of my butt?" he asked, his brow going up.

"No," I replied, then turned and raised my voice. "They just let anybody ice skate nowadays, don't they?"

A male voice called out behind us from the parking lot. The voice was familiar, but I hadn't heard it enough to recognize it. When we turned around, we saw Mika and Tom striding up.

"We heard it was someone's birthday today," Mika said, pointing to me and clucking his tongue.

I tried not to act nervous as they shook hands and slapped shoulders. They were doing normal guy stuff. It should have been comforting seeing them act human, but I could only remember how tense the last meeting with them was. Ash lingered back a little to the side, so I pretended he wasn't there.

Tom did a little bow.

"Happy birthday, Miss Talor. Sorry we don't have gifts, but we do know how to crash a party if that's of any use."

I glanced after them. I figured they'd bring dates. You know, in case they "needed" them.

"Thanks," I said. "Did you bring dates? Do you do that?"

I couldn't ignore Ash anymore. He gave an annoyed sigh and pushed himself off the wall. He tilted his head back and looked down at me.

"Well, not all of us like humans in the romantic sense like Sage does. More of a pet if you've got to feed it and pet it and take care of it, too."

Mika gave a sharp jab with his elbow.

"Be cool."

"Yeah, just shut up, man," Tom scolded.

"It was supposed to be a joke," Ash argued, shrugging. "Sorry I'm not funny, Talor."

Sage gripped the barrier between the rink and the grass and turned his head a little, shaking it. He didn't say anything. Ash blinked hard and relaxed his face.

"Yeah, all right. It's out of my system now. I'm done."

"So, if you don't have dates, does that mean you're going to skate together?" I asked, giving a playful smile. "And Ash gets to be the third wheel?"

It turned out to be the perfect thing to say. The tension evaporated. Mika and Tom laughed. Even Ash – unbelievably – gave the shortest, most caught-off-guard smile. Smirk. Grin. It *happened*. It was too fast for the normal human eye, but I saw it.

"I'll pass on that. We'll just find the loveliest ladies here and escort them around. Oh some luck," Tom said, gesturing to Azalea, Larissa, and Bex, who were skating over.

I went into something of a panic. I didn't know whether or not they were in any danger. I must have been wearing my worried face to Sage. He quickly reassured with a squeeze of my hand, soothing me just in time. Azalea was the first to speak, of course.

"Oh, Sage's band, right? All right. Hey guys."

When no one responded, she singled out Tom, who self-consciously brushed a hand swiftly through his hair.

"You have a name?" she asked bluntly. But I knew she was intrigued. I knew that tone.

"Tomahawk," he answered.

She let out that infectious, flirtatious laughter once again.

"Seriously? You can only skate with me if you come up with a better name than that."

He pursed his lips and nodded, pulling off his shoes and tossing them to the side. One of them flew at someone's face, but nobody paid any attention to the complaints.

"Does Tom work for you?"

Azalea batted her eyelashes at him.

"He better. Most guys do."

Tom ran off to get skates. Larissa and Mika hit it off and went skating off together. Only Ash was left, and he just shook his head after Mika, settling into his role as the grumpy loner.

"I'll just watch," he mumbled to no one in particular.

Bex sized him up, putting her weight against the wall and leaning halfway over to look at him.

"Yeah, I could take you," she said, grabbing at his pants leg. He blinked at her, probably shocked at her audacity. I doubted many girls touched Ash.

"No."

"You're the drummer, right? Nice. You get sweaty, don't you? Got any tattoos?"

He looked uneasy. She went around us to get to him and grabbed his shirttail.

"Hey, they want to be alone. Come with me, Mr. Can't-take-a-hint."

I didn't know how he would react to that, you know, being Ash. To my surprise, he went to get skates, too. Bex kissed her palm and pat me on the head with it as she passed by. She was so crazy and so rude, but I was never more grateful for her as a friend.

Sage and I still stood there close and cozy, smiling at each other. There was privacy to our space despite the hordes of people sliding and screaming across the ice. After a while, we just settled into a slow sliding along the wall in a hug.

"You've been so open with me, I think I need to be honest with you," I said, brushing a finger along his scarf.

"Oh yeah? What?"

"It's not really my birthday," I said, immediately covering my face.

His eyes twinkled with mischief.

"Well then, there's really only one way to atone for that."

He pushed away from the wall and pulled me out onto the ice with him. He did it fast and held me close as we did a few tight spins into the middle of the rink. I held his shoulders and closed my eyes, a squeak the only sound I could make. The cold air whooshed all around us and burned my fingers cold, but I couldn't stop laughing.

When we slowed down, I looked up at him, not even trying to hide my happiness. I was utterly absorbed in the moment, wholly selfish and relishing it.

"Oh my God, that was fun!"

"Wanna go again?" he asked, winking.

I nodded and braced myself as he pushed a leg out and spun us so fast the world was a series of streaks and fragmented sounds. He did that a few more times, and even tried to teach me how to skate backwards and do spins on my own. He had to catch me before I fell, but he always did.

We both laughed so hard every time I have no idea how we mustered the energy to try again. I think we were having more fun than anyone else on the ice that night – kids included.

I didn't notice everyone else had left until the sky was thick with stars. I couldn't believe I wasn't cold the whole time. The temperature had dropped, but Sage kept me warm. It wasn't until we turned our skates in that I snapped out of my daze. We were the last two people at the rink. When we walked away, they shut down the lights.

"When did everybody leave?" I asked.

Sage shook his jeans to wrinkle out the bottom. They had been rolled up to avoid getting wet from the ice.

"I don't know."

He slipped his hand in mine as he walked up beside me. We huddled under the lamplight of the park, the only two fools strange enough to stay out in the elements just to look at each other a little longer. It was so quiet it felt like the world was watching us. Breathing seemed too loud, too rude.

"I'm sorry my weird friends conned you into a fake birthday date with me," I said, trying to keep from feeling too charity-case about it. "And then bailed."

"Fake birthday, real date."

I laughed.

"Then it was a quadruple date?"

He laughed. When our smiles faded, he studied me for a minute, deep in thought.

"Talor?"

"Yeah?"

"I know it's not really your birthday and..."

"Um, ok?"

"And it's not raining, but..."

He was licking his lips and shrugging. I knew what he was getting at. It was a moment three months in the making. His hands came sweeping up the sides of my neck, his thumbs pushing my chin towards the sky where he seemed to be. It took the air right out of my lungs the way he did that, and I nearly crumbled in his tender hands.

He studied my face first, then my lips. My hands fell until they landed somewhere down on the back of his hips, where they hooked into his jeans. I needed to hang onto something because this wasn't about to happen. Sage wasn't really about to kiss me. His eyes went down to watch my pulse punch wildly underneath my skin. It had to be hard for him to watch the violent flow.

"It's different with me, you know?" he said, touching the vein and raising a brow.

I didn't know what he meant, but I nodded so fast it was like my neck had no bones in it. The fear that he had two tongues or some weird technique flit through my mind, but the knowledge that a kiss was coming made me willing to risk it. I couldn't hide the excitement in my voice.

"Don't care. I want this – have for – always."

He gathered me up in some sensational way, settling my curves against him. There was such an arch in my back that I never would have been able to hold had he not been doing all the work for me. He was taking my weight on like it was like nothing. The adoring way he looked at me was reassuring, so I let all my insecurities fly away with the chill that swept past.

"I kept waiting for it to rain," he said.

With that, he awarded me the lips I'd been obsessed with for months. It was a merciful domination, those sweet lips against mine. I would do whatever they asked me to. I always thought that was the case, and now I knew. He was kissing me with his lips, but his heart and soul were the ones touching. I'd never had a first kiss so sensual and pure all at once.

There was sanctuary in the way he held me. I worshipped at his altar while he baptized me in passion. It was conflicting, confounding, and comforting. Good God, there were levels to his kisses, and I needed them all. My hands clawed their way up to his neck like a feral cat.

Unable to contain myself, I pushed up on my toes and took from him again. With one hand cradling my head, his tongue teased my sanity behind a smile. I leaned back to look up at the stars, emptying my lungs with a ragged breath.

He followed, bending slightly forward and breathing in the skin on my neck – just like Spencer had done. I could barely feel his lips skim along as they traveled. It was such terrible torture for us both. After a heavy, happy sigh, his fingers stretched out behind my head and drew me back.

I thought he was going to swarm me with kisses, but he just pecked my nose and smiled, tracing a thumb against my lips. I was trying to recover from the staggered rhythm of my breath, doing my best to seem normal. I felt full of light inside, and I wanted more. But I would have to wait. He was a gentleman that night, simply taking my hand in his and walking me back to my car. He opened my door for me, as always.

As I stood in front of it, a sort of panic set in. I realized we were going to be apart for an unset number of hours. He didn't work on Mondays. It hurt to imagine time without him. I held his hand so tight, letting our skin touch as long as possible. I would need him again soon. I would. It would be ok. He must have sensed the uncertainty, so he leaned against the car and ran a hand down my cheek.

"Talor, it's ok."

"I don't know what to say. Thank you seems really stupid."

I was lying. I knew what to say. I was just afraid of sounding needy. *Don't leave. Hold me. Keep kissing me. I'm all yours.*

I looked away, mentally slapping myself. I was going to ruin a perfect moment if I stuck around too long. But I didn't want to leave. I felt exposed, vulnerable. It was weird. I was so weak. I was supposed to be a grown woman, strong and capable. I paid my own bills and could take care of myself.

I didn't like this feeling. The kiss had to be more than a kiss. He tapped into me somehow, like into my soul or something. Now I was paranoid and it almost made me angry – like he was manipulating me. I was shivering, my nerves on edge. I fought the negative thoughts as he took both of my hands in his, lacing our fingers together as he gently shook them.

"Easy. I know it's a little intense."

278

I tried to play it off. I didn't want him to think...oh, I didn't know. I was afraid I'd ruined the moment. I needed to seem in control.

"I'm ok."

He gave me a knowing look.

"We're in the same skin. I know how you feel because I feel it, too," he said, leaning his forehead against mine.

That explained the paranoia. He was technically sharing my emotional space, so no wonder. It made sense.

"Then I'm really embarrassed," I whimpered.

"I know," he said, nuzzling me.

"You can't hear what I'm thinking, can you?"

He shook his head and kissed each of my fingers before untangling them.

"No. But I like talking to you, so that's just fine. I'll call you tomorrow?"

"Ok," I replied, sending a shy smile to the ground.

He backed away slowly, pausing a second or two before letting go of my hand. We grinned at one another and looked away at the same time. He put his hands in his pockets.

"And Talor? Of all the birthdays real and imaginary, yours is the one I'm most thankful for."

I drove all the way home with such a grin on my face that whatever happened to be watching – man, God, or mythological beast – could see every single one of my imperfect teeth.

25

"Don't you get lonely?" I asked, surveying the solitary house in front of us where Sage lived.

It was a quaint cottage sitting on about two acres of land. When we drove up, I took note of the lack of streetlights. There weren't any lights on inside the cottage, either. Sage was obviously a man and a supernatural one at that for daring to leave all his lights off while living alone.

A woman would never risk it. But what did Sage have to fear, really? He could see in the dark and take down anything that tried to attack him. There was only one neighbor to the left and a small pine forest hedging every other side. It looked thick, especially in the dark. The cottage had a porch with a swing, and even a cute little chimney. It was picturesque. It seemed to be a match for him in every way: it was cute and stood alone, and he was cute and lived alone.

"I'm never here. You know, I have that job and I'm in a band and there's this girl, " he answered, smiling as he turned off his car.

When he said that, I realized how strange it was now for a supernatural creature to work a part-time job at a gym. It was never about the money. The money wasn't good enough. It wasn't about a free membership, either. He didn't need to workout to look like he did. It was about something else.

"There aren't any coffins inside, are there?" I asked. I only realized how horrible the question was once it was already out.

Sage just smiled.

"Couches are just so much cheaper."

I looked down in my lap where my fingers were busy waging war against each other. He relaxed back in the driver's seat.

"We don't have to go in. We can go get some coffee or something."

I planted my foot firmly against the floorboard of the car. I think it was a metaphor.

"Why did you come to Goodlife that day, Sage?"

He paused and opened his car door with little more than a flick of the finger.

"To meet you."

I watched him come around and open my door. When we went inside the house, the first thing I noticed was a small white Ikea couch. It was the only piece of furniture in sight. There were two throw pillows and a small Navajo-style blanket draped across the top. It was amusing. It looked like Sage shopped at IKEA.

As he made his way across the room, I thought about being alone in a dark house with a handsome vampire who was also an unsung hero of the human race. Somewhere, some lonely frustrated woman was furiously writing in her diary about this same dream.

But here I was – living it.

I could tell he was looking at me even though I couldn't see him. I hoped I looked good in the lack of light.

When he flicked on a lamp, an earthy–green colored the room. Black and white framed pictures scattered neatly across the wall. They were sights from cities all across the world, and they looked like pictures he might have taken. He let me wander along like someone in the halls of a museum. He tapped a hand on the couch excitedly once he could tell my curiosity was satisfied.

"There's something out back I want you to see," he said, ushering me to the door leading to the porch.

When we walked outside, there sat a gigantic telescope. It looked like it belonged in an observatory. I doubted it was legal to own one like that without some license or something. Not that Sage cared.

"You didn't steal that, did you?" I asked playfully.

He went over and rested a hand on it.

"God, no. I've been around for a while, remember? Did you know there's a meteor shower tonight?"

"I do remember hearing about it. I wanted to sit out and watch, but I knew I was going to be with you," I said, walking over. "Which was a fine tradeoff by me, just so you know."

"Well, now you get to have both," Sage said, shrugging. "Take a look."

I bent down and peeked through the lens. The meteor shower wasn't just sporadic specks of rushing light across the night sky like it was the last time I watched one out my bedroom window. It was a brand new experience through that telescope.

A meteor blazed across my vision, bright and brilliant. Gasping, I reached my fingers out for it. I knew I really couldn't, but for a second in

283

time, I believed I could touch it. I forgot I was thousands of miles away from what I was seeing.

"Watch out, they burn," he joked.

"It's been to the edges of the universe. God, the stories it could tell," I replied whimsically, straightening.

Sage was quiet. He gazed up with me.

"Is it weird I think about things like that, Sage?"

He was watching me, enjoying my wide-eyed wonder.

"No, it's you."

I turned to him.

"I want to hear all your stories one day. Promise me."

His eyes softened as he nodded.

"I'll tell you everything one day."

"One day," I echoed.

With that, he took out a small flashlight from his back pocket and handed it to me. Puzzled, I took it and turned it on. He put a hand on the telescope.

"If you shine light into space, it won't stop until it hits something."

I turned the flashlight towards him.

"Really? But this flashlight is so weak."

He took my hands in his and turned the flashlight to face the sky overhead between us. I could see his eyes sparkle behind the stream of light, tiny specks of stars reflecting in his eyes.

"Up there, this weak little light could go on forever in theory. Think about it: we could be on the other end of a light touching a planet or even shooting across the universe."

I followed the light beam into the sky, where it disappeared into the vast dark of space and stars. He took it and propped it up on the telescope so it was still beaming into space. He came over, brushing the fallen hair from my cheek.

"So if you looked up into the night sky, the light from your eyes would _"

He stopped. He was looking down at me, stroking a finger on my neck where he once healed it.

"Look across time. No one can see the whole universe, you know. But I think maybe you could. The stars shine in your eyes like rain drenched in light. There's a whole world in there I could just live in."

"If my eyes hold your world, your skin is my sky," I said, touching the freckles on his neck.

He smiled.

"And you said you can't write poetry."

My breath grew deep and heavy. I wanted him. He made me fearless. I found a strange courage in his arms and immortality in his lips. If I could only stay there, I'd be the happiest, most powerful being in the world.

"Why don't you sing anymore, Talor?"

My smile dissipated. I thought about not telling him, but no. I needed to. He was trustworthy, and he was good. I could talk to him and he would say the right thing, too. I brushed my finger against the necklace on my neck. He watched me.

"My mom. I can't," I said, my voice breaking.

"I understand."

I just wanted to bury my head in his chest as the tears started, but he wouldn't have it. He kissed me as I wept. I cried and kissed, sometimes sobbing and gasping for air, but always returning to him. It was probably the messiest kissing either of us had ever done.

My tears were all over my face and his, and my lips were trembling the whole time. It was something that should have embarrassed me, but I felt stronger when I pulled away from the last kiss. It was slow, and I didn't open my eyes at first. He held me close, still giving micro kisses on my swollen eyelids.

"Talor, I wrote a song for you."

"You wrote a song?"

"I want you to hear it."

I nodded. Maybe after he played the song he'd kiss me again. I hoped, anyway. It made everything better. He reached over and clicked the flashlight off before leading me back to into the house. When we got inside, he gestured to the carpet in front of the crackling fireplace. *Wait...a fire? It wasn't lit before.*

"Are you thirsty or anything?" he asked.

Sage was behind me now, easing my jacket off my shoulders. He tossed it on the couch as I watched the dancing flames in front of me. I didn't turn around and he didn't move. He was breathing in my skin, his hands soft on my arms. I couldn't help the words that came out next.

"Are you?"

He paused. I don't know if he did it for dramatic effect or if he was really trying to decide.

"No."

"Well, how often do you have to?" I asked, almost afraid of knowing. I would forever count the hours between his meals if I knew.

Sage moved away, taking the blanket from the couch and wrapping it around me. It settled on me like snow, silent and soft. He looked down at me, emotionless. I expected some brooding before a long, drawn-out confession, but he didn't hesitate. His answer was quick.

"I can stave off the craving for longer than anyone else."

In my mind, I imagined every possible horror of what he meant. How many women had he seduced? How many had he killed? Would there be more? Had he fed from someone today? Yesterday? How could I feel this way for a person who had to wound someone to eat?

"Do you like it when you do?"

"Do you really want to have this conversation right now?"

"Yes. No. Yes. I just think I should know some things," I said, standing my ground.

"Like does a vampire enjoy biting people?"

"I know. I'm sorry."

His eyes dropped.

"I like it if I don't hurt the person. They like it more that way, too."

His honesty brought me no peace. I was jealous again. I could only think of Valerie. I was glad he couldn't read my mind. I was glad my chaotic, childish, jealous thoughts were my own. I asked myself if I really wanted to know his past. It would be dark and long, and there would be no forgetting it once I knew. I wasn't brave enough to know yet.

I sunk to the floor with the blanket wrapped around me. Sage walked over to a corner and picked up a guitar. He settled down beside me. He ran a finger along the string, careful not to make a sound. Taking advantage of the silence, I looked at the seal.

"Why did your father do this to me?"

My voice was so small I wondered if I'd only thought it. But I'd asked. Sage just hadn't answered yet. He took his fingers off the strings and put the guitar to the side. He caressed the outline of my shoulder through the blanket with care. I watched his touch move along my arm, warm, soothing.

He kissed me then, sweet and desperate. He pulled away soon after, heaviness cloaking his words.

"I wish I knew," he said, his voice getting weaker at the end.

I grabbed his hand.

"I don't blame you."

"Doesn't change the fact."

He just kept running his hand up and down my arm. It calmed us both.

"Is there anything we can do?"

He couldn't answer me. He just shrugged as his eyes filled up. His hand suddenly shot out, taking me by the neck and kissing me. He wrapped his hands up in my hair and sat up before returning me gently to my back. His kiss was saturating, and I could feel him seeping into my bones.

My heart was conquered. I could find no fault in the inhuman hands that held me. The truth was, I wanted him deeper inside me than even the bones, and I couldn't kiss him enough to solidify the surrender. I would try, though. When he pulled back, he took in a sharp breath and touched foreheads.

"I want to play your song, Talor."

I nodded as I waited to be serenaded by a siren. His eyes looked deep with purpose, and I didn't know then what purpose that was – or how dangerous it would be for us both. I listened to the fire crackle behind us and coat his face with a cozy glow.

He sat up and grabbed his guitar, setting it on his lap. It was steel blue-gray in color and smooth. The reflective face had a curious design on it. Some kind of wrapping symbol curled to the left and the right and in the middle was a creature – something like a Griffin. I could tell he was collecting his thoughts.

Taking a deep breath, his fingers took their strategic places on the strings. With the first strum, he looked at me in a new way. I was drawn into his gaze completely; it was like having an outer-body experience. As he began the instrumental intro, I felt my body go rigid. It straightened so tight that I felt my bones would break with the slightest twist of the joint.

Then came his voice – that melodic perfection. Every word sent a new wave of pulses through my body. I could feel every inflection in his tone. As he built to the first chorus, I felt myself slipping into a new level of ecstasy; I could control myself no more. I was a passenger on this ride now. The words to the song haunted until they were inside me, pushing through my muscles and bones to mark their territory.

Despite my total trust in Sage, my mind panicked inside a body that would no longer obey. A cold sweat broke out across my skin. His eyes were back on me now, and they were dark. They held me hostage while his voice breathed through me like a wild wind teasing the tops of rooted trees.

That's when I noticed strands of my hair drifting up in front of me as though I were underwater, defying gravity. The lyrics continued until I could no longer stand the intensity. He had to stop. Something was wrong. I didn't react this way when I heard him at the show. I felt the fragility of my own mortality and I was afraid. Words crawled from my throat.

"Pleeease stop, Sssssage."

I saw him put aside his guitar, but a ghostly echo of the music played in my ears. I didn't know why. Sage came resting on his elbows over me. His chest lay against mine as his hand traced the curve of my hips all the way up to the length of my arm. He extended it up and it obeyed his will.

He watched me shiver before closing his eyes and kissing me. This kiss was relentless. There was no restraint. When those eyes tore open again, his fingers curved inside my own, and my wrist started to burn as bright as the fire itself.

Producing its own light, the seal cast an eerie smudged LLDR over his head. My skin began to burn as though my entire body was on fire from the inside out. It was like no pain I'd ever felt before. Like dying with no final moment for relief. It was a cycle of pain, circling, radiating, ceaseless.

My body lingered on the edge of unconsciousness, and I could only whimper, looking to him for relief. His fangs extended, and even in that hallucination of suspended reality, I knew what he was going to do. One of his hands released my fingers and slid under my head, gently turning it to the side to expose my neck. Our eyes locked.

"Forgive me."

His fangs were smooth going into the skin. I gasped from shock, not pain. His hand continued to hold mine tenderly, serving as a silent affirmation that he was not in some feeding frenzy. I didn't know why he was doing what he was doing, but I could trust that it was Sage doing it, not some bloodthirsty beast. It gave little comfort once I began to feel the effects of being bitten. A potent weakness took me as though I'd been drugged.

Reality ebbed like a wave from my conscious mind. I couldn't tell what was real from what was imaginary anymore. I didn't know if I was dying or sleeping. It felt euphoric, and I wondered how dying should be so pleasant. He kissed my neck before bringing his head up and cleaning his lips.

"Hurry," he encouraged, quickly biting his wrist and bringing it to my mouth.

The moment his blood spilled onto my tongue, his skin started ripping apart as though invisible wild beasts were tearing at his flesh. His eyes dilated as he screamed in agony. I never heard anyone make that sound before. I watched his skin try to heal, but the vicious rips were repetitive and violent, accompanied by a red-hot ornate seal searing the skin on his neck.

He pushed up on his palms, but his arms were shaking like all his bones were broken. Tears bled down his face, soaking me. I wanted to scream, but I was too weak. It got caught somewhere in my lungs. Suddenly, he collapsed, motionless.

The entire world faded out with him.

26

When I awoke, we were both still on the floor.

My hair was matted with my blood, his blood. I felt for puncture wounds on my neck, but I didn't find any. I almost thought I was dead, hovering over the scene of my demise. I felt alive and dead – odd, but it's the only way to describe it. I shivered and sat up, reaching out to touch him. He wasn't moving. I turned him on his back to see what damage had been done.

Dried blood lingered around his eyes. He was pale, but still breathing. When I tried to wake him, he didn't respond. I noticed the guitar lying on his left and tried to recall what happened. The only thing I could remember was the last few seconds before we both went unconscious.

While the memories were hazy, I remembered one thing – the passion between us. How much I wanted him. How I didn't care if he bit me. And how ashamed that made me. His phone vibrated on the floor beside him. I reached over and saw that it was Tom, so let it go to voicemail. The call log showed four missed calls. Odd.

I knew I needed to make sure Sage was ok. He hadn't moved. I didn't know how normal it was. Did they sleep? I looked at the time on the phone. It said 2:54 am. Confused, I tried to stand up so I could go to the window. My legs were weak, like I had climbed a mountain the day before. It hurt to move.

When I saw it was still dark outside, I felt sick to my stomach. We didn't get to his house until after eight. Had we been asleep for seven hours? I found my phone and checked the time. It said the same. I went back to where he was lying and touched him on the shoulder. I was hoarse, but I forced the words out.

"Sage," I groaned, touching my throat. It felt like I had a cold.

He didn't move, so I started to panic. *What if he never woke up? What if I killed him? What if –*

A loud knock came at the door. I froze, and listened to a muffled voice on the other side. The male voice called Sage's name and I hurried over. It was Tom.

"He won't wake up," I cried, pointing like somehow he'd missed the body lying on the floor.

"What happened?" he asked, the words barely making it out of his throat.

"I'm trying to remember. He was playing this song he wrote me."

He was at Sage's side so fast I felt dizzy. He looked him over and tried to wake him.

"He sang for you *again*?"

I stiffened.

"Tom, is he ok?"

294

LONG LIVE DEAD RECKLESS

Tom shook his head as tears filled his eyes.

"No, he can't...you, the seal...oh God, I think he's dying."

He cried out in pain or anger, maybe both; it wasn't clear. With that, darkness started to spread and thicken across his skin, forcing him down on all fours. His body twisted and heaved in such desperate, unnatural contortions that I was afraid he was going to break his own back.

My blood ran cold as it hit me – this is what the evo looks like. He was becoming something right now. He pawed against his skin in hysterics, trying to stop the process. I watched in suspended belief. I couldn't even scream. But when those cold, black eyes fixated my way, I knew it was time to go.

A rush of adrenaline flooded me all at once and filled my ears with a high-pitched hum. I took off at a full gallop, completely unaware of where I was heading. My arms pumped as my spinning legs had me running on air in a leap over the porch steps. I barreled across the empty yard in the dark, hair flying madly behind me. My only light was the full moon above and while it was bright enough to see by, it was no friend of mine tonight.

I bolted, giving no thought to the fact that I didn't drive. A heavy rhythmic, repetitive thud charged after me. I didn't look back. I knew who it was, but not what it was. I gulped in air, nearly choking on the breaths. With each step, I silently begged my body to go faster than was physically possible. Faster, faster, please go faster!

Nothing motivated my muscles to risk ripping apart so I could escape. I realized my mistake too late. There were no other houses on the isolated street to run for help. I had a split second to decide on taking the dirt road or the forest. I made my way into the tree line at the edge of the property. It was the longest hundred-yard dash I'd ever run, but it was probably my fastest time. Still, I never felt so slow.

I couldn't say what prompted me to seek shelter running into a dense pine forest, but I wasn't me in those moments. I was the survival instinct incarnate. The panic clouded my concentration long enough for my shoulder to halfway slam into a tree, the rough bark of the pine leaving its revenge on me in a long red scrape down my arm.

It spun me around in wobbly circles as I stumbled and tried to catch my balance in motion. During a turn, I saw billowing black fur and teeth and eyes shining as the creature pursued. The sight jolted me with a fresh batch of adrenaline.

I looked for a tree to climb or a light somewhere in the distance, but only dark pines and thorn bushes surrounded the path. Glancing up at the treetops, I could feel them watching, but they took no pity looking down on me. Weary, I weaved through the thickening trees of the forest until I looked back to see him closing in.

The sweat poured down as I made one last ditch effort to outrun the creature chasing me. My next step found me without footing as I came upon a huge drop off at the edge of the Flint River. Instinctively, I reached for a tree branch when a massive, vicious claw came swinging at me.

Falling back, I closed my eyes, expecting a blow. A blow from the claw, a blow from the water, something. But nothing came. Quiet. Just the sound of labored breathing. Mine. His. Its. Instead, I felt a tight grip on my forearm and a sudden, jerky stop.

When I opened my eyes, I saw that I was suspended mid-air by a hand reaching out from the darkness of the woods. My feet bounced involuntarily against the ledge as my legs trembled from exhaustion. I looked to see what was holding me. The hand was human. The rest was not. When I screamed, the letters on my wrist grew visible and flashed with lightning-like illumination. It was so bright I started seeing spots. Next came a sharp throb from the seal like a wave.

With a whimper, the creature submitted. I watched as Tom's body quickly changed from a massive werewolf into a man. It was like seeing animation unfold. It started from just above the hand that held me and moved up his arm to his shoulders, chest and face. The coarse, black fur flattened and dissolved into the rich olive tone I was accustomed to seeing. Once bristling wild animal hairs shortened and retracted into soft, human hairs against his skin.

His large eyes were the last to change – they contracted and swirled from a fierce animal gold to a deep green. Human eyes. Kind eyes. Once he was fully human, his other hand reached out to help ease me back on level land. I backpedaled away from him, almost unable to keep my legs under me. We held our breaths in anticipation to what the other would say.

He was the first, in broken breaths.

"I'm sorry...so sorry...please, I wasn't going to hurt you. I'm sorry."

I only half-heard him. I was still in shock. It was a lot to process, and I might have been experiencing an asthma attack. Good thing I didn't actually have asthma. He spread his hands out like he was surrendering.

"I know that was scary, but I'm just human now. Look."

I covered my eyes.

"Um, you're just naked!"

"Oh."

He blurred behind a tree, rustling the leaves and bushes at the foot of it before clearing his throat and peeping his head out.

"I forgot that happens. I don't evo often," he offered, shrugging sheepishly.

We both studied the ground for a few seconds. Maybe it was shadowy and dark, but it was the first time I'd ever seen a real naked man, and it happened to be Sage's friend. Once his lower half was safely hidden, I was able to look at him easier.

"Why did you chase me?" I asked, still breathless.

"I was trying to catch you. You're actually kind of fast for a human," he shrugged, chuckling.

"I was only that fast because a werewolf was chasing me!"

His brow furrowed as he looked down. The words were so quiet I barely heard them.

"I know, I know. I'm sorry. But I lost my head. Sage...is..."

"Tell me," I demanded, wrapping myself in a hug.

Tom sighed and straightened behind the tree, his fingers clenching the bark and relaxing. His face was in leafy shadows, but I could sense the pain on it.

"Listen, Ash and Mika are coming and it's probably best if you aren't around for that. I don't know what's happening, but I'll call you when we know."

I cringed. I wanted to cry, ask a million questions, charge back into the house and save Sage, but...I didn't do any of those things. I just gave a slow nod and stumbled away through the dark woods. I had no trouble finding my way. The infected letters on my wrist were still angry glares of embers, tiny needles of light, shooting out and shimmering like the delicate death of spider webs in the sun.

27

Sage called me the next morning.

The conversation was short and he sounded weak, but he insisted we get together as soon as possible. I almost turned him down. I was tired of the drama, the uncertainty, and the impending doom. I was emotionally spent, but when Sage asks for something, you do it. Nobody does polite the way he can, and that works some serious voodoo on a girl's heart.

He found us a nice sunny spot by the picnic grounds at Barrett Animal Park – "us" as in me and him and Tom. It was a weird third wheel situation, but I was the one who felt like the third wheel because I didn't want to be there. The park wasn't much, but I loved going out there from time to time and sprawling out on a blanket under the trees. It was quiet out there, and safe.

The day was nice and the leaves had begun to change into a beautiful shade of orange. Sage brought a basket filled with snacks for me. Tom laid the blanket and waited for me to sit down first. We were all quiet while he unpacked the basket. I had worn a dress for some odd reason. It was a new one, and I wanted to be cute.

Plus, boots and tights.

I knew we would have to face what happened, but I barely had time to recover from one crazy thing before the next crazy thing happened, and I was worn out. Still, I was trying my best to look comfortable. Sage sat across from me, one hand resting on his leg. I imagined reaching out to take it, but I couldn't.

There was something between us, and I didn't mean Tom. I was only glad Ash wasn't there to rally feeding me to the wolves in their habitat. I didn't think he'd have to try that hard anymore. Maybe even Sage would want to be rid of me at this point.

"I wanted to say sorry for the other night," Tom started, his voice cracking.

It was surprising, but it showed that he was nervous, and that helped. I straightened my back, trying to appear alert and confident. Last time I saw him, he was naked and scolding and I was bordering tears. Oh, and I'd screamed at him. Very mature memory all around.

"You really don't have to. It's ok."

Tom shook his head.

"Yeah, I do. I'm not that person. I'm really, really sorry. Mostly because you had to see me naked."

I exhaled the breath I'd been holding and dared look him in the eye. It wasn't as awkward as I thought it would be. We both laughed.

"I forgive you. If you want to be friends, though, I'd suggest maybe not chasing me through the woods as pretty much the scariest thing I've ever seen?"

He smiled nervously.

"I think that's a reasonable request. Again, sorry."

His eyes went wide as he stared at the ground. I did the same. I think Sage was smiling. Maybe even chuckling. My stomach growled. And I mean loud. It was embarrassing, but it seemed to help. Sage and Tom looked at each other and grinned.

"Better watch out," Sage replied, cocking a brow.

"Ok, ok, I promise! No need to unleash the beast," Tom cried, his hands in the air.

I laughed so hard my cheeks hurt. Sage handed me a sandwich from the basket and it took me forever to unwrap it because I was still tickled by Tom's wit. They joked a little back and forth while I started eating. One bite of sandwich in my mouth seemed too big to chew, but luckily I didn't have to talk. Sage and Tom were talking about the unfortunate naked side effects of the evo. Once the conversation died down and the sandwich was taming my stomach, I felt ready to know the harder things.

"I'm just glad you're ok," I said to Sage.

Sage tilted his head a little and gave a shy smile.

"He's good at scaring everyone. And he doesn't even have to evo to do it," Tom grinned, slapping his on the shoulder.

I shifted to sit on my knees, smoothing my skirt over them to bide my time while I found my courage.

"Can I ask what happened? I was scared that you were...um, dead."

Tom and Sage looked at each other. Tom dropped his head and clasped his wrists around his knees while he waited on Sage to respond. Sage rested back on his palms.

"But first, how's your dad?" he asked, totally avoiding everything. It would have pissed me off had I not been all too happy to report my dad's condition.

"They're releasing him next week, actually. I can't believe you could do that. Thank you."

He nodded.

"Good to hear."

I looked at him for a moment, trying to decide why he was avoiding my questions. He's the one who asked me out here to clear everything up. I gathered my hands in my lap and rubbed them together to keep warm.

"Why did it happen, Sage?" I asked again, shrugging as I looked down. I was worried he would avoid the question again and I wouldn't have the courage to bring it up.

"Because I sang for you."

I frowned, confused.

"But I've heard you sing before. Why was it different this time?"

He shifted a little.

"At the show, my voice didn't affect you because everyone else was absorbing it. This time, I was trying to remove your seal and it was a risk –"

"A stupid risk," Tom added.

Sage cut his eyes at him.

"But I had to try. Maybe it almost killed me and it was dangerous for you, but it's what I do."

I gasped.

"Dangerous for me?"

I placed my palms on the ground and cocked a brow waiting on his answer. I believed he cared about me. Possibly loved me. It made me furious that the very thing he once swore to me was a lie. I was sure there had been at least once he'd said he'd never hurt me. Yes, absolutely positive.

"Talor, it was the only option."

"It wasn't an option," Tom replied.

I thrust myself up on my feet. I'd heard enough. If I continued trusting these idiots, I was going to end up dead. Both of them had tried to hurt me in some way or another – and on the same night, too! If I was stupid enough to hang around and let them try again, I deserved my grisly fate.

I stood over them, glaring.

"Who are you, Sage? I mean, really? You think you can just bring me out here with a picnic and distract from the fact that you both tried to kill me on the same night? And somehow you think that I'd just forgive you?"

My hands were shaking from the adrenaline. Tom lifted his gaze just enough to peep out over his elbow. Sage stayed in his relaxed position, his eyes on mine. It was like I didn't know him at all, and it hurt. I expected more. He'd always been so good at more. He swallowed and parted his lips, but nothing came out.

I clenched my fists, finding that focusing on my nails digging into my palms kept me from screaming at him. I just wanted to get away. For good this time. For good. I began to march off, my knees higher with every step. I'm sure I looked ridiculous, but I was a fool. I heard Sage get up.

"I'm going to say it one more time because both of you need to hear it. He is coming. And Talor? When he does, he will take you to a world where you have no power, no friends, and no freedom. Once you're gone, you're gone, understand? Maybe no one agrees with what I did, but I was not about to be the only person in the world who has the power to try and not do it because it might offend someone."

"Offend someone? You could've killed me," I cried, whirling around.

"Not without it killing me, too."

"It doesn't change the fact that you were willing to kill me."

"I tried to save you."

I touched my hand to my heart to steady it. I knew deep down that Sage was right. I couldn't really blame him. I knew I would have agreed to it if he'd asked. I didn't know why I was angry. I breathed a little of it out, but I made myself keep moving forward.

As expected, Sage caught up with me. He took hold of my elbow and I stopped. I held my head high and stared straight ahead. He pushed his hair back past his hairline.

"It was selfish to do what I did. I'm ashamed because I know better, but I didn't do better. But God, Talor, don't forget that I'm human, too. Maybe not entirely, but I am, and I mess up like the rest of you."

"But I trusted you, and you fed from me, didn't you? You made me drink your blood. That was gross, Sage."

"What?" Tom cried from his spot by the blanket.

Sage held up a hand to quiet him.

"I have to explain. I did that because –"

"Because you wanted to and I couldn't stop you."

He put his hands on his hips and looked down.

"Is that really what you think?" he asked, frowning. There was a hint of anger in his voice, which was astounding because it was Sage.

"Yes."

"That I did what I did because I was hungry? That it was about pleasure or power and not about risking my life?"

"Well, since you never informed me of your stupid plan in the first place, what am I supposed to do, just guess?"

"What do you think I'm doing? Don't you know me by now?"

I shrugged, scoffed, and groaned all at once. Even I was impressed with myself.

"I guess not. I barely know you at all."

Sage straightened his hands in his pockets and opened his neck to the sky. He closed his eyes and stood there for a minute before opening them again. There were those gentle hazel eyes again; being the most beautiful, calming thing I would ever see.

"You do know me, just as I know you. But I'll tell you everything, Talor. Things I'm ashamed of. Things I still mourn. Things still unforgiven. I'll tell you so you can know that you know me."

I glanced back to the blanket. Tom had disappeared. I never heard him leave. Sage and I were alone.

"Go on then," I said.

"I'm sorry I didn't tell you what I wanted to do. I was scared to do it. I think I felt like if I never said anything, maybe I would chicken out. I could always just not try. But...I don't want to lose you and I didn't know what else to do."

He paused and shrugged. I knew I'd forgive him, but I wasn't ready to say the words yet. So I looked down and let him continue.

"I should've left town after I met you. Maybe that would've been best for everyone, but I'm not sorry."

I felt my throat close with emotions too strong to swallow. I finally pushed past it. I had to say things. I couldn't always cry.

"Ever since my mom died, all I've wanted is to be happy. To not always be afraid, or fighting, or sad. But ever since she died, I've felt like I was six years old again in that wave pool, drowning silently. There were people everywhere, all around me, but I would still be drowning. All I really want is to breathe just once. I really thought I had that with you.

"Part of me wishes that...I could have been off the day you came in. That we never would've met. But seeing you, it was the first time in months that I didn't go to sleep crying. I didn't feel like the world was an ocean where everyone could walk on water but me. I forgot that I was sad for a little while. But knowing everything I know now, I can't understand why we care about each other when we know what's going to happen. More than that, I can't figure out how to stop."

Sage touched a hand to his forehead and dropped it.

"I don't know how to stop, either. I only know how I feel, and that doesn't go away."

"Don't say it. You can't. We can't."

"It's too late."

I shook my head.

"You should have just left like Ash said instead of trying to fix everything. You should have just saved yourself. I don't need you to save me. I'll be fine."

"No, that's just pride talking."

He was right. I was proud. I was proud of surviving my mother's death and my father's insanity. I was proud of holding my head high when people whispered around me, proud of getting my father out of the house when he set it on fire. I was proud of standing on my own two feet when most of my friends still lived under the blanket of their parent's protection and money.

I was too proud for love. It required surrender and sacrifice. I'd already given up too much, and I didn't want anything to do with that. I shrugged his hand away and released the blanket from around me. It fell limp to the cold earth.

"Sage, what are we doing? Why don't you get out of here before it's too late?"

His voice was soft, his lips against my ear.

"There are more reasons for me to stay than go now. I have things to tell you."

I didn't care what he had to say. I could only feel his skin on mine, his body close. When he wrapped his arms around me, I just wanted to stay there and ignore the truth that we couldn't be together. But it's all we wanted. I shut my eyes as he kissed my temple.

"Keep your secrets if you want, Sage. Just don't kiss me anymore."

He slid a finger down my neck.

"But I love you, so I have to."

With that, he took my lips. It was the only ownership Sage ever believed in – the kiss.

28

Good kisses are like good coffee – they stimulate and heat from the inside, making you forget everything but the feel against your lips and the taste on your tongue.

So it was no surprise that after a rather passionate rejection of my break-up, we ended up at the Perk-U-Later Coffee Shop in downtown Cypress a few hours later. Everyone in the place was either consumed with writing a novel or snuggling on couches listening to the soothing café music courtesy of Tom.

He had taken a seat at the front of the coffee shop, chair pulled back to the far wall and guitar in hand. He had a sadness hanging about him since earlier; it was as though every motion was a struggle. I would have called him depressed if he had been human.

"Is he ok?" I asked.

Sage glanced at him and back at me.

"Yeah, he's ok."

"He just seems sad."

"We've all lost someone important along the way. Tom does this to deal. It gives him an outlet and earns some money for us to travel."

I felt a sad twinge in my chest. It wasn't so long ago that I was the one strumming a guitar in local coffee shops. But I never played because I was sad. I played because Mom and Dad were always there, always pretending to be impressed strangers talking me up to customers. Even when there were no customers, I still played and they still talked me up. Those days felt like a different life.

After we got our drinks, Sage found us a cozy corner table with high backs. A small candle in the center of the table waved hello as we sat. Sage took me under his arm so I could burrow into him. The kind-hearted Tom strummed a few chords on the guitar and no one noticed. He wasn't the siren. He was just another nameless musician in a coffee shop, and that's the way he wanted it.

"You know, I've always wondered why you ended up here in the middle of nowhere," I said, taking a sip.

Sage looked down at me from the corner of his eye. He shrugged lightly.

"It's easy to blend in. Lots of bands and bars. It doesn't seem strange that a new band would pop up overnight, and Mika and Tom are so good at circulating that people forget we're strangers. They feel like they've known us forever. Makes it easy."

It made sense, and he was right. I had only known them a few months and I forgot that until he reminded me. Tom's sorrowful tune elicited kind donations into his guitar case. It was a good song – even if he was singing in Spanish and I couldn't understand the words.

"You know, I still don't know how old you are," I said.

"I'm legal," he answered.

I rolled my eyes and stuck my tongue out at him. He scooped me into his arms and nuzzled, making me giggle. After planting a kiss on the back of my neck, he put his lips against my ear. The stubble tickled.

"Eighteen-hundred."

My jaw dropped.

"Are you seriously telling me that you are almost two thousand years old? You're too old for me!"

Tom chuckled into the microphone in the middle of his song. He was looking at us. He cleared his throat and apologized to the crowd, adopting his sad tone once again. Sage shook his head.

"No, honeysuckle. I was born in 1800. The year."

Honeysuckle?

He'd never called me anything but my name before. Oh, wait – we were already on pet names? I couldn't imagine calling him baby or sweetie or anything so silly. He wasn't actually twenty-five. He just looked it. But honeysuckle sounded kind of cute.

"What was it like living then?"

He glanced around and bunched his brows together.

"Hmmm...less clean. Lonely. Hard. But I didn't have the typical life, you know. I like now much better. Now is good," he murmured, kissing my neck.

"It is good," I said, taking a soft breath and relaxing into the lips against my skin.

I looked back at him over my shoulder, and without a word, he took my hand and we left.

Walking down the dim street late at night was never something I would do on my own. But I wasn't alone. I was under Sage's arm. A group of loud teenagers chortled their way past us, loudly prodding at each other with stolen orange street cones.

Sage switched to the outside of me before they came by. It was a small protective gesture, and sure enough, there was reason for it. One of the guys tried to jump to grab a street sign and hang from it. He caught it, but his feet flailed around and almost hit Sage in the face. The teenager cursed and jerked his feet back so he didn't hit him. He called out an apology. Sage just waved him off. I felt safe with him, truly safe. I could rest my weary soul in Sage's arms.

"I love your body," he said.

His hand tightened on my hip. I had a hard time maintaining my step. I never thought I'd be grateful for the curves I wanted to cut off with an imaginary knife. Sage's appreciation made me feel so sexy – like less of a girl and more of a woman.

"Oh. You like it, do you?" I asked, cuddling my face into his chest.

"No, I said I love it," he answered, his hands caressing even more.

"Oh, are we gonna try and out compliment each other now?" I said, swinging around to the front of him and walking backwards.

"I like it. I'll start because we already know you like the hair on my face," he said, pretending to grab and twist from his chin. "Otherwise known as a beard."

I stopped us and put my hands assertively on my hips.

"Well, maybe I was nervous! You didn't talk to me very much then. I was intimidated!"

He pretended like he was going to kiss me, but instead he picked me up from the back of my thighs and set me around his waist. I wrapped my legs around him, appreciative of a man who could pick me up and carry me around. It was nice being with someone that strong. I didn't feel self-conscious at all for not being skinny like Bex.

"Maybe I just liked listening to you," he suggested.

I don't know how he could see where we were going with me perched up on him like that. Maybe he had a sixth sense being supernatural and all. We didn't run into anything, anyway. I rested my cheek on my wrist and propped my elbow against his shoulder.

"I like your eyes, how I never know what color they are. Sometimes green, sometimes brown, but always hazel!"

He laughed.

"I like that you can admit what you're not good at. Like ice-skating. It gave me a reason to hold your hand again."

I had to kiss him after that. He stopped and brought a hand up to my hair. When we pulled apart, I hooked my arms around his neck.

"I like every single thing you say," I said.

He focused on my lips.

"I like the way you kiss."

The way he looked at me made my heart speed up. I stretched my hand back and forth across his shoulders and felt his muscles move as he walked. Inspired, he pushed us up against the shadows on the backside of the museum of Citizen's Park.

We kissed again, all lips and tongues and fingers everywhere. I giggled and put my feet down. He tried to kiss me again, so I put my hand into a knife blade against my lips like I was protecting my eyes from being poked. That made him laugh.

"Pretty please," he complained.

With wide eyes, I nodded heavily and even moved my hand, but when he leaned down again, I squealed and bolted under his arm. He froze in that bending position with a crooked smile on his lips.

"Hey! Somebody stop that girl," he called.

I ran around the building and down the stone path towards the river. I could hear him jogging up behind me. Even without his speed, he was faster than me. He caught me next to a Citizen's statue. I squawked and kicked until he spun me around straight into a kiss.

The world was wet and warm and I didn't want to run again. There I was sated, happy. We held each other against the statue, him leaning back and opening his neck for me to bury my nose in for warmth.

"Remind me. Do you like poetry, Miss Gardin?"

I groaned.

"Ugh, I hate when guys recite me poetry. It's so tacky."

He pulled me close again; this time I could feel his lips form a wicked smile. He ran a finger down the length of my necklace to where it stopped at the curve of my V-neck. My chest seemed to plump under his fingertip, but he wasn't looking there.

"She walks in beauty, like the night of cloudless climes and starry –"

I attacked him before his words set me on fire. There was too much skin and all else between us. I was slow to open my eyes, lingering on the end of a dream. With only a few fingers outlining the length of my neck to my collarbone, he walked me backwards slowly until I came against the metal bar railing lining the other side of the sidewalk. It was cold to the touch, but it did nothing to slow us down.

314

"More," I begged.

Sage touched his forehead to mine.

"I think that I shall never see something as lovely as a tree," he said, kissing the place between my neck and jaw. "A tree whose hungry mouth is pressed against the earth's two beautiful breasts."

"Those aren't the right lines," I playfully scolded.

He flashed a grin.

"Oh, they aren't? I thought you hated poetry."

"Well, I thought you were a poet's poet. Hung out with the greats and taught them genius and all that."

He placed his hands on either side of the railing around me.

"Well, I never said that, did I? Who's your favorite? I might have known them."

"Keats. If you knew him and didn't save him, I'm breaking up with you right here and now."

I took his coat collar in hand while he rested his hand over my thigh.

"Knew him," he said, grimacing.

"No, you didn't."

He grinned.

"I did. And he liked dying, actually. Couldn't convince him to stop once he started."

I slapped his shoulder and he scooped me up again. I wrapped my legs around him, resting on his interlocked hands under me and enjoying being at his height.

"So this is what it looks like to be tall. A different world, huh?"

He looked up at me for once.

"You wear heels taller than me some days. I've seen them."

"How else would you see me way down there? A girl's gotta do what a girl's gotta do to get noticed."

"Oh, I saw you."

"Do you have eyes on the back of your head you haven't told me about?"

"No, just the normal two that like looking at you."

He smiled as I slid slowly down. I meandered over to the statues and dragged my hand across them as I walked around. He followed. When I got to the last of them, his hand found my hip again from behind. I stopped, my own hand dropping from the cold concrete and taking ahold of the thigh of his jeans. His arm crawled across my stomach like a snake, encircling me in his heat.

"It's cold," I said, backing into him so there was no space between us.

He gently moved my hair and touched his lips down to my bare shoulder with a kiss.

"Come home with me."

I rested my head back on him.

"I'm scared to."

"Why?"

"Because this thing," I said, pulling back my sleeve.

It's what I wanted, too. But I couldn't risk it. I'd already knocked him unconscious once, and Spencer was still missing. I always said I'd wait until I was married to have sex. I promised mom, promised myself. That was still my plan, too...but I never wanted to marry a vampire. And one had already started calling me his wife. But Sage was the one you wait for. Even my mother, dead as she was, could see that.

"I'm cold," I told him again, shivering this time.

It was so quiet we could both hear my teeth chattering. I felt him start to take off his jacket and caught his hands. Oh, those precious freckled hands. The freckles were there, but they seemed fewer and fainter.

"No, I just want your hands. They'll do."

"Ok," he said, holding me tight.

"Why do your freckles come and go?"

"You noticed that, did you?"

"I notice everything about you," I said, blushing.

He felt so strong against me. I wanted to merge with his body and just live in it. Two souls, one skin. It felt possible in the world now. His voice was low, soft.

"Think of it like supernatural camouflage. Makes me harder to find. That's kind of important for me, you know?"

I found it fascinating watching the freckles fade as I brushed my fingers across them. I guess the more I touched him, the less he wanted to hide.

"Then you came to the right place. Cypress, I mean."

"Yeah, I did."

His beard scruff tickled my neck as he kissed it. His lips were so near my pulse.

"Is it hard for you to kiss me there?"

I felt his head move from side to side.

"No."

We looked out towards the dark river in front of us and listened to the white noise of the rush. He breathed in deep against my skin and lifted his head. I touched the place on my neck where he had been kissing.

"Is it terrible that I want to be yours?" I admitted, half-ashamed.

I couldn't believe I said that to Sage. Even worse, he seemed to feel the same way. He loosened his grip on me.

317

"What's wrong?" I asked.

"I want you to be free."

"I am free, but I'm also yours. I think I'll always be."

His hands recoiled completely, so I turned to face him. The weather was cold, but not so cold as Sage was right then. He looked like he wanted to tell me something that was hard.

"No, you belong to yourself. I want you to understand that. It's important. It's why I'm risking my life. It's the whole point of what I do, Talor."

I pushed away.

"Belonging isn't slavery, Sage. It's called a relationship."

He ran his hands through his hair.

"What is this? I thought you understood."

"I just want to be close to you."

His lips stretched into a thin line.

"I can literally feel everything you feel right now. No one else in the world can do that. How do you not feel close to me?"

"You can feel me. I can't feel you. And I never will because of this thing I can't wash off and you can't heal."

"Don't do this."

He reached out to me, but I moved back against the statue and crossed my arms.

"What am I to you, Sage? Just some girl you kiss?"

"That's not what I meant and you know it."

I blinked hard and fast. I wasn't going to cry now. He would just want to console me and not listen to anything I had to say. He came towards me, but I held him off.

"No, you're going to listen to me. I remember the night I saw you with Valerie. It nearly killed me, Sage, and that was before –" I stopped, swallowing hard, "you ever kissed me and I wanted us to only belong to each other. So don't judge me for wanting something special with you. Don't you dare judge me!"

Every movement of his was sluggish to give me time to react. He brushed his knuckles against my arm, knowing I would jerk away. I didn't want to be difficult; it was just the emotional response whenever he kissed me. They were true feelings, though. I never forgot that night. I knew it wasn't his fault. He didn't choose to be what he was.

But I was angry.

Angry he couldn't break the seal. Angry that I couldn't give him everything I wanted – my heart, my body, my blood, even. I was a china doll he could barely touch, and I wanted him so much I would gladly break. I kept from crying somehow, maybe because he wasn't touching me. But he knew how I felt, and it was all reflected in his eyes. He started talking to me like I was some animal caught in a trap.

"I wish I could say whatever you needed to hear. I wish that you were free to do everything you wanted to do. I want that kind of life for you. That's what I'm fighting for. That's what I mean. I never like feeding on humans. I don't feel held back by you because we can't do that. I feel free because it's the only time I forget – because of you. I don't judge you."

I relaxed against the statue, unhinging my elbows from their physical fortress around my heart.

"This isn't fair."

"Nothing about us is fair."

He took me into a tender kiss, lavish and desperate. It melted my anger, leaving my heart entirely his, whether he wanted it that way or not. Just

319

then, Sage's head snapped towards the walking path near the woods. He straightened, pulling me protectively behind him as his fangs extended. In that moment, I was afraid the Grigori had come and it was all over. The trees gave way after a furious rustling, swaying fight with invisible monsters.

Soon the monsters weren't invisible anymore.

29

It was Mannix. That was bad enough, but he wasn't alone, either.

"Manky," Mannix admonished, wagging a finger at Sage.

The guy with him was younger than Mannix; he barely looked old enough to drink – alcohol, not blood. He had a thick bundle of driftwood hair looped into dreads down his back. He crouched down and studied Sage.

After he was finished looking him over, he turned his attention to me. His manner changed from speculative to submissive. It was a little hard to believe the switch.

"Good evening, princess. My name is Nico."

There was that term again – *princess*. I hadn't heard it in a while, but now it started making sense. Sage stood in front of me protectively, but we all knew they wouldn't hurt me. I tried to move in front of him, but he wouldn't let me.

"Sage, please."

I held up my arm. It was visible, and the letters were illuminated. When they saw it, Nico and Mannix bowed the knee. I slowly lowered my arm, never expecting to see something like that.

"There will never be a time when it's right for you to stand in front of danger for me," Sage said simply, keeping an arm across me so I would stay behind him.

I wanted to call Tom, but he was half a mile away playing tearful songs for spare change. Not in the best state of mind for a fight, but still. Mannix and Nico paced the empty park, cracking their knuckles. Sage ignored Mannix and focused on the younger one.

"You keep poor company, kid."

"Is it true what they say about him?" Nico asked Mannix, concerned.

Annoyed, Mannix dropped his head back and sighed. Then he slapped his hands together and spread them out.

"It'll hurt, but ya heal. Pull your socks up."

Nico still looked nervous, but he nodded in agreement. Their eyes went black and fangs extended. Sage moved me back to the other side of the statue, never looking away from them. As Sage tensed up, a silver-blue fire began rising off his skin. I was touching him, and it didn't burn me.

It crackled bright in spurts, like when he drew in a breath he didn't even need. He was building up energy or something, and that's when I realized he might evo in front of me. I reached out and grabbed his arm. It was hard and cold, like something set in steel.

"Sage, don't. Come with me."

His eyes had already begun to change as he shed his shirt. His body was changing slowly, like he was fighting it. It was something I couldn't recognize. Not like a dragon or a werewolf – things I'd seen before. He looked

322

different, like something more human than animal. With that, he left me by the statue. I hid behind it.

When I looked back out, they were all three standing around, but now there was some poor woman with them. I looked harder and saw that it was Valerie. Mannix bit into her again, drinking so viciously that I was sure her throat would be torn apart. When he was finished, he let her drop to the ground. He gave a contented sigh and looked straight at me. Blood was dripping off his chin.

Not missing a beat, Sage took him by the neck and threw him. Mannix vaulted through the air and caught himself low to the ground, limbs spread wide and a maniacal laugh echoing across the empty park.

"Wanker," Mannix hissed, touching his throat.

The wound was strange. It glowed with the same kind of light as the letters on my wrist. He and Sage became a furious blur, and I could only see what happened every few seconds when one of them stopped moving to slam the other into the ground.

Nico joined in, adding his fists to the fray. I ran over to where Valerie lay lifeless on the grass, a gray sheet of ash taking over her skin. I bent down and felt for a heartbeat, but I knew I wouldn't find one. She was already gone.

Shaking frantically, I searched for my phone. When I couldn't find it, I grabbed Sage's jacket. I didn't know how fast the guys could make it, but we needed them. I found his phone and looked back to the violent scuffle still raging. Sage had Nico by the arm. He broke it, making him scream. He hurled him into Mannix, and they became a clump of bodies.

Mannix was quick to push Nico away to lunge at Sage, and both of them cut their nails against the other's bare skin. I stood frozen in the moment, unable to do anything but watch. They swiped at each other until wells of blood gushed from both. Horrendous glowing welts and slashes formed across the skin where clawed hands had been. How they were still standing was a miracle. Sage took Mannix by the leg and pulled hard enough for a loud pop, dislocating his hip.

Mannix collapsed to the ground with a throaty growl. Limping heavily, he retreated to where a huddled Nico was waiting. They swayed and shivered as they shamelessly cursed Sage's name. Sage was cut, but his wounds were already closing and theirs weren't. I think they still wanted to fight, but it didn't look like they physically could.

With a parting glare, Nico and Mannix gathered themselves up and disappeared into the woods. Sage waited until he was sure they were gone before he faced me.

"It's safe now," he coaxed, gesturing for me to come out.

I looked to where Valerie had been laying, but she was gone. I gasped, looking left and right to see where she went.

"I think they killed –"

He moved quickly around the area, searching for movement. When he didn't find any, he came back and rested his hands on his hips.

"I'm so sorry," he sighed, dropping his head.

I wiped my nose.

"But her family, Sage."

He didn't know what to say to that, so he just looked at me. I wouldn't move from the statue. It felt safe being sheltered by a large stone. Sage bent down to scoop up his jacket and shirt off the ground. I fixated on the dark entrance of the wood trail, still a bundle of nerves. I feared they were hiding there just out of sight. The murderers.

"Will they come back?"

Sage shook his head and made his way over to me.

324

"No. It'll take them time to heal."

As he walked, I watched the blood on his skin seep back inside him as though it had a mind of its own. It was eerie to watch.

"How does it do that?" I asked.

His hand went across his dry chest as he stopped.

"It just does."

Once all the blood had gone back inside him, he pulled on his shirt and let it drop over his fully healed body. I couldn't grasp what I was seeing. How could blood act like that? It was like the blood was magnetized to something inside him and it returned regardless of how much was spilt.

I shivered against the statue, the winter air finally catching in my throat and lungs after the adrenaline faded. I began to stumble over my thoughts and my thoughts began to stumble over my lips.

"You just... you're already healed? I mean, I thought you have the band as, like, bodyguards because you're wanted and everyone's trying to kill you and all, but you're...you don't even need them, I mean –"

"Hold out your arms," he said, gesturing to them.

I let go of the statue and stretched my arms out.

"Ok, like a scarecrow? Sage, that was amazing. You weren't even scared."

He wasn't acknowledging me. He seemed somewhere else as he slid his jacket over one of my arms, then the other. It was too big, obviously, but I didn't mind. He pulled it tight and looked down at me.

"I was terrified. I thought he sent them to take you. There could've been a hundred of them and I wouldn't have known. I just want to keep you as long as I can," he finally admitted, bringing a shaking hand to my cheek lightly.

I reached up and took his hand, steadying it. For once, I would soothe Sage. That's one for the record books.

"Keep me?" I asked, stroking his fingers.

"You're not afraid of me, are you?"

I brushed his arms next, going over every curve and muscle as I took in a deep breath.

"I'm not afraid."

He watched me studying his arms and sighed in relief.

"In my darkest moments, it's my father in the mirror. It's what keeps me from going too far."

He closed his eyes, ashamed. I shook my head. I didn't want to talk about his father. I wanted to ignore the shaken up version of Sage forecasting the impending doom. So I did the mature thing. I changed the subject.

"What's it like to be that strong?" I asked, feeling the muscles jump under his skin.

He tipped my chin up and touched a finger to the middle of my chest. My heart thumped against it.

"You should know."

He just took my hand and led us along the cracked sidewalk back like nothing ever happened.

30

The band house was supposed to be safe. The problem was that there were dozens of strangers making bad decisions as far out as the curb. The couches lining the porch were hardly able to bear the load of idiots on them, and the drinking games they were all playing were sure to be the end of someone's life and/or dignity.

Sage took my hand as we started the walk up the lawn to the front door – which was unhinged and all but removed. I felt safe with him as we walked through the crowd. Mika met us near the door with two beers in hand. He held them high over the crowd.

"Heyyyy, make yourselves at home."

Sage let go of my hand and took Mika close.

"A bad time to draw attention to us, Mika."

He rolled his eyes. Bloodshot eyes.

"We've been here for months playing shows. They know. Besides, never miss an opportunity to make some new fans, right? Saving the world one fan at a time? We're just trying to do our part."

It was weird having tension between those two. Sage stole a quick concerned glance at me as two teenage girls stumbled over to Mika. He handed them the beers and nodded, putting his arms around both.

"There's a quiet room in the back. I'd offer mine," he said, shrugging.

Sage blinked hard.

"But your room is the kitchen."

Sage and I looked over at a sleeping bag under the kitchen table. Without a word, Mika winked before disappearing in the crowd. I looked at Sage, who took my hand and kissed it. Someone pushed past us in a hurry, forcing Sage violently against me. He glared after them.

"Now you know why I live alone," he said.

We started trying to make our way back out, but we didn't get far. Mika began playing guitar on top of the kitchen table and everyone trampled their way inside to hear more. When Ash joined in with a drumbeat from another corner of the house, the crowd began to burst at the seams of the rooms. The song must have been one the crowd recognized because they started singing in drunk, off-key tones. Sage turned his narrowed eyes towards Mika.

"Where's the singer?" someone called.

The crowd got louder as they cheered at Mika playing wild guitar on the table. There was a strange air about the place, and even though I didn't know what was wrong, I knew something was off. Girls dragged their hands across Mika's thighs as he strummed the guitar and threw back his head to sing notes everyone else tried to mimic.

"What's wrong?" I asked Sage, trying to be heard through the crescendo and party noises.

"Mika," Sage said, ignoring me.

They were looking at each other the same way Sage and Mannix usually did. Mika gave a wink and a smirk as he jerked the guitar across his body for a loud, echoing note. He mouthed the words "can't hear you" to Sage.

When the crowd started swaying and yelling for the singer again, Sage whisked me into a side room that I could only assume was a makeshift studio. There were a few microphone stands and large headphones leaning against a tall stool. A drum set guarded the corner and several guitars were lying around. Foam padding all along the walls made it muffled from the party chaos.

"What's wrong? Something's wrong, right?"

"Yeah, listen –"

Sage stopped and turned his head quickly like he heard something. Whatever it was, it was urgent. He sprinted out of the room to the next one. With no attempt at subtlety, he kicked open the door. It was pitch black in there, but he had no trouble seeing whatever it was that made him angry.

He stood in the doorway, blocking my path, but I was able to see under his arm. It was Ash and a girl. They were lying together in the rectangular line of light from the hallway. Ash's lips were red, his eyes bloodshot just like Mika's. The girl on the floor didn't move. I couldn't tell if she was dead, and it made my heart stop. Sage looked into the room harder and pushed open the door and flipped on the light.

Oh God. It wasn't just a girl. There were several people in the room, and there was more than one pool of blood. The walls began to spin as it crossed my mind that I was looking at a mass murder scene. Without thinking, I shut the door behind us so no one would see. Great. I was an accomplice.

I slammed my back against the door.

"Are these people dead?"

"Oh, calm down, Pollyanna," Ash muttered.

I couldn't stop looking at the bodies in the room. How could they carry on a conversation in the middle of that? Sage listened to Ash bark while he calmly went around to each of them, testing for life. He would touch them on the foreheads and a soft light would go out of him into them. Soon after, they would stir.

I silently watched Ash, who was still slouched against the closet on the floor half-clothed. He wiped back his dark bangs from his face and rubbed his tongue against his teeth. He was licking the remnants of blood off them like they were cookie crumbs. He didn't even look my way; he had nothing but disdain for Sage.

"Look at you, *bràthair* – the portrait of self-control. You know the price we'll pay for being here, so don't you dare look at us like that. Leave us poor bastards alone."

Sage stood up from the last one and slowly faced Ash. He was furious, but he kept it reined in. Barely. Even Sage had limits. I was afraid of what would happen, so I wrapped my arms around Sage's neck and buried my face in his chest.

"Take me home, Sage. Sage?"

It took me saying his name twice, but his attention finally broke and he nodded. Ash scoffed as he got to his feet. He was acting like a belligerent drunk, but I knew there was no way he could be. It's not like they could get drunk. Sage took me under his arm and watched as Ash tried to steady himself against the wall. When we left the room, Sage closed the door behind him.

"I have to stay. I have to stop this before too much damage is done."

"Don't. They'll just drag you down. Please."

I gripped him at the elbows thinking I could force him to leave with me. He didn't budge.

"You saw what happened in there. Two of them were almost dead. If I'm not here, there will be bodies in the morning. Bodies I can't heal. What we're doing will be in vain if I leave them like this now."

Sage stopped and looked over my shoulder. A bunch of drunk, ridiculous girls were watching us. I began to panic. I didn't want him to be alone with girls like that. Not when everyone was acting strange.

"Sage, you aren't responsible for them. Don't stay. I'm begging you."

I looked back and saw Mika making out with multiple girls. Ugh. It made me feel sick. Then I remembered Ash in a room full of people bleeding to death. The party was only an excuse for the band to binge drink on blood. Sage was special, but he said himself that he was still human...and he wasn't above things like that, not when they were so readily available.

"Trust me. Try."

"How long will you stay? Will you come over after?"

"I'll meet you at the car. Just give me a minute here," he said, disappearing back into the crowd.

When I was leaving, I saw Tom standing near the door, so I pulled him aside. He was always the most levelheaded, the most reasonable. I could reason with him. Usually.

"Tom, Ash is hurting people."

He wiped blood from his own lips before giving me a dry response.

"Relax."

331

"I'm sorry, what? This isn't right. You can't treat people like a buffet!"

Tom sighed and took me by the shoulder, leading me out on the lawn.

"Careful now. You can't say stuff like that."

"What is going on? Ash almost killed a roomful of people in there!"

He glanced around to be sure no one heard and then grabbed at the back of his neck, wringing it in frustration.

"We can't fight our hunger all the time. We are what we are. No one's gonna die."

"Well, that's why you have the roadie, right? Isn't that what you said?"

Tom looked down at me like I was a little kid asking for more candy.

"Are you serious? One roadie? There are four of us."

"You're being disgusting right now. I can't believe you're ok with this."

He cracked his neck and let his arm drop to the side.

"Talor, this is hard to say, but you need to leave. Sage can't feed with you here and he needs to. He's weak and he won't tell you that. Someone needs to."

That hurt – imagining Sage feeding off some girls. I'd already seen it once and I never wanted it to happen again. Maybe I was Pollyanna. Maybe. But Sage was mine. I twirled his keys in my hand nervously, unable to get the thoughts out of my head. Tom's tone softened. I could tell he didn't want to hurt my feelings.

"Talor, he can't get what he needs from you. Please just go."

I finally found my voice.

"Was this a setup so he could feed? He doesn't want to. You know that."

"You're right, he doesn't. But he needs to. He's being hunted every second of every day. He needs strength. If you care about him, you'll look away."

"I do care about him, so I won't look away. You shouldn't, either."

"You need to go now."

I took a step back and bit my lip. Tom was never like this. He was more polite as a werewolf almost eating me in the woods. He knew it hurt when he said that, so he pushed his palm against his forehead and took a deep breath.

"Look, Talor. You know I don't like saying these kinds of things. We all like you. You know that, right? It's just...we were born men and monsters, and we have to feed the latter sometimes. We don't like it either."

"Then don't do it."

He shrugged.

"Don't eat, don't drink. Tell me how you feel after a few days of that. Weeks. You'd be dead. We just become dangerous and dark and can't control the evo. We aren't proud of it."

I shut up then. He was right. I was treating them like they had a choice. While they were supernatural, they still had limitations. I just looked away, tempered. Tom's tone had finally turned sympathetic.

"If there was any other way, you know we'd do it. None of us believe in feeding on humans. But eventually our bodies reject syphoned blood. It's not how we're meant to feed. It's intimate, feeding on someone. We aren't beasts tearing at flesh, Talor. It's personal, no matter how vicious it looks. It's like sex," he admitted, smiling when he said that.

I shut my eyes tightly and waited before speaking.

"I say if you're going to be different from your fathers, then be different."

Tom looked wounded, his eyes glistening. I didn't know then that he wasn't wounded because of what I said. He was sad because of what he was about to say.

333

"You know nothing about our fathers, Talor. But you will. God save you, you will."

I shook my head at him and wrapped my jacket around. I turned and left, noticing the debauchery all around me. Sage was somewhere in the mass, but I didn't try to find him. If he wanted to forget himself for the night, I wouldn't remind him. I didn't want to leave Sage, but I was afraid of what he was doing. Maybe they were right and it wasn't my place to keep them in check.

When I got around the corner to Sage's car, a sick, pale figure came shuffling out from the bushes. Had it been Halloween instead of just before New Year's, I would've believed someone dressed up as a zombie.

"Talor," it croaked, familiar and hoarse.

When I looked at the face, I could barely find words. Spencer? He had been missing for months. The police all but pronounced him dead. A myriad of emotions rolled around inside me. Whatever was closest to the top came spilling out. It turned out to be anger.

"Oh my God, Spencer? How dare you show your face! You know they almost arrested me because of you? Where have you been?"

As he stepped closer, I noticed strange crisscrossed whiplashes on his neck. There were deep red circles around his eyes like bruises and blood. He was thin. Way too thin. It looked as if he'd been starved for months. His once beautiful, sharp blue eyes were a hollow, drab shade – like oceans drying up. He had to steady himself against a tree to stay standing. I didn't know whether to help him or get in the car and drive away from all of them.

"What happened to you?" I asked, the anger fading. I was worried about him. He needed a doctor, like, now.

He waved my question away in the air like he was physically trying to slap it.

"No t-time."

I stepped closer to him, holding out my hand.

"Sage is inside. He can help you. You look so terrible."

He leaned over and retched with such a wicked sound that it resonated in my own bones. I took another step towards him. He was not okay. Definitely not okay.

"Spencer, wait here. I'll go get Sage."

"No."

Spencer dropped to his knees with a sigh, one that felt as delicate as my own emotional state. I could see his bones through his skin. I started to run back inside, but Spencer caught my leg. He shook and coughed.

"Bring me to water."

"Bring you some water? Ok, let me go and I'll –"

"No, just...bring..."

Unable to finish his sentence, he fell down on the pavement. I quickly got down beside him, checking to make sure he was still conscious. He had blood oozing from his mouth. He looked like he'd been beaten repeatedly and the whiplashes on his body seemed fresh – as if they happened mere minutes before. I touched one of them and it began to glow in sync with my wrist.

Um...

Just then, I noticed something coming out of the shadows to my left. His dark hair framed his face and covered one glowing eye. I could see his teeth, though – shining in the dark through a sick, twisted grin.

"You did this?" I asked, glaring at Mannix.

He clucked his tongue.

335

"Oh no, that was your handiwork. Now, if you don't mind, princess –"

He started towards Spencer, but I stepped between them. Mannix furrowed his brow as I glanced at Spencer, who couldn't even open his eyes. I wanted to go get Sage, but I couldn't leave Spencer there. Luckily, I didn't have to. Sage got to us so fast only the rush of wind made me aware of him. He was glowing with a misty haze on his skin. I knew it meant he could become something bigger, scarier, darker and meaner in seconds.

Mannix took a step back and narrowed his eyes.

"Your days are numbered."

"I've got more than you do, I promise you that," Sage replied.

I knelt on the ground to check on Spencer. Mannix shoved his hands in the back pockets of his jeans. His chin went high in the air.

"You're full of –"

His head was on the ground before he could finish his sentence. The guitar Sage used to decapitate him was the same one Mika had been playing minutes before. It was glowing the same color as his skin. Blood oozed from the broken strings and splintered the guitar with a hanging sour note. I guess Sage took care of two problems at once.

Sage's skin faded back to normal as he kicked the mutilated body with such force I thought it might break in half. I had a hard time regaining my breath after watching that.

"Thank God," Spencer groaned. "He needed to shut up. So damn annoying."

Sage let go of the guitar and as he hovered over the body lying at his feet. It was as though he was waiting for it to come back to life. I looked at Spencer.

"He was a Hench. Henches –" Spencer said, stopping midsentence to cough, "can suck my disappearing dick."

Sage still hovered over Mannix. I couldn't understand why he was acting like he was going to get up. Mannix was missing a head. Spencer raised his feeble hand into the air and Sage gave him a high-five without looking away. I had to smile at that.

"Talor, I want – just want to apologize," Spencer wheezed, bringing me back.

His skin was nearly bone now. The thick blonde curls that once caused such chaos in the women he crossed were withering away to white strings. I cradled his head, smoothing the hair beneath my thumb in an attempt to soothe us. Pieces fell away. Chunks.

"Did I really do this to you?"

"No, don't listen to that tool."

Sage nodded as he said that. It made me feel a little better. But then Spencer began to breathe with such labor that I knew he had little time left. Sage looked back at us over his shoulder and wiped his bloody hands off on his jeans. He walked over and knelt down beside him.

"We'll get you there."

Just then, all the guys showed up. The grave scene sobered them quickly as Sage took Spencer to his feet. He was so thin now it was probably like carrying a bare skeleton.

"He was followed," Sage warned, ushering towards the woods.

Tom rushed off to hunt while Mika began cleaning up the pieces of Mannix and the guitar. Ash came with us to help with Spencer. We drove off into the night, led by headlights and heavy hearts for the grim task ahead.

31

The river wasn't far, but I was so lost in thought watching the dark trees whizz by that we could've passed an entire state without me knowing. Spencer laid in the backseat wheezing, shuddering every now and then to let us know he wasn't gone.

Not yet.

The words felt alien even in my mind. The moon was brighter than I wanted it to be. Too bright and all too happy to cast shadows on the ground. It was blinding. The road beneath us screamed of guilt and white noise. It was my fault we were here, doing this. No one spoke.

I could tell Sage kept looking my way to check on me. I curled up in a ball against the car door, my head cradled by the thin strength of the seat-belt. My hair was trying to escape through the cracked window beside me. I wanted to fly outside with it, to escape. But even it was tethered to my terrible fate. I had all but run out of tears by the time Sage finally said something to me. His hand reached out and brushed my thigh.

"Hey, honeysuckle."

The words were quiet and sweet, but I didn't like the nickname anymore. Tears and snot blended into a sniveling cocktail on my face, and even though I was heartbroken for Spencer, I wasn't ready to be comforted. I was barely able to believe it was happening at all. I shook my head and looked back at Spencer, whose eyes were closed.

"Why did Mannix say I did this?" I whispered, knowing it was the only volume I could control my voice in. Anything louder and I'd be blubbering.

"To hurt you, Talor. The Grigori did this," Sage assured, his thumb rubbing lightly against my leg.

In the back, Spencer suddenly sputtered what had to be blood. It was a jarring sound, throwing us out of the conversation. Sage caught Ash's somber gaze in the rearview. Spencer grunted and groaned, muttering about his head hurting. Ash tenderly held Spencer's head up for him to breathe easier. It seemed to help – as much as it could help to delay the inevitable.

Spencer sounded like he was drowning in himself. I looked back as we passed under a bright lamppost along the road and saw the damage. As soon as I saw it, I wish I hadn't. Ash's forearms were covered in blood.

Spencer himself was so saturated that his head kept slipping through Ash's hands. Blood surged from his ears and nose. Ash's usual self-composure dissolved as I started to sob, finally releasing the pain I was trying to keep caged.

"Sage, get her under control! He can't take that right now. I'm barely holding him together as it is," Ash bellowed, frustration and fear dominating his tone.

"Do something for him, Sage," I cried.

"Our power has limits, Talor. We live in this world, too," Sage said, trying to stay calm and drive ridiculously fast at the same time.

He knew Spencer didn't have long. We all did. I was just the only one who was human enough in the moment to show it. I couldn't grasp how Sage could fix everyone in the world except Spencer and me. Not only could he not save him, he couldn't even ease his pain. He was supposed to be the siren. Wasn't he the only one who could anything?

"What's the point in having the power to heal if you can't actually heal anything?"

Ash eyed me, but he was looking with pity this time. I think it was because he realized how young and naive I was about their world.

"Talor, it's not that he won't. He can't," Ash said.

I searched their faces. Sage stared straight ahead, and Spencer couldn't muster the strength to form a facial expression at all. Right about then, Sage veered off into a field off the dirt road. It was bumpy and rough as the grass slapped against the tires.

Small bushes scraped the side of the car as we rolled through. He brought us to the left corner of the field and turned off the car. He ran a hand over my hair before getting out.

As he came around to my side, I sat up a little in my seat and wiped my nose. Ash carried Spencer and I hurried along beside him, holding Spencer's hand. When Spencer gave a warning kind of sound – the kind that elicits natural haste – Ash quickened pace and I had to let go.

"He's fading. Hurry," Ash urged, taking longer strides to move ahead.

My hand was slick with blood, and I stopped to watch him hurry off through the woods. It occurred to me to stay right there and wait until it was over. I didn't want to see Spencer die. I couldn't move. Luckily, Sage wrapped an arm around my shoulders.

"I'm here," he said, squeezing me.

I only walked on because he stayed with me. We came to a clearing on the banks of the Flint. Ash had already laid Spencer on the ground beside the flowing water, and he was talking to him quietly. The noises of the river were calming.

Spencer seemed to relax as his hand dipped in the river, the raspy, bloody gurgling quieting into a delicate sigh. It was the most incredible thing. It was all I wanted in the world right then – just for Spencer to feel no pain. I was never more grateful than in the few moments he laid quiet, his breathing soft and steady, and those eyes almost bright once again.

"You never sent me pictures of you in that bikini. I still think about that," he said, his voice a little stronger.

I almost allowed myself to hope in his recovery. I believed he would be ok for the longest of seconds. I knelt down beside him. All I wanted to do was hug him, but he was a withering light and the slightest touch from me would put him out.

"I guess I should have played a little bit harder to get," I said, smiling and crying at the same time.

His chapped, broken lips curled.

"Hey, Cotton Candy?"

"Yeah?"

There was a shimmer in his eyes that was fading, but it flickered for a moment.

"I caught you a little bit, didn't I?"

"A little bit," I confessed, tears blurring my vision.

Spencer was a faded autumn leaf, barely clinging to life through the wind, but he was still that bright-eyed, arrogant playboy I'd learned to call friend. I loved him in some way neither of us expected. Sage and Ash quietly moved away, giving us space. Truth is, I forgot they were even there.

"I'm so sorry," I said, whimpering.

"It's about time you apologized. My feet still hurt from being stepped on. But I wish I could've taken you all over the world, Cotton Candy," he said through shallow breaths.

They were all he could really take. It was like his lungs were shriveling up.

"You literally say that to all the girls," I said, laughing as I wiped away tears.

I kept trying to pretend I wasn't bawling. I don't know why. I guess I was afraid of the feelings. Afraid they were real. Afraid he was really dying because I had killed something that was supposed to be immortal. Afraid of what that meant. Spencer's feeble hand reached up and brushed against the wild, wind-blown hair that escaped from my ponytail.

"We really were friends, weren't we?"

"Yeah, we were."

He was quiet for a moment.

"Still in the damn friend zone."

I smiled back at him, but my lips were trembling and my tears were pooling in the cavernous cleft of what was once his muscular chest. I couldn't think of a single thing to say to him, but I don't think he expected me to.

"I've known centuries of women, but you're the one I'm most glad I knew. Wish I could've known you better."

With that, he gave a pained wink and I had to smile. Sage bent down beside me and clasped hands with him. Sage covered his knuckles with a soothing hand and they whispered to each other. Whatever language it was, Spencer seemed to understand. A faint smile found his lips one last time.

And then he was gone, and it felt like the there was no air left in the world.

Reverently, Sage and Ash took him up and together went waist deep into the dark waters. They released him and moved back as he began to glow and evo into a sea serpent – scales of an iridescent blue tinted by silver. It was the color of his eyes, their light.

We could still see him going under, the glow from his body like a lighthouse off in the distance. After that, he flickered out, and a mist rose from the water and kept rising until it was gone. It pushed the water back and splashed against us at the riverbank. The river was dark again and all of us stood silent.

I gasped and fell into Sage's arms. He wrapped himself around me as I cried. All I could think was if I had just been strong and not let Spencer kiss me, he would still be alive. I laid there in Sage's embrace with the weight of that on me. I had killed my friend.

"I mean...is that really it? Where did he go?"

"He's gone," Sage shushed.

"He can't die. You're immortal," I sobbed, my voice breaking.

Sage's arms tightened. He rested his head over mine.

"Everyone dies, Talor."

I tried to push away.

"Don't touch me. I'll hurt you, too," I cried, overcome with fear of my own body.

He held tight.

"Stop this. You can't, Talor. You can't hurt me."

344

It was good to hear those words, but I knew better. I'd already put him in a coma once. Well, technically he did that, but still. I buried myself in his chest, weeping. I just wanted to wake up from a long dream. He felt so warm against me; it was like being wrapped in a blanket. When I finally was able to look at him again, I found a gaze mirroring my despair.

He leaned down and kissed me. His fingers wiped a few tears away – ones he could catch. His eyes circled my face, aching, wishing he could help me. I could see it. Ash stood silent nearby, waiting.

When Sage glanced over at him, he started off towards the car to give us some privacy. I looked out towards the river, the quiet of it almost alarming. It was still like a pond instead of a river. I think Spencer had something to do with that.

"Come with me," Sage pleaded.

"I don't want to need you."

He took my chin in his hand.

"But you do. I know. I need you, too."

His voice broke slightly at the end. Honesty. Vulnerability. Need. I could relate to that. I decided to take his hand and follow him home. Ravaged by tears and the eternal darkness of death by my own hand, I could think of no good reason to suffer alone.

32

I stared at the sky through the wood blinds of the window, watching it get lighter as the minutes dragged on. Night eventually surrendered to day. During that time, I replayed every moment from the night before in my weary mind. My memory had to be wrong. Spencer couldn't be gone. It was a joke. Some elaborate prank, just like the disappearing act at the Victorian Gala. But I wasn't sure I could convince myself to believe that.

I knew only one thing for sure: I had to be dreaming. I wondered when I would wake up at Goodlife. Maybe I would get written up for falling asleep on the job. Spencer would harass me, Sage would watch, and I would do embarrassing things in the name of lust.

I was lost in some lucid daydream for a long time, fading in and out of reality and memories. I didn't know how I had any tears left, but the remainder rolled down onto Sage's pillow.

I was lying in his bed, but he wasn't in the room. He got up and hadn't come back yet. I smothered myself against the pillow, crying so hard that my body heaved. I felt a hand touch down on my shoulder, but I didn't bring my head up.

"Some water?" he asked, his thumb rubbing against my exposed skin. For the first time, his touch felt like sandpaper. My nerves were so raw and close to the surface even the air felt like too much.

I kept my face covered, but I brought the pillow away for him to hear me.

"Make this a dream. Make it – make it stop being real. Tell me it's not real. Tell me. I'll believe you, I promise."

He sat closer, taking me by the shoulder and turning me over.

"I wish I could."

I brought the blanket up to my head and curled up.

"I'll never be okay again, will I?"

"Here – drink this," he said, offering a cup of water.

I took it and drank, not realizing until then how thirsty I was. When I was done, he took it away and lay down beside me. I could tell he had been crying, too. His eyes were swollen.

It hadn't occurred to me that Sage had just lost someone, too. Someone he'd known way longer than anyone I ever knew. I imagined what that must be like – to know a person for centuries and lose them. I would never understand his pain, but here I was wallowing like I was the only one hurting. I reached for his hand and took it.

"I'm sorry, Sage. I know you lost him, too."

I scooted a little closer to him and pulled his hand up between our chests.

"It never gets easier," he said.

348

I stared at his lips.

"What happens to your kind when you die?"

"Talor, this isn't the time."

"What happens, Sage?"

He sucked in a strained, heavy breath as he rubbed my fingers.

"Well, once we're dead, there's no heaven or hell. There's not even a grave. We're just gone."

"So...Spencer?"

"Yeah, he's gone. Only the Grigori have the power to split us like that."

Maybe he told me that to make me feel better or to help me forget. But I didn't. Now I just knew that Spencer didn't exist anywhere. It was like he never existed at all, and I'd been the catalyst to that.

"If only I hadn't kissed him that night."

"No, don't do that to yourself. The Grigori would have discovered the truth about him sooner or later."

"What truth?"

"That he was part of the Dissent. He played both sides. Has for centuries. It was dangerous, what he did. But no one was better at it."

As Sage's kind words about him sunk in, it seemed I found out all too late how wrong I had been about Spencer. He was good. I just never knew that side of him.

"So it's their fault...and my fault?"

"No, it's not your fault at all. Spencer knew what he was doing. He just didn't care. He was always going to do what he wanted. Always. No matter the cost. And Rami, he —"

"Wait, Spencer knew about this Grigori seal? How could he see it and Ash and the others couldn't? When did he know?" I asked, knitting my brow.

"He couldn't see it. If he...when he tried to seal you for himself, he probably only knew then."

Something about his answer ached. It felt muddy, like he wasn't telling the truth. Sage knew the danger in pursuing me all along. That's why he stood back and watched. So he let Spencer...the realization sat me up suddenly. Sage followed, holding onto my wrists.

"You didn't tell him because you knew what would happen," I said, shooting a glare.

I jerked my wrists away and threw the covers off. Sage was beside me that fast.

"Talor, that's not true. I would never do something like that. Spencer was my friend."

"You were jealous the whole time, weren't you?"

He opened his mouth to answer, but I held up a hand.

"Did it ever cross your mind that he would try to bite me? That he wanted me? Didn't you think it was a possibility?"

He took a deep breath and looked me squarely in the eye. His response was so poignant, his words so heavy, if he had said it above a whisper, I would have collapsed from the force of them.

"I just – never thought that you would let him."

My heart spiraled in my chest. I didn't know what to say. No matter how I tried to twist it so that Sage was at fault or Spencer was at fault, I knew I never should have given in. The worst part was that deep down I knew I never actually wanted to be with Spencer.

I just liked the way he pursued me. I liked the thought of a jealous Sage. Spencer was dead because I wanted Sage to be jealous. I grabbed my head, trying to control the throbbing.

"Oh my God, what you must think of me now. You think...you think," I whimpered.

Sage held up his hands and tried to corral me as I wavered left and right, eyes wide and distraught. Sage thought I was smarter than I really was. He didn't tell Spencer of the Grigori seal because he never thought I would fall for him. I had no idea how to feel about that.

"No, I don't. You're just tired and you need to rest," he replied.

I shook my head, staring at the ground.

"I'm so ashamed. God, you put me up on some pedestal, Sage. I'm not perfect. I'm so embarrassed."

"Please don't."

His tone was gentle and pleading, but I refused.

"I don't know what to do. I just want to die," I sobbed.

He wrangled me into a loving hold.

"Talor, stop all this."

I broke away.

"No! I need to get away. Oh God!"

He stared at me.

"Ok, I'll take you home."

"No, I don't want to see you anymore."

"What are you talking about?"

I kept taking rapid breaths, knowing what I was building up to. It was a panic in my chest causing the ruckus.

"You have all these powers, but you can't make this right. You can't bring him back. You can't make me forget. You can't get this off my body! We just need to end this."

"This is grief. You need to feel it, not run away."

351

"No, this is me seeing things for the first time. Why does it feel like I know you less the more I learn? That's not how it's supposed to be, Sage. I think it's because we're not supposed to be."

"Don't say that."

I ignored him and gathered my things. I needed to get out of there fast or he would find a way to get me to stay. We both knew it. He closed his eyes as I passed.

"Please," he said.

I opened the house door and left. He stood there in the doorway as I fumbled my keys to get in the car. He kept his distance. It was a good thing, too, because I almost hated him right then. I never thought I could. I wanted to get somewhere safe and normal, not rampant with supernatural drama. Spencer was gone, and he was already haunting me. But after mom and the ghost at Bosh's, I could handle that.

It was Sage I could never look at the same way again.

He respected my wishes for a full day. In that time, I tried everything to feel normal. I tried reading several books, but I never got past the first page. When I thought I'd been reading, it turned out I was only staring at the page. Bosh wasn't around, so no one was able to break my thoughts up into conversations.

By the time night fell, I had worked myself into an emotional frenzy. First, it was from fearing what would happen if the detectives discovered anything about Spencer and came asking more questions. I knew things. I'd seen his death, and not only had I been a witness to it, I was an accomplice in it. I could never explain how it happened; I could merely admit that in the truest sense of the facts, I killed him.

Once I released that unfounded fear (I mean, we were talking about Cypress detectives, not Sherlock Holmes), I found a new, more gut-wrenching one to tremble under. I replayed every syllable from my breakup with Sage and soon an ominous feeling came over me. *Would I ever see him again? And if I did, would he forgive me? Would he understand why I walked away?*

And the hardest, worst, most terrifying one of them all: how would I ever live with myself if he died because I left him?

It was nearly eight o'clock when I heard a car come roaring up the driveway. Even before looking, I knew it was Sage. His car stared eerily through the windows from the driveway as the rain pelted the windshield. I peeked out the shades and my heart dropped.

I could make out Sage's silhouette in the driver's seat. He didn't get out and I didn't go out. We stared at one another through glass for a few minutes while I tried to imagine what I would say.

He turned off the car and came up to the house. We looked at each other through the glass exterior door. He was soaked to the bone, his eyes pleading. I opened the door for him. When he got inside, he pulled off his shirt and threw it down.

Of course I'd seen him shirtless before, but something about him soaked in rain, vulnerable and frustrated and lovesick...I couldn't help but stare. His freckles spanned across his body. I wanted my fingers forever on his skin.

We stared, neither able to speak. The house phone rang and startled me. Happy for the interruption, I hurried over and read the caller id. Telemarketer. They get the machine. I turned back to more important matters – Sage standing half-clothed in front of me.

"We're going to talk about this," he said.

I thought I would have more clarity by then. I'd spent a day away from the drama, but I was in worse shape away from Sage than with him. Sage didn't move from the wet mat inside the door. He just kept this intense look pointed at me, throwing around that power he wielded so tenderly.

He pulled off his shoes with gusto, flinging them against the brick. I fumbled all over words in my head, and it wasn't pretty when they finally made it out.

"Um, no – we're not. I can't. I just can't," I managed to spurt out. "I'll dry your shirt."

I snatched his shirt from the floor and marched off towards the laundry room. He followed.

"Do you really think I'd set Spencer up? I need to know you don't really think that."

I turned on the dryer.

"Tumble dry on low, right?"

He didn't answer. I rounded the corner out of the laundry room and saw him there, his hands on his hips.

"I don't think less of you because you cared about him. That isn't what I meant."

I bit my lip and gave a slow nod. Satisfied, he wiped a hand across his stubble and bobbed his head.

"Ok, good...so that's all good. I didn't want –"

"You should leave."

"No. You're scared."

"I mean, of course I am. Is there any reason I shouldn't be? I don't even know this Rami and he's going to rip me away –"

"No, that's not what this is about."

"Yes, it is. Do you even realize what you did to me? You ruined my life. You and Spencer and your father! Don't you understand that I lost my mom and my dad and now I'm going to lose everyone else in my life?"

I felt the sob start to rise, but I swallowed it whole and threw the shirt against the wall. I'd forgotten to put it in the dryer at all. The dryer hummed its electrical tune, filling the dead air between us. I couldn't look at him. It took all of my energy to contain my tears. Suddenly, he was in my space. I wanted him there, but I stopped him anyway.

"I don't want to do this, but I can't deal with everything. I can't – I just can't, Sage! I think this thing between us is a mistake. We both know how it's going to end. You need to leave before Rami comes for me."

I couldn't help but notice the nervousness in his voice. No, wait. That was my voice.

"I'm not leaving."

"Who's Adair?" I asked, suddenly remembering the name. I have no idea where it came from or why I decided to ask him about the girl right then.

Sage's forehead relaxed just as the muscles in his neck tightened.

"Who told you about her?"

"Who is she?"

"Who told you about her?"

"Wow, he really was right," I scoffed, nodding to myself.

"I don't want to talk about her. I want to talk about us."

"There is no 'us' anymore!"

"Come with me."

I paused, dumbstruck by what he just said. If we were in high school, it would be called running away together.

"I can't just run away from my life here –"

"You have to run from the Grigori, Talor."

"I have school and a job, Sage. Remember? I mean, when's the last time you went to work? Haven't you been fired yet?"

"We'll come back when it's safe."

I laughed at him.

"You mean when you figure out how to kill an immortal, right?"

I knew there was no escape from the Grigori. I was just a human, and I had no powers to fight. I had no choice. Sage was unfazed.

"I've evaded the Grigori for centuries. We can do it. Maybe it isn't the best life, but it's the only way we can do life together, and that makes it worth it to me. Come with me. We'll leave right now."

"No, I can't – my dad, Bosh. I can't just leave them."

"Then tomorrow. Come on, Talor. We can be happy. We can be together."

His confidence was intoxicating, but I had to stand firm. So I lied.

"I don't want that. I can't trust you and if I hadn't harassed you into being with me in the first place..."

He shifted his weight and toyed with the keychain attached to his belt loop.

"Are you kidding me?"

"All I know is that I can't save you and you can't save me, so we need to end this right now."

I wasn't fooling anyone – not even myself – but I was telling the whole truth and I hated it. I had done all the damage to myself that no one else could do. I wanted to block off the emotions welling up. I didn't want to let Sage in.

We had only known each other for a few months and soon he would be killed or I would be kidnapped, and there was nothing we could do to stop it. We were set on a destructive path, and this was my last chance to put on the brakes. Maybe one of us would survive.

"You're scared," he replied.

"I know," I cried, getting frustrated that I couldn't make him leave.

"Because you're in love with me."

My teeth were clenched so tight my jaw began to ache. I never wanted to fall in love. I wanted to be this strong, confident woman, not some self-conscious little girl who needed applause every time she pronounced a new word right. He eased towards me with this hopeful look on his face. I looked at him this time. I was angry, but I didn't want to miss him looking like that.

"It's scary to say, but you're brave," he urged.

My mouth went dry as he gave me a look that said he needed to hear the words. I knew it was over. The feeling right before you say I love you the first time is just like drowning. I know because I almost drowned in a wave pool when I was six.

He was all around me now, and his arms weren't pleading – they were possessing. He was both the waves and the rescue. I started to panic, so I reached a hand up for help and it caught in some of his hair. I had only a second to decide whether to breathe in death or shatter my chest instead.

"I love you."

The words inhaled us both as his lips closed over mine. There, in that moment, I breathed my last broken breath. I drowned in him and his love, and what a blissful way it was to die.

33

Sage agreed to let me say goodbye to everyone.

Of course they didn't know it was goodbye. I went to see dad. He was so happy and healthy. I bawled at the end of the visit, which thoroughly confused him. I spent the night before talking to Bosh and watching her favorite TV shows.

The day we were leaving, I got up early. I wanted to spend some time with Bosh before embarking on an adventure that meant I might never see her again. I awoke to the familiar sounds and smells of her cooking breakfast for me in the kitchen next to my room.

Bosh was always awake by four in the morning, and I regularly slept until one in the afternoon. Every now and then, she forced me awake so she could cook for me. She would burst through my bedroom door blaring praise and worship music from the old radio in the hallway. I couldn't make her understand that I had an alarm on my phone to wake me up when I needed to get up – or that I didn't work in the morning.

I think she just enjoyed cooking for somebody, like most grandmothers. I appreciated it more that day than ever before. Completely unaware of my dilemma, Bosh laid a plate full of eggs, bacon, and sliced buttered toast in front of me with a warm smile. She rubbed my upper arm swiftly as she sat down next to me.

"Tell me, Talor, how are you? I don't see much of you now. How many jobs are you working? You are too skinny. You aren't eating enough."

Bosh was always worried that I was starving myself since mom died. In her defense, I did kind of forget to eat for a few weeks. Once I moved in with her, she made sure to cook every meal for me. It didn't matter whether or not I actually wanted to eat; she always had a hot meal ready. I took the fork she handed me.

"Bosh, you know I don't go to work until three this afternoon, right? I don't need to eat breakfast this early."

She shook her head and touched the edge of her glasses.

"Well, you were up, honey. And breakfast is for the morning, not the afternoon. It isn't healthy to lie around until one o'clock. You look like you are losing weight again."

I had only lost about ten pounds in six months, but I was smaller than she was used to. I rolled my eyes.

"I'm not losing weight, Bosh. I promise."

She peered at me from over her glasses and took me by the elbow. Without a word, she led me a few feet over to the scale she kept conveniently by the kitchen table. Why she kept it there in the open kitchen instead of hidden with the shame of the bathroom, I've never figured out. She pushed me up on it as best she could – being less than five feet tall and over seventy. We both looked down at the number. I had lost weight. Five pounds. I kept my celebrations to myself as Bosh scowled.

"Your promises are no good. Sit down and eat. I will cook more."

She immediately went to the refrigerator and grabbed a tube of butter. She scooped out a spoonful and plopped it on my eggs. The yellow wax melted slowly, pooling into oily reserves on the plate. I fought the gag reflex as she pointed. I obeyed. Bosh had a way of making anyone do what she said. Tiny and feisty, that woman.

While I gobbled down butter eggs, Bosh eased herself into her recliner with the morning newspaper in her lap. I discreetly scraped as much butter off the eggs as I could and wiped it off with my napkin. The only sound in the house for the next minute or two was my fork scratching against the glass plate as I shoveled the next bite into my mouth.

While sinking my teeth into crispy toast, I spent a good minute thinking about how many miles I would have to run to work off the gallon of eggs and butter. When I finally looked at her, her face was white, her hands trembling as they held the paper.

"Bosh? What's wrong?" I asked, concerned.

She ignored me, but her eyes raced across the black and white ink. She was immersed in whatever she was reading.

"Bosh?"

The panic in my voice broke her attention away. She lowered the newspaper and looked over at me, smiling through her wrinkles. Her expression was normal, but the color in her face wasn't. Something was off.

"Yes, honey? How were the eggs? Better?"

I grimaced.

"Um, they're great...are you ok?"

Her voice was singsong, like she had just stepped inside from strolling through a garden complete with musical woodland creatures.

"I was just reading. Two more bars closed down. They went out of business. That is good to hear, isn't it, sweetheart? Do not be late to work, honey."

I cut my eyes and walked over.

"Well, what were you reading? Let me see," I said, reaching for the paper.

She quickly tucked it under her arm and sat back in the recliner. Patting me on the thigh, she then proceeded to scold me for being curious.

"Go on now. I washed your uniform. It's in the dryer. Let me know if you need me to iron your shirt. I hate when young people go around with wrinkled shirts. The sight of it."

I forced a chuckle. She was hiding something, and it was bolded on the front page of the local newspaper. It's not like I couldn't see it somewhere other than on her doorstep. I rounded the corner to the laundry room and looked back.

Bosh crinkled up the paper with such angry force that I thought I was imagining things. She tossed it in the trash and huffing, left the room. Whatever made her upset was worth digging through the trash over, so as soon as she disappeared, I scurried over to pull it out.

"Bosh, thanks for washing my uniform. I don't think I'll need you to iron anything," I called, listening for her.

Her voice answered from back of the house.

"All right, dear. Now don't be late."

I reached down and pulled the paper out as quietly as I could. I unrolled it, seeing the story about two more local bars closing from losing customers. It was strange, but not nearly as strange as the headline of the newspaper.

LOCAL FARMER DISCOVERS CROP CIRCLE.

I only had enough time to scan the article and the oversized picture beside it before Bosh found me. I jumped, not sure why I was worried about her knowing what I'd done. It wasn't as if I'd stolen money out of her purse.

"Bosh, why did you throw this away? It's probably just some kids playing a prank for attention. It isn't real."

She paused before saying anything.

"I threw it away because it was trash, honey."

I lowered the paper. Her tone was somber.

"Why did it upset you then?"

"Oh, I have heard of this before – when I was young. I never thought I would see something like it."

I shook my head.

"Do you mean a crop circle?"

Finally! I could bring up the crop circle photo. She was reluctant to answer me, of course. The look in her eyes was one of an old fear. She once lived in a world very different than this one. Whatever memory was unfolding in her eyes, it seemed fresh.

She took my hand and led me back to the table. I sat down while she paced, clasping and unclasping her hands together nervously like she was about to tell me I was adopted.

"My grandmother once told me a story of seeing one when she was sixteen. She said that she was walking to school along the road one day with her sister when they noticed it. No one could figure out how it got there. Soon after, people started disappearing."

I felt like I'd just been told a ghost story. I tried not to look spooked, but I knew something she didn't – I was about to disappear, too.

"People disappeared? Anyone she knew?"

"Yes, an old friend of her sister's. She was a few years older than them. They never did find her."

"They never found her? What do they think happened?"

Bosh looked away.

"My grandmother was a strange woman. Nobody believed her story."

I leaned my cheek in my hand and methodically ran my nails across my other thigh.

"Well, how did they explain the crop circle?"

Bosh knit her brow.

"Why do you ask that?"

I gulped.

"I saw the photo in the old album, Bosh."

She looked angry all of a sudden. So angry her lip began trembling.

"Talor. This is my house and you should not go through my things!"

I straightened quickly and turned towards her. I had to fight the urge to go stand in the corner. Bosh only ever used that tone on me as a child.

"Bosh, I didn't go through your things. Please don't be mad. I thought you took it out and it was ok to look at."

"Did you touch anything?"

Bosh's uncharacteristic response scared me, so I lied.

"No, I just looked at things."

She was still angry, but her expression softened.

"Oh honey, that is good."

"I'm sorry. I didn't mean to upset you."

"It is all right, dear."

Bosh looked out of the window, so I rubbed her hand. I could tell she was uncomfortable even recalling the story of her grandmother seeing a crop circle. But I couldn't let it go. I had to know if she knew anything else. Things like I knew.

Her blank stare at nothing outside said more than she ever would. Her gaze was fixed. I followed it to where she was looking and saw a handful of people standing by the wheat field near the house.

"Will you see what it is, honey?" she asked, touching me low on my back.

I nodded and hurried outside. When I got there, Bosh's neighbors were all pointing at something in the wheat. When I walked up to it, my heart dropped. I could see the edges of a massive crop circle – one that wasn't there the day before.

"Who did this?" I demanded, looking around at all the other bystanders.

Bosh's neighbor, Mr. Croft, shrugged. He was an old farmer. His usually sullen, aging eyes suddenly seemed vibrant.

"Never seen a thing like it in my life, darling. It wasn't here yesterday, though."

Mrs. Croft came up beside me and wrapped a hand around my shoulder.

"You don't have any friends who might like to play a joke on you, do you? Because it is still trespassing on our property."

"No, ma'am."

Another man who had been walking around the length of the circle came up to join us. He was wearing a greasy old baseball hat. When he lifted his head, I knew it was the same old man from the cemetery. My breath caught in my throat. He noticed me before I could slip away.

"You should get back inside your home, miss. Safest place for you. All of you, really," he warned, eyeing me.

Mrs. Croft fidgeted and mumbled to herself, waving her hands senselessly in the air.

"What do you think? Aliens did this? I never heard such foolishness. A bunch of young kids trespassing on private property."

Jet took off his hat and wiped his brow. He looked straight at me.

"No, ma'am. Nothing like that at all."

"Should we call the police?" Mr. Croft asked.

Jet looked back at the crop circle.

"Won't do a bit of good. I'll handle this, Larry. Alice. You folks go on back home."

They exchanged looks. Reluctantly, Mr. Croft nodded.

"Well, all right. We'll call the police to report it. Young 'uns shouldn't be roamin' on private property anyways!"

Mrs. Croft looked down her nose at me. She was a tall woman with a nose to match.

"You make sure to tell your friends that! I saw that boy driving up here the other night. Sure he didn't bring any of his friends?"

I cleared my throat, remembering my manners.

"No, ma'am. He was alone."

She nodded as they headed off towards their house. Jet put his hat back on his head and waited until they were out of earshot.

"You need to get inside a human home. Don't leave once the sun goes down. They can't enter without an invitation. The sons can, but the fallen can't."

I started to pace.

"Are you an angel?"

Jet lowered his head and touched his wrinkled hand to his heart.

"I am."

366

"Then take this off me!"

I held out my wrist. Jet looked at the shimmery skin.

"I do not have the authority."

I pointed to the crop circle.

"What is this? Why is it here?"

"It is how the fallen travel outside their strongholds. These symbols open the earth like a combination to a lock. What you see is the movement underground," he answered, squinting as the morning sun rose higher in the sky.

"Well, if it's like a door or a portal or something, can't you just lock it back?"

"It takes time. The symbol not only stirs up the earth, but all the beings within it. There are dark things coming this way, child, and even I cannot hold them all."

Staring at the crop circle made me shiver.

"Please help me."

He was quiet a moment.

"You must leave this house, this city. Go now."

"I can't leave my family!"

"You must go far from here, and waste no time. If you delay any longer, it will be too late."

I closed my eyes while I soaked in everything he said. When I opened them, he was gone. I was left standing in the middle of a crop circle alone. It felt alien and cold on that once sacred, safe ground, as though things were stirring beneath my feet that could reach up and grab me through the dirt.

I always thought that it was worse putting a dead person in the ground than facing anything that could come up out of it. Now I wasn't so sure. I kicked at the dirt, angry I'd delayed leaving. I could've gotten hundreds of miles away by now.

I watched my breath materialize in the winter air while I thought about what was coming. The crop circle was supernatural proof that I was being hunted, but I wouldn't make it easy for Rami. I didn't waste one more second standing in that field.

I took in a deep breath and prepared myself for the end. And then I ran home – too fast for even the hounds of hell that were coming after me.

34

I still hadn't figured out what lie to tell Bosh when I got back inside. The timing was terrible. It was unsettling how we had just been speaking about the crop circles when one popped up in the field next to Bosh's house. I made myself wait outside until I caught my breath from running. I didn't want to alarm her. My phone began to vibrate in my pocket, but I ignored it.

"What has happened?" Bosh asked.

"Oh, well, um," I started, but my phone kept vibrating. "Just a second, Bosh."

Frustrated, I looked down and noticed that Azalea had called me four times in a row and it was obvious she wasn't going to stop until I answered. Bosh was still looking outside where we had all been standing and I was grateful she couldn't see the crop circle from the house. As she made her way towards the door, I licked my lips so the lie could slip through easier.

"Just some trespassers. They said to stay inside until the cops came. Hey, can you make some coffee? I'm pretty tired," I asked, rubbing my eyes and yawning.

Bosh nodded and moved to the kitchen. When my phone rang for the fifth time, I answered.

"Hey, now is not a good –"

"Something's wrong with Jesse!" Azalea cried, her voice frantic.

My heart sunk.

"What's wrong with him?" I asked, closing my eyes.

"He's really sick! Please come. I don't know what to do!"

"Oh my God, call an ambulance, Azalea!"

She just started sobbing on the other end of the line, so I knew I needed to go. Whatever was happening, she needed me. Bounding into my room, I grabbed my purse and keys.

Bosh tried to catch me as I ran past her.

"Honey! What is wrong? Where are you going?"

I grabbed her around the shoulders in a fast hug, kissing her white hair and breathing in deep. Her coarse hair got caught in my lips as I pushed them against her forehead. I was afraid I would never see her again and I wanted to remember everything about her – including her smell. It was coffee grinds and cooking oil, and I fought a tear as I accepted the counterfeit scent.

"Stay inside. I love you," I said, my voice cracking.

I floored it all the way to Azalea's house. I was stressed out not knowing what I was walking into. Nothing could prepare me for the scene I found. Jesse was shirtless and pale, his hair wet and dirty. He was bleeding from gashes on his shoulders. It looked like he'd been beaten up. He stared straight through me as I froze in the doorway. Azalea appeared around the corner, shaking her head through tears.

"Thank God you're here! I think it's drugs. That's why I didn't call the ambulance. What do we do, Talor?"

Oh no. Just like Rose. It wasn't drugs, but I couldn't tell her that. I closed my eyes and looked down, trying to decide. Sage. We needed Sage. He was the only one who could do anything.

"He's in shock, Azalea. Cover him with a blanket."

Azalea whimpered and nodded her head. We moved towards the couch and grabbed a thick throw. I wrapped it snug around his shoulders and took his cold hands in mine.

"Jesse, try to focus. Did something attack you?"

For some reason, he just began mumbling to himself like the roadie Dead Reckless kept around. I knelt there for a minute listening to his senseless banter. He was talking to himself like it was one of us. He stood up and started stumbling around all over the house. I took out my phone to call Sage.

Just as I found his number, I heard a loud thud. Out of the corner of my eye, I could see something on the hallway floor. I arched to look and saw Jesse lying facedown. He wasn't moving. I ran to him and knelt down to feel for a heartbeat. He had one. I breathed a sigh of relief. But there was vomit on the floor.

"Azalea, bring a rag," I called, trying not to get sick.

I helped him over to the couch so he could lie down. As I tossed the blanket back over him, he got really emotional and started crying.

"What if I'm g-getting...sick like...your mom, Ta-alor?" he slurred, shivering.

A twinge of sadness and confusion ached in my chest. I didn't know why he would ask something like that. I paused to look at Azalea, who had returned with a glass of water and tears rolling down her cheeks. She tossed the rag on the floor and buried herself beside him on the couch.

"Then we'll take care of you," I said, subdued.

My answer made him cry more, so I'm not sure if it was the right or wrong thing to say. I hugged him. I knew I would have to call Sage, but I stared at my phone. If I did this, Azalea and Jesse would know about him. They would know what he was.

I heard the other end of the line ring once before Jesse started thrashing around on the couch and screamed like he was being tortured. Azalea tried to hold him down.

"Do we take him to the hospital?"

Jesse swallowed hard and grabbed Azalea's arm.

"No hospital. He said no hospital!"

"Who is 'he'? Who were you with? Tell us, Jesse! Who did this?" she screamed.

Before he could answer, Jesse's eyes rolled in the back of his head and he passed out. Azalea covered him with a blanket and hysterically started dialing 911. I dropped my own phone and grabbed hers, hanging it up. She nearly clawed my eyes out trying to get it from me.

"No! What are you doing?"

I grabbed her.

"Azalea! Azalea, they can't do anything for him. I called someone who can help, but you have to calm down. Things are about to get really weird and you need to control yourself if you want to help Jesse. Understand?"

"But I've seen this before," she cried, going limp in my arms.

"What do you mean?"

372

Azalea was staring at the wall.

"Remember Valerie? It was after trivia one night. She went outside to smoke, you know. I stayed inside. When she went out, she was herself. When she came back in, her eyes had changed. She became withdrawn, like she was high or sick or something. She's never been the same."

I touched her hand. Valerie was dead, but she didn't know that. It suddenly occurred to me that I'd seen so much death lately that I'd nearly been desensitized. She didn't even know her friend was dead. No one did yet.

I watched her stroke Jesse's forehead. I needed to tell her. It was time. I hesitated, but with everything coming to a head so quickly, there was no more time to keep things to myself. Everyone around me was in danger now, and they had a right to know why.

"Azalea, did you notice if there was a mark on Valerie's neck that night? Something like a bite?"

Azalea sobered up quickly. Her forehead crinkled in thought. After a few seconds, the lines flattened and she cut her eyes at my feet.

"You mean like Jill from Harvest Moon?"

"Well, actually, yeah."

"You've been keeping things from me."

"Yeah...I mean, God. I've wanted to tell you for some time, but it just never got easier. I always thought it would. Maybe once I got used to it, I guess," I answered, a bit ashamed of myself.

"If something you know can save his life, please tell me. I don't care how crazy it is."

I took in a deep breath and squeezed her hand. Then I told her everything. When I was done, she brushed her hair out of her face and sat back. She seemed to take it all in stride – maybe a little too well, actually.

"So, why didn't you tell me this? You think I'd steal your special boy-friend or something? Have I ever stolen a guy from you?"

"My God, you actually think this is about a guy? Don't you think I questioned my own sanity for a while? We're talking about vampires, drag-ons, and werewolves – things that are supposed to be fake."

She gave a short laugh and shook her head, looking up at me.

"I always thought that Spencer of yours was a demigod. He turned out to be one after all?"

I bit my lip and tried to turn away before she caught the terrible truth in my face, but I wasn't fast enough. Spencer's death was still too new, too fresh. I wasn't skilled enough to bury it from view.

"Oh my God, Talor – what happened?"

I took a few steps away. I heard her get up and come over, but I turned and flashed a smile before she got to me.

"I was kind of hoping all this would turn out to be some super realistic dream and we'd all go back to failing college. Mostly I was hoping I wasn't actually going crazy. And I didn't want you to think I was."

"After being friends for fifteen years, you really think I'd call you cra-zy?"

"How could I know? I don't know anything anymore. Not what's real, not what's fake. I don't know what's going to happen, just that I have to leave."

Azalea blinked hard a few times.

"You were just going to disappear on me?"

"I don't have a choice, Azalea."

"If there's anything I know about you, it's that you are the strongest person I know, and you're not doing this alone anymore. I'll go, too."

I hugged her.

"I wish you could come, but I don't want you involved. The only reason I'm safe is because of this thing," I replied, showing my wrist with the iridescent ornate seal.

Azalea squinted and tilted her head.

"I saw you get that. It was at their show, right? Was he there – this, um, Gregory you mentioned?"

I covered the seal. It felt like an evil eye that could see everything. Hear everything, even.

"His name is Rami. Anyway, I still don't know how or when I got this. Listen. I want you to stay away. It's dangerous."

Azalea's eyes softened. She seemed to understand. She was loyal, but she knew what I was saying was true. She stood up and took in a deep breath.

"Tell me how to help you."

"Stay away from anyone involved in this. Mannix, especially. That means me, too."

"No. You need a friend now more than ever."

She didn't question my sanity once after everything I just told her. Even after explaining how dangerous it really was, she wouldn't leave my side.

"No, not in their world. We don't have any power in it."

"You do."

"I don't have power. I'm trapped with no way out. But there's no reason for you to get mixed up in all this."

"Yes, there is. My best friend. You're my reason."

She gave a little nod before gazed at the swirling fan above with intensity. She crossed her arms in front of her and rotated the ball of her foot into the carpet. Jesse was quiet and calm for the moment.

"I need to ask you something, but I don't want you to get mad," she said.

"Go ahead."

"Could you really marry Sage's father? I mean, his *father?* That's really weird."

My lips dropped open for the words to come out, but they never formed a single word. Not one sound. Barely even a breath passed through. That moment was when I knew. All the while, we'd been skirting around the fact that I was being pursued by an immortal evil.

I had no ace in the hole besides Sage himself, and in that moment, sitting with my best friend, I knew I would rather face marriage with a vampire than watch Sage die for me. I felt Azalea's arms wrap around my shoulders and was glad for it. She held me as the tears marched down my cheeks.

When the doorbell rang, I made Azalea stay with Jesse while I went to answer it. I furiously wiped away all the tears that had escaped during my revelation. The massive door squeaked open to reveal Dead Reckless standing on the stoop. Sage was in the front resting against the doorframe by his palm. He looked out from the top of his eyes.

"How did you...come?" I asked, puzzled and tripping over the words.

Sage still had that effect. Luckily, everyone was used to me. Mika flicked his cigarette away and blew the smoke into the air.

"You still haven't hung up," he answered, pointing to the phone in the floor.

My phone. The one I used to call Sage and dropped to keep Azalea was calling an ambulance. The one that heard everything we'd said in the last ten minutes. Sage and I shared a haunted gaze.

"Azalea, hang up my phone on the floor, please," I called weakly.

Sage pushed himself off the doorframe and took his hands along the sides of his jeans and into his back pockets. His chin went into the air and looked down at me through a sigh.

"I'm here to help your friend, but then you and I need to talk in private," he replied coolly.

I felt myself flush when he said that, and it reminded me of the time he chased after me in the stairwell. Azalea was suddenly behind me peeking out. Her eyes were wide with curiosity. She looked at them like she was watching a dinosaur come alive in a museum.

"So do you need invitations to come into a house?" she asked.

Mika winked.

"No, doll. Just being polite. Who runs in a stranger's house? That'd be weird. No manners at all."

Azalea invited them in. Sage brushed my cheek as he walked by and hovered over Jesse, reluctant to touch him.

"Is this what happens when one of you, um, you know?"

"Uh, no, no, Azalea. Remember, they don't do this. They're the..."

Azalea arched her neck.

"They're the – what?"

Looking at Ash, who was always a little less than warm and welcoming in his manner, I cleared my throat.

"Good guys."

Tom leaned over the couch and watched Jesse wriggle.

"That's malicious. Someone wanted to make a point with this guy," he said, arching his brow.

Azalea fought her way to Sage's side.

"If it's true what Talor tells me, please help him!"

Sage nodded. I stood across the couch from him beside Tom. Sage took in a deep breath as he knelt beside Jesse. The mood in the room was tense and strained, everyone looking around at different things to busy their minds until Sage would reveal the cicatrix.

I held Azalea's hand as we watched, leaning against one another for support. Sage brought the cold metal of his bracelets down to Jesse's wet skin. Ash had been rubbing his chin thoughtfully, but when the seal flashed bright and sizzled, he leaned forward and raised his brows to see what it said. He asked Sage something in that language I'd heard before. Azalea and I darted glances at each other as Sage responded.

"What language is that?" she asked, her eyes growing to the size of her fists by her sides. She'd forgotten she was holding my hand and it made me yelp in pain.

"Ow! I don't know what it's called," I told her, wincing.

"It's called *Yahweh-Elata*," Tom answered. I didn't notice how close he'd been standing.

Sage looked over his shoulder at us.

"He's going to be all right."

Azalea hugged me and breathed a sigh of relief. Sage turned his attention back to Jesse. He brought both of his hands up and over him like he was feeling for something in the air. Whatever it was, he found it with speed and suddenly stood up. His hands began to illuminate with the softest light. It looked like the sun was outlining him.

He reached down touched Jesse's forehead and light passed into him. Sage exhaled and stepped back, his hands shaking. It was quiet for a few seconds until Jesse cried out in pain as he started to burn red and blister like he had chicken pox. Azalea let go of my hand and rushed over.

"What'd you do? I thought you were supposed to heal him!"

"He is healing. It'll take a little time," Tom reassured.

"It didn't look like this at the Journey," I replied, blinking nervously.

Tom and Sage looked at each other.

"We can handle this if you need to, you know, talk," Tom said, gripping his shoulder.

"Yeah, I need to say a few things," Sage said, offering his hand. I took it and followed him outside into the afternoon sun.

35

We went to the gazebo overrun with a spectacular overgrowth of ivy. Only in South Georgia could you have gorgeous ivy in the dead of winter. We inadvertently passed the same place Spencer had kissed me almost three months before. I felt such sorrow remembering the consequences of that night.

We hurried at a quickened pace to a grove of trees with sprawling arms of bone-gray bark. There was beauty in the bare oaks, the moss splayed in the limbs and the cracks in the trunks from stormy battering. They were testaments to better times and served as scars of survival. My heart bore the same marks.

Sage had been leading us along the beaten path when he suddenly turned and took me in a desperate kiss. I didn't expect him to do that, so I stumbled. He caught me fast, wrapping us up in a swell of heavenly heat. He was aggressive, pawing at my hair as he pinned me against a tree.

His fingers dug into my body, demanding obedience and surrender. I was grateful for the fleshly curve of my hips to cushion his greedy hands. I folded delicately under his advances, responding in earnest with lips and tongue as he willed.

I wondered if this is what it was like inside Sage's head all the time – the clashing of desire and desperation. I respected the strength it must've taken him daily to face such powerful demons and quench them under that gentle demeanor. It made sense that I shouldn't hesitate to obey. He wielded the quietest kind of power. His breath was hot on my cheeks as I became smaller against him so he could possess me whole.

"We never have the power we want, Talor," he said.

"What?" I asked, confused.

"I wish I could make the sun stand still forever," he said, sighing.

I had a hard time bearing the weight of his frame as it leaned against me, allowing nothing between us but deep and abiding primal instincts. I wanted him that close; needed him, in fact. When he kissed me again, he devoured what was left of my self-control. I moaned at the break, something I would never have done in my polite mind, but under the circumstances, I couldn't control myself.

I was going to let him have me right there – open air, chaos reigning, right in the middle of the day. I had a brief thought of my mom wagging a disapproving finger somewhere, but it vanished with the next sensual attack. I opened up for him, arching back; an encouraging show that I was willing to go where he would lead.

My brows hugged together as Sage laid claim to my naked neck, kissing and gripping with possessive lips. No biting. He knew better. I was melting from the inside out, and it was pooling in a fire between my thighs.

LONG LIVE DEAD RECKLESS

There was a haphazard restraint in his hands as if he was maneuvering around an invisible fence. We were acting like we would both die if he couldn't keep his hands on me. I finally gave voice to the truth mounting between us.

"I want you," I admitted, my voice fluttering with excitement and terror.

Months of burgeoning feelings finally formed resolute words in the air often so thick between us. He stiffened as he made a sound, one of division. He eased up but remained close, leaning back a little so I could look up into his eyes. I found them blazing with bright color in a soft focus, settling heavy on me. The look said he meant to do what I asked.

My eyelids were hard to hold open, but he was sexy in some new way and I wanted to watch. I braced against the great oak behind me, not from fear, but from rabid anticipation. The coarse bark clutched bits of my exposed skin in protest. I didn't care. I barely felt the snag, consumed only by the feverish way he was holding me.

Reaching one of his hands out, he traced my neck until it landed at my collarbone. From there, the fingers fanned out to cover as much skin as possible. The tips converged at my cleavage, which was advocating my will. His eyes lowered to where his fingers felt, and mine finally closed in expectancy. His hand brushed across my breast, but it didn't linger there. His thumb trailed behind, catching the farewell from my skin arched beneath the shirt.

Suddenly, his touch went away. I felt abandoned, shamelessly whimpering in protest. His hands returned, but not where I wanted them. They went to either side of my face. I felt a dip in excitement as they relaxed, barely touching. I opened my eyes, confused. He was looking at me the same, even if his hands weren't handling me that way.

"Can't," he pleaded.

It sounded like he was speaking more to himself than to me. Instead of charging on through the dazed apprehension, he lowered his head in defeat. I swallowed hard and turned my face from his, still feeling his scruff against my forehead.

"Why?"

My emotions still weren't level from the minutes before. I felt childish in my urgency, but of course what I was asking for was the very definition of adult. He shook his head. I had made myself entirely vulnerable to him and he was denying me, rejecting me...*again*! Didn't he understand what I wanted? I wouldn't let it go just yet.

"But I want you...inside...me," I whispered, barely able to say the words.

I was horrified. *Oh my God. Why did I say that?* That was a private thought. I couldn't believe I actually told him that to his face. But the sun was setting – on the day and on us. My temperature shot up twenty degrees while I waited for him to respond.

"Jesus. God, Talor," he muttered, distressed.

A peculiar groan caught in his throat and he let it simmer there, deep and raw, rolling it around. Shifting his weight indecisively, he pushed off the tree behind me and fell back a pace. He closed his eyes for a long exhale.

His attention snapped back with such intensity that it startled me. His eyes were furious and sharp, fearfully penetrating. His mouth cracked open as he reached out and touched where the puncture wounds should've been on my neck. When he kissed me again, my claws came out. They clamped down on his neck and shoulders so he wouldn't escape. He winced as he pulled away.

"Oh! I'm sorry if I..." I said, trailing off.

384

As I watched him back away and bend at the waist, I feared I'd somehow managed to hurt a supernatural creature with my fragile human hands. My nails were long, but I wasn't that strong.

"He's too close," he grunted, clenching his teeth.

He straightened, but still held a grimace as he shook his arms out vigorously. He gave an angry groan as the pain surfaced. Blisters and red rashes burned all over his skin, followed by a silver smoothness sweeping across. He turned his face towards the sky and I could see the muscles in his jaw set hard and strain. Muscles bulged as silver shot across them, the evo doing a spectacular job preserving his life.

Within seconds, the rashes disappeared. It looked like Sage could heal himself from a Grigori wound, but not someone else. But the way he labored after that, I knew he couldn't keep doing it. He lifted his eyelids and lowered his head, relaxed.

"I hurt you," I said.

"No, Talor, no. I'm fine," he said, coaxing me towards him.

I only took one timid step that way. Sage had only ever been hurt when he tried to remove the cicatrix. He bit me then, but he was only kissing me this time. A kiss shouldn't cause pain. Just like Spencer.

Oh God, Spencer.

"You can't kiss me anymore?"

In a step, he covered the ground between us and took me in his arms.

"I can," he replied, leaning down and showing me.

I pulled back quickly, almost not believing him. But he was fine. Oh, except for the heartbreak behind the eyes. There was that. He forced a smile, but his lips trembled as they touched mine. It wasn't from trepidation. It was a sort of goodbye, and I felt my heart shattering with every sip of him I took in.

"We need to get away from here," I cried, suddenly remembering what Jet said.

Sage ignored that.

"I want to explain about tonight," he said, a funny hesitation staggering the words.

I nodded, wiping my eyes and brushing my hair back.

"Ok. What's the plan?"

"The Grigori have hunted me for centuries. That's the best leverage we have. If I do what I'm going to do, Rami may release you."

I was sure I heard him wrong. No way did he just say he was going to give himself up to be killed. I took in a big breath to argue when I saw Mika and Ash come around the side of the house. Since my shirt was crooked, I made a quick attempt to remedy it. They chivalrously ignored me.

"You're giving up?"

Sage turned and tilted his head the way someone does when they're caught in a lie.

"What can I say?"

My fists clinched in adrenaline-fueled passion. Every word was a kaleidoscope of emotional bullets flying in different directions from my mouth. Part pain, part rage, and part whispers from the padded cell of my mind. I felt anger so violent that I was completely unfamiliar with the feeling.

"You don't even have a bad plan?"

Mika pointed his index finger into the air.

"I did."

Ash joined in the conversation.

"Yeah, but we took those off the table."

Mika knit his brow and fumed.

"It would work. I have an insider and–"

Sage and Ash both turned to him.

"No," they cried in unison.

He crossed his arms and narrowed his eyes at both, muttering under his breath as he stepped aside and lit a cigarette. Tom joined us outside too, but I found my focus on the ground at my feet, staring down a fallen leaf. It was faded and trampled, barely recognizable. It was torn apart by the elements, but it held its form.

I felt the same way inside knowing our choices were limited to my slavery or Sage's death. The frustration was gone now. It was replaced with sadness. Regret. My fingers traced along my neck.

"Weren't you preparing for this?"

"Listen, you negated all our plans. It's because of you that we didn't get out of here months ago. It's because of you that nothing we come up with will actually work because Sage won't risk you," Ash said, throwing a challenging look my way.

My skin prickled as adrenaline shot through me. I had enough of Ash.

"You know, all you ever do is blame me for everything," I argued, pushing off the tree.

"That's because this is your fault."

"Go screw yourself!"

"Ok, everybody calm down," Tom said.

Azalea walked outside of the circle slowly, studying each guy until she was sure they wouldn't pounce on her. By the time she got to me, even I was looking at her strangely.

"Everything ok?" I asked, touching her shoulder.

"Yeah, Jesse's still sleeping. I was interested in – whatever was happening out here, you know? Trying to catch up."

"Oh, well –" I started, but Tom made a noise for me to be quiet as he reached in his pocket and pulled out his phone. He frowned and sighed.

"Hold up – why is Ben calling – did no one talk to him about canceling the show? Mika!"

Everyone paused and looked at Mika. Mika's wide eyes went wider as a sheepish grin spread. No one else seemed to think it was funny.

"There was that, yeah."

Tom's jaw clenched as he raised the phone.

"It's your job, Mika. We don't need red flags everywhere when we're slipping out of town!"

"Just tell him our singer killed a dude with my guitar so I don't have one anymore. I think we'll be excused."

Mika was trying to be funny, but tensions were too high for that. Tom went into something that sounded like a rant in Spanish. The language change bewildered me momentarily. The way everyone was skilled at hiding accents and adapting, it was easy to forget they weren't – any of them, in fact – American. Or even close to the ages they looked. Tom's Hispanic heritage came to a halt after an aggravated swear word or two – in Spanish, of course. Mika was mad now.

"It isn't easy keeping all of you under the damn radar. It should've been Ash's job. He has plenty of time. All he does is find new ways to be pissed off at her anyway," Mika argued, thumbing at me. He added something short and sharp under his breath. Now his roots were showing.

Ash raised a brow, but didn't engage – at least not in English. It sounded like Gaelic, which was more than a little surprising because he didn't look the least bit Scottish to me. They continued delivering snarky verbal blows in various languages – Mika in French, Ash in Gaelic, and Tom in Spanish.

It was intriguing that not only could they all understand one another, but also none of them were speaking the same language and they were carrying on a three-sided argument without missing a beat.

Azalea and I stood befuddled.

"So this is your new normal, huh?" she asked.

I finally pulled my attention away from the argument and back to Sage. He had retreated twenty or so feet away, folded at the knees, fingers intertwined in hair.

I went over and dropped down beside him. I brought a hand to his forearm and he tensed up. Only minutes before, we had been flesh on flesh; minds set on the carnal needs only each other could meet. Now bickering surrounded us, and as the sun began to dip lower, there was such heavy air that no one could breathe beneath it. The ominous Grigori presence was everywhere, threatening us all.

"If I asked you to do something, would you do it?" he asked, not looking.

"Yes."

"Even if it doesn't make sense to you?"

"Yes."

"If he doesn't accept my offer, I want you to go with him."

"No."

"Don't be scared. He won't harm you, and he won't...force you to...you know," he whimpered, his lips trembling a little.

"He'll have to," I said, my own mouth contorting.

"No, he won't," he said, his voice breaking.

Neither of us could figure out which suggestion was more horrible, which thought harnessed the worst pain. Equally reeling, Sage gathered himself first. His signature calm took him.

"Love me even when it seems lost. And it will. Love me the most then. Those moments are what love is for," he pleaded.

I said nothing, but my heart was wrenching inside so much I thought I could have a heart attack.

"There has to be some way out of this," Azalea interjected. "I'm sorry, he can't just come and take her away."

"You're new to the party. There isn't. This is the Grigori we're talking about," Mika answered, a hint of sadness in his voice.

"So this evil dude – Sage's dad, eww – he wants to marry Talor, right? What would keep him from doing that? Anything?" Azalea asked, furrowing her brow in thought.

No one said anything. I couldn't even bring myself to say the only thing that was on the table – Sage offering himself. Azalea tapped her finger against her lips.

"What if they were to get married?" she cried, brightening up.

"Who – Sage? Married?" Tom asked, puzzled.

"Well, yeah! He couldn't marry her if she was already married," Azalea answered.

She brought her open hands up beside her in a shrug while she waited for applause. She received nothing but chuckles of contempt.

"Again...this is the Grigori we're talking about. Do that and not only will he kill both of them, he'll kill everyone she's ever loved. That includes you, I guess," Ash replied. "Do you want to die?"

Azalea glared at him.

"He would kill the woman he wants to marry?"

"Only if he can't have her," Ash replied.

Azalea gave an aggressive thumb's up.

"Well, that's sane. Seriously, this guy is effing nuts, Talor. We've got to get you out of this."

"He's right, Azalea. They've tried figuring something out, but there's just nothing," I said blankly.

"He's not going to come and just take my best friend away," she said, tears welling up in her eyes. "Someone has to stop him."

I gave her a hug. I couldn't say anything. I wanted to break down in someone's arms, too. After a few seconds, she composed herself.

"Well, they're not God. They have weaknesses, right? What are they? Garlic?"

"The sun," Mika said.

"And the Tears of God, but...there's not exactly any of that around," Tom added. "Pretty sure it's been gone for centuries."

"Where can we find some? In the Temple of Doom? Is it the same thing as holy water because we have about forty churches around here," Azalea said, perking up.

"No, no. It's not water from a church. It's the actual Tears of God. You know, from the flood? You have a better chance of convincing Rami to let these two live happily ever than finding a single pure drop of that on earth," Ash replied, rubbing his eyes.

"How about Alaska for the months the sun doesn't go down? It'll buy time," Azalea cried, turning to me and wriggling her fingers around.

Sunlight – the only one of its kind – was seeping away every minute. The shadows from the oak were getting leaner, the sunspots on the leaf-covered ground fading away. I hadn't noticed time passing when I came out with Sage. We must have been lost in one another's arms longer than we knew.

"That would work if it was summer," Tom said.

"Or if no one was loyal to the Grigori, but Loyalists will find her," Mika replied, his gaze settling on me.

"The only way to keep her safe is to lock her in a cell of sunlight. You wanna do that?" Ash asked.

The full weight of the truth forced all our hope into the cold earth at our feet like dead bodies interred. A stenciled branch on the ground led my gaze to Sage. I wished he could read my mind. I wanted him to take me away to some place we could live the rest of our lives laughing at the early days when the world was against us and we beat it together. But when he finally looked out from his subdued seat, his fingers separated just enough to let his sullen eyes tell the truth.

"No more," he said.

Everyone went quiet. I was so glad he said that. My heart was heavy and I was tired of everyone clamoring about it all, too. I just wanted to sit with Sage and cry, and of course he could tell. He pulled me into his chest. I didn't see them leave, but I could feel the air around us lighten.

Soon we were alone under the oak tree, collapsed together on the ground. Like once mighty branches cursed down to the earth, we were at the mercy of the place we fell. We didn't move. Couldn't move. We cradled together as tightly as safety would allow. Our weary muscles began to shake and still we were unable to let go.

"You should never have come in my life," I blubbered, half of the words incomprehensible.

"I knew the price of you before we met and I've always been willing to pay it."

We just let our tears run wild. Sage was willing to give up his life – worth a great deal more than mine would ever be – just so I could have a chance at happiness. I had been selfish and childish and even ridiculous about his decision.

I could no longer fight the man who was willing to die for me. I was wrong, and I wanted him to know it. I offered an apologetic kiss, and he accepted with feverish forgiveness; immortalizing the moment we could not bring ourselves to leave.

36

I cried in Sage's arms until my eyes were swollen. I started thinking of Bosh and dad as the sun crept lower behind the trees. I couldn't go the rest of my life without seeing them. I would die of heartbreak.

"What will happen to my family?"

He leaned up, rolling to his side and resting his weight on his elbow beside me.

"They will be looked after."

"How do you know?" I asked, hoping for a little more information to ease my mind.

Sage sighed and scratched his fingernail against the sleeve of his jacket.

"The truth is, they're safer now than they ever were. His seal mandates protection of anyone who shares your blood."

That made me feel a little better, but it just reminded me of the ever-circling issue. Either he would die or I would be carried away to be some slave – all because of a seal. I had one more question, and it was one I hadn't asked yet because I couldn't bear knowing.

"Are you going to die if I leave with him?"

Sage's gaze fell hard on me then, and everything in his face said yes. It was only a second in time, but I knew he was trying to invent some lie that would make me feel better. I knew the look because it was the same one the nurse had when she came to get me from the couch outside mom's hospital room. It's a look you remember forever. He never got to answer.

Azalea came racing around the corner of the house with a wild look in her eyes.

"He's gone! He's gone!" she yelled, pointing towards the long, tree-lined gravel road leading through Beaty property.

"Jesse?" I cried, scrambling to get up in a hurry. Apparently, I wasn't fast enough. Sage pulled me to my feet and seemed to focus on something far off in the distance.

"Yes! I went to the bathroom and came back and he was gone," she explained, out of breath.

Sage and I looked at each other. We knew where he was going. I couldn't make my feet move, so Sage took me by the arm and led me over to Azalea.

"Get inside, Talor. Stay there until I come back."

He blazed off at impressive speed. I couldn't see him anymore, but my heart was beating at the same pace as his feet. Azalea and I were suddenly alone in a big, scary world. We both glanced around at the trees and woods surrounding her house. Trees who had guarded our playground parameters our entire lives had become untrustworthy shadows looming over us and darkening with the sky. Henches could be hidden behind any of the gnarled arms reaching overhead.

"Come on," Azalea urged, hooking our arms together and running indoors.

Ten minutes turned into an hour and still no one had returned. The day had dwindled to dusk and the feeling of looming calamity hung heavy in the kitchen where we retreated. Azalea finished making tea, convinced busying herself would avoid anything bad happening.

She fumbled with the teapot and teacups, searching high and low for saucers we wouldn't use. Her hands were shaking as she poured the tea. I sat at the high bar and surprisingly felt little tension. My energy was drained from the events of the day, so I folded my hands on the bar as I waited for her to pass my cup to me.

Azalea brought my cup and sat down facing me, hunching over.

"Where are the guys?"

Truth is, I knew why they weren't guarding me. Sage was the one actually in danger. I was a lost cause and everyone knew it. I didn't want to scare Azalea, so I lied.

"I don't know. You'd think one of them would've stayed behind," I said.

"This is all really surreal, you know? I can't believe you've been dealing with all this on your own," she said, shaking her head and taking a sip.

"Really surreal?" I asked, giving a weak smile.

"I'm just trying to say that I wish I'd known sooner so I could've been there for you."

"Be glad you didn't."

Azalea's perfectly plucked brows tensed up in concern.

"I wanted to ask you...are you ok? I mean, the stuff you've been through with your mom and dad and now all this? And Spencer. God, it's just too much for anyone."

"No, I'm not," I answered, drawing my lower lip into my mouth and biting down on it. The tears would stay put. They wouldn't fall again. I was finished crying for the day. Month. Year. Forever, really. Done with tears.

"I wish we had curtains for those windows," she said, a tremor in her voice. "The world's pretty scary when you know what's really out there. Maybe we should sit where we can't see outside at all."

She cut her eyes to the large glass window to the left of where we sat. It had a view of the woods and in the growing darkness, little else. I took a sip of tea and nodded. I glanced out of the corner of my eye and nearly had a heart attack when I saw something move by the window. I knew I wasn't imagining it. Someone was out there.

"Azalea, did you lock the doors? And the windows, too?" I asked, trying not to seem alarmed.

She spun around and nearly spilled her tea.

"They're always locked. He can't come in, can he? Isn't that the whole reason you had to get inside?"

I straightened and placed the cup down on the counter. I walked into the foyer of the mansion, a place with no windows and only one door. We could see the long hallways from that single spot, so we couldn't be surprised. Azalea followed closely.

When the sound of a key sliding into the lock filled the vacant air, my blood ran cold. The tumbler in the lock clicked in obedience, allowing the key holder unrestricted access. Azalea moved to a small closet where she grabbed a set of Mr. Beaty's shoes and jammed each one under the doors. It was a weird tactic, but it worked. Azalea jerked me away from the door with such force my shoulder almost went out of joint. I had little time to complain.

She dragged me off down the hall. We only got a couple dozen steps away before the front door exploded behind us. No, not just the door – the wall, too. We felt the force and tumbled forward, hitting one side of the hall.

We toppled to the floor as a deafening screeching sound bellowed from the doorway and heavy feet thundered into the foyer. The weight of whatever it was cracked the marble and shook the foundation. Sounds of something large and angry slamming into walls echoed through the house.

Azalea pushed me to my feet.

"Run! Go!" she cried.

I grasped the chair rail that spanned the length of the wall and found my feet. I prayed for Sage – for anyone – to get back to us in time. I looked back, eyes wide and hands so sweaty they were slipping off the chair rail.

Whatever creature was in the house, it was nearly upon us and there was nothing we could do to stop it. It could kill Azalea, but not me. It wouldn't hurt me. I knew what I would have to do. I was so afraid that even my insides were trembling. I had to stop the onslaught before the mansion caved in on top of us.

"They won't hurt me, Azalea," I replied, pulling her up. "Find Sage!"

I pushed her a little ahead of me as I turned to face the creature. I heard her footsteps retreating and a door slam. I was now alone in the hall, the sounds of the massive beast growing louder as I drew closer.

My hands were shaking as I neared the end of the hall. I stopped just short of the landing where I knew the creature would see me. I saw a large shadow cast off the chandelier. The beast was on its haunches, that much I could tell. There were layers to it and horns.

"Stop."

I looked down to see the LLDR in an incandescent red glow. It pulsed in a single ripple and faded out once again. When I stepped into the foyer, a shirtless young man was kneeling there, his fist drawn to his shoulder. He was saluting someone. Something. I recognized him as the guy with Mannix when they attacked Sage in the park.

I took the moment to survey the damage. The walls were gutted and shredded, floors splintered into points. It was going to be hazardous to walk through. I would never make it without falling through the floor, which was mostly gone except for the edges. After venturing around the room, my eyes fell back on the guy still kneeling.

Nico. That was his name.

"Why did you do this?" I asked, waving a wild hand around to the carnage.

"I am sorry, princess," he answered, bowing his head lower.

I wanted to scream at him for destroying Azalea's historical landmark house with his bulldozing, but he seemed penitent. Besides, what I saw behind him just outside on the lawn made me reconsider. Mannix had Azalea. She was cuddling into him as he wrapped a tentacle around her and turned to face me.

"Ah, here comes the bride," he said, his accent thicker, his voice lower. "Your husband's come a long way to collect you."

"Let her go."

He caressed Azalea's head like a dog. "I've a mind to keep my pet, but it's your call."

He jerked her close and exposed her neck. His fangs dropped as he stared at me, waiting. My lip trembled too much to form a full word, but I found I could still nod, so I did that. He dropped his head to the side, disappointed.

"Off with you," he said, waving Azalea off while winking at me. She was still sporting a smitten smile.

I scowled at him, irate that I couldn't actually say anything. I wouldn't risk Azalea. Mannix was too unpredictable. I moved towards where the front door used to be. Now it was a large hole and I felt like I was walking into a cave the closer I got to outside. I had to watch my step so I didn't slip or trip up on the wreckage.

Alarmingly, Nico was beside me, offering his hand to help. I pulled my hands away from him and onto the wooden beams exposed through the wall. He joined Mannix outside and they waited for me.

Azalea was about to walk right past me without even noticing. I caught her by the arm. She stopped and looked at me, searching my face through dilated, unfocused eyes. Mannix could have her forget my face, my name, all of it. Maybe that was best in light of the circumstances.

Mannix impatiently snapped his fingers. I ignored him and took her in a hug. She didn't hug back. When I released her, she walked straight back inside.

"I hate you," I told Mannix, stepping onto the front porch.

He scratched behind his ear and yawned.

"Yeah, I don't care."

"If you touch her again, I'll have you killed."

He did a mock bow and flung his arm around in a large circle as he straightened like he'd swung a golf club. He waited for me to walk ahead of him and practically skipped along behind me, all the while whistling an upbeat tune.

I glanced over my shoulder to see Nico trailing us, eyes searching the grounds for any threats. I caught the haunting shadow of Azalea sitting up against the windowsill with a lamplight behind her. It was the last time I would see my best friend for a long time.

We walked through several acres of Beaty land before I saw Jesse. He was standing in the middle of another crop circle murmuring gibberish. I tried talking to him when we first arrived, but it was useless. It was clear he wasn't himself. Mannix and Nico were searching the surrounding darkness of the field. I couldn't see like they could, but I knew Sage would come. They were a little unsettled while we waited for Rami to show. I guess they could sense the others.

"Come out, you wankers," Mannix challenged.

Something moved in the wheat nearby and we all turned towards the sound to see Ash break away from the darkness. All I could see was his reflective eyes. The others started filing out around him. Sage appeared near the front of us. I moved towards him, but Mannix thrust his arm in front of me.

"Careful, princess. Their kind might have mange. Ya never know."

"Try and keep her away from me," Sage told him, low and severe.

Mannix held his hands up in the air and his brows went high and wide as the corners of his mouth. Then he laced his hands behind his back as he stepped to the side, clearing my path.

"Ah, he'll be dead soon, anyway."

Sage tipped his head up slightly. I rushed over to him.

"I'm sorry, Sage. I had to. I mean, he had Azalea and I – couldn't risk," I started, my tone so remorseful it seemed silly even to me. Sage pulled me close and touched my lips, shaking his head.

"You didn't do anything wrong. I should never have left you."

He held me tight as he smoothed a hand over my hair. Mannix chuckled as Sage's skin began to glow.

"Right. You just gonna take off my head again?"

"I don't aim for the head," Ash said coolly, stepping between Mannix and us. I didn't know what that meant, but knowing Ash, it probably meant he would tear his heart out of his chest.

Mannix and Ash stood close and stiff, their jaws locked tight and shoulders thrown back. Usually Mannix was a sarcastic bully, but his expression grew earnest as he spoke.

"I pity you most. Mixed up in the Dissent. You were one of us."

There was a rare glint in Ash's eye. Without hesitation, he lopped off Mannix's head and flung it to the side. We watched his body topple over – first knees, then chest. Next, Ash glowered as he turned to Nico, who made no attempt at aggression.

Convinced he wasn't a threat, Ash turned to us and shrugged at Sage.

"I changed my mind about the head. He talks too much."

Sage kissed my forehead, looking across the field to the Beaty mansion.

"We need to get you indoors," he said, rubbing his hands up and down my arms for warmth. The temperature was dropping and I forgot my coat at Azalea's.

Nico cleared his throat.

"Princess, your husband will do whatever he must to get to you."

"Shut up or you'll lose a head, too," Ash replied, turning his cold stare on him. Nico didn't even pay attention to him. He was still looking at me.

I held up my wrist.

"I know what this seal does. He wouldn't hurt anybody I love."

Nico looked at the ground.

"That only protects blood, not him," he thumbed to Jesse, who I'd completely forgotten about until then. He had ceased his muttering and was sitting cross-legged on the ground right in the middle of the crop circle.

My heart dropped as I stared at the back of his head, knowing his life was literally in my hands. Suddenly, the crop circle began to vibrate and move beneath us and a red mist rose off the earth. The guys began to scatter, flanking Sage and me. Sage took off at a sprint towards the mansion, dragging me along behind him.

"What about Jesse?" I cried, my lungs heaving as he quickened pace.

Mannix appeared fast in front of us, blocking our path. Sage let go of my hand and using his momentum, hit Mannix so many times it looked like he had ten hands. Mannix was either caught off guard or slower than Sage, so he felt every hit. His body jerked left and right through heavy cracking sounds. Bones had to be breaking.

Sage was on the backside of him then, taking him under one arm and heaving him with ease over his head. Mannix sailed through the air with speed and tumbled along the field in a sickening, flailing contortion of limbs and torso, kicking up dust and rolling into the distance. Sage watched him disappear into the darkness and lowered his body to ready for an assault I couldn't see.

"Talor, keep going," he shouted, waving me off.

While I didn't want to leave Sage, I knew I needed to get inside. He was fighting for me, so I needed to do what I could do. A human house was the only place Rami couldn't enter, so I sprinted towards it as fast as my legs would take me. I only made it halfway to the end of the field before I heard rustling race up behind me. I shut my eyes and pumped my arms until they were so spent that I could barely swing them. The sound was too fast – it was in front of me now.

I almost tumbled over trying to stop. A dark shadow hovered level to my face. It had no face or limbs, but it gave the air of alien space, loneliness and utter despair. I screamed, bringing Sage in haste. He got between us, extending a hand out front to keep it at a distance. It seemed to work. The shadow swayed back and forth, seeming to test the boundaries, but it didn't charge head on while Sage kept his hand raised.

I buried my face in his chest.

"Sage, it came after me once. Kill it!"

"Wait. It's a soul shadow – one of the cursed first," he answered thoughtfully, turning his head to each side to get different perspectives of it. "I haven't seen one in a long time."

Sage seemed more curious than alarmed, so I dared look at it again. It floated above the ground, a misty dark thing with a feisty will. He spoke to it in *Yahweh-Elata*, and while I had no idea what he was saying, I knew it was a command based on his tone. The shadow grew larger in response. I guess it didn't like that tone.

"Show me," Sage commanded.

The soul shadow hissed at him, so Sage grabbed it by the top where the neck would be. It was amazing that Sage was able to touch the creature and I was only able to swipe through it. It screeched at such an alarming decibel that I had to drop down and cover my ears. Unaffected, Sage reached out to subdue the thing and it was able to slice his forearm open.

That had to be incredibly painful, but somehow he kept his grip. When his arm adopted the silver fire on it, the creature stopped fighting him and tried to get away. It started to drag Sage along the ground, but he held onto it. It dove down, trying to escape into the dirt beneath us. Sage held it fast, grunting. When it started to slip through his hands, he fell to one knee, straining.

"*Son-cede!*"

When he said that, something dropped from the soulshadow and fell to the ground. Satisfied, Sage released the soul shadow and let it seep back inside the dirt at his feet with a chittering growl. Sage was silent for a moment, staring at whatever it was the soulshadow had dropped.

Then he turned and reached for my hand, lifting me up and checking me for injuries. When he was satisfied that I was unharmed, we both directed our attention to at the ground where the object was relinquished.

It was a small glass vial the size of a nail polish attached to a long necklace. It didn't look like much. It wasn't glittery or glowing, but a dull gray; still, whatever it was, Sage was stunned. He reached down and took it in hand, wholly consumed.

"Tears of God," he exclaimed.

A whooshing sound came from overhead and something hot and bright dropped down in front of us at the edge of the field. It was a lava-like fire, and it splashed high and wide, nearly spraying out at us.

Sage jerked me back and spun me around, racing back towards the interior. A black dragon – someone who wasn't Ash – was burning the field at its borders and driving us back towards the crop circle. Never none to miss out on a fight, Ash quickly evoed into a dragon with blue scales and shot off skyward. He tore into the black dragon with frightening fury, and when they clashed it emitted a cracking, terrible, ungodly kind of sound.

I could feel the heaviness of them in the air over us, my heart pounding at the power and weight somehow suspended over our heads. At any moment, liquid fire could shower us and that would be the end of it all.

As if the thought called the exact action to life, a bright, hot flash spread across my field of vision and with a cry, Sage gripped me tight and went full evo just in time to cover us from the thick vats of dragon fire raining down. Sage and I tried to get away from the battle, but the damage was done. The immediate field around us caught flame and we were trapped in a small space of dry dirt.

Seeing our predicament, Ash screeched and beat his gigantic wings to soar high in the air before curling into a ball. Incredibly, he turned down towards the black dragon still focused on us and became a missile of claw and muscle, slamming the unlucky creature from the sky.

The unexpected hit rendered it unconscious as he hurled to the earth in a ground-shaking thud. Fire drooled from the dragon's open mouth before he automatically evoed back into a man, and it spread quickly across the field. Finding a path through the devastation, Sage led us a safe enough distance from the edges of the blaze, but it was getting harder to breathe.

"Cover your mouth," Sage said, noticing my labored breathing.

I nodded, but my eyes were starting to burn and my hand only got as far as my mouth to cover my coughing. He started to pull my scarf up over my nose and about then, Tom and Mika came running up through the pillars of smoke crowding the air.

"They're everywhere, Sage," Tom said.

"We're surrounded," Mika added.

Ash went evo midair and landed on his feet. Even his breath was ragged, his chin quivering. He pulled on his pants behind some wheat while everyone stared at each other. I wondered what no one was saying.

Then Sage gave voice to it.

"He's here."

37

Everyone turned slowly, carefully.

Sage took me behind him before I could even look. It was the only thing done with speed. I hid there, my fingers gripping deep into his sides, hoping, praying, coughing. He was soaked in sweat, so my cheek stuck to the warm muscles tensing through his cotton t-shirt. I cowered into his comforting strength and it felt a little safer there. I watched as the guys moved closer together before peeking out the side of Sage's arm – and I saw a fallen angel.

Rami.

They were right. Once you see one, you just know. As if obeying him, the smoke billowed back away from us all as he came forward, clearing the air entirely. I could breathe easily again, but I held my breath because I couldn't stop staring at the creature that had been hunting me. He looked nothing like the figure I had in the back of my mind. The way they talked about him – the timid respect mixed with deep-seated disgust – he should have been an evil-looking monster.

I guess I expected a menacing-looking man dressed all in black robes or something, but he looked nothing like that. I expected black, moldy wings, honestly. I expected everything but what I saw – a display of beauty and power in the way he held himself.

There was nothing about him that suggested he was malicious or even inhuman. Looked to be in his late thirties. He was tall and wiry, built purely of lean muscle. He stopped some distance from us, searching each face around with a focused brow. His eyes were a friendly set, not filled with the hardened black pearls of ice I thought he should have.

There is no way to describe the color, but it's safe to say that they don't make it on earth. I lingered too long at them and my curiosity betrayed me. Like a beacon, it drew his gaze until I was the only thing in it.

The colorless eyes widened slightly and then fixated. It should have intimidated me. It should have terrified me. Instead, it made my clasp on Sage loosen. All at once, I felt an overwhelming need to get nearer. It was like stumbling on something undiscovered in the wild, something you had to get closer to and touch if you could. It was bewitching, and I needed to be nearer to him.

I scanned his features, imagining them against my skin. I was ashamed of the thoughts I found stirring. I was grateful that he looked nothing like Sage. But then again, I didn't think he would. The Grigori were true shape shifters. I doubted Rami wanted to look like the son he loathed anymore than I wanted to be reminded of Sage every time he…would kiss me?

Oh God! I was going to let this demon kiss me? My chest felt like it was hollow, yet heavy, so heavy. The pain was searing deep and fanning out into all my muscles. I needed to breathe.

I forgot to breathe?

I gasped just as black spots dotted my vision. Shaking my head, I tried to break the lock he had on me. I couldn't understand. How could I be attracted to the creature threatening Sage's life and seeking to bind me in supernatural slavery?

I was aware of my weakness then more that I had even been. It was a double-sided comfort knowing it was a spell of sorts that had me feeling that way. They weren't true feelings, but what chance did I have against the type of magic that could ply my will with no effort?

I felt like I was lifting off the ground and no matter how I tried running in place to touch a single toe back down, I was lifting higher and higher. My heart and my mind, everything was bending towards him. I knew I'd have to go to him or I'd shatter like glass. Something in my soul would break, like we were supposed to be together no matter what.

While he was attractively misleading, I couldn't deny there was darkness to his presence. Standing near him felt like standing up against a closed door with something terrible on the other side. There was no way to know when the door would burst open and the creature lurking behind would fill its space.

"Hello, my love," he said, tilting his head.

His voice harmonized with the rest of him. It was the perfect depth and dialect; it vibrated sweetly in my ears and churned my maddening blood, bringing it rushing to the surface in a furious, delirious flush. I felt deep and hot, flustered like I'd been caught doing something only done in private.

"H-hello."

It twisted half a smile on his lips, revealing fangs. Fangs that didn't retract.

"Don't talk to him, Talor," Sage barked.

411

When Sage spoke, Rami's eyes narrowed. The whole band seemed to tense up in a single breath. I knew the danger in facing off against a Grigori. They couldn't be killed. Rami wasn't even acting threatening, but he could kill us all in seconds.

I moved my fingers from Sage's back to his arm. I was shocked to find it shaking. He was trying hard to control it, but he was trembling. Sage was never afraid. It set me into a quiet panic.

"Free her and I'll go with you," Sage offered, a nervous tremble finding his vocal chords and hanging on.

Rami's thick brow drew together.

"I am not here to make a deal."

"What about the others? Would they agree to you taking her over me?"

Rami shifted his weight to take a step. Just one. But the band reacted as if he was charging them. They circled around Sage in a defensive posture, everyone glowing to evo on high alert. I retreated behind Sage, my eyes closed tight this time. I tried to pray, but the thoughts were everywhere.

I couldn't catch enough of them to form a sentence to send God. Honestly, I wasn't even sure that it would have mattered. I didn't know where God fit in everything happening to me, or even if he cared. All I knew was that Sage's sacrificial offer was refused. The only plan B we had failed.

Rami, while unthreatening at the moment, might not have much patience. I could walk away with him and leave them all behind alive. Or, I could continue clinging to Sage and get them all killed. Finding my courage, I opened my eyes.

Taking in a deep breath, I looked out from behind him again.

"Why do I feel −"

Sage stopped me, whirling around and putting his forehead against mine.

412

"Don't talk to him, Talor. Don't talk to him. Just look at me. Please," he begged.

I nodded, resting my hands on Sage's chest. I could feel his heart raging inside him. It scared me that he was so unlike himself.

"Why do I feel like I know you?" I asked.

"Because we belong to one another," Rami replied.

Sage glared at Rami over his shoulder.

"She doesn't belong to you. She doesn't belong to anyone."

"I have come for my wife."

Sage shook his head, unwilling to part with a single inch of my flesh. While he clung to me, I came to terms with the ugly truth. I did want to go to Rami. I was sure I was going mad. It was almost as if Sage knew that. His loving hug turned into a painful hold.

"Why won't you just take me?" Sage groaned.

Tom touched his shoulder, but Sage didn't pay him any attention. He was gripping me the way a child does their favorite puppy from the litter just before someone takes it away to a new home. His hands were nearly white with the strain. The hug hurt, but I bore it because I knew Sage was floundering inside, breaking. I knew if I took a deep breath, I might shatter our fragile shell. Tom tried to reason with him again.

"*Ella está en el dolor*," he murmured, gesturing to the distressing signs of his embrace.

"I will not say it again," Rami said.

When I looked up at Sage, I could see tears streaming down his face. He loosened his grip a little, but he didn't want to let go anymore than I wanted him to. I needed to make him feel better. He was always making me feel better, always healing my wounds. But when the tables were flipped, I was helpless. Sheer panic set in when I realized then that I might never see him again.

"Tell me what to do. Sage, tell me what to do. Will you be able to find me where he takes me?"

I didn't recognize my own voice. It was hurried and frantic, hushed and wavering. Sage couldn't answer me. He could barely lift his head from leaning against mine. He just whimpered and cried, trying to contain his pain and quiet it down.

When he found the strength, he planted a quivering kiss on my forehead. He lifted my chin and paused before kissing my lips. He whispered something strange. Although I didn't understand, the words calmed me.

"What did you say?" I asked, focusing on his lips.

"Just that I love you," he said, our eyes catching.

I thought I knew pain. Everything that I'd been through until that point in time had served me only as a fire poker to my soul, merciless and cruel as it continued to stab, weakening and bleeding me until I had a hole for a heart. Pain was a companion, a friend of sorts.

I learned to linger in it so that the next wave, the next stab, would hurt a little less. But Sage's eyes were filled with a pain I had never known – not watching my frail mother wail as the cancer spread inside her bones. Not watching my father scrub mud on his body as he knelt in front of our burning house. I had known pain, but Sage knew something beyond that.

My fingers rested on the cross around my neck while Sage closed his eyes and kissed me. It was so tender and loving that I nearly dissolved in his lips. We were seamless, he and I. The lips were a portal of goodness – every laugh, every kiss, every kind word spoken. Every beautiful bit of us was in that perfect kiss. I was his, he was mine, and we were happy.

When the kiss came to an end, reality rushed in so fast it made me dizzy. Without Sage's warmth, I was overcome with a debilitating hollowness. He was saying goodbye to me, to us. His tears were still on my face when he brought his hands up to my jaw, cupping it like he was afraid to push too hard into my skin – like it would break.

And it probably would have. He was searching me with unparalleled intensity and focus, like he was looking for the last time and wanted to remember every single detail. I stood there in his arms, trying not to die. There was such agony in his face at first, but soon the corners of his lips started to soften. Peace seemed to take him, and the longer he looked at me like that, the more it spread to me.

"Remember us," he said.

"What?"

"It's ok," he urged, letting his hands drop away.

"Have you lost your damn mind?" said Ash, sneering.

"Sage, you know what'll happen to you. You know what'll happen to *her*," Tom said, leaning in.

Sage knew what my leaving would mean. He had been willing to fight for me just that afternoon. He'd been willing to die for me only a few minutes before. But now he was just fine with me being whisked away by his enemy? I was stunned. Hurt. Broken. It jerked my heart around in my chest. Whatever peace I had a minute ago, it was dissolving, and fast, too.

"Ash, Tom – please do something," I begged.

I was met by only sympathetic stares. They would always do whatever Sage told them to, and he was saying to let me go. I didn't want a life without him in it. It wasn't in me to do what he wanted.

I started shaking my head so hard I was sure it would fly off. Something switched inside him. He wanted me to leave? I wouldn't do it. I started to choke up as he took me in a hug and leaned his lips against my ear. His voice was so calming.

"Don't be afraid to cry often. Cry hard. It will keep you alive. As long as you're alive…"

He didn't finish his sentence. He just ran a hand down my cheek. Shaking his head, he stepped arm's length away from me, kissing my hand and shutting his eyes tight. His smile started to fade now. Maybe he was finally realizing what he was telling me to do.

"Remember how I loved you. Let that hold you in the dark," he said, letting me go.

Once the last bit of his skin separated from mine, my blurry, tear-filled eyes turned towards Rami. The seal under my skin started to illuminate, and the longer I tried to refuse it, the more intense the longing. Rami stretched a hand towards me.

"It is time, my love."

I reached up and touched the tears Sage left on my cheek. Holding the remnants of them in my palm, I brought my hand to my chest and brushed them across my skin. I savored the fleeting comfort of knowing they were once his and they were a part of me now.

When I got a foot or two from Rami, I stopped. He gave a satisfied smile as he closed the distance between us. When I looked up, he brought his lips against my forehead. The kiss struck me right in the heart this time.

A rush traveled across the surface of my skin to my wrist, bubbling up as the letters disappeared and the seal reemerged like braille. It was no longer a brand. It was one with my skin. Organic. Alive. Rami took my hand in his and kissed my open palm, catching me in a gaze I couldn't shake. I watched his lips take shapes, transfixed.

"Siren, enjoy your last days while I enjoy my wife."

Sage collapsed to the ground as Mika, Tom, and Ash all gathered around him, affording whatever comfort they could. Blood and tears drenched his wobbling arms, dropping thick to the ground like a holy rain. When he raised his head, I could see the beautiful hazel I had grown to love already dimming. In that moment, the foggy final words of his serenade played across my memory.

If confused I ever be
About just who you are,
I'll know you by those eyes so bright
They caught a falling star.

As much as I wanted to run to him – to hold, save, and comfort him – when Rami started walking, my feet took me in the opposite direction. I could feel some part of me remaining with him, beating in that precious heart of his bleeding out on the ground. He was dying, we were dying, and still I moved forward.

But that's what you do when death comes – you move forward and leave your soul behind. Some people call that dying, but that's all living is to me.

Want to read more of *LONG LIVE DEAD RECKLESS*?
Enjoy this sneak peek from the next book in the series!

for the ages

CHAPTER 1 of FOR THE AGES

The cold cry of dead leaves underfoot.

That's what I focused on. It was better than the annoying voices of Mannix and Nico, who were behind me carrying on a conversation made entirely of cackling. I just watched my feet move forward, amazed they could continue when I only wanted to crumple up in a heap and die.

Before long, we stopped at a stringy dirt road between fields. I kept my eyes down while I waited for the pull from the wretched braille seal that stained my wrist and my soul. Rami's name in my skin was an invisible chain both seductive and sickening in its manner, like a feather with razor edges.

I should have guessed the fallen angel the name belonged to would treat me exactly the same way

Keep your cross hidden.

The words felt like wind moving inside me, so I obeyed and quickly tucked my cross necklace under my sweater. They were the last words mom said to me. Even broken and numb, I obeyed her from a memory.

Meanwhile, Rami's cackling henchmen trudged past me on one side, hauling a stumbling pair of jeans along. It took me a minute to realize the jeans were Jesse. I could only assume that they were bringing him along to keep me compliant, but holding my best friend's brother as a hostage wasn't part of the deal.

"No, wait," I croaked, calling after them.

But they were already gone. As far as I knew, they were going to murder him in the fields on the edge of Beaty Mansion. If I'd had one more ounce of courage, I'd have demanded Jesse's release. Instead, I wiped my chapped nose again with my numb fingers. The late December wind was brutal as it swirled through the open field around us, stinging my eyes with its bitterness. A new year was merely days away and I was going to spend it in a world without Sage.

As I wiped a worthless tear from my cheek, Rami and I caught eyes. His were shining again in that creepy way of reminding me he wasn't human. The longer ends of his wavy hair were whipping in the wind across his bearded cheek and over his collar, looking like black fingers reaching out from their graves. Reaching for me. We held the gaze for several seconds before his tall frame moved forward once again.

Shivering, I dared look over my shoulder towards Cypress, almost expecting to turn into a pillar of salt as punishment. As much as I hated my hometown because it's where mom died, it felt like my heart was being buried alive as I left. Even though mom was gone, Dad was well again thanks to Sage's healing. It was cruel that I finally had him back and I would probably never see him again. Knowing I was only a mile away from Azalea's house and everything so familiar made my heart flutter and ache all the way down to my tingling toes.

I could try running back to everyone. They weren't far. Sage was probably still bleeding out on the ground, still alive for a little longer. But he was the siren, and there was only one way to kill one. I had done that willingly. Instead of making a run for it, I turned back towards Rami and saw him waiting for me just inside a crop circle about fifteen feet away.

"Have no fear," he said, offering a hand.

When I looked at the lines glowing at my feet, I was absolutely sure the ground was breathing. As if that wasn't terrifying enough, everything outside of the symbol seemed dark and foreboding. Evil seemed to descend all around in the dark spaces I couldn't see, and my wrist assured me that to be with Rami was the only way to be safe.

As soon as I stepped inside, a quivering jolt shook me. It felt like being baptized with fire in my bones, and for a moment my nostrils clogged with water. Fire and water were together inside and all around me, so I panicked and flailed, certain I'd just walked into a supernatural landmine. I lurched inside the crop circle, gasping and whimpering as I touched my face to be sure I hadn't burned. I only relaxed when I saw that I was completely unharmed.

When I looked up, I saw Rami smiling at me in this tender way. At the time, I thought it was because he enjoyed watching me break, but that wasn't it at all. As I gathered myself and took trembling steps towards the center, the crop circle began to shrink behind me.

There was no going back now. Rami wanted me to know that. When I was only a few feet away, there was a momentary glow like a flash of lightning behind me. I whipped around to see a wall of air and energy that moved like glass. It was a sort of doorway for sure, and I knew that's what I'd passed through. When Rami whispered to it, the mirrored veil shivered before dropping into the earth at our feet. The water fizzled out like fire, scorching the ground.

Seconds later, the ground began to shimmy and groan. It was so violent, my insides vibrated. My focus shifted quickly as things began to change all around us. The earth began bending and turning, scenery changing and cracking, folding like origami all around us.

My first instinct was to grab something, to hold on, but there was nothing, not even the ground. While the world around me was flipping and switching, Rami and I remained perfectly still and supported as though the ground was still under our feet. Still, my chest tightened; afraid the next motion would bury us.

I couldn't understand how it was happening. The earth didn't work like this. Layer folded over layer and slammed down into place, a kaleidoscope of fields, streets, even buildings. Finally, the furious turning slowed to stop and the crop circle faded away. With it went the light. But I knew where we were, and there were lamps overhead lighting the pathway down.

We were standing on the steps of Radium Springs, one of the most haunted and beautiful places in Cypress. It scared anyone with sense. I'd only been once or twice in my entire life; mostly because water that temperature probably gave more than a few people hypothermia.

People had been disappearing from here for decades, and suddenly I knew why. The water's eerie black shimmer chilled my core. It's said there is a cave system at the bottom of the beautiful abyss; complete with frozen bodies of lost divers.

At least, that's the stories we always heard growing up. Someone was always drowning in the springs, but of course they could never find a body. The city finally closed down this entrance several years ago.

Weeping willows hung over the foreboding water, daring only to dangle breathlessly just out of reach. Even they wouldn't tempt the wicked pool. Massive rocks lingered below the shivering surface like earthy icebergs latched to the edge of the world.

Large shadows seemed to move through the moonlight under the surface, making my blood thicken like icicles pushing through the veins – a burning hollow.

Rami walked down the cragged steep stones a few feet and stopped. Somehow he sensed I wasn't following.

"Come, my love."

Heart beating wildly, I stood on the edge of the hypothermic murder pool.

"I almost drowned once."

"I know."

I wanted to ask how he knew, but I didn't. I watched the water push away from him by a good foot on all sides. Water was falling up, so I decided if the water did that for him, I shouldn't push my luck. I didn't want to, but I knew my only choice was to follow. He led me through the deepening, darkening cavern.

The only light was the moon glowing through the waters around him, bewitched with his power. I nearly slipped on the steps once or twice from trying to move too carefully, as odd as it sounds.

Once we stepped into the first cave, Rami raised his hand and brought the water down. It crashed back into itself, thundering loudly as it covered the pathway and slammed into an invisible wall in front of us. The cave walls ruptured and shook, but none of the debris hit us.

It was humbling to witness, but I tried to act like I wasn't holding my breath over every single thing he was doing. Out of the corner of my eye, I noticed a glistening spider web extending across the entire cave up ahead.

It didn't look like a normal spider web. Forget that it would require a gigantic underwater spider to patrol it. It moved like the glass in the crop circle. Rami walked through it as though it wasn't there, so I did the same. No jolt this time.

Once through, I looked back out into the dark water still churning from being pushed back. As shadows sailed by, their empty eyes landed on me. Gaping mouths gave silent screams, making me stumble back. Rami just looked at me and then at the water. I felt stupid as I gathered myself, and we continued in silence.

The cave had more turns than I expected, and every time I looked back, the water had begun to quietly rise behind us, filling the spaces with darkness. It was so alien down there, I worried that maybe Jesse was the lucky one. Maybe I was the one to die. Maybe that's all the Grigori ever really wanted.

No one would ever find me in Radium Springs.

After what felt like forever, out of the darkness there appeared in front of us several men standing around talking. There were at least half a dozen of them, and they had a glow about them like the sons before an evo. I stood and stared at the enemies of God and man. It was surreal seeing them in person after hearing so much legend and mystery.

There was nothing terrifying or menacing about them. They looked like a group of men talking together after coming out of a restaurant. They were all different nationalities. Some were dressed in suits, others in casual street clothes.

When we approached, they all fell silent. I glanced up quickly to see eyes of fire. You wouldn't know there was anything different about them at all if it weren't for the burning behind the eyes. It's a burning even the blind can see; every color reflected and refracted through an ancient anger. Unyielding, unsettling, and fixated firmly on me. I shut my eyes as tight as I could, praying they wouldn't burn through.

Rami spoke to them in some strange tongue made up of sounds jumbled like a puzzle to the senses. I'd heard the band speak it (I learned it was called *Yahweh-Elata*), but never in full sentences, just words. It was odd to hear a new language – or rather, the oldest one. I stood a few feet behind them, but once Rami finished whatever he was saying (probably how they should murder me), he turned and ushered me forward.

"Some of my brothers may speak to you now. Do not fear them."

I came a foot or two closer and did something like a nod. Not quite a nod because I didn't want to agree to talk to anyone.

Suddenly it hit me again that Sage was lying across town dying. Dying because I didn't stay. Dying because I went with Rami. Dying because of me. It took everything in me not to cry.

"It's a lot to handle in one day, isn't it?" asked one of them, offering a handkerchief.

I took it, catching a quick look at him as I did. He wasn't imposing; he was a comfortable presence with a tender, vague sympathy in his eyes. Eyes that didn't burn. They were dark brown.

"Your name's Talor?"

I nodded, wiping my nose as daintily as possible. I didn't want to dirty up his gesture of goodwill by wiping my emotional snot all over it.

"Ah, *Ta-hime*. I'm Okabe," he said.

I stared at him, not sure what to say. Did he expect me to comment on his name? He shrugged as he pointed to the handkerchief.

"Don't be shy about using that, *Ta-hime*. You've got a situation."

"Thank you," I mumbled, wiping my nose more liberally.

Just then, another one approached, but his manner was quite different. His eyes were like gold – reflective, sharp, captivating. Chestnut hair tumbled down the sides of his chiseled face, suggesting a carefreeness he didn't actually have. There was this perpetual look of disgust disguised beneath masterful layers of regal neutrality.

"Rami, she's too young and she has blood on her soul," he commented coldly, staring like he was trying to explode me with his mind.

It seemed a bit rude considering we'd never met, but I wasn't exactly in the place to argue about manners. He looked like someone you had to pick your battles with, so I stayed quiet. That was wise.

"I know, Saiza," Rami said.

The one he called Saiza tilted his head as he looked me over again – a little less murderous this time.

"She will be troublesome to you."

Rami didn't respond. He just glanced at me. In the uncomfortable silence, Saiza straightened and shifted his focus to Rami.

"You could have a more suitable wife. This one is –"

"My choice. This one is my choice, Saiza."

Saiza ran his hands lazily up his forearms, pulling back the sleeves.

"Let us take the siren now while he is unhidden and weak. Let us end your pain, brother. You have suffered long enough."

Rami took in a deep breath. One corner of his lips curved up as he narrowed his eyes at me. Whatever he said next made everyone murmur. Saiza turned towards me, scrutinizing a little harder. He brought a hand to his chin and started rubbing it thoughtfully.

"Is that true, woman? Did you love the siren?"

I was almost afraid to answer him, but it felt like it would be worse to ignore him. Besides, our love wasn't past tense.

"I do love him."

"Then he will die," Saiza said, a smile flitting across his face.

I had done very well up to that point controlling my emotions, but when he said that, I buried my face in my hands. My wobbly legs gave out and resigned me to the cold, damp ground.

"You need rest," Rami replied.

"I need to go home please," I said, whimpering as my tears splashed against the handkerchief still clutched in my palm.

His hand lowered into my field of vision.

"I will take you."

I slid my hand into his so he could bring me to my feet. When I rose, we were alone in the cave. His fingers began to curl loosely around mine, but before they could get comfortable, I jerked my hand away.

I don't know why I imagined he would return me to my front door like we'd been on a date. I guess I needed to believe that to keep going. So I followed him deeper and deeper into a dark cave, and it would be a long time before I came out the other side.

Ready to read the rest?

You can purchase FOR THE AGES (LLDR, #2) on Amazon!

~ **Thank you for reading!** ~

As you know, authors rely on readers like you to get the word out about their books! If you enjoyed *Long Live Dead Reckless*, please consider leaving a review so other readers can find novels like this.

Made in the USA
Monee, IL
10 February 2020

21432485R00252